MY
CYNTHIA HAND
PLAIN
BRODI ASHTON
JANE
JODI MEADOWS

HARPER TEEN

An Imprint of HarperCollins*Publishers*

HarperTeen is an imprint of HarperCollins Publishers.

My Plain Jane
Copyright © 2018 by Cynthia Hand, Brodi Ashton, and Jodi Meadows
All rights reserved. Printed in the United States of America.
No part of this book may be used or reproduced in any manner whatsoever without written
permission except in the case of brief quotations embodied in critical articles and reviews.
For information address HarperCollins Children's Books, a division of HarperCollins
Publishers, 195 Broadway, New York, NY 10007.
www.epicreads.com

Library of Congress Control Number: 2018933339
ISBN 978-0-06-265277-5 — ISBN 978-0-06-287227-2 (special edition)
ISBN 978-0-06-287986-8 (special edition)

Typography by Jenna Stempel-Lobell
18 19 20 21 22   PC/LSCH   10 9 8 7 6 5 4 3 2 1
❖
First Edition

For everyone who's ever fallen for the wrong person, even though we agree that Mr. Darcy looks good on paper . . . and in a wet shirt.

And for England (again). We're really sorry for what we're about to do to your literature.

"He made me love him without even looking at me."
—Jane Eyre, *by Charlotte Brontë*

"I am just going to write, because I cannot help it."
—Charlotte Brontë

Prologue

You may think you know the story.

Oh, heard that one, have you? Well, we say again: you may think you know the story. By all accounts it's a good one: a penniless, orphaned young woman becomes a governess in a wealthy household, catches the eye of the rich and stern master, and (sigh) falls deeply in love. It's all very passionate and swoonworthy, but before they can be married, a—gasp!—terrible treachery is revealed. Then there's fire and despair, some aimless wandering, starvation, a little bit of gaslighting, but in the end, the romance works out. The girl (Miss Eyre) gets the guy (Mr. Rochester). They live happily ever after. Which means everybody's happy, right?

Um . . . no. We have a different tale to tell. (Don't we always?) And what we're about to reveal is more than a simple reimagining of one of literature's most beloved novels. This version, dear reader, is *true*. There really was a girl. (Two girls, actually.) There was, indeed, a terrible treachery and a great fire. But throw out pretty much everything else you know about the story. This isn't going to be like any classic romance you've ever read.

It all started, if we're going to go way, way back, in 1788 with King George III. The king had always been able to see ghosts. No big deal, really. He didn't find them frightening in the least. Sometimes he even had amusing conversations with long-deceased courtiers and unfairly beheaded queens who were floating about the palace grounds.

But one day, disaster struck. The king was walking in the garden when a mischievous ghost rattled the branches of a nearby tree.

"Who's there?" called the king, because, as it happened, he was without his spectacles.

"Look at me," answered the troublesome ghost in its most stately voice. "I'm the King of Prussia!"

The king immediately dropped into a bow. Quite coincidentally, he had been expecting a visit from the King of Prussia. "I am most pleased to meet you, Your Highness!" he exclaimed.

Then he tried to shake the tree's hand.

This, again, would have been no big deal, but for the dozen or so lords and ladies who had accompanied the king on his walk in the garden, who didn't see the ghost, of course, only the king mistaking a tree for royalty. From that moment on, poor George was referred to as "Mad King George," a title he greatly resented.

So George assembled a team made up of every kind of person

he thought could help him be rid of these irksome ghosts: priests who specialized in exorcisms, doctors with some knowledge of the occult, philosophers, scientists, fortune-tellers, and anybody, in general, who dabbled in the supernatural.

And that's how the Royal Society for the Relocation of Wayward Spirits was established.

In the years that followed, the Society, as it came to be called, functioned as a prominent and well-respected part of English life. If there was something strange in your neighborhood, you could, um, write the Society a letter, and they would promptly send an agent to take care of it.

Fast-forward right past the reign of George IV, to William IV ascending England's throne. William was practical. He didn't believe in ghosts. He considered the Society to be nothing more than a collection of odious charlatans who had been pulling the wool over the eyes of his poor disturbed predecessors for many years. Plus it was a terrible drain on the taxpayers' dime (er, shilling). So almost as soon as he was officially crowned king, William cut the Society out of the royal budget. This led to his infamous falling-out and subsequent feud with Sir Arthur Wellesley, aka the Duke of Wellington, aka the leader and Lord President of the RWS Society, which was now underfunded and under-respected.

This brings us to the real start of our story: northern England, 1834, and the aforementioned penniless, orphaned girl. And a writer. And a boy with a vendetta.

Let's start with the girl.

Her name was Jane.

ONE

Charlotte

There was no possibility of taking a walk through the grounds of Lowood school without hearing the dreadful and yet utterly exciting news: Mr. Brocklehurst had been—gasp!—*murdered.* The facts were these: Mr. Brocklehurst had come for one of his monthly "inspections." He'd started right off by complaining about the difficulty of running a school for impoverished children, the way said children were always, for whatever reason, annoyingly asking for more food—*more, sir, please may I have some more?* Then he'd settled down by the fire in the parlor, devoured the heaping plate of cookies that Miss Temple had so kindly offered him, and promptly keeled over in the middle of afternoon tea. Poisoned. The tea, evidently, not the cookies. Although if he'd been poisoned by the cookies the girls at Lowood school felt it would have served him right.

The girls didn't shed so much as a tear over Mr. Brocklehurst. While he'd been in charge they'd been very cold and very hungry, and a great many of them had died of the Graveyard Disease. (There are many terms for this particular illness over the course of history: the Affliction, consumption, tuberculous, etc., but during this period the malady was most often referred to as "the Graveyard Disease," because if you were unlucky enough to catch it, that's where you were headed. Anyway, back to Mr. Brocklehurst.) Mr. Brocklehurst had believed that it was good for the soul to have only burnt porridge to eat. (He meant the poverty-stricken, destitute soul, that is; the dignified, upper-class soul thrived, he found, on roast beef and plum pudding. And cookies, evidently.) Since Mr. Brocklehurst's untimely demise, conditions at the school had already improved tremendously. The girls unanimously agreed: whoever had killed Mr. Brocklehurst had done them a great service.

But who *had* killed Mr. Brocklehurst?

On this subject, the girls could only speculate. So far nobody—not the local authorities nor Scotland Yard—had been able to uncover the culprit.

"It was Miss Temple," Charlotte heard a girl say as she crossed the gardens. Katelyn was her name. "She served the tea, didn't she?"

"No, it was Miss Scatcherd," argued Victoria, her friend. "I heard she had a husband once, Miss Scatcherd did, who died suspiciously."

"That's just a rumor," said Katelyn. "Who'd marry Miss Scatcherd with a face like hers? I still say it was Miss Temple."

Victoria shook her head. "Miss Temple wouldn't hurt a fly. She's so sweet-natured and quiet."

"Oh, tosh," Katelyn said. "Everyone knows it's the quiet ones who you have to watch out for."

Charlotte smiled. She collected rumors the way some girls liked to accumulate dolls, recording the juicier details into a small notebook she kept. (Rumors were the one commodity that Lowood had in spades.) If the rumor were good enough, perhaps she'd compose a story about it later, to tell to her sisters at bedtime. But the death of Mr. Brocklehurst was much better than mere gossip passed around by a gaggle of teenage girls. It was a genuine, bona fide mystery.

The very best kind of story.

Once outside the walled gardens of Lowood, Charlotte pulled her notebook from her pocket and set off into the woods beyond the school at a brisk pace. It was difficult to walk and write at the same time, but she had long ago mastered this skill. Nothing so insignificant as getting from one destination to another should impede her writing, of course, and she knew the way by heart.

It's the quiet ones who you have to watch out for. That was quite a good line. She'd have to work it into something later.

Miss Temple and Miss Scatcherd were both reasonable suspects, but Charlotte believed that the murderer was somebody that no one else would ever think to consider. Another teacher, who had until recently been a student at Lowood herself. Charlotte's best friend.

Jane Eyre.

Charlotte climbed down into the dell and spotted Jane near the brook. Painting, as usual.

Talking to herself, as usual.

"It's not that I don't like Lowood. It's that I've hardly been anywhere else," she was saying to the empty air as she made a series of quick, short strokes onto her canvas. "But it's a school. It's not real life, is it? And there are no . . . boys."

Jane was a peculiar girl. Which is part of why Charlotte and Jane got along so well.

Jane let out a sigh. "It is true that things are so much better here, now that Mr. Brocklehurst is dead."

A thrill shivered down Charlotte's spine. Never mind that this was (as we have previously reported) what every girl at Lowood had been saying regarding Brocklehurst's untimely death. There was just something so satisfied about the tone in Jane's voice when she said it. It seemed practically a confession.

It had been no secret that Jane had detested Mr. Brocklehurst. There'd been a particular incident the week that Jane had first come to the school, when Mr. Brocklehurst had forced her to stand on a stool in front of her entire class, called her a liar— *worse than a heathen*, he'd said—and ordered the other girls to avoid Jane's company. (Mr. Brocklehurst had really been the worst.) And Charlotte remembered another time, after Mr. Brocklehurst had refused their request for more blankets, when the girls were waking up with chilblains (we looked this up, and a chilblain is a red, itchy, painful swelling on the fingers and toes, caused by exposure to cold—gosh, wasn't Mr. Brocklehurst the *worst*?), when Jane had quietly muttered, "Something should be done about him."

And now something had decisively been done about Mr. Brocklehurst. Coincidence? Charlotte thought not.

Jane looked up from her painting and smiled. "Oh, hello, Charlotte. Lovely day, isn't it?"

"It is." Charlotte smiled back. Yes, she suspected that Jane had murdered Mr. Brocklehurst, but Jane was still her best friend. She and Jane Eyre were kindred spirits. They were both poor as church mice: Jane a penniless orphan, Charlotte a parson's daughter. They were both plain—they even somewhat resembled each other—both exceedingly thin (at a time when the standard of beauty called for ladies to have a pleasant roundness to them), with similarly sallow complexions, and unremarkable brown hair and eyes. They were the most obscure type of person—the kind people's gazes would pass over without notice. This was also partially on account of the fact that they were both little—that is, short of stature, diminutive, *petite*, Charlotte preferred.

Still, there was beauty inside of them, if anyone cared to look. Charlotte had always known Jane to be a kind, thoughtful sort of person. Even when she was committing murder, she was thinking of others.

"What's the subject today?" Charlotte stepped up beside Jane's easel and lifted her spectacles to her eyes to examine Jane's unfinished painting. It was a perfect facsimile of the view from where they were standing—the dell dappled with sunshine, the leafy boughs of the trees, the swaying grass—except that in the foreground of Jane's painting, just across the brook, there was a golden-haired girl wearing a white dress. This figure had been featured in many of Jane's paintings.

"That's quite good," Charlotte commented. "And you've captured a sort of intelligence in her expression."

"She thinks she's intelligent, anyway." Jane smirked.

Charlotte lowered her glasses. "I thought you said she wasn't anyone in particular."

"Oh, she's not," Jane said quickly. "You know how it is. When I paint people they sometimes come to life in my mind."

Charlotte nodded. "The person who possesses the creative gift owns something of which she is not always master—something that at times strangely wills and works for itself."

Jane didn't reply. Charlotte lifted her glasses to look at her. Jane was staring off at nothing. Again.

"You're not leaving Lowood, are you?" Charlotte asked. "Are you going to be a governess?" (That was really the only viable career choice for girls at Lowood: teaching. You could become a village schoolmistress, or an instructor at some institution like Lowood, which is what Jane had done, or a governess in some wealthy household. Being a governess was really the best any of them could hope for.)

Jane glanced at her feet. "Oh, no, nothing like that. I was just . . . imagining another life."

"I imagine leaving Lowood all the time," Charlotte said. "I'd leave tomorrow if the opportunity presented itself."

But now Jane was shaking her head. "I don't wish to leave Lowood. That's why I stayed on, after I graduated. I can't leave."

"Why ever not?"

"This place is my home, and my . . . friends are here."

Charlotte was beyond flattered. She'd had no idea that Jane had stayed at Lowood simply because she hadn't wished the two of them to be separated. Charlotte was, as far as she could tell, Jane's only friend, thanks to Mr. Brocklehurst. (Charlotte had never given a fig to what Mr. Brocklehurst had dictated concerning Jane.) Friendship was indeed the most valuable of possessions, especially for a girl like Jane, who lacked any family to speak of. (Charlotte was the middle child of six—which she counted as both a blessing and a curse.)

"Well, I think you should go, if you can," Charlotte said gallantly. "I would miss you, of course, but you're a painter. Who knows what beautiful things there are to behold outside of this dreary location? New landscapes. New people." She smiled mischievously. "And . . . boys."

Jane's cheeks colored. "Boys," she murmured to herself. "Yes."

Both girls were quiet, imagining the boys of the world. Then they sighed a very yearning type of sigh.

This preoccupation with boys might seem a little silly to you, dear reader, but remember that this is England in 1834 (think before Charles Dickens, after Jane Austen). Women at this time were taught that the best thing that could ever possibly happen to a girl was to be married. To a wealthy man, preferably. And it was really good luck if you could snag someone attractive, or with some kind of amusing talent, or who owned a nice dog. But all that truly mattered was landing a man—really, any man would do. Charlotte and Jane had few prospects in this department (see the above description of them being poor, plain, obscure, and little), but they could still imagine themselves swept off their feet by handsome strangers who would look past their poverty and their plainness and see something worthy of love.

It was Jane who broke the spell first. She turned back to her painting. "So. What marvelous story will you write today?"

Charlotte shook the idea of boys out of her brain and took a seat on the fallen log she always perched on. "Today . . . a murder mystery."

Jane frowned. "I thought you were writing about the school."

This was true. Before all of this business with Mr. Brockle-hurst, Charlotte had begun writing (drum roll, please) her Very-First-Ever-Attempt-at-a-Novel. Charlotte had always heard that it was best to write what you know . . . and all Charlotte really knew, at this point in her life, was Lowood, so the First Novel had been about life at a school for impoverished girls. If you'd flipped through Charlotte's notebook, you would have found page after page of her observations of the buildings, the grounds, notes on the history of the school, detailed renderings of the individual teachers and their mannerisms, the girls' struggles with cold, the Graveyard Disease, and, above all, the abominable porridge.

Consider the following passage from page twenty-seven:

Ravenous, and now very faint, I devoured a spoonful or two of my portion without thinking of its taste; but the first edge of hunger blunted, I perceived I had got in hand a nauseous mess: burnt porridge is almost as bad as rotten potatoes; famine itself soon sickens over it. The spoons were moved most slowly: I saw each girl taste her food and try to swallow it; but in most cases the effort was soon relinquished. Breakfast was over, and none had breakfasted.

That had all been fine, Charlotte thought, especially that bit about the porridge. But this was supposed to be a NOVEL. There had to be more than just simple observation. There had to be a story. A plot. A level of intrigue.

She was on the right track, she was fairly certain. The main subject of Charlotte's novel was a peculiar girl named Jane . . . Frere, a plain, penniless orphan who must struggle to survive in the harsh environment of the unforgiving school. And Jane was smart. Resourceful. A bit odd, truth be told, but compelling. Likeable. Charlotte had always felt that Jane was the perfect protagonist for a novel (although she hadn't told Jane that she had the honor of being immortalized in fiction. She was waiting, she supposed, for the right time for that conversation). So the character was good. The setting was interesting. But the novel itself had been somewhat lacking in excitement.

Until the death of Mr. Brocklehurst, that is. It had been a

most fortuitous turn of events.

"The girls are beginning to theorize that it was Miss Scatcherd. What do you think?" Charlotte lifted her glasses to her eyes again to watch Jane's face for any telltale reaction, but Jane's expression remained completely blank.

"It wasn't Miss Scatcherd," Jane said matter-of-factly.

"You sound so certain," Charlotte prodded. "How do you know?"

Jane cleared her throat delicately. "Can we talk about something else, perhaps? I'm so weary of Mr. Brocklehurst."

How doubly suspicious that now Jane wanted to change the subject, but Charlotte obliged. "Well, I did hear a good bit of news today. Apparently the Society is coming here."

Jane's brow rumpled. "The Society?"

"You know, the Society. For the Relocation of Wayward Spirits. There was a 'Royal' in there somewhere, too, at one time, but they had to drop it on account of their falling out with the king. Which I think must be a terribly interesting story."

Jane's brow was still rumpled. "Well, of course I've heard of them. But I never—"

"Do you not believe in ghosts?" Charlotte chattered on. "I believe in ghosts. I think I may have seen one myself once, back in the cemetery at Haworth a few years ago. At least I thought I did."

"What I'd like to know is, what do they do with them?" Jane said gravely.

"What do you mean?"

"The Society. What do they do with the ghosts they capture?"

Charlotte tilted her head to one side, thinking. "Do you know, I've no idea. I've only heard that if you're having a problem with a ghost, you send for the Society, and they apparently all wear black masks that are quite striking, and then they come and . . ." She gestured vaguely into the air. "Poof. No more ghost. No more trouble."

"Poof," Jane repeated softly.

"Poof!" Charlotte clapped her hands together. "Isn't it exciting that they're coming?"

"They're coming here." Jane pressed a hand to her forehead as if she was suddenly feeling faint. Which didn't alarm Charlotte, as young women of this time period felt faint regularly. Because corsets.

"Well, they're not coming to Lowood, specifically," Charlotte amended. "Apparently the Society has been hired to do some kind of exorcism on Tuesday night at the Tully Pub in Oxenhope—you know the one they say has the shrieking lady over the bar? That's what I heard this morning from Miss Smith. But perhaps they *should* come to Lowood. Just think of how many girls have died here of the Graveyard Disease." Two of those girls had been her older sisters, Maria and Elizabeth. Charlotte cleared her throat. "The school must be bustling with ghosts."

Jane began to pace.

"We should request that they visit Lowood," decided Charlotte. Then she had a thunderous idea. "We should ask them to solve Mr. Brocklehurst's murder!" She paused and peered through her spectacles. "Unless there's some reason you can think of that we wouldn't want to solve Mr. Brocklehurst's murder."

Jane put a hand to her chest, as if she was now having true difficulty breathing. "How could they solve Mr. Brocklehurst's murder?"

"They can speak to the dead, apparently. I imagine they could simply ask him."

"I have to go." Jane started to gather up her painting supplies, in such a hurry that she smeared paint on her dress. Then she was practically bounding up the hill in the direction of the school. Charlotte watched her go. She opened her notebook.

It's the quiet ones who you have to watch out for, she read.

Jane Eyre had the opportunity and the motive to kill Mr. Brocklehurst, but could she have actually done it? Was she capable of cold-blooded murder for the good of the school? And if not, then why was she so agitated about the news of the Society? If not a murder, what else could Jane be hiding?

It was a mystery.

One that Charlotte Brontë intended to solve.

Jane TWO

Jane stood across the road from the Tully Pub, her gaze fixed upon the door. The scent of pork scratchings and pickled eggs wafting from the building made her stomach cramp painfully. Her supper of a spoonful of porridge and a half glass of water were hardly adequate sustenance for a girl of eighteen. (But at least the single spoonful of porridge tasted better now that Mr. Brocklehurst was dead, she thought, which was a small comfort.)

A man came down the road. Jane checked for a mask, but he was a regular man, wearing regular clothing and walking in a regular manner. He glanced in her direction but did not notice her, and then he swung the door to the pub wide open—inside was warm firelight and more men and a burst of raucous laughter and music—and disappeared into the room, the door slamming shut behind him.

She sighed. Before she'd arrived, she had expected to see a sign across the door of the pub reading "Keep out! Exorcism of Screaming Ghost Lady, and other Regular Maintenance." Surely a "relocation," or whatever it was called, would be a big to-do. But she'd been standing there for nearly half an hour, and in that time men had been freely coming and going out of the pub as they would any other night. Young women like Jane didn't belong in pubs, but she *had* to know if there was a ghost, and she *really* had to know what the Society would do to said ghost.

Jane, you see, had always believed in ghosts. When she was a small girl she'd lived with her horrible aunt Reed and two equally horrible cousins, and one night her aunt had forced Jane to sleep in the "Red Room." (This room had red wallpaper, red curtains, and red carpets—hence the name "Red Room.") It was creepy, and Jane had always imagined it was haunted by some shadowy, evil spirit. When Aunt Reed locked her in there, Jane tearfully begged to be let out, then screamed until she was hoarse, and finally fainted dead away—her heart, unbeknownst to Jane, actually stopped beating, so great was her terror.

She literally died of fright, if only for a moment. And when she opened her eyes again her late uncle was kneeling next to her, and he smiled at her kindly.

"Oh, good, you're awake. I was worried," he said.

"Uncle? How . . . are you?" She couldn't think of anything else to say to him. She knew she was being terribly rude, since clearly her uncle wasn't doing very well due to the fact that he'd been dead for years.

"I've been better," he replied. "Can you do me a quick favor?"

In the morning, when she was finally let out of the Red Room, Jane had marched right up to her aunt and informed her that Uncle Reed was quite perturbed. He had loved Jane—and as he was dying he'd made Aunt Reed promise to take good care of her, to "love her like a daughter." But Aunt Reed had obviously interpreted those words to mean "treat her like an indentured servant, and maybe starve her a bit for your own pleasure." For starved Jane had been, and generally mistreated, and Uncle Reed had taken note of it all from beyond the grave, and now he demanded that Aunt Reed make amends.

"He wants you to remember your promise," Jane explained. "He'd just like you to try to be a bit nicer."

Aunt Reed had responded by calling Jane a "liar" and a "devil child" and sending her away to Lowood, where Mr. Brocklehurst had also labeled her a "disobedient heathen girl who was headed straight for hell." But Jane never questioned what she'd seen. In her heart she knew that she'd really conversed with her dead uncle because it was the only moment of Jane's rather tragic life when she'd felt that she'd been part of a real family.

She never spoke of her uncle now, of course. Not to anyone. In Jane's experience, talking about it usually led to some form of punishment.

She stared at the tavern, her stomach grumbling loudly.

"Are you hungry, too?"

The soft voice startled her. She turned to discover a raggedly dressed little girl standing beside her. A street urchin.

"I'm hungry," reported the child. "I'm always hungry."

Jane glanced around. The street was deserted, save for herself and the urchin.

"I'm sorry, but I've nothing for you to eat," Jane whispered.

The girl smiled. "I want to be pretty like you when I grow up."

Jane shook her head at the wildly inaccurate compliment and turned her attention back to the pub.

"Are you going in there?" asked the girl. "I've heard it's haunted."

Yes. There was a ghost in there, and since nothing was happening outside, Jane must go in to see it. "Stay here," she said to the urchin, and then hurried across the road. She took a deep breath and pushed through the door of the pub.

She'd done it. She'd gone inside.

The pub was packed. The scent of liquor mixed with body odor assaulted her senses. For a moment she felt paralyzed, unsure of what to do now that her waning burst of courage had propelled her into the tavern. There was no ghost that she could see. Perhaps Charlotte had been wrong.

She should ask. Of course, that would mean she would have to *speak to a man*. Jane had wistful fantasies about boys, but these were men. They were hairy and smelly and huge. It seemed utterly impossible to have a conversation with one of these drunken men lurching about the pub.

She did not belong here. She lowered her head, slyly pinched her nose to shut out the dreadful man smells, and barreled through the crowd toward the bar. (At least, Jane would call it barreling. We would describe it as delicately weaving.) At her approach the barkeep glanced up.

"Can I help you, miss?" he asked. "Are you lost?"

"No," she said hoarsely. "No, at least I don't think I'm lost. Is this the . . . establishment . . . where . . ."

"Where what?" asked the barkeep. "Speak up. I can't hear you."

Her corset felt horribly tight. (It was. That was rather the point of corsets.)

"Here. On the house." The barkeep poured a glass of brandy and slid it over. For a moment Jane looked utterly scandalized that he should offer her such a thing. Then she snatched up the glass and took a sip. The liquid fire seared down her esophagus. She gasped and put the glass down. "Is this the place where the—"

She had just started to pronounce the word *ghost* when an unearthly shriek filled the room. Jane jerked her gaze upward to behold a woman in a white nightdress hovering in the air above the bar. The woman's hair was raven black, floating all around her head like she was caught in an underwater current. Her skin was almost entirely translucent, but her eyes glowed like coals.

She was perhaps the most beautiful ghost Jane had ever seen. And Jane had seen her share of ghosts.

"Just ask your question, miss," the barkeep was saying, his eyes still fixed on Jane. "I haven't got all night, you know."

He obviously didn't see the ghost.

"Never mind." Jane took another sip of the brandy and backed away from the bar to better regard the unhappy spirit.

"Where did they take him?" the ghost moaned. "Where did they take my husband?"

Jane felt a tug of pity for the woman.

"Where is he?" cried the ghost.

How awful, Jane thought, to be parted from one's true love, to be so cruelly severed from one's other half, like losing a part of your very soul. It was terrible. But also . . . terribly romantic.

"I know he's here somewhere!" shrieked the ghost. "He always is. I've got a few things to say to him, I'll tell you what. That good-for-nothing Billy-born-drunk!"

Oh. Oh, dear.

The ghost raised her arm and swatted at Jane's brandy glass. It went flying, whizzing past Jane's left ear, and crashed into the back wall.

"Cricum jiminy!" exclaimed the barkeep, because he had obviously noticed the flight of the brandy glass. "The Shrieking Lady's back!" He glanced up at the clock on the wall. "Right on schedule."

"Not worth a rap!" bellowed the ghost. "The boozer!" She swept around the room in a whoosh of cold wind and then back to the bar, knocking the clock off the wall for good measure. "The muck snipe!"

"Where's the blooming Society?" the barkeep groaned. "They're supposed to be here."

"I know you're hiding that ratbag!" The Shrieking Lady

grabbed the bottle of brandy and lobbed it at the barkeep's head. Her aim was true. Down he went, without another word.

This wouldn't do at all. Jane ducked so that she would be less of a target, and crawled and slid and scurried until she was safely tucked away behind the bar, where she could use the unconscious barkeep as a shield. (Always thinking of others, that Jane.) The hem of her dress was sticking to the booze-soaked floor, which was unfortunate, but unpreventable at this point.

She peered around the incapacitated barkeep to watch the ghastly scene continue to unfold. The Shrieking Lady kept demanding to see her degenerate husband, all the while hurling things about the room. The bar patrons were cursing and bumping into one another in their haste to steer clear of the ghost, although they didn't seem to be particularly interested in vacating the pub. They were probably used to it.

What a mess, thought Jane glumly as the Shrieking Lady sent a huge jar of pickled eggs crashing to the floor. By now she was feeling markedly less pity for the woman. This ghost is definitely troublesome, she concluded. So where was the blooming—oh dear, pardon her French—Society?

At that exact moment, as if her thoughts had conjured him, a man in a black mask jumped onto a table in the center of the room. He took a small object out of his pocket and threw it against the wall.

It exploded with a flash and a bang.

The crowd stilled. Then all faces turned to stare in

open-mouthed silence at the masked man.

Jane caught herself staring, too, her breath catching—although, again, that could have just been her corset. She shoved the barkeep aside to get a better look.

The agent was a young man—even wearing the mask, that much was clear—although Jane wouldn't call him a boy, either. Most of the men of this era had a mustache or, at the very least, sideburns, but he had neither. Jane wouldn't call him handsome. (In the pre-Victorian age, a truly handsome man should be pale—because being out in the sun was for peasants—with a long, oval-shaped face, a narrow jaw, a small mouth, and a pointy chin. We know. We can't believe it, either.) This young man's jaw was decidedly square, and his hair was too long. But he was obviously of the upper class, wearing a fine wool coat and expensive-looking leather gloves.

"Everybody out!" he shouted, and Jane ducked behind the bar.

The crowd immediately exited in an orderly fashion. The room was now empty save for another masked man, this one younger than the first, definitely a boy, and wearing a much shabbier suit. Apparently they came in pairs.

The one with the exploding thing jumped down off the table.

"Now pay close attention," he said to the second agent. "First we clear the room. Then we confirm the identity of the spirit."

The spirit. Jane had almost forgotten. She glanced up to see the ghost. The Shrieking Lady had long since stopped shrieking, too busy staring at the agents.

The one in charge produced a small, black leather-bound note-book from an inner pocket of his coat, and a pencil. He opened the book gently, in a way that reminded Jane of Charlotte, and turned to a marked page.

"Tell me your name, spirit," he directed at the ghost, sounding almost bored.

The Shrieking Lady pressed her back against the ceiling but refused to answer. The other agent, the short one with the mop of red hair and glasses—which Jane noticed he wore *over* his mask—stepped forward. "You should really answer him," he said, looking at the ghost. "Please."

The one in charge shushed the redhead. He turned to the ghost again. "You are Claire Doolittle, are you not?"

"I lost him," the ghost whispered. She sounded suddenly forlorn. "They took him."

"Took who?" The agent consulted his notebook. "Your husband? He was thrown into debtors' prison, if I'm not mistaken. A gambling problem."

The ghost swayed from left to right, but said nothing.

The agent glanced down at his notebook again. "His name was Frances Doolittle."

"Frank," the ghost sneered. "He was a hornswoggler."

"Frank," said the agent, jotting that down. "Hornswoggler." He reached into his pocket again and drew out a silver pocket watch. "All right," he said to the second agent, "now observe this closely. When capturing a spirit—"

The ghost let out a wail so loud and so mournful that Jane's stomach twisted with a new wave of pity. Then the Shrieking Lady snatched the watch from the agent's grasp. At least that's what she tried to do, but failed, as the watch passed through her insubstantial hand and clattered onto the floor.

The next events happened in quick succession:

The agent in charge reached for the pocket watch on the floor.

The ghost sensed an escape window and darted downward from the ceiling.

"She flees!" cried the redhead.

The agent in charge leapt nimbly through the air and landed beside the ghost. "Get the watch! It's—" But he couldn't finish the order because the redhead clumsily lunged forward and dove to tackle the ghost, but instead of tackling her, he—naturally—flew right through her and landed in a pile next to Jane's hiding place behind the bar.

At which point Jane shot to her feet.

All eyes fell on Jane, including the ghost's.

"Uh, good evening." Jane waved. "I was, um . . . sleeping . . . sweeping . . . then sleeping."

A moment of complete silence passed. Nobody moved, except the redheaded one, who groaned and rubbed his temple. But the ghost began to drift purposefully toward Jane.

"Sleeping," the first agent said skeptically.

"I . . . I . . ." Jane stammered. "I was drunk. From the drinking of . . . the brandy."

"Right."

By now, the Shrieking Lady was uncomfortably close to Jane, who tried with all her might to pretend she couldn't see the wayward spirit.

"Hello," the ghost said.

Jane could feel the masked man's eyes on hers. She quickly glanced at the ceiling. A table. The painting on the wall. Anywhere but at the ghost.

"You are so beautiful," the ghost breathed.

Jane's cheeks went red. She never knew how to answer to this, mostly because living persons had been telling her all her life how very plain she was.

What a commonplace girl.

And . . .

Oh dear. I do hope she can secure a position . . . somewhere.

And . . .

Oh goodness. How unexceptional. (She always wondered why, if she was so unexceptional, did people feel the need to comment on it?)

To ghosts, however, she was the epitome of beauty.

This left Jane to believe that something was seriously askew in the afterlife.

"You're so like my Jamie," the Shrieking Lady continued. "With the sun setting behind him." Jane didn't know who this Jamie person was, but the dead woman obviously felt entirely different about him than she had about her husband. "A soft breeze ruffling his red hair," she cooed.

Jane's hand, almost of its own accord, reached up and brushed away a few strands of her unexceptional hair from her unexceptional eyes, as she tried desperately, tenaciously, to ignore the ghost.

The agent in charge glanced from Jane to the ghost and back again, his head tilted to one side.

"Oh my, would you look at the time." Jane gestured to where, until a few moments ago, the clock had been hanging on the wall. "I must go."

The dratted ghost breezed even closer. Jane had seen this type before. This could turn into a fly-on-flypaper situation. Which she could not let happen now.

She took another two steps back. The ghost floated two steps forward. "I've never seen anything so lovely," she said in a sigh. "You're truly radiant." She wrapped her arms about Jane.

Jane smiled nervously at the men. "I wouldn't want to interrupt your important work. So I will just stand here. Not moving."

The agent in charge frowned at Jane in a puzzled way. Then he bent and picked up the pocket watch from the floor. He walked cautiously toward Jane and the ghost. When he reached the apparition he whispered, "Spirit, you are hereby relocated."

"What are you doing?" Jane asked.

He didn't answer. Instead he raised the pocket watch high into the air and bopped the ghost on the head with it.

(We understand, reader, this is an extremely pedestrian way to describe something, this "bopping on the head." But after numerous revisions and several visits with a thesaurus, that really is the most adequate description. He bopped it on the head.)

A frigid blast of air blew Jane's hair from her face. The silver pocket watch glowed, and then, to Jane's horror, sucked the ghost in. Poof—Claire Doolittle was gone. *Gone*. But where?

Jane stared at the pocket watch, hoping the ghost was all right, but the watch vibrated and shook and jerked away like the ghost was trying to escape. The agent dangled the watch by its chain until it stilled. Then he made a move to toss it to the redhead, but at the last moment seemed to think better of it, and wrapped the watch in a scrap of fabric before returning it to his pocket.

It was all so sinister. "Where did she go? Is she in there?" For a moment Jane completely forgot herself.

The agent turned to look at her sharply. "So you *did* see her."

Drat. Ever since the Red Room, Jane had operated by the following set of rules:

Rule #1. Never tell anyone that she could see ghosts. Never. Ever. Ever.

Rule #2. Never interact with or speak to a ghost in the presence of a living person.

Rule #3. No matter how tempted she was, no matter how interesting the ghost, no matter how pressing the situation seemed to be, refer to rules #1 and #2.

"No, I—I didn't see her," Jane stammered. "*It*, I mean. I saw nothing."

The agent narrowed his eyes. "Who are you?"

"No one, sir."

"You're obviously someone," he countered. "You're a seer, at the very least. And you came from somewhere. Where?" His notebook was in his hand again. Jane felt a surge of panic. In spite of her strict adherence to the rules concerning ghosts (which were more like guidelines, really), she was not a very good liar.

"I assure you, sir, I am no one worth noting," she said, although this did nothing to stop his obvious noting of her in his notebook. "If you'll excuse me, I'm very late." She gave a quick curtsy and started for the door, but the agent stepped into her path.

"You're late? Who could be expecting you at this hour?"

"My students," she blurted. "I'm an instructor. I am teaching maths."

"You teach mathematics in the middle of the night."

"Yes," Jane agreed. "Imagine how worried my students must be."

The agent frowned and was obviously about to question her further, but at that moment the barkeep (having only now regained consciousness) stood up from behind the bar. "What happened?" he asked groggily.

The agent narrowed his eyes at the barkeep. "Who are you, sir?"

"I'm Pete. Obviously." He rubbed the goose egg on the back of his head. "I own the place. You're wearing a mask. You're from the Society. Did you get the ghost?"

"Yes," the agent said.

"I'm sorry I missed it." Pete surveyed the destruction of his pub. "Good riddance, I say."

The agent turned back to Jane, who had been silently sidestepping toward the door. "At what school do you teach?" he asked her.

She stopped. "Oh, I'm sure you've never heard of it."

"There is a school nearby," the redhead piped up from behind them. "Do you teach at Lowood? Perhaps you are acquainted with—"

"I suppose now you'll be wanting to be paid," the barkeep interrupted, clearly impatient to get on with his business of straightening up the pub and reopening it. He scratched his chin. "Ten pounds, was it?"

"Fifteen," the agent clarified, reluctantly turning his attention away from Jane as Pete the bar-owner went to fetch his purse and then slowly, grumpily, counted the coins off into the agent's hand. In shillings, not pounds, which was going to take a while.

That was all the opportunity she needed. Jane fled, pausing only to swipe a pickled egg or two from the floor on her way out, because she had learned never to leave a room with free food without grabbing some.

"Wait, I still wish to speak with you," the agent called after her as Pete continued to count out the cash with excruciating slowness. "Wait!"

But Jane was out the door. The street urchin was still standing in the exact spot where Jane had left her.

"Did you see a ghost?" the child asked.

"Run, urchin, run!" Jane cried. The little girl sprinted away, and Jane ran, too.

* * *

The moment Jane stepped across the school boundaries, Mr. Brocklehurst appeared.

"Miss Eyre! What are you doing skulking about at this hour! I've caught you!" He pointed to the ground beneath his feet. "You shall be made to kneel on Cook's cornmeal!"

The scars on Jane's knees prickled at the thought. But happily Mr. Brocklehurst was dead.

Which, sadly, had not made him any less annoying.

"You know, I had a wife," he said, wiping a nonexistent tear from his nonexistent face. "And children. What will become of them now?"

Jane considered feeling bad for him, but then a few victims of the Graveyard Disease floated by, and she decided against it.

"You're looking well, Miss Eyre," Mr. Brocklehurst noticed, his eyes narrowing. "Please don't tell me they have increased food rations at the school. I'll have Miss Temple's hide for this!"

Jane's stomach growled. The pickled eggs had done little to take the edge off. She pushed past the ghost and headed for the second floor.

"Come back here at once!" Mr. Brocklehurst shouted. "Miss Eyre!"

"Oh, leave me alone," Jane muttered. "You can't hurt anyone anymore."

Mr. Brocklehurst huffed, but to her relief he did not follow.

In the stairwell she came upon Charlotte curled up with a

candle, writing. She was always writing, always, oblivious to the rest of the world, scribbling away into that notebook she carried around. Jane was exceedingly fond of Charlotte. The girl was a bit peculiar, but that only made Jane like her more. Charlotte was Jane's favorite non-dead person at Lowood, but Jane was too frazzled for conversation at the moment.

She had almost passed by unnoticed when Charlotte looked up from her notebook.

"Did you say something about hurting someone?" Charlotte asked. "Tell me more."

"Oh, Charlotte, good evening. I didn't see you there." Jane thought fast for a diversion. "Did you happen to notice the moon tonight?"

"Yes. Very round. Did you say something about hurting some-one?" Charlotte held her pencil at the ready.

"Did you *write* something about hurting someone?" Jane replied.

And just like that, they seemed at an impasse in a contest of some sort, where the opponents had no idea what the contest was about.

"I do apologize, Charlotte, but I'm rather tired. I think I'll go to bed."

"Is that Charlotte Brontë?" came Mr. Brocklehurst's muted voice from downstairs. "Skulking about in the middle of the night? Disgraceful. She should be punished!"

Jane was glad that Charlotte couldn't hear him.

"Did you go to the pub?" Charlotte asked. "I thought you might. It's what I would have done, if I were allowed to leave the grounds."

The girl apparently missed nothing.

Jane attempted to look scandalized. "Why ever would I go to a pub? A young woman of my position does not belong in such a place. So . . . no, no, I certainly did not go to a pub. I was taking a midnight stroll."

Charlotte nodded. "Was the ghost there? Did you see the men from the Society? Did they capture the ghost? Was it very exciting?"

For a moment Jane was tempted to share her secrets with her friend, but that would definitely be breaking Rule #1, so Jane simply said, "I assure you, it was only a walk in the moonlight. You know I like walking. Well. Good night, Charlotte."

She made her way up the stairs and to her tiny room.

Where Helen Burns was waiting. Her best friend and favorite ghost in all the world.

"Thank goodness you're back! What happened?" Helen asked, her translucent cheeks flushed with the fever that had killed her so many years ago.

Jane dropped her face into her hands. "It was terrible. He just . . . bopped that poor ghost over the head." And then the entire story spilled out of her in a rush.

"So the Society can do all the things the papers claim," said Helen after Jane had finished talking.

"They can." Jane kicked off her shoes and began to struggle out of her various layers of repressive clothing. "And they're cruel. They didn't even bother talking to the ghost much. They were simply intent on capturing her. And she wasn't so very troublesome. . . ." Jane recalled the brandy glass smashing against the wall. The clock. The jar of pickled eggs. "Well, she did need help. But she didn't deserve to be trapped in a pocket watch."

"A pocket watch. How awful," Helen said with a shudder. "It must be so cramped. And think of the ticking."

Jane finished dressing and blew out the candle. The two curled up together on Jane's small, lumpy bed, as they had always done, even though sleep was only required by one of them. For a long while Jane stared up at the dark ceiling, then suddenly said, "The Society might come tomorrow."

Helen sat up abruptly. "Here?"

Jane sat up, too. "Yes. The agents seemed very curious about me. And one guessed that I teach at Lowood. If they come, you must stay hidden."

"I'll stay out of sight," promised Helen.

Jane paused for a moment. "It's time to leave this place. This time I'm serious."

Helen's lower lip trembled slightly. "You would leave me?"

"I will never leave you! I meant both of us would leave. Together, as always."

Helen had been Jane's first true friend, her only friend at Lowood until Charlotte had come along. Helen had stood by Jane when everyone else shamed and punished her. And despite Jane's excessive plainness and her many other inadequacies, Helen had loved her.

But Helen died when she was fourteen. That spring a particularly nasty version of the Graveyard Disease had descended on Lowood. By May, forty-five of the eighty pupils lay in quarantine, Helen among them. One night Miss Temple helped Jane sneak past the nurses into the room where Helen lay dying.

Jane had climbed into Helen's cot. "Helen, don't leave me," she whispered.

"I would never," Helen promised. "Hold my hand."

Jane clasped her friend's hand tightly, trying to ignore how cold Helen's fingers were. They fell asleep like that, and when she woke the next morning, Helen's body was pale and still.

And standing above it was Helen's ghost.

"Hi," she said with a mischievous smile. "I think I get to stay."

It was always hit-and-miss with ghosts as to which ones stayed and which ones left for some great beyond. But Helen had stayed with Jane, true to her promise. And Jane promised, in return, that they would never be parted. Helen was the closest thing to a sister Jane had ever had. She could not—would not—abandon Helen. But now she worried that the Society would storm Lowood tomorrow. And if it wasn't tomorrow, it was only a matter of time. There were so many ghosts here, one was bound to cause a problem. Mr. Brocklehurst, probably.

"It's not as if we have anywhere to go," Helen was saying.

"I could get a job."

"What job?"

"I could be a seamstress."

"Your sewing is terrible," Helen pointed out. "I love you, but you know it's true."

"I could wash clothes and press them."

"Think of how chapped and red your little hands would get."

"I could be a governess."

Helen nodded thoughtfully. "You are a good teacher. And you like children. But you're far too beautiful to be a governess."

Helen was no different from the other ghosts in this regard. She thought Jane was beautiful, even though it was Helen, with her porcelain complexion, blue eyes, and long golden hair, who would have turned heads if she were still alive. "What does my appearance have to do with anything?" Jane asked.

"You're so lovely that the master of the house wouldn't be able to help falling in love with you," Helen explained. "It would be a terrible scandal."

Jane didn't think that sounded so terrible. "I could handle it."

"Trust me. It would end badly," Helen said stubbornly.

"Please, Helen. We must do this. Say you'll come with me. Say you'll try."

"All right. I'll come with you. I'll try," said Helen.

They fell silent again. From outside Jane heard the mournful coo of a dove. Daylight was fast approaching. In a few hours, she had a French class to teach. She was quite good at French. And some

Italian. She could conjugate Latin verbs. She could do maths. In spite of Lowood being such a hard place to grow up, she'd received a good education here. She'd studied classic literature and history and religion. She knew the rules of etiquette. She could embroider a pillowcase and knit socks (well, she'd only ever been able to finish one sock—two seemed overwhelming). She was adequate on the pianoforte, and more than proficient at painting and drawing and any kind of art. And she *was* a good teacher, she told herself. She'd make an excellent governess.

"You want to be a painter," said Helen, as if she'd read Jane's mind. "That's what you should do. Be a famous painter."

Jane scoffed at the idea of being a famous anything. "Yes, well, people aren't posting job advertisements for famous painters at the moment."

"They aren't posting job advertisements for governesses, either." This was true. Every week Jane scoured the job ads in the newspaper, seeking her escape from Lowood, and there had been nothing for governesses lately. It seemed that all the wealthy children in England were already being cared for.

"So we won't be going anywhere at the moment," Helen said.

"No," Jane agreed glumly. "I suppose not."

THREE

Alexander

The moment he stepped onto the grounds of Lowood, Alexander Blackwood was surrounded by ghosts.

Twenty-seven of them, in fact. An unusually high number.

Now, Alexander was no stranger to ghosts. Ghosts were his job. (His main job, that is. The job that paid the bills. His side job—well, more about that later.) But he wasn't here for ghosts. He was here for a girl, the one he thought could be a seer. But instead he ended up with twenty-seven ghosts, twenty-six of whom were young girls, and one of whom wanted his murder solved.

"Are you listening?" asked the ghost. "I've been *murdered*."

Alexander made a note in his notebook: *Twenty-seven ghosts. One claims he's been murdered.*

The girls were all different ages, with different color hair and skin and eyes, and different—uh—names, too, presumably (although Alexander didn't bother to make formal introductions), but the one thing they all had in common was the sad expressions that spoke of short, difficult lives without affection.

Well, that and the fact that they were all dead.

"Mr. Brocklehurst killed me," said a transparent girl wearing a dress of colorless burlap. Her lips were tinged blue, as though she'd been very cold when she'd died. "He locked me in a closet for five hours. By the time anyone came to find me, I was dead."

Alexander's eyebrows rose.

"You needed to think about what you'd done," said the ghost of Mr. Brocklehurst.

"He killed me, too," claimed another girl. This one had red welts all over her arms and neck, with angry slashes across her skin like she'd tried to scratch the welts right off. "I'm allergic to burlap."

(Hey, reader, it's us again. We did some digging, and it seems as though burlap wasn't produced until 1855. At least, that's the popular theory. We did a little *more* digging and it turns out that Brocklehurst actually invented burlap just to make his students miserable, but it wasn't widely known about until much later. Now you know.)

Alexander looked at the ghost of Mr. Brocklehurst, who just shrugged.

"Itching is good for the soul," he said. "It inspires prayer."

As Alexander walked up the stairs to the crumbling school

building, the ghosts continued offering grievances against the late Mr. Brocklehurst, who countered every accusation with an excuse of some sort.

The door squeaked open before Alexander could knock, and another girl squinted out at him. This one was alive, we should mention.

She raised a pair of thick spectacles on a wand. "You must be from the Society! I recognized you by your mask. Everyone says people from the Society wear masks so the ghosts can't discern what they look like. Is that true?"

"My name is Alexander Blackwood. I'm here to speak with one of your teachers."

"Are you here about the murder?" she asked tightly.

"I could tell you about the murder," said the ghost of Mr. Brocklehurst. "I was there, after all."

"I'm here to speak with one of your teachers," Alexander said again.

"Which teacher?"

Well. That one was harder. He hadn't caught the teacher's name. "I'd like to see all the teachers." He was fairly certain he'd recognize the girl from the pub if he saw her again, although if he'd been asked to describe her, he wasn't sure about her hair or eye color. She was small in stature, he recalled. And her coat had been gray.

"Shouldn't there be another agent with you?" the girl asked, and peered around him as though someone might be hiding in the tall weeds that lined the walkway. "I've heard that you work in pairs."

"I don't need an assistant today." He cringed at the thought of last night. Who tried to *tackle* a ghost? They'd almost failed the assignment because of that dunce.

"Interesting." The girl traded her spectacles for a notebook and began scribbling into it.

"That's Charlotte," supplied Mr. Brocklehurst. "And if I weren't dead, I'd—"

"Stop," Alexander interrupted. He didn't want to hear what kind of punishment would be dealt to the girl. In fact, he was rather coming to understand why someone might have wanted to murder Mr. Brocklehurst.

The girl looked up from her notebook. "Excuse me?"

"Stop delaying, I mean." Alexander pointedly looked around her, peering into the foyer. "I'm on a schedule. Miss . . . ?" He had learned that her name was Charlotte, but of course it would be improper to address a young woman by her first name.

"Sorry." She stowed her notebook and pencil and stepped aside so he could enter. "I'm a writer, you see. Charlotte Brontë, at your service."

"A pleasure to meet you, Miss Brontë." Alexander went inside, the ghosts of dead students trailing behind him. "What do you write about?"

"Everything," Miss Brontë said. "But murder, lately."

"A popular subject." He looked at her more closely; murder

(and the avenging of) was one of the topics he was most interested in, himself. "Have you been writing about this murder in particular?"

Her face went blank and her voice flat. "I suppose you could say that."

"And what have you concluded?"

"That it's generally agreed upon that we're better off now that Mr. Brocklehurst is gone, so who cares who did it?"

"I'm standing right here!" cried Mr. Brocklehurst.

"Whoever killed him did us a great service," Miss Brontë went on, not hearing the ghost, of course.

"I see. So you won't tell me who you think did it?"

She shook her head.

He found that commendable, in a way, but solving the murder made an excellent excuse to gather the teachers together. He didn't want anyone to get ideas about him coming to see a young lady he'd met at the pub.

"Very well. I'll solve your murder."

"It's not *my* murder," Miss Brontë insisted. "It's *our* murder, in that it benefits us all."

"Then will you please allow me to see the teachers?"

"Of course I want the murder solved!" Miss Brontë collected herself. "I mean, please follow me."

"Miss Brontë thinks Miss Eyre poisoned me. I read her notebook over her shoulder." Brocklehurst sighed. "They're friends. Makes sense, if you ask me. They're both ungrateful little liars."

"You believe Miss Eyre did it, don't you?" Alexander asked. To confirm the ghost's claims, and definitely not because he enjoyed shocking people.

Miss Brontë's face turned white. "Of course I don't. Why would I think that?"

Alexander took out his own notebook. *Student suspects "Miss Eyre" may have poisoned Brocklehurst,* he wrote. And then, to Miss Brontë, he said, "All right, please gather all the teachers together."

Miss Brontë lifted her chin. "I'd rather not do anything until I know whether you're going to arrest my friend."

Alexander frowned.

"You don't scare me."

Alexander kept frowning.

"Not even with that mask."

More frowning.

"Fine. But remember, she's my friend, and even if she did kill him, she helped the school. You have no idea how bad things were. It was self-defense."

"I know about the burlap."

"Daisy was allergic to burlap!" Miss Brontë pulled out her notebook and scribbled what looked like *He knows about the burlap.* "All right, go ahead and solve the murder, but don't arrest anyone I like."

He tried not to smile. "I make no promises, Miss Brontë."

Several minutes later, Alexander found himself in the center of the parlor, with teachers and students (both living and dead) all standing in a circle like an audience. It was quite crowded, and everyone seemed to be talking at once, going back and forth about the murder, the improved situation since, and the latest theories about who'd done it.

And . . . there was an even more uncomfortable topic spreading from the back of the room. More uncomfortable than murder. More uncomfortable than the murderer likely being in the room with them. And that was—

"A *boy*," one of the girls said, and she didn't exactly say it quietly enough to avoid Alexander's notice. "A boy *here*."

"I've never seen a boy so tall." That was another girl in the back. "With hair so black."

"You've never seen a boy, so you don't know if this one is tall or not."

"He looks like someone straight out of a story."

"Do you think he's come to marry one of us?"

"He's probably here to marry a teacher."

"Miss Scatcherd? Or Miss Smith?"

"No, probably Miss Temple. She's so pretty. Imagine what beautiful babies they'd have."

Alexander felt his face going red under his mask, and it wasn't long before the living half of the girls were finger-combing their hair and pinching one another's cheeks. Some of the dead girls started, too.

Quickly, he found the line of teachers near the door. One was definitely a Miss Scatcherd, if the sour expression on her face was any indication. The second was a tall, lovely woman, possibly Miss Temple. The third might have been a Miss Smith. And the fourth was the girl from the pub.

Their eyes met, and the young lady blushed and looked away.

"You," he said, approaching her. "What's your name?"

Her mouth moved, and some sort of sound came out, but it was too soft to hear under the students bouncing where they stood.

"Oh my gosh!" one of the girls whisper-screamed. "He's here to marry Miss Eyre!"

Miss Eyre. The same girl Miss Brontë thought killed Mr. Brocklehurst.

Alexander sighed, but at least he'd found her. "Miss Eyre," he said, "may I speak with you privately?"

Miss Eyre didn't say a word, but when he went out of the room, she followed after a bit of prodding from Miss Temple.

Just before he closed the door, Miss Brontë caught his eye. *Do not arrest her!* she mouthed.

"Miss Eyre," he said once the door was closed and they had the hallway to themselves. "I've come to speak to you."

"To me, sir? Everyone says you're here to solve the murder."

"Not originally," he said. "I came here to see you."

"Why me? I didn't do anything."

Well, she might have murdered Mr. Brocklehurst, but that was beside the point.

"Of course you did nothing wrong," he said quickly. "I'm with the Society for the Relocation of Wayward Spirits. You may have heard of us."

Miss Eyre said nothing.

"Well, I assume you've heard of us. Is that why you came to the pub last night? Because you learned we would be coming?"

Miss Eyre said nothing.

Alexander cleared his throat. "I know you were able to see the ghost. That would make you what we call a seer."

Miss Eyre . . . still said nothing.

He tried a new tactic. "You shouldn't be ashamed of what you can do. It's actually a rare and valuable gift. It makes you unique. Special."

Her brow rumpled, but still she said nothing.

"At the Society we are in great need of such talented individuals. Normally we don't employ women, of course, but in this case I think an exception could be made."

Nothing.

"I'm trying to offer you a job," he said. "At the Society."

Her eyes widened slightly. That was obviously not what she'd been expecting.

"What do you think, Miss Eyre?" he prompted.

"I think . . ." She frowned.

Of course she must be overwhelmed, to have such a sudden, wonderful turn of her fortunes.

"I think I must decline. I'm going to be a governess," she said.

Alexander's mouth dropped open. "A governess! Why?"

"It's my life's dream. I've always wanted to be one. I think children are adorable."

"But . . ." He was completely flummoxed. "What are your qualifications for being a governess?" Because she *clearly* had the single most important qualification to be a Society agent: she could see ghosts.

"My qualifications?" Miss Eyre shook her head. "Why, I was meant to be a governess." She rattled off a list of things she could do: something about Latin verbs and pianoforte and high marks in classic literature.

He frowned. "I'm afraid I don't understand."

"I'm going to be a governess," she said. "Thank you very much."

Alexander scowled. "Are you sure I can't persuade you to join the Society? If you'll just come with me to London, I can show you—"

"I'm going to be a governess!" Miss Eyre pressed her hands to her mouth. "Excuse me. Can we get on with the murder investigation?" She turned on her heel and opened the door to the parlor.

Several girls jumped back (Miss Brontë included) and scattered to the other side of the room, as though they definitely hadn't been trying to listen at the door. Fortunately for Alexander, he hadn't been speaking about the whole seer and job thing with much volume. By now, the students had probably decided on names for the children they imagined he and Jane Eyre would create.

Awkward.

Confused over the less-than-favorable response to his job proposal, Alexander turned to leave.

"Wait," called one of the girls. "Did you solve the murder?"

Alexander glanced from Miss Eyre to Brocklehurst to the door and back to Miss Eyre. "Should I?"

"*Yes,*" several girls cried.

"No!" said Miss Brontë.

The latter was outvoted. Alexander strode into the center of the room. His eyes landed on Miss Temple. "Please tell me what you know about the poisoning." Now that the seer had turned him down, he wanted to get back to his inn.

Miss Scatcherd prodded Miss Temple. "Go on. He wants to talk to you."

A couple of the students in the back whispered that he'd left Miss Eyre for Miss Temple, and what a scandal it was. "This is like a real live romance novel," one girl said. "I can't stand the tension. Who will he choose?"

Alexander couldn't wait until his life revolved around ghosts again. "Miss Temple," he said gently, "if you'd tell me about the day Mr. Brocklehurst expired, I'd be so grateful."

"He'd be sooo grateful," sighed one of the girls.

Miss Temple was trembling as she stepped forward. "Well, Mr. Brocklehurst came for one of his monthly inspections—"

"Pardon me," Alexander said. "We can skip that part. I know enough about the school under Mr. Brocklehurst's care."

Miss Brontë was standing near Miss Temple, and the student

leaned forward just enough to mutter under her breath, "He knows about the burlap."

"Ah. Very well." Miss Temple clasped her hands together. "Mr. Brocklehurst had demanded tea and cookies, so the girls and I made them while he napped in front of the fire. After he awakened, I served the refreshments. A short time later, he expired, though I didn't realize it at first. I thought he'd just gone back to sleep."

"Very interesting," said Alexander. He turned to Miss Scatcherd. "Please bring me the teacup."

Miss Scatcherd pressed her lips together and frowned, then turned toward a girl nearby. "Anne, fetch the teacup."

"Which teacup?" asked the girl.

"The one Mr. Brocklehurst drank from!" Miss Scatcherd huffed. "Of course."

"All the teacups are the same." Anne pressed both fists against her mouth.

Alexander hated when his clients were difficult and he had to embarrass them, but he needed that teacup. "Miss Scatcherd. The teacup. Now."

Her face reddened, and after a tense moment with everyone staring at her, she turned and vanished down a hall.

"Why do you want the teacup?" Brocklehurst asked.

Alexander ignored him. Instead, he looked at Miss Eyre. She was so obviously a seer. And, quite strangely, she was surrounded by adoring ghosts. One of the dead girls whispered that she liked

Miss Eyre's hair, and another inquired about her skincare regimen.

How could she *not* want to work for the Society?

"Look," whispered one of the living girls. "He's pining."

"I *really* hope it works out for them," said another girl.

Abruptly, Miss Eyre excused herself and headed toward the door, slipping through the crowd of people (avoiding stepping inside any of the ghosts, too, he noticed).

Miss Brontë caught Miss Eyre's arm. "Are you all right?" asked the former.

Miss Eyre shook her head. "I don't feel well."

Just as Miss Eyre left the room, Miss Scatcherd returned with a cart full of teacups.

"Perhaps you misunderstood my request?" Alexander said. "I only needed the one."

Miss Scatcherd rolled her rattling cart through the crowd and parked it against a wall. There had to be at least thirty teacups. They were chipped and worn, with the paint rubbed off most of the ceramic. "Yes, well." The teacher came to stand by Alexander, but landed partly in Mr. Brocklehurst.

Brocklehurst shuddered and jumped away, and all throughout the room, girls gasped and rubbed their arms, as though chilled.

"The cup was washed and put away with the rest." Miss Scatcherd shook her head. "I didn't realize you were going to ask about our teacups. How am I supposed to know which one was *the* one?"

"The teacup held poison and you just *put it away*?"

"We *washed* it." Miss Scatcherd shrugged.

"Very well." Alexander approached the cart of teacups and glared, like glaring may reveal which teacup potentially held poison.

"I'd have served his tea in the one with the fewest chips," offered Miss Temple.

That did narrow it down some. Alexander picked out the five cups with the fewest number of chips and showed them to Brocklehurst. "Do any of these look familiar?"

"They all look the same!" The spirit of Mr. Brocklehurst slammed a fist on the cart, making several cups jump. One crashed to the floor. The girls yelped.

This was bad. Alexander had to get the spirit under control before anything worse happened. The living couldn't usually tell what the dead were doing—not unless they were like him—but when spirits became emotionally charged, the boundaries of what was possible shifted.

"Why do you care so much about *which* cup it was?" asked a dead student.

"Because." Alexander seized one of the potentially poison-bearing cups and tapped Brocklehurst on the forehead with it.

The ceramic went right through.

Everyone was staring. The living were clearly questioning their faith in his ability to deal with ghosts. The ghosts of students past just frowned and muttered that it was rude to put things *through* ghosts. And Mr. Brocklehurst himself just seemed confused.

"Don't do that again."

Alexander did it again, this time with a different cup. Again, though, it had no effect.

"If you would all be so kind as to leave the room," Alexander said to the living students and the teachers. Clearly, this was going to get ugly.

"I don't know what's going on," said one of the students.

"No one does," replied Miss Temple, nudging the student toward the door. "But I think we should leave."

"Why are you hitting me with cups?" Brocklehurst's face and neck turned red, in spite of the fact that he was dead and didn't have blood anymore. "I demand that you stop!"

Alexander did it again with a third cup.

Nothing.

Maybe it wasn't a cup, then. But he'd been *so* certain. Of course it had to be a cup, didn't it? What if it had been the cookies? He'd have no clear talisman. It could be a spatula, a mixing bowl, or even the oven.

As Alexander reached for a fourth cup, Brocklehurst lashed out and struck a painting off the wall.

At once, screams filled the parlor. The ghosts stayed in place, but the living moved toward the exit at top speed.

Brocklehurst, for his part, threw more things onto the floor: cups, pens, books.

Alexander had to act quickly. Brandishing the fourth cup, he pursued the angry ghost.

"Stop hitting my head with cups!" screamed Brocklehurst.

"Not until I know which cup it was!" Alexander tried again, and this time the ceramic thudded firmly against the ghost's forehead.

Immediately the ghost of Mr. Brocklehurst was sucked into the teacup. The ceramic trembled in Alexander's gloved hands, like the ghost was struggling to escape.

"Please work," Alexander whispered. And then there was a flash of light and the shuddering stopped. He'd trapped Mr. Brocklehurst.

Carefully, he wrapped the teacup in a scrap of burlap. Handling these talismans was a delicate business, and why he always wore gloves: touching a talisman could lead to possession by the ghost trapped within. Society agents always wore gloves, to be safe.

"Are you going to make any arrests?" Miss Brontë asked, returning to the now-empty parlor.

Alexander shrugged. "My job isn't actually to solve murders. I capture ghosts. Though sometimes that involves solving murders. I just didn't need to this time."

Miss Brontë pressed her lips together. "Mr. Blackwood, are you going to relocate the other ghosts in Lowood? I imagine there are a lot after all these years." There was a look in her eye. A sadness, as though she'd lost people she cared about.

Alexander shook his head. "I can relocate any the school finds troublesome, but to relocate them all would take a lot of time and it's not strictly necessary, unless the spirits begin causing problems."

The girl's shoulders relaxed. "No, no. I mean, unless they

want to go with you. But perhaps they're happy here. Even though they're dead."

"Perhaps." Alexander's encounters with ghosts were rarely happy ones. People never called him because of *friendly* ghosts.

"Well, good day to you." Miss Brontë pulled out her notebook and wandered away, busy with whatever story she was telling now.

Alexander just hoped it wasn't a romance.

Back at the inn, Alexander pulled out a pen and slip of paper to send a note to the Duke of Wellington.

> *Sir, I've encountered a seer. Her name is Jane Eyre. Unfortunately, she has declined my initial offer to join the Society. I will endeavor to persuade her. —A. Black*

When the ink was dry, he sealed the paper closed with a drop of wax and secured the note to a pigeon's ankle. Soon, the bird was off to London and the Society headquarters.

Alexander had dedicated his life to the RWS Society at the tender age of four, when three important things had happened: (1) His father was killed. (2) He gained the ability to see ghosts. (3) The Duke of Wellington took him in and began training him to become the best agent the Society had ever seen.

This was where the side business came in. Yes, Alexander was the star agent of the Society, and usually that was good enough for him, but his father hadn't just been killed.

He'd been *murdered*.

This meant that Alexander's side business was actually the

revenge business, though to be completely honest he had just the one customer: himself.

For fourteen years, he'd been working toward avenging his father's murder, but he didn't have much to go on at the moment, only the fuzzy memories of a frightened young boy. Which made revenge quite difficult. So he poured himself into his day job at the Society, tracking down troublesome ghosts, reading newspapers in search of new recruits, and generally trying to keep the struggling Society on its feet.

Reading a newspaper was how he'd found his apprentice, who'd been the perfect age to join the Society, and at the perfect place in his life. He'd had no other attachments that might prevent him from doing his job. (Sometimes people did.) And he'd had the gift. (Not everyone got it, even under all the right circumstances.) Over the years, Alexander had offered jobs to several people, and most were happy to join. But ever since the king cut funding, recruitment had been far more difficult.

Just as night fell, and Alexander finished writing up a formal report to go along with the teacup and Brocklehurst incident, a pigeon arrived with a note from Wellington. (Yes, this does sound like a remarkably fast reply for the day, and it was. But Arthur Wellesley, the Duke of Wellington, possessed the fastest racer pigeons in all of England. One could even say that they were almost supernaturally fast.)

Alexander snapped the wax seal and unfolded the note.

I trust you. —A. Well

For the next several minutes, Alexander thought back to his approach to the job offer. Everything had been hectic. She'd been flustered, he thought. Perhaps an impromptu relocation hadn't been the best time or place for such a proposal (no matter that he'd gone there with that intention in the first place).

Very well, then. He'd go back and he'd try again, and this time he would get it right.

FOUR
Charlotte

As you, dear reader, could have probably guessed, the students at Lowood school were no longer remotely interested in the murder of Mr. Brocklehurst. Now all they wanted to talk about was the dashing and impossibly enigmatic Mr. Blackwood—*sigh, Mr. Blackwood*—with his fine wool coat and his fine black hair. That such a person—*an actual boy!*—had taken an interest in Jane Eyre—*the most unremarkable girl, so plain!*—was the most sensational gossip ever to grace the halls of Lowood. Even if Mr. Blackwood wasn't exactly handsome, per se (his jaw was simply too square), he was definitely wealthy—*I mean, look at his coat*—which was all that truly mattered. *And there's just something about him, don't you think, that makes him the most interesting person you've ever encountered? That coat. That hair. That mask, so very mysterious, framing those piercing eyes.* (There'd been

54

a fierce argument over the color of those piercing eyes. Some said they were a deep and mossy green; others said a storm-tossed blue.) And let's not forget the way those piercing eyes had gazed at Jane Eyre—*so intently, so very, well,* piercing—*sigh—Don't you wish someone might gaze that way at you?*

Charlotte was a bit weary of the gossip, truth be told. Of course she was interested in Mr. Blackwood. She'd noted that he had quite an arresting manner and very shapely hands. But her main interest in Mr. Blackwood was on account of his position as a member of the RWS Society. He had the best job in England, in Charlotte's opinion. The idea of traveling the country, gathering information, taking notes, tracking down ghosts, capturing them: it was the most glamorous form of employment that Charlotte could envision. She could only imagine the stories she'd collect at such a job.

Mr. Blackwood had returned to the school twice after the initial visit. He'd presented himself the next morning and requested to be given a private audience with Miss Eyre. To discuss his earlier proposition, he said. (At this point, several of the girls had fainted in sheer delight—a proposition!) But Jane had refused to see him.

Undeterred (*he must be so very besotted with her,* speculated the girls), Mr. Blackwood had reappeared the following morning. Same time. Same reason.

"I have nothing to say to him," Jane had said stiffly. "Please tell him to go away. Politely."

Charlotte couldn't fathom that Mr. Blackwood had actually

asked Jane to marry him. They'd only just met. Charlotte believed in love at first sight, of course—she dreamed that one day, at some unexpected moment, such a thing might even happen to her—but she firmly disapproved of marriage at first sight. Instead she thought that this whole business with Mr. Blackwood and Jane must have something to do with Jane's night at the Tully Pub. Something significant must have happened.

There was a story there. She could feel it in her bones. Something that perhaps she could work into her Very First Novel about Miss Jane Frere.

"Perhaps," Charlotte had relayed to Mr. Blackwood back in the parlor, "if you could enlighten me as to the nature of your request, I could entreat Miss Eyre on your behalf?"

Mr. Blackwood shifted uneasily on the sofa. "I'm not at liberty to discuss the details with anyone but Miss Eyre. I simply wish to know if she has reconsidered my . . ."

Oh, my, perhaps he *had* proposed. Charlotte lifted her spectacles to see his face. His cheeks were slightly flushed. And his eyes, she noticed, were a deep sable brown.

She leaned forward. "Yes?"

". . . if she would reconsider my offer of employment at the SRWS."

Charlotte blinked at him. "You wish to employ Jane Eyre? At the Society?"

"Yes."

"Am I to understand that the Society is recruiting new

agents?" She leaned forward even further. "*Female* agents?"

"Yes."

He was rather monosyllabic, wasn't he? But never mind that. This was wonderful news.

"Well, sir," she said rather breathlessly. "Jane seems to have made up her mind." (Jane was mad, clearly. What could she be thinking, refusing such an offer?) "I know her well, and once her mind is made up about something, there's little changing it." She was thinking in particular about Jane's response that time when Mr. Brocklehurst wanted to cut the girls' hair so that they wouldn't become vain. But then she didn't want to bring up Mr. Brocklehurst.

Mr. Blackwood exhaled—a small, frustrated breath—and scratched at the side of his face. Charlotte got the impression that *no* was not something that this man was used to hearing. "I did not anticipate that she would refuse to even see me. If she would only hear me out, I'm sure I could—"

"No, sir," Charlotte said gently. "If she said no, she most likely means it."

He looked crestfallen. And also like he was trying to hide how crestfallen he was. He straightened. "Well. This is most unfortunate. Not many people would pass up such an opportunity."

Charlotte completely agreed. She gave a nervous laugh. "I wonder—" She took a fortifying breath and summoned her courage. "I wonder if you might consider employing someone else."

His eyebrows furrowed. "Someone else?"

"One of the other girls at Lowood." She was now leaning so far forward in her seat that she almost tumbled to the floor. "Namely, me, sir." Before he could reply, she rushed out with her qualifications. "I'm at the top of my class. I'm a quick study—I could pick up any skill you required with veritable ease. I'm hardworking. Resourceful. And I've a keen eye." She thrust her dratted spectacles into her pocket and squinted at him. "I could be entirely useful."

Mr. Blackwood cleared his throat. "I'm sure that you are a bright and enterprising young woman."

"I am. I really am, and I'm not just saying so because it's terrible here, and I'm desperate to leave."

"Tell me something." Now he was leaning forward, too. "Are we alone?"

She pulled out her glasses again to glance around the room. "Relatively," she answered. "Miss Scatcherd is standing just outside the door, of course, to chaperone, but other than that, we're quite alone." Her heart thundered in her chest. He must be about to tell her something confidential.

He nodded as if confirming something he already knew, then sighed regretfully.

"The offer is for Miss Eyre, I'm afraid. No substitutions." He stood and gave a stiff bow. "Miss Brontë."

Disappointment clawed at her. She stood, too, and curtsied. "Mr. Blackwood."

"I hope you'll urge Miss Eyre to reconsider. She knows, I

suppose, where to find me if she changes her mind."

"Yes," she managed. "Yes, I shall urge her."

He did not return. The girls at Lowood had decided therefore that they were witnessing some great romantic tragedy, and that Jane had been jilted and was now probably going to die of a broken heart. Which was nonsense, Charlotte knew very well. Jane was the jilter, not the jiltee. And this was not about romance. This was about ghosts, Charlotte was certain. Adventure was knocking at Jane's door! But to Charlotte's utter dismay, Jane stubbornly refused to open it. And even worse, she offered no further details about the mysterious job offer.

"It's a simple misunderstanding," she said to Charlotte for the umpteenth time as they sat down to breakfast a few days later.

"A misunderstanding of what, exactly?"

"It's of no consequence."

"It's of great consequence!" Charlotte argued hotly. "Why must you be so deliberately obtuse?"

The dining room had fallen silent. The other girls were staring. (This was the inception of a particular rumor that Charlotte Brontë was also madly in love with Mr. Blackwood, and she and Jane Eyre would now be forced to compete for the man's affections. Bets were then taken regarding which of the girls would win Mr. Blackwood's heart. Most thought it would be Jane. *Both girls are plain, but at least Jane is not blind as a bat. Those spectacles are simply dreadful.*)

"Why must you be so melodramatic?" Jane whispered.

Charlotte was almost pleading at this point. "What happened in Oxenhope that night that so affects you? Why did the Society seek you out? I must know."

"Then you must get used to disappointment." Jane's mouth tightened into a line as if she were sealing her lips with glue, and Charlotte knew she'd been defeated. Since then, Jane and Charlotte had hardly spoken at all. But Charlotte had continued to watch Jane closely, and Jane had continued to speak to *herself*, more than ever, when she thought no one could hear her. She'd been distracted during lessons, sometimes drifting off mid-lecture, lost in thought. And she had left off painting, which to Charlotte was the greatest indication of all that Jane was not herself.

"All right," Charlotte had heard Jane cry out this morning in the washroom. "You're even worse than Charlotte. If you don't stop talking about that horrible Society perhaps I'll poof *you* into a pocket watch!"

Jane knows something troubling about the Society, Charlotte scribbled into her notebook. *She also has a pocket watch.* She glanced up from her writing to look at Jane, who was now demurely seated in the study near the window, away from the students who were doing their needlework and not-so-subtly gossiping about her love life. Jane was angrily darning a single sock.

Miss Temple appeared in the doorway. "The newspaper is here."

The girls all sat up straight and tried to catch Miss Temple's eye. Every week, only one newspaper was delivered to Lowood, and this one newspaper had to be shared by more than fifty girls. Miss Temple always chose a special student, a girl she wished to reward for good behavior, to look at the paper first. Then it was a matter of seniority—the older girls, then the younger. Sometimes the paper was in tatters by the time Charlotte got to read it, but she always read every sentence on every page.

Miss Temple glanced around the room. Charlotte smiled up at her hopefully.

Miss Temple turned to Jane. "Miss Eyre, would you like to read the paper? I know I typically pick a deserving student, but I thought . . ."

Miss Temple was so kind. She knew that Jane had suffered a trying week.

But Jane shook her head. "I'll stick to my sock."

This was also a sign that something was off. Normally Jane loved to read the newspaper almost as much as Charlotte did.

"All right." Miss Temple sounded a bit offended. She scanned the room again. "Miss Brontë, then. You've been so helpful lately."

She handed the newspaper to Charlotte, who laid it carefully on the table next to her notebook—she'd be taking notes on current affairs now, of course, to find the best stories—and unfolded the pages, relishing the heady aroma of the fresh-printed paper and ink. Then on to reading. There was something about King William having yet another row with the Duke of Wellington over some political disagreement or other. An impassioned essay by a young man named Charles Dickens about the state of the poor in London.

A list of persons who had recently died from the Graveyard Disease. A recipe for plum pudding that made Charlotte's stomach rumble. But not much that she found newsworthy.

She turned to the advertisement section last, in which she came upon this notice:

WANTED: A GOVERNESS FOR ONE ADORABLE CHILD.

THE YOUNG LADY IN QUESTION SHOULD BE AT LEAST EIGHTEEN YEARS OF AGE, WELL EDUCATED, PROFICIENT IN THE PIANOFORTE, ABLE TO CONJUGATE LATIN VERBS, AND WELL VERSED IN CLASSIC LITERATURE. MOREOVER, IT IS PREFERRED THAT SAID YOUNG LADY HAVE A CHEERY DISPOSITION, ROSY CHEEKS, AND ABSOLUTELY NO WARTS. SHE SHOULD BE AMENABLE TO PLAYING GAMES (ALL SORTS).

IT IS ALSO IMPERATIVE THAT THE YOUNG LADY IN QUESTION SPEAK FRENCH.

TO APPLY FOR THIS POSITION, PLEASE CONTACT MRS. FAIRFAX AT THORNFIELD HALL.

Charlotte read the advertisement again, because it struck her as so unbelievably specific. That, and it nearly perfectly described someone she knew. Not herself, of course, as she was only sixteen and not remotely interested in becoming a governess. And not the rosy cheek part. But everything else.

She bit her lip. Coming upon this ad at this precise moment had an air of providence to it. Some might even call it destiny. But surely the position Mr. Blackwood had offered Jane was a great deal better than being a mere governess. Surely, given time, Jane would realize that. She'd try for a larger destiny. She'd . . .

No. Jane was not going to change her mind. She had set herself against it, and would not be unset.

Charlotte stood and walked over to Jane, who was still furiously darning her sock by the window.

"Darn," Jane muttered. "Darn. Darn."

"Jane," Charlotte said.

Jane looked up with a little sigh. "Yes, Charlotte?"

Charlotte held out the paper. "You should have a look at this."

The other girls began to whisper excitedly among themselves, certain that a quarrel over Mr. Blackwood was imminent.

Jane shook her head. "I know you mean well. But I've already said that I—"

"No, this." Charlotte pointed to the advertisement, her finger landing neatly on the word *ROSY* in *ROSY CHEEKS*.

Jane took the paper from her hands. "Wait. What's this?"

Charlotte intuitively felt that she was about to lose her best friend. And that she was about to lose a story that could have been *the* story. She swallowed down the lump in her throat. "I believe this is meant for you."

* * *

A week later Charlotte walked Jane out to the main gate at Lowood, Jane dragging a small trunk crammed with her belongings and various art supplies. Jane seemed a bit of a mess. She kept glancing over to one side and whispering, "We're going to be all right. You'll see."

"Yes, we're going to be all right," Charlotte assured Jane. Things had been better between them since she'd spotted the advertisement. Settled. Boring. But better. "I shall miss you."

"And I, you." Jane took a deep breath and stepped past the main gate and officially off the Lowood grounds.

"Come on," she said. "We're almost there."

Charlotte nodded and followed her to the waiting carriage. Jane opened the carriage door and paused, as if she were hesitant, in this final moment, to actually leave.

"We can do this," she breathed.

"Yes," Charlotte agreed. "We can."

Then all at once the tension drained out of Jane's shoulders, and she climbed up into the carriage.

"Good-bye, Jane." Charlotte straightened and said with confidence, "We shall meet again, one day, under far better circumstances." She'd written this into her notebook earlier. It was a good line, a hopeful line, though in this moment she doubted it was true. She wondered if she would ever see Jane Eyre again.

Jane reached down to briefly clasp Charlotte's hand. "Good-bye, Charlotte."

"Good-bye."

The driver of the carriage, a hairy man with a tattered top hat, walked heavily over and closed the carriage door, pushing Charlotte aside and parting the two friends. He took Jane's trunk and slung it onto the roof of the carriage, where he fastened it down. Charlotte stepped back through the gate, clutching her notebook to her chest, still looking at Jane.

"All right, miss," the driver said. "Are you ready to go?"

Jane's eyes were shining as she took one last look at Lowood. "We're ready," she said.

FIVE

It became clear from the moment she arrived: something was amiss at Thornfield Hall.

First of all, no one from the estate had come to meet Jane at the train station. She'd needed to hire a carriage, which became so full that Helen insisted on riding up front next to the driver. (Ghosts didn't like to be permeated by humans. They considered it most inappropriate, crossing all sorts of boundaries of pre-Victorian propriety.)

Secondly, when Jane and Helen had exited the carriage, the driver sped away without payment.

"How strange," Jane had said, befuddled but happy to hang on to any extra shillings.

Thirdly, though it was well into evening, the house seemed

empty. Thornfield Hall was massive. The turrets loomed. The darkened windows gaped black beyond the entrance, and the spires at the east and west wings rose upward as if the house were raising its arms to grab the sky.

Helen shivered next to Jane. "Perhaps we should return to Charlotte. She probably misses us."

"*Us?* Charlotte doesn't know you exist."

"Well, if she did, she would surely miss me."

"Come, now." Jane dragged her trunk to the entrance. The door was rounded at the top, and in the middle of its thick oak facade sat a large, ornate knocker that Jane wasn't sure she'd be able to lift. Not that there was anyone inside the house who would be around to hear it.

"It's haunted. It's haunted," Helen said, pacing back and forth. "It's so obviously haunted. If we looked up 'haunted' in that one book . . . what is it?"

"The dictionary?" Jane guessed.

"Yes. If we looked up 'haunted,' there would be a painting of this house."

Jane sighed. "You've been around ghosts your whole life—er—afterlife. What are you afraid of?"

Helen shook her head. "I think it might be haunted by the living."

"If that were the case, every house would be haunted."

"Every house *is* haunted."

Jane closed her eyes and blew out a breath. She had never quite understood Helen's fear of unfamiliar live people. "The living don't haunt," she said, opening her eyes just as a backlit shadow crossed behind the window of the uppermost room in the east turret. Darkness returned before Jane could figure out what exactly it was she had seen, but the fleeting glimpse sent a cold chill down her back. She tried to keep her face blank, for she didn't want to upset Helen, but she did make a mental note to ask Mrs. Fairfax about ghost activity at Thornfield Hall. She desperately hoped there was none. She didn't want anything to draw the attention of the Society and their dangerous pocket watches.

Jane lifted the giant knocker and let it fall.

"No one's coming," Helen said. "They're probably all dead."

"Give them a chance," Jane said pragmatically. "It's a large house. Who knows how many rooms one must pass through to get to this door?"

Helen shrugged and turned away, muttering, "I'm not sure I want anyone answering the door anyway."

"What, you want to set up a tent on the porch?" Jane ribbed, hoping to lift Helen's spirits.

Footfalls sounded from inside, followed by a flicker of light under the door.

"Someone's coming," Helen lamented.

"Well, which way do you want it?" Jane said. "Someone coming or no one coming?"

With a loud creak, the door opened, and there behind the light of a candle was a pleasant face belonging to a plump woman in a black uniform with a white cap. She held a candelabra.

"Can I help you?"

"Good evening," Jane said, her heart racing. "I'm Jane Eyre. I answered the advertisement for a governess position here."

"Miss Eyre! My, you're plain." She held the candle closer to Jane's face. "No rosy cheeks," she observed.

Jane put a hand to her face. "They tend to get rosier when it's cold. But I don't have warts. And I am proficient in French—"

"Never mind the rest. I am glad you're here. Please, come inside. Your note said you weren't to arrive until tomorrow."

If Jane had been the type of young lady who cursed, she would have. In her haste to leave Lowood (and the RWS Society), she must have written the wrong date. "I do apologize, Mrs. Fairfax. I hope we're not causing too much trouble."

"We?"

"Uh—" She didn't usually let things slip like this; it must have been nerves. "Forgive me. I haven't slept or eaten much." For her whole life.

"Of course. Cook shall prepare something at once." Mrs. Fairfax rang one of the several bells that lined the wall. "Come, come."

Not quite half an hour later, Jane was sitting comfortably by the fire in a spacious but cozy kitchen, sipping tea, surrounded by a dozen servants, from Mrs. Fairfax down to a young soot-covered boy, who was in charge of lighting fires in bedchambers. Cook placed a large bowl of hot stew beside Jane.

"Do eat," Mrs. Fairfax said.

Jane tried to be as ladylike as possible as she shoved spoonful after spoonful into her mouth. It was the most delicious stew she'd ever had. It was the *only* stew she'd ever had.

"Well, Miss Eyre, this is the entire house staff, and were Adele not asleep, I would introduce her as well. I know you must be tired, but would you please tell us a little about your background? From where do you come?"

Jane was about to answer, but then an eerie scream pierced the air.

Jane and Helen both startled. No one else moved.

"What was that?" Jane said.

"What was what?" Mrs. Fairfax said.

"That scream!"

"What scream?"

"The one just now," Jane exclaimed.

"The one that pierced the air!" Helen added.

"Oh, that would be the wolves," Mrs. Fairfax said cheerily, as if a bloodcurdling scream from a wolf wasn't only *slightly* less terrifying.

"That did not sound like an animal," Jane said.

"Oh, well, then it was the wind. Come along, dear. Everyone, time for bed."

"But . . ." Jane glanced around the room, confused at the utter lack of alarm. "But shouldn't we make sure no one is hurt?"

"Why, dear? The entire household is here. So, you see, it couldn't have been a human. And if it were a human, they would probably scream again. But no, there was just the one scream."

"What if they can't scream again?" Jane said with a tone of dread.

"Well then, there's not much to be done about it is there?" She headed for the doorway. "We should all turn in. Thank you, Miss Eyre, for delighting us tonight. Isn't it a prodigious thing indeed for someone so plain to be so clever?" Mrs. Fairfax held open the door. "Now, off to bed!"

Mrs. Fairfax instructed the soot-covered boy to start a fire for Miss Eyre. A scullery maid then led Jane and Helen to a bedchamber on the third floor. The room was big and warm, and the bed was comfortable, and after everything that had happened that day, all Jane could focus on was climbing under the covers and going to sleep.

"You might want to lock your door," the maid said on her way out.

"Why do you say that?" Jane asked.

"It's nothing to alarm you, miss. Grace Poole sometimes wanders the hallways." With that, she shut the door.

"I don't remember a Grace Poole among the servants, do you?" Jane asked Helen.

"Maybe she's a ghost."

"I'm sure the servant would have mentioned that small detail."

Helen frowned. "I told you this place was haunted."

Jane rubbed her forehead. "Grace Poole is probably on night

watch. And the sound could have been a wolf," she said mid-yawn.

"And I might be the Queen of England," Helen said.

"Hush, dear," Jane whispered. Helen went quiet.

Jane slept restlessly that night, stirring at the softest of noises. At least Helen was sprawled out beside her. Because the bed was that big.

The next day, Jane tried to ask Mrs. Fairfax again about the scream, but the woman wouldn't have it.

"There's an entire house and all of its quirks to learn," she said. "No time for speculating."

But Jane couldn't help speculating as Mrs. Fairfax ushered her from room to room.

The estate probably could've housed ten Lowood schools, it was so big. The only part of the house they didn't tour was the east wing, which Mrs. Fairfax said was boarded up for restoration. When the tour ended it was mid-morning. And time for tea in the kitchen.

"When am I to meet Adele?" Jane asked.

"Tonight," Mrs. Fairfax answered.

"And Mr. Rochester?"

"Who knows when the master will return. He often stays away for months at a time."

"Hmpf," came a grunt from the doorway of the room.

Jane startled and turned. In walked a woman wearing servant's clothes. Her apron sash sat askew on her hips, and her hair looked like it had barely survived a windstorm. A strong jaw and extreme eyebrows gave her a menacing appearance, which intensified when the candle by the doorway lit her features in such a way to cast a long shadow up her forehead. She strode over to the teapot, poured herself a cup, and strode back toward the doorway all the while making very little noise.

At the doorway, the cat blocked her passage and hissed. The woman leaned down and hissed back, revealing a mouth full of black and brown teeth. The cat sprinted away.

Jane considered this to be very strange behavior, but Mrs. Fairfax didn't even glance up from her tea.

"Who was that?" Jane asked.

"Grace Poole," Mrs. Fairfax said. "She works in the east wing."

"But I understood it to be boarded up for restoration?"

"Never mind about Grace Poole. Do you have any further questions for me, Miss Eyre?"

Helen raised her hand. "What do you mean she works in the east wing? Is *she* doing the restoration?"

Jane tried her best to ignore her friend. "Yes, what can you tell me about Mr. Rochester?"

"Oh, well," Mrs. Fairfax said. "He is a very good master, if somewhat unpredictable of mood. He is loyal and he pays our wages in a timely fashion, which makes it easier to forgive his sometimes dark manners and mostly rare but sometimes often outbursts of anger."

Jane could not figure out if Mrs. Fairfax liked her master or feared him.

"Now, Miss Eyre, if you could possibly post these letters." She grabbed a stack of envelopes from the table and thrust them toward Jane. "It's just down the road."

Jane had the distinct feeling she was being summarily dismissed.

Mrs. Fairfax ushered her out of the kitchen and toward the servants' entrance.

"But I'm unfamiliar with the area," Jane said.

"I'm sure you'll figure it out," Mrs. Fairfax said.

And with that, Jane and Helen found themselves out the door. Alone. On a dirt road. Which was blanketed in a thick fog.

"This is going so well," Jane said.

"We're all going to die," said Helen.

They walked in silence for a long time. For Jane's part, she was quiet because she didn't want to alert anyone (or anything) to her presence. But she'd never admit that to Helen, who was next to her, shaking uncontrollably.

"These woods are haunted," Helen said.

Jane forced a smile. "I've decided to believe Mrs. Fairfax. It was probably a fox."

"She said it was a wolf."

"Right. That's what I meant."

Helen looked skeptical. It wasn't Helen's fault she was holding on to this fear. Wayward ghosts always held on to feelings longer than necessary. It was how they became wayward in the first place.

Maybe she just needed a distraction.

"Helen, tell me the story of the first time we met," Jane said.

"You don't remember?"

"Of course I do, but I love to hear you tell it."

Helen smiled. "Well, I couldn't wash my hands that morning, for the water was frozen. Miss Scatcherd called me to task for it, and struck my neck with a bundle of sticks."

"Not that part!" Jane hated that part.

"But it's the reason you came and spoke to me that day, isn't it?"

"Yes," Jane allowed.

"So I will never resent that memory," Helen said simply.

The living Helen had been such a good person. Better than Jane. And though the ghostly Helen could be a bit precocious and paranoid, she was still a better person than Jane.

"You told me that day that it was not violence that overcomes hate, nor vengeance that heals injury," Jane said. "And it's a good thing you did, because I had formulated a plan to escape Lowood and beat my aunt Reed with a very large stick."

"No!" Helen exclaimed.

"No, of course not," Jane said. She would never. Not with a *large* stick.

Suddenly, they heard galloping hooves coming from somewhere deep in the fog.

"What is that?" Helen said, alarmed.

"Probably just a horse," Jane said in a trembling voice.

"What if it's a Gytrash?" Helen asked.

Jane sighed. She shouldn't have told Helen about the Gytrash, a northern ghost that appeared as a horse or a very large dog. Helen hadn't stopped pacing for days after that story.

"Gytrash aren't real," Jane said. But her voice wavered.

"You said Bessie told you about it and you said you believed her!" Helen said.

"That was a long time ago."

"That was last week."

The sound of hooves was getting louder. Jane's pulse quickened. Maybe Helen had a point.

"The legend also says no one rides the Gytrash, so if this horse has a rider, we know it's not a Gytrash." There, that should soothe Helen's nerves. Wild, unbridled horses were rare in this part of England.

To prove her point, Jane faced the sound of hoofbeats, just as a huge dog shot out of the mist and barreled toward her.

"Gytrash!" Jane exclaimed.

The dog was followed by a large black horse, with a large dark rider.

"Unfamiliar human!" Helen exclaimed. Her terror was so great that—for a moment—she appeared in the middle of the road, looking as solid and alive as Jane.

The horse neighed and skidded, but couldn't stop in time. He raced right through Helen, then reared up and bucked. The rider dropped to the ground.

Helen turned translucent again.

"Damn!" The rider sat on the ground a few meters away, his back to Jane.

Jane rushed forward. "Sir, are you hurt?"

He groaned and grabbed his ankle.

"Sir, can I be of help?"

"You mean, helping me with something other than throwing me from my horse at very great speeds? What are you, witches?"

Oh, no. *Witches.* Plural. He'd seen Helen.

Helen mouthed, *I'm sorry.*

Jane turned toward the man, who had been watching her, and promptly forgot what she was going to say, because she caught sight of his face, and it was easily the most handsome face she'd ever seen. Pale and oval in shape, sideburns all the way down to his pointed chin (which would technically make it a beard) and framing the most perfectly tiny lips she'd ever beheld.

"Witches," he snarled again. He was even handsome when he was calling her names.

"Sir, I believe you mean witch in the singular. There is no one here but me."

He frowned. "So you admit to being a witch?"

"No. I just meant if I were a witch, there would be just one of us. Of me. Sir, if you cannot move, I can fetch someone from Thornfield Hall. I live there."

At this, he raised his eyebrows.

"I do. My name is Jane Eyre. I can get help."

"You live at Thornfield Hall, witch?"

"I'm not a witch; I'm a governess. I'm employed by Mr. Rochester."

"Ah," he said. "Do help me up."

Helping him up would require more height and girth than Jane had. She looked left and right, hoping by some miracle that someone more muscular than she would appear. No one did.

Helen shrugged. "He doesn't look so hurt."

Jane shot her a look.

"All you must do is stand by my side and help me to my horse," the rider said.

Helen put a hand on her hip. "How are you supposed to do that? He's twice your size."

"Um . . ."

The man frowned. "Conversely, you could bring the horse to me."

Jane glanced at the dark beast. "No, let's try it your way."

The large dog bounded toward the rider again and licked his face. "Down, Pilot."

"Aw, he's such a cute puppy," Helen said.

Granted, he wasn't as scary as before, but Jane would hardly call him a cute puppy.

The man climbed to his feet and draped an arm around Jane's shoulder; he smelled of brush and pipe smoke. It was quite nice, not at all like the sour stench of the drunken louts in the Tully Pub.

She blushed. This was the closest she'd ever been to a man,

besides the unconscious barkeep, and we promise she was only using him for a shield. Had this extremely handsome man not been wounded, their contact would have been considered very inappropriate.

Jane helped him to his horse.

"Are you acquainted with this Mr. Rochester?" he asked.

"No, sir, I've never met him."

"What do you know of him?"

"He is loyal and pays his staff in a timely fashion, and the bursts of anger are rare. Mostly."

At this, he tilted his head. And his hair flopped. She'd never seen a man's hair flop so adorably. Admittedly, she'd never seen a man's hair flop before, but surely this was something special. Jane's cheeks flushed.

"Sir, if you are recovered, I should return to Thornfield."

"As you wish," the rider said. He hoisted himself onto the beast. "Farewell, Miss Eyre, if that is indeed your name."

"Why on earth would that not be your name?" Helen asked.

The strange man kicked his horse and the beast galloped away, trailed by the dog.

"Goodness," Helen murmured, "he was . . ."

"Tall? Dark? Brooding?" Jane filled in. He was just like the men in the great romances. He was just like Mr. Darcy. "I agree."

"I was going to say angry," Helen said.

"Well, he had a right to be. He was spooked by a couple of witches!" Jane replied.

Helen gave her a quizzical look. "Did you hit your head as well?"

Back at Thornfield, Jane removed her muddy shoes and scurried past the master's study. The door to the study had been shut the night before . . . but now it was wide open. And there was a fire. And a large dog.

"Pilot!" exclaimed Helen. The dog whipped his head toward her. "He heard me!" Helen clapped.

Jane threw a hand over Helen's mouth, hitting—of course—nothing but air. What was the rider's dog doing here? Unless . . . it was at that moment that the rider—Mr. Rochester, it must be!—stepped through the doorway of the study.

"Miss Eyre," he said.

Jane froze with her arm out at a strange angle, still covering Helen's mouth.

"You're Mr. Rochester," Jane said in disbelief, slowly lowering her arm.

"Don't you think it's a bit strange that he didn't mention the fact that he was your employer back there on the road?" Helen said. "I mean, it would've saved us a lot of mystery."

Jane shot her a look.

But Helen kept talking. "Four words: 'Mr. Rochester? That's me!' Then you could've been introduced and had a laugh about it."

"Shut it," Jane said through gritted teeth.

"Pilot will agree with me, won't you, boy?" Pilot whined and trotted over to Helen's feet and flipped onto his back.

"That's strange," Mr. Rochester commented. "First, you bewitch my horse. Now you've bewitched my dog."

Helen smiled widely. "Maybe we *are* witches!"

"Pilot!" Mr. Rochester barked. The dog reluctantly returned to his master. Between the sudden reveal of Mr. Rochester, and Helen's commentary, Jane was at a loss for words.

"You are much quieter than you were earlier," Mr. Rochester said.

"Maybe that's because you're suddenly Mr. Rochester," Jane said.

"It's not so sudden for me," he said. "It's been coming on for quite some time."

Jane laughed nervously. Handsome and witty. She glanced down at her fidgeting hands and forced them to be still.

"Well, Miss Eyre. Good day."

"Good day, sir."

He shut the door, and Jane walked slowly on.

"Are you all right?" Helen asked.

"I am more than all right. I feel as though I have just had the most exciting day of my life."

Helen frowned. "You didn't find him to be—"

"Quite possibly the most intriguing person I've ever met?" Jane interrupted. "Yes, my dearest friend. I did."

SIX

"You are quite possibly the most annoying person I've ever met," Alexander shouted above the beating hooves as the carriage careened wildly along the road. He and his assistant were not currently riding in the carriage, as normal people are meant to do, but clinging to the back as a ghost in a top hat laughed maniacally from the driver's seat, spooking the already spooked horses.

It had been a bad day. A bad week, really.

"I'm sorry, sir," shouted Mr. Branwell. "Please don't tell Mr. Wellesley. I didn't know he was a ghost."

Alexander cursed as a rock flew past his head. "How could you not know? He was transparent. You could practically see through him."

"My vision's not the best, sir." At the moment, Mr. Branwell's spectacles were dangling from his nose upside down, snagged on his mask.

"Fine. I'll take care of it." Alexander struggled to lift himself to the roof of the carriage, but then fell back again. They were moving too fast. The wind was blowing. The moon was in his eyes. Otherwise, he could have climbed up no problem.

And then it started to rain.

Things had been going wrong for Alexander since the mysterious Miss Eyre had rejected him at Lowood. First, his bumbling new assistant had contracted a man cold (which in pre-Victorian England they believed to be far worse than a lady cold). Then Mr. Branwell had proceeded to share said cold with Alexander. His nose was still red. And it hurt. He resented this.

Then Branwell had almost burned down the inn in a misguided attempt to make Alexander a bowl of chicken soup.

After that the innkeeper had understandably wanted them to leave. So Alexander had decided they should return to London and report to Wellington.

And oh, yes, he meant to report all of this to Wellington.

They'd been going along just fine toward London, when the carriage driver had stopped to rest the horses and water the shrubbery. That was when Branwell had noticed the figure standing on the side of the road: a somber-looking elderly gentleman with a top hat and a cane.

Alexander, of course, had known immediately that the man was a ghost. But squinting out into the foggy night, Branwell had called out, "Oh, hello, sir. It's quite cold tonight. Would you like to come inside the carriage to warm yourself?"

The ghost floated in and sat across from Branwell. (Which, unfortunately, was right next to Alexander. He considered saying something then and there. He should have, really. But by then Branwell was already engaged in a one-sided conversation with the ghost.)

"I work for the Society. Normally it's all very hush-hush, but you look trustworthy," said Branwell.

Alexander dragged his hand down his face.

"I don't know if you're aware," Branwell continued. "But you are in the presence of the star agent of the Society, Mr. Alexander Blackwood himself!"

Perhaps Branwell wasn't *so* bad.

Branwell pointed at Alexander and grinned. "He's a ghost hunter extraordinaire. No ghost is safe around this guy!"

And that's when, as they used to say, the dung hit the crosswind.

The ghost stood, his translucent body expanding to fill the carriage.

"Um, sir, are you all right?" inquired Branwell.

The ghost opened his mouth and a stream of flies buzzed out. Alexander had to confess he'd never seen that before. Then the ghost sprang through the roof of the carriage and into the driver's seat. He let out a bone-chilling cackle. The horses reared and bolted, taking the carriage with them. Alexander and Branwell attempted to climb around to the driver's seat, but then they hit a pre-Victorian pothole. And that's how they ended up clinging to the back of the carriage. And now you're caught up.

"I can help you, sir," offered Branwell even as his fingers began to slip off the railing one by one. "I can give you a boost."

"No! God, no! Under no circumstances are you to ever give me a boost." With renewed determination, Alexander tried again (by himself) to get to the roof of the carriage. This time he succeeded, only to crash through the fabric that was stretched over the top. Now he was *in* the runaway carriage. Which was only slightly better than hanging off the back of it.

But how to stop the ghost? Good question.

At that moment, the carriage struck a pre-Victorian speed bump, and an object from the floor of the carriage smacked Alexander in the head.

It was a cane, he ascertained when he woke up moments later. Oh, how embarrassing. He was never going to tell Branwell about this.

A cane. Neither he nor Branwell used a cane. What was it doing here? It had come in with the old man. But it was obviously real. He could only hope it would work as a talisman.

Alexander grasped the cane and climbed through the hole he'd so conveniently made for himself in the top of the carriage. He glanced back. Branwell was still dangling from the rail.

"Hello, sir!" Branwell almost waved but then remembered he was hanging on for dear life. "Don't worry about me, sir! I'll wait here."

Alexander nodded and then turned to the ghost, who was still laughing manically and goading the horses. Alexander brandished the cane.

"You, sir, are hereby relocated."

Bop.

Somehow they reached London alive.

Most people probably would have been quite impressed by Westminster, which housed the Society headquarters. After all, it was where Parliament ruled the kingdom. It was a grand sight, and a privilege to be there, Alexander supposed, but to him, the headquarters was simply his second home.

So Alexander rarely stopped to take in the glory, because he came here all the time, but we'd like to pause a moment and paint the picture for you.

Imagine an enormous stone palace with square towers, round towers, and elegant peaks. Add a couple dozen archways on the first floor, and even more windows above, and a few chimneys with smoke trickling into the blue sky. Now surround all that majesty with a cobblestone sea and horse-drawn carriages, and you have the House of Lords and Commons.

All in all, it was a very fancy place. We hope you're impressed.

Back to Alexander.

He just strolled through all of that, like it wasn't a big deal. He went through the secret halls, gave the password to the doorkeeper, and headed into the great library where Sir Arthur Wellesley kept his office.

Usually, he arrived with a smile on his face, but today his head hurt and his nose was still a bit raw and sniffly. And usually Alexander had succeeded in whatever task he'd been given. This time, shamefully, he'd failed. Oh, sure, he had the pocket watch and the teacup and a random cane containing the ghosts he'd captured, and they could be safely stored away in the collection room, but he had not persuaded Miss Eyre.

He knocked on the door and then entered the library to find the Duke of Wellington and Mr. Mitten—the Society's former liaison to the king—engaged in a conversation by the fire.

"My boy." Wellington stood, not bothering with a formal greeting. "Come in, come in." He shot a glance at Mr. Mitten, who got up and started for the door.

Alexander nodded. "Good day, Mr. Mitten."

"Good to see you, young man. I swear, you're the spitting image of your father."

People said that sort of thing to Alexander regularly, and it made his heart squeeze every time. "Thank you, sir."

Mr. Mitten smiled and was out the door.

"I'm glad to see you've returned. Have a seat." Wellington motioned to the chairs by the fire. "I'll call for tea."

Alexander smiled gratefully and pretended to study the spines of books while Wellington ordered tea. Then, when his mentor returned, they sat together.

"Now"—the duke leaned back in his chair—"tell me about our new agent."

"Branwell is perhaps one of the most enthusiastic agents I've ever met," Alexander said carefully. "His desire to learn and succeed is unparalleled."

Wellington nodded slowly. "Enthusiasm and desire to learn are well enough. Tell me about his capacity for such success."

There it was. This question was the reason Alexander had sent Branwell back to his flat, once they returned to London, rather than bringing him to the Society headquarters.

"Well, sir." Alexander hated giving Wellington bad news, but Branwell had almost gotten him killed. Twice. He could still see the boy clinging to the back of the carriage, his red hair flapping in the wind. "He struggles."

Wellington frowned deeply. "Am I to take it that you do not view Branwell to be a competent agent?"

Alexander shifted. "Perhaps more training." Lots more training. Years of it. Unfortunately, there were only a few people in the Society who could train a new seer, and Alexander was one of those.

"More training." Wellington narrowed his eyes. "Tell me the truth, Alexander."

How frustrating that Wellington could always see right through him. "I'm afraid I don't believe Branwell will ever become a proper agent of the Society, even though he seems a decent fellow. He has shown little improvement."

"That's most unfortunate." The duke seemed genuinely sad about it. "I'd hoped Branwell would prove a fine agent, but it sounds as though I was right to be uncertain."

"What do you mean?"

"There's something about Branwell you should know, Alexander. Something I didn't tell you because I wanted you to be honest with me about the boy's progress."

"Sir?"

"Branwell is—ah—" The duke glanced at the floor. "Well, the boy doesn't know this, so please do not tell him, but he is my sister's son. She married poorly, you see, and this is the result."

Oh.

Alexander's redheaded menace of an assistant was Wellington's nephew, which meant two things: (1) Alexander was immediately a teeny-tiny, itty-bitty bit just a smidge jealous. And (2) he needed to find something nice to say about the boy. Fast.

"He tries very hard," Alexander blurted. His face went hot with embarrassment. "I've never met someone so enthusiastic."

Wellington just sighed. "What about when you went to the school to recruit Miss Eyre? How was his behavior then?"

"I left him at the inn when I went to Lowood. I couldn't predict what he might say to Miss Eyre, and I didn't want to risk his"—Alexander winced—"enthusiasm causing her to refuse my offer."

"A wise choice. The most important thing is finding a new seer, especially if Branwell isn't going to work out."

Alexander winced again. "About that."

Before Alexander could admit the ugly truth, the tea arrived.

Alexander took his teacup, warming his hands on the ceramic while the fragrant tea steeped.

"When will Miss Eyre arrive?" Wellington asked.

"She won't." Alexander slouched a tiny bit. "She declined."

"How could she decline?" Wellington shook his head. "Tell me exactly what you said to her."

Recounting the conversation was easy. It had been so completely baffling, the way she adamantly did *not* want to join the Society. "She said her life's dream is to become a governess. After that, she refused to see me, though I went back to the school several times."

Wellington frowned. "Well, you tried. At least you took care of the incident at the Tully Pub. I suppose that went well enough."

In spite of Branwell, yes. But . . . "There was something a little strange about that."

"What is it?"

Alexander tried to recall exactly how it had happened. "In the pub, when Miss Eyre first appeared, the Shrieking Lady reacted . . ."

"Yes?" Wellington prompted.

"Oddly." It was just so unusual, Alexander could hardly find the words. "The ghost immediately stopped shrieking and began"—he shrugged—"hugging her?"

"Hugging Miss Eyre, you say?"

"Yes, sir. I know it sounds bizarre. But that is what happened."

Wellington leaned back in his chair and crossed his arms. "That is interesting. Did anything else happen with Miss Eyre in the presence of ghosts?"

"Come to think of it, the ghosts at Lowood kept asking her for skin-care tips."

"Ah." The duke stroked his beard. "Tell me, Alexander, have you ever heard of Beacons?"

The word was familiar to Alexander, of course. The definition and whatnot. But he sensed Wellington meant Beacon (capital B) in a specific way. "No, sir."

Wellington nodded. "We haven't had a Beacon since you were small. You wouldn't remember, I suppose."

"What is a Beacon?"

"A Beacon, my boy, is a seer with, shall we say, extra abilities. Our previous Beacon could command ghosts with a word. From what I understand, ghosts often comment on the Beacon's attractiveness, as though there's some sort of supernatural glow about them, visible only to ghosts. The Beacon was an invaluable—you might say necessary—part of what we do here."

"We haven't had a Beacon in years, though?" Alexander frowned. He'd always tried so hard for the Society, but now he learned he would never be enough, no matter how much he gave?

"Oh, we can function without a Beacon, Alexander. We have been functioning quite well, as you know. Considering that our funding has been slashed and we have so few seers . . ." Wellington took a sip from his tea and stared across the room, deep in thought. "The Society is in trouble, my boy. More trouble than I wanted you to know about. The continued existence of the Society depends upon seers like you. And this Miss Eyre, if she is indeed a Beacon. We need her to join us."

A chill ran up Alexander's spine. "Sir?"

"Promise her whatever you must. Better pay. Better lodging. We need a Beacon."

"Sir, I know there aren't many seers at the moment, but we still have Mr. Sussman and Mr. Stein. They're both fine agents—"

"They're dead." Wellington sat up straight and placed his teacup on the tray once more. "They've been killed in the line of duty. It's just you and Branwell now."

What a sobering thought.

"You must persuade Miss Eyre," said the duke. "She could be the key to restoring the Society to its former glory."

Alexander drained his tea and stood. "Then I shall return to Lowood at once."

The duke nodded and shook Alexander's hand. "I know you won't fail me again."

"I won't, sir. You have my word." He departed, having completely forgotten to turn in the ghost-filled talismans in his haste. Oops.

SEVEN
Charlotte

Charlotte woke in the dead of the night to find a strange boy sitting on the edge of her bed. (Don't get too excited, dear reader—it was only her brother.)

"Bran," she gasped, sitting up so fast she nearly cracked heads with him. "What are you doing here?"

"Can't a brother stop by to see his favorite sister?" he whispered.

She forced herself to remain stern. "Not at an all-girls boarding school," she admonished. "If Miss Scatcherd sees you here, we're dead." She glanced down the long row of beds at her two sleeping sisters. "Am I truly your favorite?"

He grinned and pushed his mass of unkempt red hair out of his eyes. "Actually my favorite sister is Anne. But you're a close second."

They retreated down the hall to a corner of the library where it was less likely they'd be discovered. Then Charlotte lifted her spectacles to her face so she'd know where to punch him in the arm. "What are you really doing here?"

"I happened to be in the neighborhood, and I thought I'd surprise you," he said. "Ow. Oh, I suppose I've missed you, too, Charlie."

"Don't call me Charlie, Bran*well*. You're supposed to be at home, helping Father with the parish. However did you—"

"Actually I've come to tell the most marvelous news," he said. "It's really the best news, ever. Can you keep a secret?"

"Of course." It was Bran who couldn't keep a secret to save his life. As evidenced here.

He straightened his shoulders, his chest puffing out a bit. "I've been recruited into the Society."

That was not what she'd been expecting him to say.

"The Society for the Relocation of Wayward Spirits," he elaborated when she didn't immediately respond. "It's an elite group of distinguished persons who locate and extricate ghosts—"

"I know who they are," she said. "But . . . why? Why did they recruit you?"

(It should be noted here that Charlotte loved her brother. He was only a year younger than she was, and he was a dear. But he was also—hmm, how do we put this nicely?—the family foozler, which was a pre-Victorian word for "screw-up.")

"They heard about my accident," Bran explained a bit nervously.

Charlotte frowned. "Accident?"

He blushed and pushed his spectacles up on his nose. (Bran, unlike Charlotte, actually wore his glasses on his face, instead of on the end of a wand.)

"Don't tell me you agreed to another dare," Charlotte chided. Just in the last six months he'd nearly died falling out of a tall tree someone had dared him to climb, he'd nearly choked to death on blackberries during an impromptu pie-eating contest, and he'd singed his eyebrows off in some incident involving a lit candle and a handful of gunpowder.

"Well, there was this old bridge, see, and this boy from the village kept saying I was lacking the proper spine to try to cross it. I was doing fine until I got to the middle. No trouble at all. But then the train came, and I had to jump."

Charlotte closed her eyes. "You jumped from a bridge. Was it over water, at least?"

He nodded. "It wasn't a terrible drop, and the river was quite deep, so I didn't break my neck."

"How wonderful."

"But I did—temporarily, mind you—drown. For a few moments. My heart stopped beating. But then it started again," he added cheerfully. "So I met the Society's criteria."

Charlotte stared at him. "What? Just . . . what?"

He laughed at her obvious confusion. "They are desperate to enlist young men who've been technically dead for at least a full minute, and then brought back. They learned of my accident at the bridge—it may have been in the local newspaper—" He coughed.

95

"And now here I am, the newest initiate in the Society for the Relocation of Wayward Spirits. Why, just this month I participated in my very first relocation not far from here."

"With Mr. Blackwood?" Charlotte couldn't believe what she was hearing. "You were at the Tully Pub?"

He grinned. "It was dreadfully exciting, Charlie. I did make a bit of a mess of it, but it turned out all right."

She whacked him in the arm again. "Why do all the good things happen to you?" A brilliant thought occurred to her. "Earlier I did ask Mr. Blackwood if they might take me on as an employee, and he refused, but perhaps if you were to speak for me . . ." She trailed off because Bran was shaking his head.

"The Society is comprised entirely of men," he said. "No women allowed."

She frowned. "But that doesn't make any sense. I know for a fact that they—"

"Besides, even if you weren't a girl," Bran continued, "you wouldn't qualify. Like I said, they're interested in those certain persons—male persons, that is—who've experienced death first-hand."

"But why? What's so important about brushing shoulders with death?"

Bran pressed his lips together. "I really shouldn't say."

She waited.

"You see, when you die and come back, it can change your perspective," he informed her gravely.

"Naturally," she said, and waited.

"I see dead people," he blurted out.

She blinked. "Pardon?"

"After you die, temporarily, anyway, you can see the dead and commune with them," he said. "Well, sometimes. Seers are rare—not everyone who dies comes back with such an ability. Which is why the Society seeks us out. It's a gift, they say, and a great responsibility."

"Oh." Charlotte swallowed down a lump of disappointment in her throat, both because she was a wretched female and because she had never died, not even once. It all felt so wildly unfair.

"I'm the new apprentice to Mr. Blackwood," Bran said. "He is the star agent—"

"Yes, I've met him," Charlotte said. "He is impressive. Long coat. Brown eyes."

There was a noise from the hall. She and Bran froze. Then a pair of small dark shapes appeared from around the corner. Charlotte lifted her spectacles. Drat. It was her sisters. (Normally she quite enjoyed the company of her sisters, but this news of Bran's was just very good and she wanted to grill him about it, which she couldn't very well do with her little sisters standing there. Double drat.)

"Bran," the younger girl cried. "I knew I heard your voice!"

"Annie, my little mouse." Bran dropped to his knees and opened his arms as she ran to him. He reached out a hand to Emily. "Em."

"What are you doing here?" Emily asked, frowning deeply. "If Miss Scatcherd sees you . . ."

"Bran has been given a new employment . . . opportunity," Charlotte explained quietly. "He was working nearby and decided to pop in to see us. Isn't that nice of him? But now he has to go before he gets us all expelled."

"What kind of employment opportunity?" Emily never could mind her own business. (In that way, she was entirely like Charlotte.)

Anne gazed up at Bran. "Aren't you going to be a parson, like Father?"

"No, darling, I'm going to be—"

"Actually, he can't tell us," Charlotte interrupted. "He's been sworn to—"

"I'm an agent for the SRWS," he announced.

Charlotte sighed.

Anne's mouth went into a little O. "The Society? However did you manage that, Bran?" Anne was precocious for a twelve-year-old. Charlotte sometimes thought Anne was smarter than all the rest of them put together.

"It's, er, kind of a funny story," Bran said.

"So you're a ghost hunter, then." Anne took her brother's face in her small hands and looked at him with the utmost seriousness. "You'll be careful, won't you?"

"There's no danger. Ghosts can't harm the living," Charlotte said. "Unless you're the sort who'd be scared to death."

"No, I mean, you won't scare away Maria and Lizzie, will you?" Anne asked earnestly.

All four Brontë children fell silent. They never spoke of their older sisters. Their father couldn't even bear to hear their names. He'd wanted to bring them all home after the Graveyard Disease had taken the two oldest and so many others at the school. But they couldn't afford it.

"They keep me company sometimes," Anne said. "Don't make them go, Bran."

"I . . . won't," Bran stammered. He glanced around quickly. "Have you seen them here at the school, Annie, dear?"

She smiled but said nothing.

"What do you mean, has she seen them?" Emily crossed her arms. "She can't have seen them. They're gone." (Emily was the no-nonsense one of the family. She didn't believe in ghosts. Not yet, anyway.)

"What does Father have to say about this whole Society situation?" Charlotte was suddenly keen to change the subject.

"He doesn't know. He thinks I'm studying business in London." Bran ruffled Anne's hair. "You won't tell on me, will you?"

Anne shook her head. (Unlike Bran, she was quite capable of keeping secrets.)

The clock in the hall chimed four.

"I must be off," Bran said, extricating himself from Anne's thin arms and rising to his feet. "But I shall return tomorrow, dear ones. If Mr. Blackwood allows me to accompany him this time, but I think he will. We're becoming quite bonded after all we've been through together. So you'll get to see me in my official Society capacity. Hard at work. I won't be able to converse with you directly, but I will see you in the morning."

He crossed to the window and was halfway out of it before Charlotte could process what he'd said.

"Wait!" She caught him by the arm and pulled him back into the room. "Why is Mr. Blackwood coming here tomorrow?"

"We're recruiting a new member. Extremely confidential business, though. Don't tell. Mr. Blackwood returned to London, but now we've been sent back. So I've got to make sure his clothes are pressed and laid out for tomorrow's engagement with Miss—"

Charlotte clapped a hand over his mouth. "Don't say the word 'engagement' so loudly around here, Bran. Especially when it has to do with Jane Eyre."

His brown eyes widened theatrically behind his glasses. "How did you know we are seeking out Miss Eyre?"

"I'm a genius," Charlotte said impatiently. "That, and Mr. Blackwood's already been to see her three times. So it's rather predictable, wouldn't you say?"

"You're going to press Mr. Blackwood's clothes?" Emily, as usual, had gotten stuck on the insignificant detail. She smirked. "You know how to press clothes?"

"I'll do whatever he asks of me," Bran said brightly. "And if I don't know how, I'll learn. I think very highly of Alexander . . . Mr. Blackwood. I'd like to impress him if I can."

"But Mr. Blackwood cannot see Miss Eyre," Charlotte said. "It is quite impossible."

Now it was Bran who frowned, an expression that did not

come naturally to his face. "Why is it impossible?"

"Jane landed a position as a governess. She's gone from Lowood."

"She left last week," Anne said mournfully. "She was my favorite teacher."

"Charlotte's been moping for days," Emily added.

Charlotte swallowed. It was all so obvious now, what was ailing Jane. Jane Eyre could see ghosts. She must have died once. She, like Bran, was a seer. This was why Mr. Blackwood had attempted to recruit her. It was also why Jane so often appeared to be talking to herself, Charlotte realized. She must have been speaking to figures that others could not see.

Why had Jane not told her? She'd thought they were friends— best friends—so why would Jane keep something so vital from her?

Perhaps, Charlotte thought, she didn't know Jane Eyre at all.

"I should inform Mr. Blackwood of this news at once." Bran was grinning again—Mr. Blackwood would be pleased with him for bringing this vital information. And Charlotte had given this information to Bran. She'd been somewhat useful, then.

The girls took turns hugging and kissing their brother. Bran slipped out the window, shimmied his way awkwardly down an adjacent tree (but miraculously avoided injury), and disappeared into the fog.

Charlotte walked her sisters back to bed.

"Bran looked well, didn't he?" Anne sighed drowsily as Charlotte tucked her in.

"Yes, dear. He did." He *did*, Charlotte thought. His eyes had been bright, his cheeks flushed with excitement. It was good to see her brother with a purpose. But it made her all the more keenly aware of her own lackluster future.

She tried sleeping, but after a time gave up and went to her hiding place in the stairwell with a candle and her notebook. A series of rapid thoughts were cycling through her brain, and she felt compelled to write them down. Mostly on the subject of the sheer injustice of being withheld from all the truly worthwhile forms of employment simply because she was a girl.

Women are supposed to be very calm generally: but women feel just as men feel; they need exercise for their faculties, and a field for their efforts, as much as their brothers do, she wrote, her pen flying across the page. *They suffer from too rigid a restraint, too absolute a stagnation, precisely as men would suffer; and it is narrow-minded in their more privileged fellow-creatures to say that they ought to confine themselves to making puddings and knitting stockings, to playing on the piano and embroidering bags. It is thoughtless to condemn them, or laugh at them, if they seek to do more or learn more than custom has pronounced necessary for their sex.*

She took a deep breath and felt some of the tension drain from her. Writing could let out the pent-up emotions the way a doctor might bleed his patients. But it also made her feel empty, like this writing was all that she would ever be permitted to have. Could she subsist on only these thoughts and dreams, these hastily scribbled wanderings of her mind? A shiver worked its way down Charlotte's spine. No. No. She would not tolerate it. She would—how had Jane put it?—she would imagine a different life. She would seek it.

She hurried back to the bedroom, dressed quickly, and slid a carpetbag out from under her bed, in which she packed her meager possessions.

"What are you doing?" Emily whispered.

Charlotte was unable to keep the quiver of excitement out of her voice. "I'm going to work for Mr. Blackwood. He wanted Jane, but he's going to get me, instead."

"You think he'll accept you?" Emily sounded both worried and envious. "Didn't he already refuse?"

"I will persuade him."

"But what about school?"

"I have learned enough here." Charlotte laid her notebook, a tightly sealed bottle of ink, and a handful of pens on top of her clothes and shut the carpetbag. The handle was broken on one side, but she could manage it. She smiled.

Emily sat up. "But it's not proper, Charlotte. You're a girl. It's not dignified to run about begging for a job."

Charlotte's chin lifted. "I would always rather be happy than dignified," she said, her cheerful tone returning, and out she went.

Jane EIGHT

"You must put on your finest dress," Mrs. Fairfax said, combing through Jane's wardrobe, which consisted of two gray dresses, so the combing consisted of choosing the dress that looked the least worn. "I guess this one will have to do." Jane had been called down to the parlor to "be presented" to the master of the house, and update him on her progress with Adele.

Mrs. Fairfax laid the dress on Jane's bed and then fluffed the pillows and shook out the bed skirt. Mr. Rochester had been away for a few days, and his sudden return had put the housekeeper in a state of flurry.

Jane's cheeks flushed, partly because of her lack of fine things, but partly, she suspected, in anticipation of seeing Mr. Rochester again. With his dark eyes. And his tall ways.

"I hope Pilot will be there," Helen said, pretending to admire herself in the mirror, even though she had no reflection. "I think he likes me."

"Do not be late, Miss Eyre," Mrs. Fairfax said. "The master values promptness above all else. Except order. And discipline."

"I will not be late," Jane said.

Mrs. Fairfax flurried out of the room, dusting as she went.

A full fifteen minutes early, Jane was sitting in the parlor, waiting, with Helen by her side. Moments later, Mr. Rochester walked in carrying a satchel. Jane's art satchel. Jane had given it to Adele to look at, but somehow Mr. Rochester had it.

Jane shot to her feet. "Sir," she said.

"Miss Eyre. Please sit."

She complied and Mr. Rochester sat on the other side of the sofa. Helen scooched toward Jane just in time to avoid him sitting through her.

"Rude," Helen said.

Jane wasn't sure what to say or do. Even though they sat on opposite ends, it still pushed the boundaries of propriety for a single woman and a single man to occupy the same sofa. It was a comfort for Jane that Helen sat between them.

Mr. Rochester placed the satchel at his feet.

"So, Miss Eyre. From where do you come?"

"Lowood school, sir," Jane said.

"And who are your parents?"

"I have none."

"Brothers and sisters?"

"None."

Mr. Rochester studied her face. "Friends?"

"One or two," Jane said.

"Does he ask these questions of all his servants?" Helen said.

"One or two," he repeated. "Are you referring to the other witch?" The corner of his mouth twitched up.

Jane didn't know what to say, but it didn't matter because Mr. Rochester continued on with his string of questions.

"And what did you learn at Lowood school?"

"Starvation," Jane said, without thinking. She then added, "And the usual maths and history."

Mr. Rochester tilted his head thoughtfully. "I understand Mr. Brocklehurst runs the school. He did not feed you?"

"No. He considered feeding the students a waste of food. And keeping them warm a waste of coal. But his opinion matters little now. He is dead."

"Thank God," Helen said. She'd been twisting her head back and forth, following the conversation the way one might watch a tennis match.

"You are very opinionated for someone who has spent her entire life at one place."

"Yes," Jane said.

Mr. Rochester sighed and then reached down toward Jane's satchel. As he bent over, a necklace with a key on it fell out of his shirt. He quickly stuffed it back inside, then opened the satchel and pulled out a handful of Jane's beloved art.

Jane drew in a breath, and Mr. Rochester seemed to notice. He held the pictures gently, and then spread them out on the table.

"You did all of these on your own?" Mr. Rochester said.

"Of course," Jane said, somewhat indignantly.

"I meant no offense," Mr. Rochester said.

"I meant to take none," Jane said.

He turned back to the paintings. Most of them were landscapes. Some of them featured a golden-haired girl.

Helen leaned forward. "I love me in this one," she said, pointing to one where she stood in front of a hill.

"Were you happy when you painted these, Miss Eyre?"

"I was not unhappy."

"So, you were happy?"

"I was on a break from school, during which I stayed at the school because I had nowhere else to go. I was content."

"Why do you avoid saying you were happy?"

Jane shook her head. *Because I've been starved. Because my best friend died in my arms. Because I have no family.*

At that moment Mrs. Fairfax flurried into the room, with Adele, who was wearing a green dress and frilly pantaloons.

At the sight of Mr. Rochester, Mrs. Fairfax froze. "Sir, I do apologize for my tardiness."

Adele stepped forward. "I have prepared a song in my native tongue. Would you like to hear it?"

"Of course," Jane said.

"My *maman* taught me to perform. She used to sing in an . . ." She put her finger on her cheek, searching for the word.

Mr. Rochester cleared his throat. Mrs. Fairfax shifted uncomfortably. "Opera house," the housekeeper said.

Mr. Rochester grunted.

Adele shook her head. "Oh, no, I do not think that is right—"

"*Opera house,*" Mrs. Fairfax insisted.

"Opera house," Adele said, frowning.

Mrs. Fairfax took a seat near the sofa. Adele took her place in front of the audience and began to sing.

"Miss Eyre, perhaps you can tell me what she's saying?" Mrs. Fairfax said. "The only other person in the house who speaks French is the master, and he hates to translate anymore."

Jane glanced at Mr. Rochester, but he stared straight ahead.

Jane listened to the song. "The first few lines are about a famous dancer . . . in a club. . . . She wore flowers in her hair and a dress that . . . oh." Adele sang in detail about how much the dress covered. Or didn't cover.

Jane blushed and glanced at Mr. Rochester, searching for a reaction to the scandalous lyrics. But he just listened. Not scandalized.

"So, yes, the dancer wore a dress," Jane continued, with slightly less detail. "And she was in love with a . . . dealer. Of cards. And at night, they . . . oh my."

Adele sang of a *very* special hug.

Jane's cheeks flamed. "Perhaps Mr. Rochester should translate."

She turned to Mr. Rochester, who coughed. He waved his hand. "Please continue, Miss Eyre. You're doing such a fine job."

Now Adele sang of the woman's roving eye, and another man visiting her while her lover was away.

"They continued to love each other," Jane said quickly, maybe a bit desperately.

In the last verse, the boyfriend found out about her infidelity, and stabbed the dancer and her other lover.

"That escalated quickly," said Helen. She also spoke French, but no one had asked her to translate.

"And they both lived happily ever after," Jane blurted. She was going to have to teach Adele some new songs.

"How sweet!" Mrs. Fairfax declared. "I am excited to see what you can do with her."

Jane smiled awkwardly.

Adele sang two more songs: one about a French dance that involved the lifting up of skirts and kicking very high, and then another about a lady of the night. Jane had to wonder who had been in charge of Adele's education up to this point. Someone at the, ah, opera house, perhaps? She stopped translating.

After Adele was finished, she looked expectantly at Mr. Rochester. "Where is my present?"

"Ah, I am back from traveling, and therefore, she expects a gift," Mr. Rochester said. "Because she values gifts above all else. Do you love gifts, Miss Eyre?"

"I wouldn't know. I've never received one. But I assume they are considered generally pleasant things."

"No gifts?"

"Unless you count learning to live with little to eat a gift."

Mr. Rochester took in a deep breath. Then he walked over to the wall and rang a bell labeled "kitchen." A few moments later, Grace Poole strode into the room. She had ash or soot on her face, and her expression was dark.

"Mrs. Poole," Mr. Rochester said. "What are you doing in the kitchen? Why are you not—" He cut himself off abruptly.

"Not in the east wing for the *renovations*," Mrs. Fairfax said.

"Yes," Mr. Rochester said. "That's what I was about to say."

"I was in the kitchen getting food for the . . . *renovations*." Grace Poole did not call him *sir*, nor did she exhibit any of the other genuflections servants at that time should have.

Jane expected her to face some sort of chastisement, but none came.

"Ah, well, please bring Miss Eyre something to eat," Mr. Rochester said.

Grace Poole cut her gaze to Jane. Sized her up. Jane sat a little taller, trying to look deserving of food.

"Never mind," Mr. Rochester said. "It is late. Miss Eyre, please put your charge to bed."

Grace Poole shrugged. "If you're sure. I can whip something up in the cauldron."

"Do not eat anything she whips up in a cauldron," Helen whispered.

"Thank you, but I should put Adele to bed." Jane couldn't

stop the quiver in her voice. "Good night. Adele, come with me."

Mrs. Fairfax walked a ways with them. When they were out of earshot of the master, Jane said, "Mr. Rochester seems to change temperament abruptly."

"I am used to his ways," Mrs. Fairfax said. "I hardly notice. But he does brood. And with good reason. He has had much strife in this life. He lost his older brother to the Graveyard Disease, and there was some sort of other family treachery."

"Like what?" Jane said.

"Never you mind," Mrs. Fairfax said. "Sleep well, Miss Eyre." With that, she scurried away down the corridor.

Sleep seemed impossible that night, as Jane and Helen lay in bed. Helen was shaking so badly, the bed vibrated.

"Grace Poole is evil," she said.

"Don't be silly," Jane said, trying to convince herself as well.

"Who calls a pot a cauldron?" Helen said.

"I'm sure she misspoke."

"Something is amiss here," Helen said.

"Go to sleep, dear," Jane said. She turned her thoughts from Grace Poole to her evening with Mr. Rochester, and the tender way he held her sketches, and the way he almost ordered her food.

NINE

Alexander

"She's gone." Alexander stared at Branwell, who'd just burst into his room in the dead of night.

"That's what I said, sir. Miss Eyre has left the building." He cocked his head. "Sir, do you sleep in your mask?"

"Doesn't everyone?" Alexander slumped back to the foot of his bed, still trying to wake up, and still trying to comprehend those words: *she's gone*. "I don't understand," he muttered. "Why would she leave?"

"To fulfill her life's dream of becoming a governess?" Branwell cocked his head the other way, as though trying to remember if he'd said that already. (He had, but poor Branwell wasn't used to Alexander having a hard time keeping up, so he had to question everything now.)

Alexander nodded slowly. "Do you know where Miss Eyre has gone?"

Branwell sagged a little. "I'm sorry, Mr. Blackwood, I forgot to ask."

"But we *must* go after her." Alexander rubbed his temples.

"I suppose I could go back to Lowood. . . ."

"Wait." Alexander shook off the last of his sleepiness. "Why were you at an all-girls school?"

Branwell startled. "Um."

This was terribly improper. If anyone found out that a member of the Society had been so inappropriate as to sneak into a girls' charity school in the middle of the night, the crown would never even *consider* reinstating their funding. The association alone was enough to not only destroy Alexander's career, but Wellington's as well, if it ever got out that Branwell was in fact Wellington's *nephew*. (Alexander still couldn't quite believe this fact.)

Branwell's face had turned bright red. "Sir, I—"

"Say no more!" Alexander grabbed his luggage out from under the bed and opened the lid. "Return to your room. As soon as it's dawn"—which wasn't far off—"I'll go to the school and request Miss Eyre's forwarding address. You're to remain here and gather your things. As soon as I've interviewed every girl and ghost in Lowood and know where Miss Eyre has gone, we'll go after her."

"I'm terribly sorry, Mr. Blackwood. I thought—"

"Not now, Mr. Branwell. Return to your room and get some rest. I'll fetch you when it's time." How would he explain Branwell's behavior to Wellington? It was bad enough to tell the duke that Branwell was a mediocre agent with no potential for advancement, but to tell the duke that his nephew might have caused a scandal?

But oh, what fire his return would add to the girls' theories of romance. He shuddered, remembering his previous visits.

Was it worth it to discover the whereabouts of Jane Eyre?

Probably.

Maybe.

Branwell slouched toward the door, pulled it open, and stopped short. "Oh. Charlie. Hello?"

And now someone named Charlie was here?

This was why Alexander preferred to work alone.

He dropped his clothes back into his suitcase and looked up to find Branwell throwing his arms around a young woman in the corridor.

And worse, *she returned the embrace.*

Beneath his mask, his face flushed. A young lady was hugging *his apprentice.* Of all people. Such a blatant display of affection! At this hour! In the hallway!! (In pre-Victorian times, and also Victorian times, and for quite some time later, even hugging was considered Too Much. And yes, Hallway Hugging definitely deserved two exclamation points.)

Even when they finished hugging, the two stepped back to hold hands. That's when Alexander saw that the young woman was Charlotte Brontë, from Lowood.

"Why did you come here?" Branwell asked, grinning at her.

"And how long have you been standing outside the door?" Alexander crossed his arms, rather wishing he'd slept in his shirt and trousers, too. His long nightshirt felt awfully revealing at the moment.

"A short while." She broke away from Branwell and lifted her glasses back to her face to peer down at her notebook. "Just long enough to overhear you're going to interview every girl and ghost in Lowood school in order to find out where Jane Eyre has gone. And here I am, ready to be interviewed."

Alexander frowned, first at Miss Brontë, then at Branwell. "You two know each other?"

"Of course!" Branwell grinned. "I've known Charlie—"

"Don't call me Charlie."

"—my whole life!"

Wellington was going to kill Alexander for this.

"Charlotte is my sister, Mr. Blackwood."

Alexander's mouth dropped open. "But how?"

"Well, sir, when two consenting adults—"

"Stop!" Alexander could see the resemblance now, though. They were both small of stature but big in excitement. They had similar noses and skin tones, and wide eyes that tried to take in everything. "What I meant was, Mr. Branwell—"

Miss Brontë burst with laughter. *"Mr. Branwell?* Really?"

"Isn't that your last name?" Alexander glared at Branwell. "Everyone calls you Branwell, and Branwell is a last name."

"My name is Branwell Brontë, sir."

Well, this was just embarrassing. First, that Branwell Brontë had a last name as a first name. Might as well call him Smith Smith. But even more, why had no one ever told Alexander? "Lord," he muttered. "There are two of you."

"Four, actually," Branwell said. "You saw our sisters Emily and Annie at the school."

"I'm so glad. Let's try to get back on track." Alexander shifted his glare to Miss Brontë. "Why are you here?"

"To help you, of course!" She smiled brightly. "You don't have to go to the school again. I know it makes you uncomfortable."

Oh, no.

"And I've realized," she went on, "that if I'm to be your assistant, I must show initiative."

Alexander scowled. "I already have an assistant." Unfortunately.

"Right!" Miss Brontë pointed a finger at him, then turned to Branwell. "I'm going to be your assistant's assistant."

"I'd really rather you not." His frown deepened, but Miss Brontë didn't seem to notice.

"And when Jane is recruited and becomes a full agent, she'll probably need an assistant, too, and I think she and I would make an excellent team."

"We don't even know where Miss Eyre has gone," Alexander said.

"But, oh," Miss Brontë said, "I do know."

"Then tell me."

"Let me come with you." She stuffed her notebook and pen into her pocket. That was when he noticed the carpetbag resting at her feet. Packed for adventure, no doubt. "I'll be an asset. You'll see."

"You're definitely not coming with us," Alexander said. "Not a chance."

Reader, Miss Brontë definitely went with them.

Not that it had been easy for her. On their way downstairs and then out to the carriage, Alexander ran through the same few phrases several times:

"Go home, Miss Brontë."

"I can't afford any more delays, Miss Brontë."

"Please stop talking, Miss Brontë."

Nevertheless, she persisted.

She followed along as he and Branwell prepared to depart, and was about to step into the carriage when Alexander held out a hand to stop her. "Go home, Miss Brontë."

"I don't have a home, Mr. Blackwood," she argued. "I mean, my place of residence is Lowood, but I've never considered it my true home. How could it be? It's a place as lacking for any person with imagination as . . . well, as one can imagine. And I suppose I could consider my family's house in Haworth as home. . . . It's where I was born and where my father still lives. . . ."

Ah, yes. Now he could see how she and Branwell were related.

"I'm going to help you, whether you like it or not."

"You can't help me," he sighed. "You're just a girl."

But she refused to step down from the carriage. "That makes no sense. My gender has nothing to do with my helpfulness in this situation."

"That's not what I meant," he said. "You're only sixteen."

"You're eighteen," she shot back. "And Bran is fifteen. What's your point?"

Alexander turned sharply to Branwell. "You're fifteen? You said you were seventeen when you were inducted."

Branwell's cheeks were red as his hair. "I may have exaggerated my age a bit."

"Miss Brontë . . ." Alexander dragged his hand down the front of his face.

"Mr. Blackwood," she returned. "I'm coming."

"But why?"

"Because, quite simply, you need me."

"Why would I possibly need you?" he asked wearily.

"Answer me this, Mr. Blackwood. What was your plan?"

"My plan?"

"Exactly. You don't know where Jane is. I do."

He frowned. "I could just go to Lowood and ask them."

"If you do," she said, "I shall tell everyone you're there to arrest Miss Eyre for murder and then they'll never tell you."

He dragged his other hand down his face. "Miss Brontë."

"Anyway"—Miss Brontë lifted her chin—"were you going to try recruiting her the same way you have three times already?

Because none of those times have ended with success."

"But I've been authorized to offer her better accommodations. A grocery budget."

"I didn't know those were options," said Branwell from inside the carriage.

Miss Brontë was shaking her head. "Not to be rude, Mr. Blackwood, but what could you possibly know about a girl like Jane Eyre? Perhaps the request would be better coming from a woman who she knows has her best interests at heart."

Alexander couldn't really say anything to that.

"Jane is my best friend," Miss Brontë went on. "If anyone can persuade her to accept your offer, I can."

"So you need to go," he said. "To persuade her."

She nodded. "And because I'm not going to even tell you where she is unless you let me get into that carriage."

There was a long moment while he thought about it. Then he sighed again and stepped back, leaving the door to the carriage open so she could pass. Miss Brontë bounced down onto the seat next to her brother. Alexander settled carefully across from them and called out the window.

"Where to?" asked the driver.

Alexander sent a pointed look at Miss Brontë. Maybe once she told the driver, he could stop by Lowood and deposit her back at school first.

"Head south." And then *she* sent a pointed look to *him*. "You'd leave me behind if I said where she was."

"Would not," Alexander said.

"Would too," Miss Brontë said.

"Absolutely would," Branwell muttered.

Alexander would never admit to sulking, but that's probably the most accurate description of what he did the first hour of the drive. Branwell had gone to sleep (not having slept yet), and Miss Brontë was happily writing in her notebook.

"I'm excited to work with such a distinguished organization," Miss Brontë said. "I heard that decades ago, there was a gang of ghosts terrorizing the shopkeepers of London. They kept robbing the shops and singing 'God Save the Queen' so loudly that even normal people could hear it. Then a single Society agent chased the entire gang through the Tower of London and tricked them into being relocated. Is that true?" Her pen was poised over the paper, though how she could write in the bouncing carriage, Alexander could not begin to guess.

"It's true," he said. "But it's unlikely we will ever be able to accomplish such feats again. At least now that the king has cut funding. I don't see how we can continue for much longer unless we can persuade him of our usefulness. Our *importance*."

Branwell cracked open an eye—not asleep after all—and said, "The Society is doomed."

"I'd read that the king's cut funding." Miss Brontë lowered her pen. "And just as I come on as an assistant. This is terrible. Please explain."

Alexander most certainly didn't have to explain anything.

Society agents never explained themselves. But the determination on Miss Brontë's face was so genuine, just as real as her eagerness to work for the SRWS.

He sighed. "Very well. I'll tell you what's going on, but you must swear to keep it to yourself."

"And my notes," she said, lifting her pen again. "Go on, Mr. Blackwood. If that is your real name."

"Of course it's my real name! Why wouldn't it be?"

She blinked at him. "I was only joking."

"Right." Alexander leaned back in his seat. "Earlier this year, His Majesty decided to balance the royal budget."

"He kept Meals on Wheels and the National Endowment for the Arts," Branwell said, "because we aren't animals, for pity's sake. But the Society . . ."

"The Society had to go," Alexander said. "Arthur Wellesley fought hard to keep the program funded. But King William doesn't believe in ghosts, or the need for our services. He cut the program, saying that Wellington could find alternative funding for the Society if he wished. He suggested we ask France to pay for it."

"What did France say?" Miss Brontë's pen skittered across the page.

"They said no," Alexander said. "That's when we started charging for our services, but I still believe ghost relocation should be free for everyone, not just the wealthy."

"So what you're saying," Miss Brontë said, "is that the Society can't pay assistants well, but it does pay some."

How was this the main thing she'd managed to take away from the Society's money problems? "Wellington has sworn he'll do whatever it takes to keep the Society running," Alexander said. "No matter the cost. But it may be futile if we can't recruit more seers."

Miss Brontë lifted her glasses and studied him with that keen gaze of hers. Then she made a few more notes and shut her notebook.

"What are you working on?" Alexander asked. "The story about murder from before?"

"Not this time." She patted the leather cover. "This one is about ghosts and the people who bust them."

"I don't want to be a character in a novel," he said.

"Of course not." She smiled slyly. "The hero of this novel is taller."

TEN

Charlotte

They arrived in a town called Bakewell, where Mr. Blackwood paid for three rooms for the night. Charlotte could tell that he had every intention of sending her back to school in the morning. She, of course, was determined not to go. But now she had no choice except to disclose Jane's whereabouts at the nearby estate called Thornfield Hall.

After an afternoon of snooping about town and speaking with the locals, Charlotte discovered the master of the house was a man by the name of Mr. Rochester. With that information in hand, Mr. Blackwood's first order of business was to send a letter.

The communication between Mr. Blackwood and Mr. Rochester went as follows:

Dear Mr. Rochester,

I'm writing to inquire about the governess you recently hired, a certain Miss Eyre. I believe she may be of great importance to the RWS Society, and I would appreciate the opportunity to speak with her.

Sincerely,

A. Black

A reply was delivered rather quickly:

Dear Mr. Black,

No.

Edward Rochester

Mr. Blackwood would not be deterred so easily, so naturally he tried again:

Dear Mr. Rochester,

Please. It's important.

A. Black

Only one word came in return:

No.

What this meant was that they needed a plan.

Not just any plan, but a good plan. A smart plan. A plan that would guarantee success and end happily for everyone. Mr. Blackwood clearly needed one of *Charlotte's* plans.

"You must get into Thornfield Hall," she mused, turning this last one-word response over in her hand. "But the master of the house has denied you."

"Twice," Bran added.

Mr. Blackwood sighed. "How very observant of you." They

were all sitting in a sectioned-off space of the inn's dining room, where they could speak privately, but still in public so that no one would think anything untoward was happening, given the two masked men sitting with a young lady. Mr. Blackwood, Charlotte was coming to learn, was quite the stickler for such things.

"Perhaps Charlotte could write Jane a letter?" Bran suggested.

Charlotte tapped her pen on the edge of the table. "Who's to say she would get it, especially since Mr. Blackwood has been asking about her? It'd be suspicious. And clearly we can't just stroll up to the house and call on her. We'll have to be smarter. Sneakier."

Both men were looking at her, and finally Bran said, "You have a plan, don't you, Charlie?"

"Branwell. Dear. I have asked you repeatedly not to call me Charlie. Please try to remember." She turned back to Mr. Blackwood and infused her voice with confidence. He would see her value. He *would*. She lifted her glasses and found the part of her notes she was searching for. "Ah, yes, here it is. There is a lady currently residing in the Leas, a Miss Blanche Ingram, who is said to be a possible match for Mr. Rochester."

"A possible match?"

"Everyone in town is talking about how the two of them—Mr. Rochester and Miss Ingram"—she enunciated carefully—"are probably going to be married. It is likely that, within a fortnight, they say, she will go to Thornfield Hall to pass the time with him and to see if he will, indeed, ask for her hand—that much is well known in the village."

"What does this have to do with our mission?" Mr. Blackwood

asked. "Why do I care who Mr. Rochester intends to marry?"

"Because she's our ticket to Thornfield Hall. We'll request the Ingrams' help on the matter. We'll say we're members of the Society on a secret mission, and ask if they might allow three people to join their ensemble for a short time, stay at Millcote and accompany them when they go calling on Mr. Rochester."

"Three people?"

"Yourself, Bran, and me, of course. But I'm going to need a mask."

"Wait, wait, wait." Mr. Blackwood was frowning again. "Why would you need a mask?"

"Because I'm going to pose as a member of the Society along with you. Until I can become an official member of the Society, later."

"No. No mask." Mr. Blackwood folded his arms.

Miss Brontë looked at him coolly.

He looked back.

She didn't blink.

His mouth twisted unhappily.

"It actually does sound somewhat brilliant, as plans go," piped up Branwell.

Charlotte smiled at her brother gratefully.

Mr. Blackwood sighed yet again. (With all that sighing, air might soon be in short supply inside the inn.) "All right," he said at last. "I do have an extra mask."

* * *

Everything turned out exactly as Charlotte had planned. (Just kidding. As skilled as Charlotte was at concocting wild-but-ingenious schemes, they almost never turned out as she planned. Remember this for-future reference, dear reader.)

The first snag they hit was that Mrs. Ingram was not at home. Upon their arrival they were allowed into the parlor for receiving but informed that the mistress of the house was out for the entirety of the afternoon. Would they like to wait for her? It was uncertain when she would return.

"We would," Charlotte answered just as Mr. Blackwood asked, "Is there anyone else we can converse with?"

So they were presented to the young Miss Ingram, the daughter, the one Charlotte had understood to be marrying Mr. Rochester sometime soon.

"Well, isn't this a droll little circus troupe," the young lady drawled from where she was reclining on a satin-upholstered chaise in the drawing room. She looked Charlotte up and down with an expression of utter disdain in her large black eyes. She was beautiful, Miss Ingram—that much was undeniable. Charlotte had probably never seen a more attractive person. Her crown of carefully braided hair was glossy and black, her bust was tall and fine, her neck swan-like, her complexion perfect—any part of Miss Ingram could have inspired poetry. Charlotte immediately jotted down a few notes for a future character sketch. But she also found Miss Ingram unkind in the way she glanced over at Bran wearing his glasses over his mask and smirked at how silly and nervous he looked. Then her gaze landed on Mr. Blackwood, and she smiled more brightly.

"Who are you, exactly?" she asked.

Charlotte started to answer, but Bran cleared his throat. Which meant *allow Mr. Blackwood to speak for us, please*, which she knew was the proper thing to do. So she clamped her teeth together and listened to Mr. Blackwood explain that they were members of the Society, who had been tasked with a secret mission of the utmost importance.

"What kind of mission?" Miss Ingram wanted to know.

"The secret kind," Bran said.

Charlotte flashed him a warning glance.

Miss Ingram gave a hard laugh. "Oh. The secret kind. Which would involve you staying in our home and helping yourselves to our food and being part of our company." She stared at Mr. Blackwood again. "Although I don't suppose I'd mind if *you* stayed."

"The Society would be willing to compensate you for any expenses we might incur." Mr. Blackwood's jaw was tight, Charlotte noticed. He didn't like Miss Ingram, either. A show of his good character.

"Would you always wear the masks?" Miss Ingram asked.

"No," Alexander explained patiently. "We'd like to be introduced as new acquaintances of yours who are visiting at your request. We'd use false identities. And again, as I mentioned, it would only be for a short time."

"It sounds rather scandalous," she said.

"We'd act in perfect civility," he promised. "We'd only be

present—for a short time, as I said—to listen and participate in certain group excursions. You will hardly notice we're here."

Miss Ingram wasn't convinced. "This is just so strange a request."

"The Society would be most grateful for your cooperation. They would never send us here on such a task if it weren't imperative."

"I'd agree if it was only you, perhaps," Miss Ingram said, staring up at his face again. "You're charming enough."

He shook his head. "No. It must be all three of us."

She sighed. "Then I'm afraid I must refuse. We don't allow strange individuals the run of our home. We are a very prestigious family, and can't afford any little slip that might tarnish our reputation."

They would have been sunk, but just then the dowager Mrs. Ingram swept into the room in a flurry of black satin and pearls.

"Oh my goodness," she exclaimed when she saw the three masked persons standing there. "Are you members of the Society, by chance?"

"We are, madam." Mr. Blackwood gave a short, graceful bow, followed by an awkward bow from Bran and an even more awkward curtsy from Charlotte.

"We don't have any ghosts here at the moment," Mrs. Ingram said, coming to stand beside her haughty daughter. "But several years ago we had quite a problem with the spirit of Mr. Ingram's grandfather. He refused to leave the house—caused us all kinds of humiliation before the Society was kind enough to relocate him. Honestly, I can't thank the Society enough. What can I do for you, sir?"

Alexander smiled. "Madam, I am so glad you asked."

Within the hour, it had been agreed upon that they would accompany the Ingrams on their visit to Thornfield Hall. It'd also been decided that they were to be introduced as the "Eshtons," a family who had only recently moved to the Leas.

Charlotte was wearing a new dress. It was white and gauzy with voluminous, puffy sleeves and a blue sash. She'd never worn something so fine in all her life, and she could not help lifting her spectacles to stare at her reflection in the mirror. If only she didn't need the blasted glasses, she might have considered herself attractive.

"You look pretty," Bran said when she came out to present herself. "What's your name supposed to be, again?"

She held out a hand to him. "Amy. Amy Eshton, pleased to make your acquaintance."

"And I'm your dear brother, Louisa," he said.

"Louis."

"Right."

"This is so exciting," declared Mrs. Ingram from her grand chair in the corner. "My late husband would have been so pleased. He adored keeping up with what the Society was doing."

Miss Ingram sniffed conspicuously from her place at the

piano. "I think the Society is entirely odd, what with their focus on the supernatural and those distasteful ghosts and the like. This whole thing seems very questionable, if you ask me."

"Nobody asked you, dear," Mrs. Ingram said.

Charlotte lowered herself carefully into a chaise. In order to fit her into this lovely gown, they'd had to cinch her corset extra tightly. She couldn't exactly breathe. In some ways, she might have preferred burlap.

Mr. Blackwood entered the room briskly. He looked uncomfortable, too, as if he'd prefer to be wearing his mask. This was the first time Charlotte had ever seen him without his mask, in fact. He had a nice face, she decided, lifting her glasses up to her eyes, almost like one of those classic Greek statues in the angles of his cheekbones and nose, with large dark eyes and neatly combed black hair.

He saw her and approached.

"Amy, is that correct?" He seemed flustered to call her by her first name, even this false one.

She nodded. "And you're my dear cousin, Mr. Eshton. The new magistrate."

"And I'm Louis," reminded Bran.

Miss Ingram sniffed again.

"So when do you think we might go to Thornfield Hall?" Mr. Blackwood turned to ask Mrs. Ingram, the senior. "We're most eager."

Mr. Blackwood—Mr. *Eshton*, Charlotte tried to rename him in her mind—looked a bit pale. The idea of bamboozling Mr.

Rochester still didn't sit well with him. For someone who lived his life so shrouded in secrecy, he seemed surprisingly unaccustomed to deceit.

Miss Ingram stood up. "Tell me exactly what your business is at Thornfield. Does this have to do with Mr. Rochester?"

Bran turned to Miss Ingram with a sympathetic expression. "You're fond of him, aren't you?"

Mr. Blackwood and Charlotte exchanged looks of alarm. What was Bran up to?

"Yes," Miss Ingram said stiffly. "One could say that."

"Can you keep a secret?" Bran asked.

Charlotte reached for her brother's arm. "Bran—er, Louis," she hissed near his ear.

He shook her off gently. "Well, can you?" he prompted Miss Ingram.

Her dark eyes flared with curiosity. "Of course."

He bent his head closer to hers. "You're not to tell anyone," he murmured conspiratorially near her ear.

"I . . . I promise," she agreed. She seemed almost frightened. "Is there something wrong with Mr. Rochester?"

"Can I have a word with you?" Mr. Blackwood said tightly.

Bran, incredibly, ignored him.

"No, nothing like that," he said to Miss Ingram. "Nothing wrong with Mr. Rochester himself, that is. He has a ghost, is all."

"A ghost?" She frowned. "You mean to say that there's a ghost in Thornfield Hall?"

"That's exactly what I mean to say," Bran confirmed. "And Mr. Rochester is actually fond of this ghost, as it turns out, but it's a disruptive ghost. A malevolent ghost, in fact."

"That would explain a lot," Miss Ingram mused. "Who is the ghost, did you say?"

"Uh. . ."

Bran had no idea. Charlotte looked to Mr. Blackwood. He had no idea. Charlotte lifted her chin.

"It's the ghost of his brother," she said. She'd heard, in her rumor-gathering session in the village, that Mr. Rochester had been at odds with his brother at the time of his death. Something about an unfortunate incident in the West Indies many years ago.

Miss Ingram's large eyes were round as saucers. "Of course. His brother."

"We've been sent to remove this apparition from Thornfield," Mr. Blackwood filled in smoothly. "But we mustn't let Rochester know that's what we're doing. And we mustn't alert the ghost to our presence, either, because the more upset a ghost becomes, the more difficult it is to remove it."

"I understand." Miss Ingram shook her head. "You should have told me that from the start. I wouldn't have made such a fuss. I'll send word that I want to visit him as soon as possible."

"Perfect," Mr. Blackwood said. "Thank you."

After Miss Ingram was gone, Bran sighed. "She smelled really good, didn't she?"

Charlotte kicked him in the shin.

"Ow. She did, though."

"You have no business smelling Miss Ingram." She turned to Mr. Blackwood. "So it's all turning out well, isn't it?"

"Yes," he admitted grudgingly. "It seems to be."

Charlotte thought about Jane, so close by, unaware of this great surprise that was about to befall her. She wondered what Jane was doing now, and if she was content in her place as the governess. Charlotte hoped for her own sake that Jane was not content. Charlotte had a great deal riding on the idea that she'd be able to waltz into Thornfield Hall, take Jane aside, and convince her friend to become an agent in the Society.

She'd been working on what she was going to say, but she wondered if it would be enough. If Jane turned them away again, then Charlotte knew that her own ambitions to become an agent—or if not an agent, exactly, an assistant or employee of some sort—would most likely fail.

That night she got on her knees beside her bed and sent up an earnest prayer.

"Dear Lord," she whispered. "I've been thinking. Please, if it's not too much to ask, could you cause something to happen to Jane at Thornfield—nothing too serious, mind you, but something, please, to cause her to rethink her position there." She stopped. She'd never wished ill on anyone before. But this was serious. Both Jane's and Charlotte's futures were hanging in the balance. "Please," she said again. "Could you send Jane just a bit of trouble?"

Jane ELEVEN

Rochester's bed was on fire.

Literally, Rochester's bed was on fire, and he was in the middle of it, in a deep sleep.

Let us back up a bit. Jane had been working at Thornfield Hall for several days, rarely seeing its owner. On this particular night, she had gone to bed with a full stomach and warm feet. Sleep had come quickly, for it was the kind of sleep that came to a comfortably warm and fed person.

But a strange noise in the middle of the night woke Jane with a start. Helen popped upright as well.

"Did you hear something?" Jane said.

"Yes. Did you?" Helen said.

"I must have, considering I'm awake. Let's be quiet and listen."

They both sat in the bed, perfectly still. Floorboards creaked down the hall. The faint sound of laughter floated in from the corridor. Or maybe it was the normal sounds of an old mansion.

After a few moments, another sound, as if something had swept the panels of the bedchamber door.

"It's right outside," Helen whispered.

"You're a ghost," Jane whispered back. "You don't have to whisper. And since you're a ghost, why don't you peek out into the hallway?"

Helen shivered, and the bed shivered along with her. She must have been very afraid.

"You think this is something alive, and not something . . . not alive?" Jane asked. Helen didn't like the word *dead*.

Helen nodded.

"It's probably Pilot," Jane said. "The other night, he came and scratched at our door, looking for you, no doubt. It's probably him," she repeated, as though repetition might make it true.

The brushing sound came again.

"Then *you* go out there," Helen said.

"You wouldn't want to disappoint Pilot, would you, dear?"

They both sat frozen, so long that Jane's mind began to imagine she heard the noise again.

A maniacal laughter broke their trance. It seemed to come from the keyhole of their door. Jane and Helen jumped out of bed.

"Who's there?" Jane asked.

A door from somewhere down the corridor squeaked and then slammed shut.

Jane flew from her bed and flung the door open.

"No!" Helen exclaimed.

The hallway was murky, with only two lit candles obscured by smoke. Jane ran down the hall, following what she believed to be the source of the smoke. She turned and dashed down another corridor and ended up in front of a door, at the bottom of which still more smoke was pouring out. It was Mr. Rochester's bedchamber.

She threw the door open, propriety be darned. But right before she did, she made sure her nightgown was buttoned all the way up, because propriety shouldn't be totally darned.

A fire was licking at the fringe of one of the drapes that hung from the four posters of Mr. Rochester's bed. It cast a warm light through the gloom, illuminating his face while he slept. The glow became him; as the fire danced, its darting light softened the severe lines of his brow and lip.

"Please fall in love with me," Jane whispered. It shouldn't be totally out of the realm of possibility. After all, Mr. Darcy fell in love with the nearly destitute Elizabeth Bennet. It could be like one of those stories Charlotte and the other girls at Lowood were always telling—the ones with rich, handsome suitors, not the ones about murder.

Wait.

Murder.

The bed was still on fire.

During her admiring, the flames had grown onto the canopy, and one burning piece of fabric had dropped to the bed, igniting the blankets.

"Sir!" Jane screamed. "Sir, wake up!"

She wanted to shake him, to rouse him, but she couldn't reach him without becoming engulfed in fire herself. "Helen," she cried. "Help me!" She didn't really believe Helen would come, though, as Helen was more afraid of getting hurt than anyone Jane knew.

But suddenly, Helen leapt through the flames and onto the bed. She looked at Jane. "What do I do?"

"Jump!" Maybe, if she was afraid enough, she could shake the bed, as she'd done in their room not ten minutes ago.

Helen nodded frantically and began to jump, but she was only able to jostle the sheets a bit.

"Sir!" Jane exclaimed again. Mr. Rochester didn't budge. How could someone sleep so heavily through a raging fire? Perhaps he'd had too much wine at dinner.

The flames crawled across the bed, closer and closer to the master of the house.

Jane rushed to his washbasin. Fortunately, it was filled with water. She carried it over and deluged the bed, hitting Mr. Rochester's face as well. Still, no movement. Jane hurled the basin up and over the flames.

It hit Mr. Rochester squarely on the forehead.

"Ah!" he grunted. "What the devil?"

It took him a moment to figure out what was happening; then he was on his feet, ripping off sheets and curtains and using them to smother the remaining flames.

The room fell into smoky darkness.

"Jane Eyre, is that you?" he said gruffly. He coughed a few times.

"Yes, sir."

"Did you just hit me with something?"

Helen scoffed. "That should be the least of his worries right now."

"You were almost burned alive," Jane said. "I heard a noise, a laugh, and I followed the smoke to your bedchamber." She squinted, willing her eyes to adjust to the dark. Then she remembered the lit candles down the hall. "Be right back."

"You're leaving me here alone to stumble about?" he said.

Jane rushed out the door, followed closely by Helen.

"Stumble about," Helen said. "As if he's never walked in the dark before."

Jane shushed her and fetched both candles from the corridor. She returned to Mr. Rochester's room and handed one to him.

Their candlelit faces stared at each other for a long moment. The glow had a certain way of illuminating his features that made Jane decide then and there that his face should only ever be lit by candlelight.

Much better than bed-firelight.

Helen glanced from one face to the other. "What are we looking at?"

Jane ignored her. "Sir, someone's tried to kill you. You need to find out who. Shall I fetch Mrs. Fairfax?"

"What the deuce is Mrs. Fairfax going to do about it? No, let her sleep." He grabbed his robe and draped it over himself. "Stay here, Miss Eyre. Stay here and I'll find out what's going on."

"But . . ." Jane shivered.

"Are you cold?" Mr. Rochester asked softly. He took the robe from around his shoulders and placed it on Jane's. He then led her to the chair in the corner of the room, sat her down, and put her feet on the stool. "I'll be back momentarily. Please, stay here until I return."

With that, he left.

And Jane's racing heart began to slow.

Helen plopped down on the stool beside Jane's feet. "How odd," she remarked.

"What's odd?" Jane said.

"What's odd?" Helen repeated. "Um, maniacal laughter, scratching at our door, bed fire. And now he wants you to just sit here and wait?"

"Of course he does. It makes perfect sense." Jane grabbed the robe and held it to her face, inhaling his scent, as she gazed wistfully out the door. Reader, it smelled of fire.

"How does it make sense?" Helen waved her hands above her head. "A lunatic attempted murderer is on the loose *inside* the walls of Thornfield, and he leaves you here, *at the scene of the crime*, by yourself, unprotected."

"Everyone knows the arsonist would not return to the scene of his crime so quickly." Jane felt her cheek at just the spot where Mr. Rochester's hand grazed it. Her skin was warm under her fingertips.

Was it from the excitement or his touch?

"I don't think that's true," Helen said. She flapped her hands and glanced nervously at the door.

"You don't think what's true?"

Helen groaned. Jane stared at the door, each second growing longer and longer. The hallway beyond was pitch-black. Where was he? Did the culprit catch up to him in another part of the house? Was he lying on the floor, bleeding somewhere?

At last Mr. Rochester appeared, and Jane sighed in relief. She stood and went to him. She felt strangely weightless every time she was near him.

"I figured out what happened," he said breathlessly. "It is as I thought."

"What was it?"

He folded his arms and looked at the floor, and then said in a peculiar tone, "Um . . . I forget. Who did you say you saw in the corridor?"

"No one," Jane said. "I only heard someone laugh."

"And you have heard this laugh before?"

"Yes. I think it was Grace Poole."

He nodded. "Yes, Miss Eyre, you have solved it without any help from me. It was indeed Grace Poole. It is near four in the morning. Servants will wake in the next couple of hours. I will sleep in the library. And, Jane, I expect you to say nothing of this. I will explain everything. Now, please return to your own room."

"But, sir," Jane protested.

"Please, do as I say," Mr. Rochester said. Jane found his commanding attitude to be quite dashing.

"Yes, sir. Good night," Jane said. She stepped backward.

"Wait, you would leave me so?" he said, a complete turnaround from what he had just ordered her to do.

Jane immediately slid forward. "You asked me to go."

"Not like that, though. You saved my life tonight, and you were about to walk on by as if I were some stranger you met on the road."

Helen said mid-cough, "He *is* some stranger you met on the road."

Jane elbowed Helen in her ribs, hitting nothing but air of course.

"At least shake my hand," Mr. Rochester said. He held out his hand. Jane took it, and then he covered her hand with both of his. A shock thrilled through her at their touch, and she wondered, and hoped, that maybe he would pull her closer.

"I knew you would do me good from the first moment I laid eyes on you," Mr. Rochester said, his fierce gaze piercing her soul.

"Wasn't that the same moment he called you a witch?" Helen said.

Not now, Jane thought. For the first time in her life, she was having a Moment! For the first time since meeting Helen, she wished to be alone. Not *alone* alone, of course. Alone with Mr. Rochester. Obviously. Sure, this might not be the Moment she'd dreamt about, what with the fire, the strange laugh, the frightening noises, the lingering odor of smoke, the fear for her life, and the strange need Mr. Rochester felt to lift her feet onto the stool as if she couldn't do it herself. But it was a Moment, nonetheless, and she wanted to enjoy it.

"Is someone going to say something?" Helen said.

Mr. Rochester sighed. "But if you must go, you must. Good night, Miss Eyre. I am in debt to you."

"You owe me no debt." She tried to leave, but Mr. Rochester's grip on her hand remained tight.

"So does he want you to go, or doesn't he? I'm confused," Helen muttered.

"Why do I find myself reluctant to let you go?"

Jane's breathing was ragged, and she could find no words.

"Jane, promise me this incident won't scare you away."

"Why do you think I would ever leave?"

"You are young. Young people love to travel. Have adventures."

"Young people with means, maybe," Jane said. "But I am not leaving."

He finally released her hand. "Sleep well, Miss Eyre."

Sleep was nonexistent for Jane. She could not help but remember each moment. Her fear upon entering his room, that he might already be dead. Her panic trying to wake him. The sound of the basin bonking him on his head. The way his fingers grazed her cheek as he placed his robe around her shoulders.

The warmth of his touch, as he cradled her hand.

"Who would want to hurt Mr. Rochester in such a way?" Helen said, breaking Jane's reverie.

"Shhh," Jane whispered. "I'm sleeping."

"Oh. Okay."

Jane returned to her contemplation. Mr. Rochester was everything one could want in a match. He was handsome, kind, interesting, thoughtful.

"He *does* have a nice dog," Helen said.

These were all reasons he would never go for someone poor and plain, like Jane. He could have any number of eligible ladies in far better financial situations. Even Elizabeth Bennet wasn't so poor as to not have servants. She didn't require employment, as Jane did.

Jane turned away from Helen, and pulled the soft sheet above her head.

They'd had a Moment, though, hadn't they? He held on to her as if he never wanted to let her go. And then he asked her to go. But then he'd seemed unwilling to let her go.

It was all so very confusing. But romantic?

She'd saved his life. That had to mean something.

(Reader, your narrators understand Jane has fallen for Mr. Rochester rather quickly. The reasons for this could be threefold: first, it was pre-Victorian England, and courtships could last the length of an egg timer. Second, Jane's lack of experience with men. And third, Jane's *perception* of men, which was gleaned mostly from books and art that tended to glorify tall, dark, and brooding ones. The broodier the better. And Mr. Rochester was among the broodiest.)

Back to Jane Eyre. Yes, she had fallen hard, and yes she had romance on the brain, and for the first time in her life, she allowed herself to believe that maybe, just maybe, she deserved a happy ending.

Jane woke after luncheon. She was surprised no one had come to rouse her, but maybe Mr. Rochester had said something to Mrs. Fairfax. How thoughtful of him.

"You slept a lot," Helen said.

Jane stretched her arms above her head. "I know."

Jane made her way downstairs, an extra hop to her step. She hoped to catch a glimpse of Mr. Rochester, but there were no signs of the master of the house. Perhaps he was catching up on sleep as well. She went to the kitchen, again hoping to run into Mr. Rochester, but again she was disappointed. Mrs. Fairfax was conferring with one of the maids. A plate covered with a towel sat on the table. Jane assumed it was for her.

Helen whooshed through the door. "Oh, look! Food. For you. Again. My, they just keep feeding you here, don't they?"

Jane smiled and started over toward the plate, when movement in the corner caught her eye. It was Grace Poole, sitting in a rocking chair by the fire, mending the curtains from Mr. Rochester's bedchamber. (Given the size and violence of the fire, we're as surprised as you that there was anything left to mend but we did the research, and Grace Poole was indeed mending the curtains. Somehow.)

"Afternoon, miss," Grace said, not looking up from her sewing. She didn't look anxious or remorseful or delinquent, or any of the other ways Jane thought a person who had committed arson would look the day after.

"What's happened?" Jane said.

"The master fell asleep with his candle still burning. It toppled and lit the curtains on fire. The master woke and doused it before it spread."

Grace Poole said this in a disinterested way, nothing vexed about her tone.

"That's not right," Helen said. "Jane doused the flames."

"Is he all right?" Jane said, and then added in her head, *Did he say anything about me?*

Mrs. Fairfax interrupted. "Prepare yourself, Miss Eyre, for I have word that Mr. Rochester plans for a party of people to descend upon Thornfield Hall this very evening when he returns."

"What? Where is he?" Jane tried not to look too anxious, but then she knocked over her goblet of water.

Mrs. Fairfax raised her eyebrows.

"I meant, he's not at Thornfield?"

"No, he has gone to town to speak to his accountant. But he sent a messenger and we must prepare."

"Who is in this so-called party of people?"

Mrs. Fairfax tilted her head as if this was a strange question to ask. "A few prominent families from the village. They are to accompany the Ingrams." She leaned close to Jane. "The daughter of Lady Ingram, it is believed, will soon be betrothed to the master."

"Who?"

"Blanche Ingram. She is from a wealthy family. She is widely known to be a great beauty and very accomplished."

All the things Jane was not.

"He's to marry her?" Jane blurted. Just last night he'd been holding her hand. He'd talked about the good she was going to do him. They'd had their Moment.

"Mr. Rochester is an eligible and, if I might add, financially solvent bachelor, which makes him extremely attractive."

Jane stomped her foot beneath the folds of her dress. "Why don't we all just marry him!"

Mrs. Fairfax raised her eyebrows, but Jane stormed out.

Once in her room, she rummaged through her things (which only filled one drawer, so not much rummaging was involved) and took out her canvases and brushes, and began to paint her feelings.

She imagined a young woman, dressed in the finest silk gown with the puffiest sleeves, the shiniest white shoes, the laciest parasol. The skin on her face was porcelain and perfect, her cheeks rosy. Her hair was black and arranged in an intricate braid, so there was no question that a servant, or maybe even two, had attended her. She emerged from Jane's brush with a knowing smile.

Then Jane set an easel next to her mirror and painted herself. Brown hair that any lowborn girl could have done without help. Brown eyes that never danced, no matter what the light. Skin that was tan in places where she'd had no choice but to work in the sun. Ribs and collarbone that were not softened by years of adequate nutrition. Shadows under her eyes.

When she had finished, she stepped back to assess her work. Helen peered over her shoulder.

"What are you doing, dear?" Helen said.

Jane frowned. "Reminding myself."

TWELVE
Alexander

They arrived at Thornfield with much more fanfare than seemed necessary. Carriage after carriage pulled in to the long drive of a dark, looming house. It looked cold. Definitely haunted. (Alexander was something of an expert at identifying haunted houses, after all.)

A knot in his chest tightened as the carriages stopped, riders dismounted, and a housekeeper opened the front door to allow the party entrance.

And what a party it was. There was Lady Ingram and her two daughters, Blanche and Mary. Sir and Lady Lynn, along with their sons Henry and Frederick Lynn. Colonel Dent and Mrs. Colonel Dent. And of course there was the "Eshton" family, Mr. Eshton (Alexander), and his cousins Amy (Miss Brontë) and Louis (Branwell).

All in all, it was more of a crowd than Alexander liked, and he didn't understand why the Lynns and Dents had to come along.

To be fair, they probably didn't understand why the Eshtons had to come along.

"You seem distracted." Miss Brontë kept her voice low as the group all walked to the door. She looked very well today, he couldn't help but notice. The day dress she wore suited her, forest green with ivory trim, and a bit of proper food and sleep had given her complexion a healthier cast than when he'd first met her.

She lifted her gaze to him and raised an eyebrow.

It probably wasn't proper to notice how well she looked today.

"Just eager to get through this." He ducked his face to hide the creeping blush. Without his mask, he felt all his thoughts were plain on his face, evident for anyone to see. But especially Miss Brontë. Even without her glasses, he knew she missed nothing.

Ahead, the other families entered the house, greeted by a dark figure within. Rochester. A man most protective of his governess.

Miss Brontë touched Alexander's shoulder. "We will persuade her," she said. After a week in Millcote together, he was rather coming to appreciate her presence. Even Branwell's, to a point.

The feeling of being watched tugged his attention, and he glanced up.

Two faces peered out a second-story window. One was a young girl, with little ringlets framing her angelic face. The other was Jane Eyre.

"Don't look," he murmured to Miss Brontë, "but your friend is up there."

"I'm sure she'll be shocked to see me."

It must have been difficult for her not to look. Miss Eyre surely wouldn't recognize Alexander—not in this different context and not without his mask—but he still needed to be careful. He had to give Miss Brontë plenty of time to talk with Miss Eyre and persuade her to their cause, and then help arrange a graceful exit.

Just before Alexander dropped his eyes to the door again, he caught a hint of someone behind the two girls in the window. A third girl, perhaps four or five years younger than him, and there was something off about her. She wasn't exactly . . . solid.

A ghost.

Then Miss Brontë and Branwell passed through the front door, and Alexander had to follow behind them.

And again there was Mr. Rochester, standing on the far side of the room, greeting his guests. There was something familiar about him, though Alexander couldn't place it. Certainly he hadn't encountered the man recently, but . . .

A flash of memory struck: this man sitting across the table from Alexander's father, laughing at one of those jokes his father always told. *Had* always told.

Had they been friends?

Ahead, Rochester clasped Lady Lynn's hands, and they kissed each other's cheeks. Then Colonel Dent greeted him, followed by Miss Blanche Ingram, who fluttered her eyelashes in his direction, as if he wasn't twenty years her senior.

The man himself was tall. Too tall, some might say. (No one, in fact, would say this. As we've mentioned before, exceedingly tall was considered attractive in this day, and Alexander was quite aware that he was of average height.) In addition to a vertical advantage, Rochester had dark, dark eyes. Those eyes now turned toward Alexander, and he waited for some spark of recognition, considering all his life he'd been told he was the spitting image of his father.

But there was nothing.

Then Lady Ingram introduced him, Miss Brontë, and Branwell as the Eshton family, and Alexander smiled. "Good evening," he said, and extended his hand. "A pleasure to meet you, sir."

Rochester took the offered hand and shook, and that was that. They had gained entrance to Thornfield. Miss Brontë's plan had worked. Now she just needed a moment with Miss Eyre.

That afternoon, the entire party went out on horseback, which made it impossible for Miss Brontë to get away from the group and locate Miss Eyre.

It wasn't until dinnertime that they returned to the house, but Miss Eyre—naturally—was not at the table.

After dinner, the group moved into the drawing room. "Oh, what a love of a child!" cried one of the ladies when she saw a little girl—the child Miss Eyre had come to teach.

Alexander took a seat toward the center of the room, where he could appear to be part of every conversation, but actually be involved in none. He preferred to observe the group. But even before everyone had come in, the space had been occupied by three girls, two living and one dead.

Miss Eyre sat next to a ghost in the window seat, the possessor of a fine view of the room, but also out of the way. She seemed unusually subdued tonight. Not that he really knew her well enough to make that kind of observation, but his memory of her popping out from behind the bar in Oxenhope was still very vivid. Given what he knew of her, though, the grand surroundings and even grander company might have something to do with it.

Still, her hair was plaited and she'd donned a much nicer dress than he'd seen her wearing in the Tully Pub and Lowood school.

Then both girl and ghost saw Miss Brontë.

"It's Charlotte! It's Charlotte!" The ghost clasped her hands and hopped. "Let's go say hello!"

For Miss Eyre's part, she looked surprised to see Miss Brontë, but then she shushed the ghost and muttered, "Yes, it's Charlotte, but she obviously disguised herself for a reason. Just sit."

The ghost dropped to the floor.

Alexander forced his expression into blankness. Miss Eyre and the ghost were *friends*? That complicated things.

The last thing Alexander needed was for Branwell to have seen that exchange and start up a conversation with the ghost, which, as we all know, would end in disaster.

But Alexander didn't have to worry about Branwell. The redhead was fully occupied by a discussion of flower arrangements with Mary Ingram and Mrs. Dent.

"Texture," he was saying. "It's so important to have a variety of textures in order to add visual interest."

"Oh, I agree." Mrs. Dent picked up a vase of wildflowers, and the three of them began to critique the contents.

Meanwhile, Miss Eyre's young student was surrounded by a court of men and women she mistakenly believed were admiring her, because they'd lead with comments such as "What a pretty dress!" and "Adorable ringlets."

"Rochester, I thought you were not fond of children." Blanche Ingram looked at the girl as one might a rabid squirrel.

"Nor am I." Rochester hardly took his eyes off the young lady everyone said he was going to marry.

"Then what induced you to take charge of such a little doll as that?" She pointed at Adele. "Where did you pick her up?"

"I did not pick her up; she was left on my hands."

From across the room, Miss Eyre leaned toward the ghost and whispered, "Isn't that good of him? So compassionate."

The ghost frowned. "He talks about Adele like she's a stray dog. He often calls her 'the brat.'"

Miss Eyre just shook her head and continued gazing at Rochester.

"You should have sent her to school." Miss Ingram seemed unaffected by Rochester's generous nature.

"I could not afford it: schools are so dear," replied Rochester.

Alexander glanced around the lavishly decorated house, which had to have at least twenty bedrooms and two kitchens, a stable, orchards and fields and gardens surrounding, and not to mention a carriage house filled with vehicles all bearing the Thornfield crest.

Oh, yes. Schools were so dear.

"But you hired a governess. That's even more expensive. You have to keep them both. You know how governesses like to take over the house, and children demand so much food and then refuse to eat any of it." Miss Ingram sent a scathing glance toward Miss Eyre, who seemed to be shrinking in her window seat. "Oh, look, she's right here. Why do you think she's down here, socializing, making us take care of her charge?"

"Because," said the ghost, "he *ordered* her to come down here!"

Miss Eyre leaned forward again, as though waiting for Rochester to defend her, but the master of the house looked indifferent to the subject.

"Well, she's here," he said.

"He cornered her in the hallway earlier," continued the ghost. "She tried to say she wanted to stay upstairs, but she was given no choice!"

"Oh, it's not that bad," Miss Eyre murmured, her gaze still locked on Rochester. "I don't mind. Think of how much better this is than Lowood."

Alexander leaned toward Miss Brontë, wanting to tell her that now might be a good time to speak to Miss Eyre, even if ladies of "Amy Eshton's" station didn't interact with governesses. But then the conversation moved a little too close for Alexander to privately convey his instructions.

Blanche Ingram turned toward her sister. "Remember how our governesses used to call us villainous children? Oh, they hated us so."

"All fifty of them!" Mary Ingram laughed as she looked at

Miss Brontë. "What about you, dear Amy? Did you have many governesses?"

Miss Brontë gave a nervous laugh, pitching her voice slightly higher than normal. "Oh, Louis and I had only one over the years, and she didn't mind us. She let us get away with anything. We regularly destroyed her desk and books, and she gave us candy."

The Miss Ingrams both giggled. "That is too good," said Mary Ingram. "Too good."

Alexander glanced toward Miss Eyre to see what she'd thought of Miss Brontë's story, but she was watching Rochester, as though waiting for him to put a stop to this rude conversation about her kind.

Strangely, Rochester did nothing. He did not defend the breed, nor ask his guests to be less rude, or even turn to acknowledge Miss Eyre. That was odd, though, because he'd been so protective of her when Alexander had written. And he'd acted warmly earlier, but here, he was cold and close to cruel.

What a confusing man. Did he like his governess or did he hate her? It was impossible to tell.

"They're always so plain, too, don't you think?" Miss Ingram gazed at Miss Brontë, whose mouth dropped open, but no sound emerged. "This one is particularly plain. Why, I've never seen such a plain girl in all my life."

Miss Eyre's cheeks went red, her eyes darting between Rochester and Miss Ingram.

"What?" The ghost balled her hands into fists.

Meanwhile, a few of the guests desperately tried to change the subject. "We should do something fun," said Lady Lynn. "Let's play a game."

"Charades?" asked Branwell/Louis. "I like charades."

"Excuse me." Toward the window (Alexander tried very hard not to look directly), the ghost paced back and forth in front of Miss Eyre. "Is no one going to deal with the fact that earlier today Rochester ordered you to come down here and now he's just ignoring you? Which is especially rude because you look *amazing* today, but I guess no one cares?"

"Oh, Helen. I look as I always look. You know that." Though Miss Eyre kept her voice low and her face downward, tears filled her eyes.

"Charades can be fun," said Colonel Dent. "I don't think I'd mind."

"I. Mind!" Helen stomped her foot, and suddenly the floor trembled. "Jane is the best and you're all the worst!"

Abruptly, the merriment on the popular side of the room halted. "What was that?" asked one of the others.

"It was me!" Helen screamed.

"Helen," Jane hissed. But this time, the ghost's scream had actually been loud enough, and emotion-filled enough, for everyone to hear . . . something.

"What a strange sound." Lady Ingram glanced pointedly at Alexander before turning to Rochester. "My dear, something is very wrong here."

"Like what?" Rochester looked around, as though completely lost as to why the subject had changed from games and humiliating governesses. "I didn't hear anything."

"I heard it," said Adele. "It was a scary noise."

"My friend," said Colonel Dent, "there was a truly unearthly wailing sound that came from over there." He pointed toward the window where Miss Eyre sat.

All eyes swung toward Miss Eyre. "It—it wasn't me," she stammered.

"Stop being mean to Jane, you awful . . . You see? This is why no one likes the living. Humans!"

Alexander tried not to look directly at the ghost. No one else could see her, except Branwell, of course, and Branwell wasn't doing a very good job at hiding the fact that he saw her as plain as day. Not that *she* noticed. Helen was shrieking now, calling everyone names, hurling insults, and generally being the type of ghost that Alexander was paid to relocate.

"Mr. Rochester," Alexander said, "have you ever heard a noise like this before?"

Rochester shook his head, visibly frightened, though his fear was probably because he knew this was an actual ghost situation, not just a strange whistling of the wind over a crack in the window.

The Ingrams all shot one another understanding looks. As far as they knew, this was the ghost the Society had come here to catch. Alexander could almost see them deciding that the Society agents would clear this up any moment now. Mary Ingram even went so far as to lean toward Miss Brontë and whisper something too soft for Alexander to hear under Helen's screams.

"You're so mean to her," Helen continued. "How dare you call her plain!" Just then, the wildflowers Branwell and Mrs. Dent had been discussing—as well as every other flower in the room—exploded in showers of orange and pink and green. Plant sludge splattered on the floor.

Awkwardly, Miss Eyre crept away from the window. "My word, what a storm outside."

Through the glass, the sky was perfectly clear.

"It wasn't a storm!" Helen shouted. A vase flew across the room, whizzing past Rochester's head before it shattered against a wall. "It was me!"

"Helen," Miss Eyre hissed. "Sit down and stop being a pest."

Helen immediately plopped onto the floor, her mouth pressed into a translucent line.

"Mr. Rochester," announced one of the Lynn men. "I believe it's time to call for the Society."

Helen's eyes went round. Miss Eyre, too, looked pale.

"What Society is that?" A faint tremor entered Rochester's voice.

"Why, the Society for the Relocation of Wayward Spirits!" answered Mrs. Dent. "Everyone knows that."

"And everyone knows the Society has fallen out of favor." Mr. Rochester's gaze darted around the room, as though he might find the ghost . . . or a Society agent hiding behind the curtains.

"Out of favor doesn't mean out of business," said Lady Ingram. "They could still be called upon."

"Clearly you have a problem here," added Lady Lynn. "Didn't you see the flowers?"

"I don't think there's a problem." Rochester spoke too quickly. "What use would the Society be here?"

"They could relocate the ghost," said Colonel Dent.

"I don't have a ghost!" Rochester shouted. "The Society isn't coming here, and the noise is just a storm, and the vase fell over because of the wind. And that's all!"

On the other side of the room, Helen glared daggers at Rochester, but there was real fear in her expression.

Miss Eyre looked from Helen to Rochester, her face perfectly white. "It's the storm," she agreed. "There are no ghosts here. I asked Mrs. Fairfax when I first arrived."

"See?" Rochester surged to his feet. "It's confirmed. The storm did it."

Everyone went quiet for a moment, listening. Outside, beyond the curtains, Alexander could hear the faint twitter of birds singing evening's approach.

"All right," said Miss Ingram. "The noise seems to be over anyway. The storm must have passed."

"Quick storm," muttered Lady Ingram, gazing at the plant sludge on the floor.

"Odd," agreed Branwell/Louis.

"So." Colonel Dent cleared his throat. "Maybe there is no

spirit here. But maybe we should summon one and ask it questions."

Immediately, Adele found the "talking board," (what we in this day and age would call a Ouija board) but even as the party gathered around a table to summon ghosts, Alexander continued to watch Miss Eyre, his mind echoing with his recent conversation with Wellington.

All the signs were there. Jane Eyre was definitely a Beacon.

THIRTEEN
Charlotte

While the party was occupied with the talking board, Charlotte took the opportunity to duck behind the curtains near where Jane was sitting. This was Charlotte's chance.

"Jane," she whispered urgently. "Over here, Jane!"

Jane didn't turn around.

"I'm behind the curtain, Jane," Charlotte whispered a bit more loudly.

Jane scratched her nose.

"Jane! Jane!" More frantic whispering from Charlotte.

Nothing. Then Jane stiffened like someone had poked her in the ribs. She looked around and spotted Charlotte peeking out from behind the heavy velvet drapes. Charlotte waved at her, then ducked entirely behind the curtains. A moment later Jane slid in beside her.

"It's me!" Charlotte announced, then remembered they were supposed to be hiding, and she lowered her voice. "Surprise!"

Jane looked not so much happy to see her as terribly confused. "I knew it was you. But what are you doing here?"

"I disguised myself as a highborn lady in order to gain entrance to the house." Charlotte gave Jane a quick hug. "And it worked."

Jane didn't hug her back. "Why would you do that?"

"I came to speak with you, Jane."

Jane drew away. "Why would you desire to speak with me? You heard what they said about governesses."

Charlotte stared at her. Jane's eyes were cold, and with good reason. The ladies had been cruel just now. And Charlotte had played a part in that. The thought filled her with shame.

"That was horrible," she said. "They should never have spoken about you like that. I shouldn't have—"

Jane nodded. "So what do you want, Charlotte?"

"Um . . ." She'd been so certain about what she was going to say, until this moment. "I've come about the job. At the Society."

Jane threw her hands up in the air. "Oh, for heaven's sake! Are you still going on about that ridiculous offer of employment? I already told you—"

Charlotte pressed on. "This is more important than you realize, Jane. I've come with Mr. Eshton . . . Mr. Blackwood. He's the agent with the Society for the Relocation of Wayward Spirits. He's . . ."

"That agent!" gasped Jane, pressing her hand to her forehead as if the very thought of Mr. Blackwood made her head ache. "The one with the evil pocket watch! I knew there was something familiar about him."

Charlotte didn't know anything about evil pocket watches, other than the fact that Jane seemed to be obsessed with them. "Mr. Blackwood—Mr. Eshton, here—is most desperate to have you as part of the Society, Jane. It turns out that they are in dire need of new agents. The Society is on the decline, you see, and it is most imperative that . . ."

Jane was firmly shaking her head. "Charlotte, it's no use. I don't even know why they would want me. It's a mistake."

Charlotte grabbed Jane's hand. "Do you see dead people?"

Jane's mouth closed so fast there was almost a snap. She met Charlotte's eyes.

"Tell me the truth," Charlotte implored her. "We're friends, aren't we?"

"Yes," Jane murmured. "Yes, I see them."

Blast, Charlotte wished she had her notebook on hand. There'd be so much to write.

"Don't tell anyone," Jane said.

"That's why they want you, silly. It's an incredibly valuable gift that you have, Jane. Mr. Blackwood has instructed me to give you the following offer—if you would come to London, be initiated as an agent into the Society, you would receive a decent salary. You could negotiate the exact sum, but it would be more than a woman could make doing anything else. Once you've gone through all the necessary training, you'd be given a mask (and they're terribly comfortable—I can tell you from personal experience), so you could carry on your job incognito, as it were. And you'd be provided with your own private living quarters."

Jane stared at her mutely. For a moment, it seemed like Charlotte might have finally gotten through to her. Because who could resist such an offer? Most jobs didn't come with a flat in London, let alone such a stylish uniform.

But then Jane's expression became, if anything, slightly horrified.

"Well. The job does entail interacting with ghosts," Charlotte went on, because she could see how the ghost element would not exactly be appealing to everyone, "but you wouldn't have to talk with them, just capture them and return them to the Society headquarters. That's what Mr. Blackwood does. I find the whole thing vastly exciting. You'd get to travel the country, you know."

Jane's mouth opened. And then shut again. Finally she said, "I wish to be a governess."

"You do not. No one *wants* to be a governess."

"I do."

"I don't believe you. Think of the prestige you'd gain, working at such a highly respected institution. You could afford to buy a nice dress and good shoes. You'd live in London. Think of the food, Jane. Just *think of the food*."

Jane shook her head. "I'm well fed here."

"But you'd earn a salary! A decent salary!"

"I make a decent salary."

"But—"

"No, Charlotte. I'm sorry you had to travel all this way. But my answer is still no. I want nothing to do with the Society."

"But why?"

"They make it their business to imprison defenseless ghosts, ghosts who've done nothing wrong but express themselves perhaps a little more enthusiastically than they should. I've seen it with my own eyes."

"At the Tully Pub?" Charlotte guessed. "What exactly did you see at the Tully Pub?"

"Enough to understand that the Society is evil."

"The Society is not evil. Why, my own brother is an agent!"

"It is evil."

"It is not."

"Is too."

"Is not."

"What if you could see for yourself?" Charlotte changed tactics. "Come with us, inspect the Society and its headquarters, meet the Duke of Wellington, judge by fact, and not one fleeting encounter that you must have misunderstood."

Jane frowned. "So are you an agent of the Society now?"

Charlotte's chin lifted. "I expect to be. Any day." Depending on Jane's answer.

"But I thought you wanted to be a writer."

"I can be both," Charlotte pressed on. "You're wrong about the Society. They need you, Jane. Really and truly need you. How often is someone like us actually needed? Won't you at least give it a chance?"

Jane's mouth was pressed into a line, but she didn't say no again. That was something.

"Please, Jane," Charlotte added. "At least say you'll consider the offer. Give it time. We're going to be here for three more days, I believe. At the end of the three days, you can give your final answer."

"Very well. But don't get your hopes up." Jane cocked her head to one side as if she could hear something Charlotte did not. "They're looking for you. You'd better go."

"So we're agreed, then?"

Jane squeezed her hand. "We're agreed. I will tell you no again in three days."

"Or you'll tell me yes." Charlotte stepped out from behind the curtain. Then she thought of one last thing she wanted to say. She stuck her head back in.

"I'm really sorry about earlier. I've missed you."

She was gone before Jane could reply.

"Ah, there you are," said Mr. Blackwood when she rejoined the party. "We were beginning to worry." He leaned close to whisper. "So? Did you speak with Miss Eyre?"

"I went for a brief walk in the garden, dear cousin," she said, then whispered back: "She is considering the offer. She said she would give us her answer in three days." Although what they could do to convince Jane in three days, she had no idea. Jane seemed to have absolutely made up her mind. Charlotte definitely needed some time to rethink her approach. "How was your conversation with the dead?" she asked Mr. Blackwood more loudly.

He blinked for a few seconds before he caught on that she was referring to the talking board. "Oh, very interesting. As a man of science, I find the idea of communing with the deceased unlikely. But amusing, to say the least."

"You're playing this part very well," she whispered.

A smile touched his lips. "Thank you," he whispered back. "You're not bad, yourself."

She felt herself blushing, and for a moment became uncharacteristically tongue-tied. Then she remembered that it was her job to be reporting on Jane. "She also said something about an evil pocket watch?"

He looked puzzled. "An evil . . . Oh, the talisman. From the Tully Pub. I'll tell you about it later."

"Oh, I am most eager to hear about what transpired in the Tully Pub," Charlotte exclaimed.

A high, fake laugh tinkled from across the room. Charlotte and Mr. Blackwood turned to see Miss Ingram practically draped over Mr. Rochester's shoulder. Then they watched as Bran tripped over the edge of the carpet and doused his face with his own cup of punch, which got nearly everybody in the room laughing at her poor dear little brother. Mr. Blackwood didn't laugh at him, though, which Charlotte was grateful for. He was still staring at Mr.

Rochester, his eyebrows drawn together.

"There is something very off about that man," he said, almost to himself.

"What do you mean?"

He turned back to her. "Nothing. Just a feeling. So tell me more about your conversation with Miss Eyre. Did she at least seem amenable to the idea of joining us?"

Us, he'd said. She gave a little sigh. *Us*, as in, part of the collective *we*. As if Charlotte were already a member of the Society.

"Well . . . no," she admitted, glancing at the floor. "I told her there would be a salary, and the mask, and her own lodging, but she did not seem impressed. She seemed . . ." Charlotte stopped. How had Jane seemed? Different, somehow. Something had changed in the few weeks since Jane had left Lowood. Like she had grown up from a little girl into a woman in the space of a month, not as thin or homely, either, with more confidence, more bearing. And there'd been something else about her, too. A kind of glow.

Her cheeks had been rosy, Charlotte realized. Jane was happy here at Thornfield.

But why? Charlotte agreed with Mr. Blackwood that there was something definitely off about the master of the house. He was creepy, no doubt about it. And he'd stood by and said nothing when he was the person who could have stopped the ladies from attacking Jane. Surely he and Miss Ingram deserved each other. The little girl, Adele, was cute and all, but not particularly charming. Everyone around Jane seemed to treat her with that level of mild disdain reserved for serving women, when they weren't treating her with outright contempt. Charlotte thought guiltily of her own part in the mocking of Jane earlier. So how could Jane possibly be happy here?

It was yet another mystery surrounding Jane Eyre. Charlotte didn't know if she could take any more mysteries. Her novel was becoming so convoluted as it was, on account of the ghost stuff.

"Did she have Helen with her?" Mr. Blackwood asked.

Charlotte blinked up at him. "Helen."

"Her ghost friend."

"Her what?"

Mr. Blackwood nodded. "Oh, you didn't know. Of course you didn't. You can't see anything. Both times I've seen her here, Miss Eyre has been accompanied by the ghost of a young woman—perhaps thirteen or fourteen years of age. Golden hair, white dress."

Charlotte knew immediately who he was talking about. The girl in Jane's paintings. She was real. She was a ghost. Charlotte felt a series of painful jolts deep inside her, first at the way Mr. Blackwood had said, "You can't see anything," and then at the idea of Jane having a ghost for a friend—a real live ghost! Or, not *live, but real all the same*—at Lowood, too, and Jane had never told her.

"Are you ill?" Mr. Blackwood asked, gazing at Charlotte's rapidly whitening face.

"Helen?" Charlotte croaked. "Did you say the ghost's name was Helen?"

"Yes . . ." Mr. Blackwood cleared his throat as if addressing a young woman only by her first name physically pained him. "That's what Miss Eyre called her. She did not give a surname."

"Burns," Charlotte murmured. She had never met Helen Burns—the girl had already succumbed to the Graveyard Disease before the Brontë girls had come to Lowood. But the other students had spoken often and reverently of Helen Burns as the cleverest, prettiest, kindest, and most pious girl who'd ever been enrolled at the school. In fact, there was a school saying regarding Helen, whenever a girl failed in some way. What was it? Oh, yes. *We can't all be Helen Burns, you know.*

Charlotte's mind raced. She quickly put everything together: Helen Burns was the friend—not Charlotte, after all—whom Jane had not wished to leave at Lowood. It had been Helen Burns who Jane was talking to as Charlotte had walked her out of Lowood that last day. Helen who she was talking to every time it seemed that she was talking to herself. All this while Charlotte had thought she was Jane's only friend in all the world, but it turned out that Jane had another friend. A prettier friend. A best friend.

"Miss Burns was the spirit that made itself known in the parlor earlier," Mr. Blackwood was saying, while Charlotte's heart quietly broke. "It was she who shattered the vase and did that crazy thing with the flowers. Through watching Miss Eyre's interaction with Miss Burns I've become quite convinced that Miss Eyre is truly a Beacon."

Charlotte dabbed her eyes briefly on her sleeve and glanced up. "A Beacon? I thought you said she was a seer?"

Mr. Blackwood proceeded to enlighten Charlotte about the

nature of Beacons. Normally Charlotte would have found the topic fascinating—a person who could attract and command spirits—how thrilling!—but the most she could muster as a response was a stunned nod and a blank smile.

Charlotte wanted to be happy for her friend. She did. She should think it wonderful that it had turned out Jane was more than just a seer. Jane was rare. Jane was special. Jane possessed powerful, mystical abilities related to the spirit world. Jane was going to be so useful to the Society. She could right everything, Mr. Blackwood explained, that had been going wrong there. Mr. Blackwood's job would be saved. Bran's job. And if Jane would only agree to be an agent (and how could she refuse, when Charlotte told her how important she was?) then Mr. Blackwood and Jane would carry on in their important duties as the most integral agents of the Society, Jane and Alexander together, Alexander and Jane, righting the wrongs of the world.

And Charlotte had never felt quite so utterly unnecessary.

Jane FOURTEEN

Jane (oblivious to the angst she was causing Charlotte) was in the garden, painting. Helen stood awkwardly by the stream, posing with her arms intertwined, the palms of her hands facing upward as if she were hoping a butterfly would land softly upon them.

"You've never asked me to pose before," Helen said, trying not to move her lips.

Helen was right, but secretly Jane had asked her to pose, and hold very still, so she would stop talking about Mr. Rochester's quote unquote strange behavior and Charlotte's revelation that Alexander Black . . . Esht . . . whatever was at Thornfield to try to recruit her to the Society. Jane had lived a boring life up until this point—a life where the most exciting thing she participated in was trying to not die from the Graveyard Disease. But now there was a little too much excitement.

"Stay still, dear," Jane said, tension seeping into her words. "Talking ruins your lines of . . . grace." *Lines of grace?* Jane didn't even know what that meant. "It's a new technique I'm practicing."

Jane had awoken early this morning to put her feelings onto canvas. Adele was still in bed, having stayed up very late, and Jane was in no mood to converse with Charlotte again, so she had packed up her easel and canvas and brushes and departed just as the sun was rising.

"Aren't you so excited Charlotte is here?" Helen said.

Jane's brush jerked, giving the swallow she'd been working on a giant mustache.

"Silence, please, dear. Or else you might ruin everything."

Helen didn't seem to notice Jane's irritation because something had caught her attention. Jane turned to look, and saw Mr. Rochester riding his horse away from the house, and toward her. Jane watched as he got closer and closer, and his hair got blowier and blowier, the tails of his riding jacket whipping behind him as he went. She waited for him to turn down the lane that would lead into town, but he didn't. He came straight toward her. She reached up to tame a stray hair.

"Jane Eyre," he said. "What are you doing?"

"Painting, sir." She gestured to the brook.

She assessed her painting, and winced. Her mind must have been otherwise occupied because it was the worst painting she'd ever created. Even before the black mess, the picture was rife with harsh strokes and prickly crosshatches, and a butterfly that looked more like a flying centipede, and rays of sunlight that promised destruction to whoever stepped near them.

Mr. Rochester regarded the art with a raised eyebrow. "It's very . . . elegant."

Jane scrunched her nose. "It's a warm-up."

"Ah."

A light breeze blew between them, as they said nothing.

Rochester looked around. "Thornfield is a beautiful place in the summer, isn't it?"

"Yes, sir."

"People get to a place, become settled, and then they wish to leave again. Do you feel that way, Miss Eyre?"

Jane wondered if he had any inkling that Mr. Blackwood was here to recruit her for the Society.

"No." Jane wanted to add that she was reluctant to be apart from him, in particular, but that would have more than pushed the boundaries of propriety. That would have broken them. Or, more accurately, lit them on fire and burned them to the ground.

Mr. Rochester tilted his head. "Farewell, Miss Eyre. I will return. And promise me that you will be present in the parlor this afternoon with the rest of the guests."

Jane nodded.

He touched his hand to his heart, so subtly that Jane didn't know if it was an innocent movement or a deliberate gesture. She let herself imagine it was the latter.

Mr. Rochester and horse galloped away.

"Strange that the master of the house is set to leave again. Where could he be going?" Helen said. "And while he has guests. Who *does* that?"

Jane ignored her. As she watched Mr. Rochester disappear down the road, she put her own hand to her heart.

Jane kept her promise and sat in the parlor with the other guests for afternoon tea. Blanche Ingram sat close to the fire and shot Jane nasty looks followed by hushed comments to her mother. She was most likely talking about her contempt for the presence of the help, judging by Charlotte's uncomfortable glances toward Jane. For Jane's part, she was more concerned with how elegant a lady could appear while being so nasty. Of course, Mr. Rochester would want someone so elegant as his wife.

Jane wondered if Miss Ingram had received a private farewell from Mr. Rochester as well. Did he put his hand on his heart as he took his leave of her? Did he do something more?

Mr. Blackwood also eyed Jane, and seemed fidgety. No doubt he wanted to address her about the stupid Society gig, but was impeded by the pre-Victorian rules about the highborn speaking with the servants.

Tea had just been served when a loud knock sounded at the main entrance of the manor. Soon after, the door to the parlor blew open.

Jane shot to her feet, expecting to see Mr. Rochester. Instead, a stout man rushed in, followed by a servant breathing hard to keep up. Jane sank back down.

"Mr. Mason," the servant announced.

The new arrival—Mr. Mason—paused momentarily, scanning the room as though looking for someone. He then gathered himself and bowed.

"Good day," he said. "I am here to call on Mr. Rochester."

The party stood, bowing and curtsying, and then Miss Ingram stepped forward. "Mr. Rochester is away on business, but he will return this evening. Please do sit."

Jane thought it seemed awfully presumptuous of Miss Ingram to take it upon herself to do the welcoming.

When the guests and Mr. Mason had settled, and the proper introductions were made, Lady Ingram spoke.

"Do tell us, Mr. Mason, how are you acquainted with Mr. Rochester?"

Mr. Mason shifted in his seat. "We . . . have traveled together."

"Ooh, exciting," Blanche Ingram said.

Helen glanced at Jane. "Is it?"

Jane shrugged.

"And where did you travel?" Lady Ingram said.

"Here and there. About." Mr. Mason cleared his throat.

"Ooh, thrilling," Helen said.

"Mr. Mason, you are indeed piquing our curiosity," Miss Ingram said. "You must tell us more."

"What would you like to know, Miss Ingram?"

Miss Ingram clasped her hands together. "Why do you visit

Mr. Rochester now? What brings you here?"

Mr. Mason frowned. "I'm here for the . . . weather." Just then a thunderclap shook the windows. "The hunting weather."

"Ah," Lady Ingram said.

Everyone looked very puzzled. Mr. Mason grew even more uncomfortable, and kept an eye on the entrance to the parlor, anxious for Mr. Rochester's return. Almost as anxious as Blanche Ingram. Almost as anxious as Jane.

Then there was Charlotte and Mr. Blackwood, both of whom kept stealing glances at Jane. They were obviously anxious to talk to her, but they were not given the chance.

So, between Miss Ingram and Jane and Mr. Mason and Mr. Blackwood and Charlotte, the room was . . . anxious.

FIFTEEN
Alexander

It was a dark and stormy night.

After everyone went to bed, Alexander penned a letter to Wellington. He wrote by the light of a single candle, keeping the scratch of metal on paper to a minimum. In the bed by the door, Branwell was already sleeping; Alexander didn't want to wake him, as things were generally safer when Branwell was asleep.

The letter read:

> *Dear Sir,*
>
> *I've pursued Miss Eyre to an estate called Thornfield Hall. Having seen her command the dead on several occasions, I am more convinced than ever that she is a Beacon.*
>
> *While I am confident she will be persuaded to join us, I'd like to offer her £5,000 a year. I realize that is rather exorbitant, but with*

her being a Beacon, I believe the expense would be worth it.

I am your obedient servant,

A. Black

When the ink dried, he fastened the letter to one of the Society pigeons and opened the window. The bird left, and Alexander tried to sleep.

But Branwell's nasal snores prevented sleep from reaching him, and Alexander lay in his bed going over every moment of the day.

Rochester remained absent from Thornfield, which made sense with the storm, but why had he abandoned his guests in the first place? Something was still troubling him about the man.

Alexander searched through his earliest memories, those fragments of his childhood before the explosion had killed his father.

He could remember his father taking him for walks by the River Thames, pointing out different shops he'd taken Alexander's mother to before she succumbed to the Graveyard Disease, and then Westminster, which loomed over the water with its towers and arches and bells. His father knew everyone in the city, it seemed, from the merchants whose boats bobbed in the current to the boys who sold papers on every corner. When the crowd grew thick and Alexander couldn't see over the heads of all the adults, his father would set him on his shoulders. Perched up there, Alexander had felt so big and tall and safe. When the breeze rustled through his hair, scented with the odors of smoke and people and trash in the river, Alexander had imagined he was flying.

He could also remember going into Westminster, seeing Wellington, who'd patted his head, and then stopping by an office where one of his father's friends worked. That was Rochester, he was certain. The man had been younger then, with fewer lines around his eyes and mouth, but he'd seemed warm and generous to little Alexander, offering a sweet and then making him laugh by saying something in French.

And now his father was dead. And gone.

Not everyone became a ghost, of course. And it was better, wasn't it, that a spirit moved on to find peace? But still, an ache lived within Alexander. He'd searched for his father's ghost at first, convinced he must be out there somewhere, waiting for Alexander to find him. But gradually, he'd had to admit the truth. His father was gone. Forever, it seemed. He remained only in memories, and Alexander's desire to avenge his murder.

"One day," Alexander whispered into the night. "I promise."

Branwell's snoring was getting worse, rivaling the thunder outside. There'd be no sleeping like this.

Wearily, Alexander pulled on his robe and stepped out the door, into the candlelit hall. For a while, he wandered the maze of the house, letting his feet take him where they pleased. His head was back in those memories, that feeling of being held aloft on his father's shoulders, high above the world and everyone in it.

He'd been thinking of his father a lot since coming to Thornfield—from the moment he'd realized Rochester had been his father's friend.

"What are you doing out here?" The voice came from the translucent figure of Miss Burns, who was floating toward him from the opposite end of the hall.

Alexander glanced around before replying; they were alone. "I couldn't sleep."

"Me neither."

They stared at each other, having reached some sort of impasse with that brief exchange.

"Well." He cleared his throat. "I suppose I'll let you get back to haunting the halls."

"Are you going to trap me in a pocket watch?"

He frowned. "No. Why would you think that?"

"Jane is worried that you will. She doesn't trust you or your pocket watch, and I agree with her."

"Then there's nothing to worry about. I'm not here to relocate you, only to offer Miss Eyre a job." Perhaps this reassurance was all that Miss Eyre needed to change her mind. (Regarding the exploding flower incident, Alexander could keep a secret.)

"That's good to know."

"Will you tell her that?" he asked.

"I don't have to do anything you say. You're not the boss of me."

"That's why I phrased it as a question, Miss Burns."

She tapped her finger against her chin. "Perhaps I'll tell her. If the topic comes up again." She floated away.

In the direction he needed to go.

Reader, you know that feeling when you say good-bye to someone and then you walk in the same direction with them, but you've already said good-bye and everything is awkward?

Alexander was desperate to avoid that. He turned the other direction.

Just then, he spotted someone else. Toward the east wing, a man fully dressed in a deep gray suit tested a doorknob, but it was locked. The man glanced over his shoulder, then pulled something from his pocket. A lock pick gleamed in the candlelight—just an instant before he fumbled and the sliver of metal clattered to the floor.

As the man rushed to find the fallen lock pick, Alexander strode forward. "Good evening," he said. "Mr. Mason."

The other man shot up. "Oh, Mr. Eshton, right? I didn't see you there."

"Couldn't sleep?" Alexander nodded toward the other man's day clothes.

"Hmm? Oh, yes. I'm something of a night owl." He took a step to one side, as though to block the door he'd been trying—and failing—to open. "And what about you? You look preoccupied, if you don't mind me saying so."

Mr. Mason was behaving awfully shiftily, but Alexander hadn't become the star agent of the Society by showing his hand. He'd let Mr. Mason believe he hadn't been caught trying to break into the east wing. "I was pondering how strange it is that Mr. Rochester left mere days after receiving a houseful of guests."

"Very strange," Mr. Mason agreed.

"You've known him a long time, I take it." Alexander shoved his hands into his pockets. "Has he always been like this?"

Mr. Mason hesitated. "It's been some time since I've seen the man, I must admit, but I recall him being more—ah—attentive in the past."

"What kept you away?"

Mr. Mason shifted his weight. "N—nothing in particular. That is, years ago a favor was asked of me and it's been so long. . . ."

Alexander waited for him to finish.

"It's family business. I shouldn't have said anything."

How intriguing. Alexander barely restrained himself from reaching for his notebook. "Worry not, sir." Alexander forced himself to smile. "I'd better be off to bed. Good night, Mr. Mason."

When Alexander returned to his room, a wet pigeon waited on the windowsill, its feathers singed by lightning and a letter tucked around its ankle. Apparently it was still raining. Gently, he removed the note and offered the bird a bit of bread, then watched it fly back into the storm. (These Society birds were as tough as nails.)

Branwell's snores filled the room. He slept deeply enough that he didn't even stir when Alexander struck a match and lit a candle.

The note read simply:

Return to London immediately.

That was strange. More than anyone else, Wellington knew the importance of having a Beacon join the Society. And what was more, Alexander still had two days to persuade Miss Eyre.

No, Wellington must have misread his note. (No matter that this had never happened before.) Wellington must have missed the part where Alexander confirmed she was a Beacon.

It was perhaps the first time Alexander deliberately disobeyed orders from Wellington, but *perhaps* it was the first time Wellington had ever been so wrong.

Alexander would not leave Thornfield Hall without Jane Eyre.

SIXTEEN

Charlotte

"Five thousand pounds!" Charlotte stared up at Mr. Blackwood, her mouth hanging open in shock. "Wait. What would Jane's assistant make?"

Five thousand pounds was an enormous sum. Charlotte could not conceive of what Jane would do with such an amount. The only thing she'd ever known Jane to spend money on was painting supplies, and five thousand pounds would practically buy Jane the Louvre.

She tilted her head. "I thought you said that the Society was experiencing financial difficulties."

Mr. Blackwood nodded tightly. "So I did."

"But the Duke of Wellington approved offering Jane five thousand pounds a year?"

Mr. Blackwood scratched the back of his neck and glanced away. They had slipped out to the garden before breakfast to discuss their plans of recruiting Jane. One day had passed since Charlotte had made her initial offer behind the parlor curtains. Which meant there were two days left before Jane would give her final answer.

But Charlotte was certain that she'd only need today. No one could refuse the offer of five thousand pounds.

"Um . . ." Mr. Blackwood was being uncharacteristically inarticulate. "Well . . . We'll cross that bridge when we come to it."

"But, Mr. Blackw—"

"I find all this talk of money inappropriate, don't you?" he said.

Inappropriate? She frowned. The last thing she wanted was to be inappropriate, but how could they discuss their plans for Jane without discussing—

"So how will you approach Miss Eyre this time?" he asked. "We are meant to go on a picnic later. Perhaps we can find a reason to bring Adele along. And therefore Miss Eyre."

"I thought, instead, that I might stay behind," said Charlotte. "I could say I have a headache or am otherwise feeling ill."

"Yes, do that," Mr. Blackwood said faintly. "That's good."

At the strained sound of his voice she lifted her glasses to look at his face. There was a small cut on his chin, where he must have nicked himself shaving, and shadows under his eyes. His expression was drawn, thoughtful.

"Are you all right?" she asked.

He did not answer.

"Mr. Blackwood?"

He gave a weak attempt at a smile. "I'm fine. I had difficulty sleeping last night, is all."

"The storm was quite loud."

"Yes."

She could tell, though, that there was something more on his mind than the lack of sleep.

"Mr. Rochester has still not returned?" she asked.

His smile faded. "No."

"That's odd, don't you think?"

"Quite."

It was quiet for a moment, Mr. Blackwood frowning, deep in his thoughts, and Charlotte observing him. Then she lost patience and just came out with her question. "What is it about Mr. Rochester that you're not telling me?"

His gaze flew up to her face. "What?"

"Ever since we've arrived here, you've been troubled by something. Someone. Mr. Rochester, I think. You stare at him whenever he's present in the room, and your expression in those moments . . ." She looked away, suddenly embarrassed to reveal how carefully she'd been observing him. "You obviously have a heightened interest in Mr. Rochester. Why?"

"I—" Mr. Blackwood seemed taken aback by the bluntness of her question. Then he sighed. "Mr. Rochester was, I believe, a friend of my father's."

"Was?"

"My father died." He bent his head as if the sight of his feet intrigued him.

"I'm sorry," she said simply. "When?"

"Fourteen years ago," he said. "I was just a boy when it happened, but . . ."

She was tempted to put a hand on his shoulder, but there were people walking about the garden who would have found that gesture inappropriate, even between supposed cousins. So instead she offered a sympathetic smile.

"I know something of how it feels to lose a parent. My mother died when I was around that same age. I was so young I hardly remember her, besides a few flashes." Like once when she'd had a fever. She could remember the coolness of her mother's hand against her face, how very comforting that single touch had been.

She glanced up again at Mr. Blackwood. He was looking at her now, his brown eyes fixed on her face. She felt her cheeks heat.

"Anyway," she continued. "Mr. Rochester knew your father?"

"They were best friends, I think. More and more is coming back to me." Mr. Blackwood gasped. "I can even remember dinners here, at this very house. Mr. Rochester and his . . ." He paused. "His wife. He had a wife. I thought she was so very beautiful."

"She must have . . ."

"Yes, she must have died," Mr. Blackwood said. "A shame."

"And now he's going to marry Miss Ingram. An even greater

shame," Charlotte added. "Being that she's such an insufferable human being."

Mr. Blackwood gave a startled laugh. Charlotte laughed, too. Then they smiled at each other, the somberness between them broken.

"So will you tell Mr. Rochester that you are your father's son?" Charlotte asked.

Mr. Blackwood nodded sheepishly. "I have been expecting him to recognize me. I know that sounds absurd, but I have the look of my father."

"But if you were to tell Mr. Rochester about your connection, it would reveal that you are not, in fact, Mr. Eshton," Charlotte pointed out. "So it's fortunate that he hasn't recognized you."

"Yes," he agreed. "Fortunate."

She was about to say more, but then Bran appeared before them like a happy puppy.

"We're going on a picnic!" he said excitedly. "I adore picnics!"

Mr. Blackwood and Charlotte exchanged amused glances.

Charlotte smiled. "I think I feel a headache coming on."

After the others had gone, Charlotte sought Jane out and found her in the library, where Adele was conjugating irregular verbs.

"Oh, hello, Charlotte," Jane sighed when she looked up to see Charlotte standing before her.

"Do you have a moment?" Charlotte asked. "To talk?"

Jane sighed again. "I suppose."

They went off into a corner where they would not be overheard. Charlotte straightened her shoulders and took a deep breath.

"I do wish you wouldn't bother," Jane said before she could get a word out. "Nothing has changed since the last time we spoke."

"Oh, but it has," Charlotte said eagerly. "Jane. You won't believe this. But the Society is willing to offer you five thousand pounds a year to become an agent."

Jane just stared at her.

"Did you hear me?" Charlotte asked. "Did you hear me say five thousand pounds?"

"Yes," Jane said in a small, strangled voice. "But why—"

"Do you remember Sarah Curshaw, from Lowood?"

"The one with the green eyes?" Jane said.

"Yes. And how she went into that church that random day and met Mr. Bourret, who was so immediately taken by Sarah and her green eyes that he simply had to marry her? It was the biggest scandal, because Sarah's family was penniless, and Mr. Bourret brought in four thousand pounds a year."

Jane looked weary. "What's your point, Charlotte?"

"If you became an agent, you'd be richer than Sarah Curshaw, the richest girl we know. You'd be set for life."

"I don't understand," Jane said. "Why would they be willing to pay me such a sum?"

"Because you're special, Jane," Charlotte answered, pressing down the stab of jealousy she felt in her chest. "You're what's called a Beacon. You can—"

Jane held up her hand. "Stop. No more, Charlotte. I don't want to hear it."

"But—"

"I am no one special," Jane said. "I am just a girl. I can see ghosts, yes, but it has only ever brought me trouble!"

"But, Jane, if you would only—"

"No. I don't need another minute to give you my final answer. No. No, no. Go away, Charlotte. Stop playing your little game."

Charlotte felt the heat rush to her face. "You're a selfish girl, Jane Eyre. You've been given an opportunity that some of us would—well, not exactly kill for, but desire very much, and be willing to work incredibly hard to attain. And this *miraculous* chance is offered to you, freely, but you turn your nose up at it. You're throwing it all away, Jane! You're a fool!"

There was a moment of thunderous silence. Then Jane said, under her breath, "I'm sorry. I didn't mean it. You know I didn't mean it. You're not trouble."

Charlotte thought Jane was trying to make amends, but then she realized that Jane was not speaking to her. She was speaking to Helen.

"She's here right now, isn't she?" she asked. "Helen Burns?"

Jane's eyes flickered with surprise. "How did you know?"

"Mr. Blackwood can see her. He's not here to relocate her," she added quickly, as Jane's face filled with alarm. "I wish you would have told me yourself. I thought . . . I thought we were friends."

"We are," Jane said.

"Tell me the real reason, then, that you won't accept the Society's offer."

Jane bit her lip. "There's no real reason. I am simply content to stay at Thornfield Hall."

"But why?"

"It's warm here—so warm, my toes are nice and toasty every night, no chilblains, ever—and the food is very good, and I am becoming so fond of my little pupil, and then, well, there's . . ." Jane sighed. "Rochester."

"Rochester?"

"Rochester is a good and decent man. He's been so kind to me. He's not what you might consider classically handsome, I know, but he's tall and dark, at least. And there's something so appealing about his broody mannerisms. His scowl is so . . . attractive. And sometimes when we talk I feel that he's the only person who really understands me. It's like my soul communes with his. It's like he—"

"Oh, blast. You're in love with Rochester," Charlotte observed. And then everything suddenly made much more sense.

Jane's face colored. "No. Of course I'm not in love with Rochester. That would be entirely inappropriate. He's my employer. He's . . ." Charlotte stared at her. "Is it that obvious?"

"Jane," Charlotte began.

"I know he's a bit older than I am. But that just makes him wiser, don't you think?"

"Oh, Jane." This was a distressing development. Charlotte

could contend with Jane's low opinion of herself, her unfair prejudice against the Society, her unwillingness to picture herself as respectable or wealthy. But if Jane was in love, well, that was that. Jane would not be coming to London with them or joining the Society.

Love trumped everything in a woman's life. More than ambition. Respectability. Common sense. Love, they'd both been taught, conquers all.

"So you're in love with Rochester," Charlotte said with a little sigh. "When did this happen? How did this happen?"

Jane shook her head helplessly. "I don't know. He made me love him without even looking at me."

Charlotte wasn't sure how that worked, but she said, "And you think he loves you, in return?"

She nodded. "Once, he put his robe around me when he thought I might be cold."

Charlotte gasped. "That is romantic. And scandalous. Jane!"

"I saved him because his bed was on fire," she confessed, and then she recounted the entire story of her time with Mr. Rochester, including their unusual introduction on the road, the strangeness that was Grace Poole, the incident with the fire, and their moment yesterday in the garden. By the end of the tale Charlotte, too, was convinced that Jane and Rochester were indeed soul mates.

"And then he said, I knew you would do me good from the first moment I saw you," Jane finished up.

Charlotte propped her head in her hand and sighed dreamily.

"He said that? That sounds just like Mr. Darcy."

"I know! That's what I told Helen! He's said it more than once, actually. So you see, I am needed here. I am doing him good."

Charlotte frowned. "But why, then, is he leading everyone to believe that he's going to marry Miss Ingram?"

Jane stared off into the distance again. Her hand, Charlotte noticed, was trembling.

"So it's true, then? Mr. Rochester is going to marry Miss Ingram?" she whispered.

"Yes, they're getting married. At least that's what everybody says. Including Miss Ingram."

"She's not even that pretty," Jane muttered. "Who needs such glossy hair, anyway? And her neck . . ."

"Swanlike," Charlotte sighed.

"People really shouldn't have necks like swans," Jane said. "It's absurd. She's a bird neck, is what she is."

"Plus, Miss Ingram is the worst, haughtiest, most unkind of persons. I'd feel sorry for anybody who ended up with her," Charlotte added.

Jane looked at her and smiled brilliantly. The smile transformed her from very plain to quite pretty in an instant. "Oh, thank you for saying that. That makes me feel much better."

"Anytime." Charlotte really did believe that Jane was a greatly superior human being compared to Miss Ingram. "But Miss Ingram definitely has the impression that she's to be Rochester's bride. . . ."

Jane grabbed Charlotte's hand. "But *why* does Miss Ingram

think she's marrying Mr. Rochester? Has he asked her? Surely he hasn't asked her, or he wouldn't act so friendly with . . ."

"He hasn't asked her," Charlotte said.

Another transformative smile. "He hasn't?"

"She thinks he will ask her on this visit."

Clouds darkened Jane's expression. "Oh, she does, does she?"

"Don't you worry about Miss Ingram," Charlotte said generously. "I'm sure it will work out. It sounds like he loves you."

"It does, doesn't it?"

"Yes. I see, now, why you can't leave him."

"But you won't tell anyone? We're friends, aren't we?"

"Yes. We're friends. I'll just tell Mr. Blackwood that it's no use. You've made up your mind," Charlotte said.

She could only imagine how he was going to take the news.

Jane
SEVENTEEN

The guests came back from the picnic and still Mr. Rochester hadn't returned. Jane mulled over her conversation with Charlotte. She couldn't believe her feelings for Rochester had been so obvious. More disheartening was the fact that everyone in the party thought Rochester would propose to Blanche Ingram sooner rather than later.

And the third most disheartening thing was the pressure she now felt to join the ghost-hating Society.

"Five thousand pounds," Helen said.

Jane was trying to focus on her work with Adele, but Helen's pacing and frequent outbursts about the money were making it difficult.

Still, she'd rather try to teach Adele than meet up with the guests in the parlor. Mr. Rochester wasn't back. He would never know that she wasn't there.

"Do you know what you could do with five thousand pounds?" Helen said.

"Do tell," Jane whispered. Adele was still conjugating verbs and didn't hear her.

"You could . . . you could . . . buy all the burlap in the world and then burn it in one big bonfire, which would also keep you so cozy warm."

Jane couldn't help smiling.

"Besides that, Mr. Rochester is by no means a sure thing, but five thousand pounds is."

Jane couldn't help frowning.

A knock came at the door, and Mrs. Fairfax entered.

"Miss Eyre, I have a rather peculiar request. An old fortune-teller has come to Thornfield. She has entreated that all of the ladies in the house visit her in the master's study to have their fortunes revealed."

Jane gave her an incredulous look. "I have no fortune, Mrs. Fairfax, let alone one that could be told."

"Not yet," said Helen. "But if you go with Mr. Blackwood—"

"Please, Miss Eyre. She is quite persistent, and you're the only lady yet to be seen."

"Why the ladies?" Jane asked.

Mrs. Fairfax ignored the question and made a shooing gesture toward the door.

Jane glanced toward Helen, who shrugged. Perhaps Jane needed something to take her mind off Rochester. And Charlotte. And the Society. And the blasted Ingrams.

"Very well. I will come down at once."

Mrs. Fairfax led the way to the study, followed by Jane and Helen.

"Well, this is all very exciting," Helen said. "Perhaps she'll tell you some glamorous thing that lies in your future. Like five thousand pounds."

Jane didn't answer.

When they arrived at the door, they found it closed and locked. "I believe Miss Ingram is finishing up," Mrs. Fairfax said.

Sure enough, moments later, the latch unhinged and out came Miss Blanche Ingram. Her face was dark, and her frown pronounced.

"Miss Ingram, are you feeling all right?" Mrs. Fairfax inquired.

"I am quite well," she said in a curt voice. "Only it is unfortunate I wasted away a quarter of an hour listening to nonsense."

She stomped away to join the others in the library.

Mrs. Fairfax turned toward Jane. "She certainly seems upset by her future. Now, Jane, be certain not to take this fortune-teller's words to heart. She is almost certainly full of lies."

"Do not worry, Mrs. Fairfax. I won't listen."

Inside the study there hung a tapestry, separating the door half of the room from the window half. A lone chair sat by the drape.

"Ah, the last of the single ladies of the house. Please do sit," came a gravelly voice from the other side of the tapestry.

Jane sat, and Helen knelt beside her.

"Are you shaking, girl?" the old woman asked.

"No."

"Why not?"

"Because I'm not afraid."

"Are you not worried about my supernatural powers?"

"I don't believe in them," Jane said.

"You speak most confidently, for someone who hides such a large secret."

A breath caught in Jane's throat.

"There now," the fortune-teller said. "I see this affects you."

"I don't have a secret," Jane said, though her voice quivered.

"I know you're an orphan."

Again, Jane took in a breath.

"Wouldn't you like to sit closer to the fire?" the fortune-teller asked. "I think at Lowood school, you were starved for heat."

Okay, this was getting ridiculous. And just a touch frightening.

Helen stood and walked through the curtain. What if the fortune-teller truly had skill in the occult and could see Helen?

But Helen returned almost immediately.

"It's Mr. Rochester!"

Jane raised her eyebrows in question.

"Yes! It's him. It's him! I promise."

"Did you hear me, girl?" The fortune-teller/Mr. Rochester said. Now that Jane was listening for it, she could definitely hear a marked resemblance to the master's gruff voice.

"I did. Yes, I do appreciate fire, but I'm sure there are very few who don't. Except maybe Mr. Rochester, who was nearly burned in his sleep a few nights ago."

There was throat clearing on the other side of the curtain. "And what about this secret of yours?" Rochester asked. "Is there no one you can confide in?"

"No. Not really," Jane said, wondering what secret Rochester was referring to. Surely he didn't know she could see ghosts.

"What do you think of this party of guests here at Thornfield? I think there is one in the party who does occupy your thoughts, isn't there? Someone you might have feelings for?" Mr. Rochester nudged.

Jane couldn't deny the fact that it was his face, lately, that had dominated her thoughts.

It was a good thing Mr. Rochester couldn't see her, or hear her racing heartbeat. "No one's face, in particular. Although Mrs. Fairfax always looks pleasant."

"But what of the master of the house? What do you think of him?"

Jane knew better than to mine her own heart for this answer. She thought back to Mrs. Fairfax's description that first day. "He is a good master. Loyal. Pays his staff in a timely fashion, though he owes me fifteen pounds that I have yet to see. But that's between you and me."

Mr. Rochester coughed a few times. "But what of the master's character?"

"I'll leave his character description to the woman who's captured his heart." She paused for dramatic effect. "Miss Ingram, of course," Jane continued. "I believe their engagement is as good as settled. So I intend to advertise for a new place of employment."

The curtain flew to the side, and out stepped Mr. Rochester. "You are not leaving!"

Jane frowned. "Mr. Rochester, I knew it was you."

"Hah!" he cried. "You are a witch."

Jane rolled her eyes. "I've no intention of going anywhere until necessary. But, sir, pretending to be a fortune-teller to get me to talk?"

Rochester opened his mouth as if to argue, but then shook his head and smiled. "No, you are right, Jane. It is not fair. But how else am I to find out what's going on in your mind?"

Helen stomped her foot and the end table near her rattled. "Can't he simply ask you? Converse with you? Acknowledge you in certain company? There are a million things he could've done to figure out what was going on!"

"I would do anything to know what you are thinking," Mr. Rochester said.

Jane blushed. Why would someone like Mr. Rochester care what was inside the head of a lowly servant? She was at a loss for words. What was she to say? The silence dragged on.

Helen knew exactly what to say. "Never in any Jane Austen novel did the love interest pretend to be a fortune-teller," Helen said. "Why would someone do that? Jane, you must confront him."

Jane was having a difficult time ignoring her friend. Surely they couldn't expect any real person to compete with Mr. Darcy.

"Did you know there is another visitor to Thornfield?" she blurted.

"No," he said. "Who is it?"

"He says he's an old friend. A Mr. Mason."

Mr. Rochester's expression remained blank. "I see. You may go."

Jane frowned.

"I must attend to my new guest."

Jane walked stiffly to the door.

"And I expect you in the drawing room."

"Yes, sir," Jane said.

"Well, that was strange," Helen said. "Even you must admit it."

Jane nodded slowly. "I admit it."

The two of them went to the drawing room, where Jane took a seat next to Adele, partially hidden behind a panel.

Yes, for the umpteenth time, someone is hiding behind a panel. Apparently in pre-Victorian England, there were panels everywhere, and people hid behind them. Frequently. From what we could discover during our thorough research of the subject, panels were advertised by how well someone might hide behind one.

So, Jane was sitting behind a panel, as usual, when Mr. Blackwood entered.

"Mr. Blackwood!" Helen exclaimed, waving. "Hi! Do you have employment for a ghost? I can be most useful."

Jane shot her a confused look and said, "Sit down, dear."

Helen dropped to the floor. Before Jane could question Helen about her sudden enthusiasm for Mr. Blackwood, Mr. Rochester threw open the drawing room door and strode inside.

"I am sorry for my absence, my esteemed guests. The storm kept me."

Mr. Mason crossed the room, his hand extended. "Rochester, my dear fellow."

Mr. Rochester's eyes narrowed and he took the tiniest step back. "Mr. Mason."

Mr. Mason hesitated at the cold reception, and the two men stiffly shook hands.

"Very well," Mr. Rochester said. "I understand you all had fortunes told. I can't wait to hear about it, but for now, dinner is ready. If you'll follow me."

He held his elbow toward Miss Ingram, and she took the offered arm, a little less enthusiastically than she had in the past, Jane thought. She and Adele watched as the party went, two by two, out of the drawing room. Mr. Blackwood and Charlotte made the final pair, and both of them looked over their shoulders at Jane as they exited.

Helen watched them leave and then shook her head. "Five *thousand* pounds."

EIGHTEEN
Alexander

As a general rule, Alexander found everything suspicious. Like, why didn't women's clothes have pockets? And why did most mammals walk on four legs while humans used only two? And especially why did we see only one side of the moon? What was the other side trying to hide?

And then there was Rochester, who did suspicious things all the time. And Mason, who skulked about the house in the middle of the night. What was their relationship? Their greeting had been so odd and uncomfortable, as though the two men didn't agree on their shared history. And after dinner, Mason had tried to pull Rochester aside, but the latter just hissed gruffly, "She's not here. You should go home."

That wasn't the sort of warm friendship Mason had indicated when he'd arrived.

Then, when Mason and Rochester separated, Mason caught Alexander's eye and saw he'd witnessed the exchange. "Family business," he muttered, frowning, but he seemed more confused and hurt than anything.

Family business probably wasn't Alexander's business, but what did that mean about Mason and Rochester's relationship?

All of this might have been Alexander's suspicious nature; as we said, he found everything worth raising an eyebrow at. Nevertheless, it was enough to keep him up a second night in a row. (That and the fact that he hadn't worn his mask in more than a week. The lack of his mask made him feel exposed. Practically naked.)

On the other side of the room, Branwell snorted in his sleep, groaned, and turned over.

Resolved to find answers, Alexander dressed and started out of the room, only to realize Branwell was suddenly standing in the doorway. Fully clothed.

"What are we doing?" asked the apprentice.

"Snooping."

"I love snooping."

"I don't think—"

"I'm coming along." Without waiting for an invitation, Branwell was out the door with Alexander.

It would have been better, he thought, if he had to have "help," if that help could have come from Miss Brontë; the young lady had proved her cleverness in getting them in to Thornfield

Hall, though tonight she'd seemed to avoid him before dinner, and during dinner, and then when he tried to corner her after dinner, she wanted to talk about the tomato soup. But it wouldn't have been proper, him sneaking around the house with a young lady. He shuddered to imagine the talk.

"Who are we snooping on?" inquired Branwell as they slipped through the hall.

"You should have asked before you decided to join."

"I didn't say I'd rescind the offer of help. I was just asking for details."

"Rochester."

Branwell gave a little hop. "I can't wait."

Shortly, they reached Rochester's study, and Branwell stood watch while Alexander picked the lock with his penknife. At first glance, they found . . . everything in perfect order. No strange memory-altering artifacts. No device that removed the ability to speak French.

"What are you looking for?" Branwell at least had the presence of mind to keep his voice low.

"Anything that tells me about his relationship to my father, or why Mr. Mason is here and behaving so squirrely."

"Squirrely, sir?"

"It's a word, Branwell."

"I know, but it's not one I thought you'd use."

"There are lots of squirrels in London. I'm familiar with how they behave. And Mason is behaving like a squirrel."

Branwell nodded. "What about Rochester? Are you turning him into an animal as well?"

Alexander clenched his jaw. Really, he would have preferred to come in here alone, if Branwell was going to interrogate him like this.

"Maybe he's not really a bad chap and you just don't like him because you don't like people," Branwell mused as he dragged his finger over the spines of books on a shelf.

"That's not true. I like plenty of people." Alexander was focused on the large mahogany desk, opening drawers and flipping through papers.

"Who do you like?" Branwell asked. "Name one person."

Alexander had to think about that. There was Wellington, a man he deeply respected, though respecting someone wasn't the same as liking them, he supposed; he didn't know Wellington well enough on a personal level to say he *liked* the man, just that he didn't *dislike* the man.

And, well, there was . . .

"Ah!" In searching through the drawers, Alexander had come across a false back. He removed the pens and jars of ink from the front, then used his penknife to open the secret compartment. It was filled with old letters, the papers yellowed with age.

"What is it?" Branwell abandoned his search of the bookshelves and brought his lamp close. "Did you find something incriminating?"

Alexander riffled through the pages, skimming names and dates. He removed several of them, long enough to glance over the text. "Most of these are about Rochester's late wife," he said. "Her illness, treatments, something about a woman named Grace Poole. Nothing that would be remotely useful for us to know."

But then he paused. On one of the letters in the back, a familiar name jumped out: his father's.

"Who's this?" Branwell asked. "Do you know him?"

"No one of consequence," Alexander muttered. "This is nothing. There's nothing here."

Branwell frowned. "You seem really upset about something that's nothing."

"I'm sorry, Branwell. You should go back to bed."

"So I helped you break into Rochester's study for nothing?"

"I'm afraid so." Alexander's hands were shaking as he stuffed the letter into his pocket. Branwell could see it, surely, but the assistant didn't comment. Instead, the boy just left the study with a concerned frown on his face.

Finally, Alexander was alone in the room. He swallowed, then traced a finger across the bottom of the letter where the name N. Bell had been carefully signed. That was his father's signature. There were so few items of his father's left after the explosion, and here was a letter in his own hand.

He swayed a little, then leaned on the side of the desk. The letter begged to be read, but if he looked at it now, there would be nothing new for Alexander to have. No more anticipation.

He closed his eyes and breathed, trying to calm himself. He'd suspected something strange about Rochester. That was why he'd sneaked into a gentleman's study and riffled through his desk.

But memories were persistent, funny things. They lifted up at the most inconvenient times.

Alexander's father had been part of the Society for the Relocation of Wayward Spirits, years and years ago, back during King George III's reign. He'd worked in the treasury, not as an agent; as far as Alexander knew, his father hadn't been able to see ghosts. But he'd believed, and he'd done his part to improve the lives of citizens of England.

The day his father died was seared into his memory. He'd replayed it in his mind for years, polishing it until he felt he could recall every detail. Wellington had warned him that some of those details might be fantasies. He'd been so young. How could anyone remember everything exactly? But Alexander knew the truth. He'd heard the argument between the killer and his father. He'd felt his father's anger as the killer left the house in a fury. And he remembered the impacts of his footfalls as he, a young boy, went racing after the killer.

Then. The explosion.

At that moment, the man had turned. And he'd looked triumphant.

And while the killer had watched Alexander's house explode, and his father's life extinguish within, Alexander had gone racing back, as though he could save him.

He'd returned to the house, coughing at the smoke, ashes stinging his eyes.

It was there he'd died.

For a moment.

That was when Wellington had found him and rushed him to a doctor. He'd breathed in too much smoke, that was all, and Alexander had been (physically) fine after that. But he'd died. Briefly.

That had been the trigger. After that, he'd been able to see ghosts.

But not his father's.

And now Alexander held this letter from his father. To Rochester. It was dated mere weeks before the explosion.

He took a deep breath and began to read.

My dear friend Rochester, the letter began.

Alexander had been right; his father had known Mr. Rochester. They'd been friends. Not just acquaintances or passingly friendly, but *dear.*

The beginning of the letter was all formalities, updating Rochester on the activities in London and their mutual acquaintances. There was even a note about Alexander—*My son is full of energy and curiosity. I fear I won't be able to keep up with him*—which Alexander read over and over, burning the words into his heart. He wanted to remember forever some of the last thoughts his father had about him.

Then: *I know you and I have not agreed in the past about what to do about AW, but I'd still like to avoid violence if we can. We should meet in person to discuss how we might save the Society and bring this travesty to an end.*

Alexander read the letter five more times. A hundred more times. Slowly, the pieces began to fall into place. Rochester had come to London to see Alexander's father. To discuss something about the Society. To avoid violence.

But there *had* been violence. The explosion.

Perhaps the disagreement had been stronger than his father had realized.

What if his father had died at the hands of Edward Rochester?

NINETEEN
Charlotte

The candle was almost burnt out, but Charlotte kept writing. She'd felt a rush of inspiration ever since this morning's conversation with Jane. It was a new story, a better one than she had ever attempted. The mystery of Mr. Brocklehurst had flown from her consciousness. This story she was writing now—the one she'd been waiting for—the one, she knew, she was *meant* to compose, was not a murder mystery. Murder mysteries were rather base, weren't they? It was not a ghost story, either, although it may have supernatural elements, Charlotte supposed. No, this new story was a romance. It was drawn in large part from Jane's situation. It had come to Charlotte all in a rush as she'd listened to Jane reflect on her relationship with Mr. Rochester. There'd been this gleam of love in Jane's eyes. Jane Eyre—little plain Jane—was in love. She had no right to be in love, of course, a girl of her status, especially seeing as the man of interest was the master of the house. But in love, Jane was. And it sounded as if the love were, at least in some aspect, reciprocated.

Charlotte could imagine it all so well. Jane and Mr. Rochester were bound together, no matter how improper it appeared. She sighed. Someday, perhaps, she'd find love, too. Or it would find her, as it had with Jane. How was it that Jane had described it? "He made me love him," she'd said, "without even looking at me."

For now, Charlotte would have to be content to write her own version of their story. She'd already filled a quarter of her notebook with her tiny, laborious scrawl about Jane in love. At the moment, as the candle burned perilously low, she was trying to write the perfect description of Mr. Rochester.

The fire shone full on his face, Charlotte wrote, drawing her lip between her teeth and holding it there as her mind whirled with words. *I*—she'd been writing it so far in first person because it felt more natural to her to try to feel as she thought Jane must feel, and to give her a voice—not the voice of some wise, presumably male narrator, judging her, but her own, pure voice, speaking for itself. (And also, if we're being honest, Charlotte could live through Jane a little, if she wrote that way.) *I knew my traveler, with his broad and . . .* She frowned . . . *jetty* . . . yes, jetty . . . *eyebrows, his square forehead, made squarer by the horizontal sweep of his black hair. I recognized his decisive nose, more remarkable for character than for beauty.* She smiled at the line, dipped her pen into the inkwell and carried on in trying to describe his face. *His grim mouth, chin, and jaw—yes, all three were very grim and no mistake.*

She paused. There was indeed something grim about Mr. Rochester. Something ominous. She'd felt it every time she'd been in the man's presence. But this was the man Jane professed to love. Charlotte, as Jane's friend, should try to be supportive. And love was blind, was it not? Mr. Rochester possessed all the qualities that a young lady should yearn for. He was rather old, she could admit, but not feeble or senile. He was wealthy. He had an amusing talent—he was a decent actor, she'd seen when they'd played charades earlier. And he owned a very nice dog.

He would do. And Jane loved him, which was what truly mattered.

Charlotte turned back to her work. *His shape, now divested of cloak—I suppose it was a good figure in the athletic sense of the term—broad chested and thin flanked, though neither tall nor graceful.*

She paused again. For some mysterious reason her mind drifted to Mr. Blackwood. Mr. Blackwood *was* graceful. In her mind she conjured the way he walked, so purposefully and yet light on his feet. How he folded his hands when he sat. His serious expression—but then there was the way he tried not to smile even when something struck him as humorous—the way his eyes would give him away and the tiniest upturn in the corner of his mouth would appear for a flicker of an instant before he'd banish it. She did like the smile, even though it meant that he might not be taking her seriously, she supposed. Lately when he'd told her to "Go home, Miss Brontë," that hidden smile had been present, too, as if he were only saying it out of habit now, but he didn't mean it. He wanted her there.

Charlotte brushed an errant curl from her forehead. *Focus,* she told herself. Back to Mr. Rochester. She concentrated on picturing the man's face, his stern features and heavy brow, his eyes and gathered eyebrows looking . . . *ireful and thwarted.* Yes.

But Mr. Blackwood . . . he could appear stern as well. Tonight, for instance, he'd borne an air of sharp determination as he'd pursued her about the house. He'd wanted to speak with her about her conversation with Jane. He expected her to report on Jane's answer to the proposition of five thousand pounds.

And Charlotte had, well, avoided him. She wasn't ready to tell him yet, that their endeavor to recruit Jane was futile. Jane had just divulged all the deep secrets of a woman's heart. Mr. Blackwood couldn't possibly understand.

And he was clearly wrestling with his own feelings concerning Mr. Rochester.

She sighed. Perhaps she was not ready to admit to herself yet that this had all been for nothing. That Jane would not become an agent, and therefore Charlotte's life was likely to return to the way it had been before. Boring. Starving. Languishing at Lowood.

And she and Mr. Blackwood would have no reason for further contact. She would never truly get to know him, the way she had lately been feeling she was coming to know him.

Ahem. *Mr. Rochester.* Charlotte turned back to her writing. She supposed that if Mr. Rochester had been too good-looking, Jane would have been intimidated by him. She nodded to herself, then wrote, *I had hardly ever seen a handsome youth; never in my life spoken to one. I had a theoretical reverence and homage for beauty, elegance, gallantry, fascination; but had I met those qualities incarnate in masculine shape, I should have known instinctively that they neither had nor could have sympathy with anything in me, and should have shunned them as one would fire, lightning, or anything else that is bright but antipathetic.*

Charlotte sat back and stretched her arms, feeling pleased with herself. (But she was a writer, so while she did get this moment of thinking herself somewhat brilliant, it would soon be offset by a crippling doubt that she had a gift of words at all. Such is the way with all writers. Trust us.) She liked what she'd written because it felt true. Better that a boy not be overtly handsome, she thought, if one was plain. Better that there were simply individual parts of said boy to admire. Like the shape of his hands. Or a smile. Or . . .

There was a soft tapping at her door. Charlotte startled, nearly upsetting her bottle of ink. It was the dead of night, the house entirely still. Perhaps she'd imagined the sound. She listened. It came again, a gentle rapping, rapping at her chamber door. She stood and put on her dressing gown and went to open it. Then she lifted her spectacles to see who it was.

Mr. Blackwood was standing there—not in his nightclothes, but fully dressed, though uncharacteristically rumpled, frowning this troubled little frown.

"What's wrong?" she asked immediately. "You look as if you've seen—"

Well, it would be ridiculous to say he'd seen a ghost. He was accustomed to seeing ghosts, after all.

"This is inappropriate," he said dully. "I . . . I shouldn't have come. I . . . I just . . ."

She didn't know what to do. She should definitely not invite him into her bedroom.

She stepped back and held the door open for him. "Come in."

He strode past her and straight across to the other side of the room, as if keeping some distance between them might preserve some semblance of propriety. He drew back the curtains and stared out the window into the moon-filled night. Charlotte closed the door gently.

"Do you wish to sit?" she asked, gesturing to an armchair.

"Yes." He crossed to the chair and sat, then stood up again. "No. No, I can't."

"Are you all right?" she asked.

"Rochester murdered my father." He rubbed his hand across his face. "Well, I think he did."

She felt instantly cold. "Mr. Rochester."

"He was there, that night, the night of the explosion. They argued. There was shouting. I remember it."

"The explosion?"

Mr. Blackwood quickly relayed the details of his father's death, his voice wavering. Her heart swelled, picturing the little boy he had been. What he'd been through.

He drew a letter out of his pocket and handed it to her. She read it. "So they had a falling-out, over the Society, it seems. But . . ."

"Rochester's a traitor," Mr. Blackwood spat out. "He's a

villain of the worst kind. I . . ." His hands were shaking. "It must have been him. Who else would have reason to hurt my father? There's no other explanation."

"Oh, Alexander, I'm sorry," she said.

His expression hardened. "He's the one who will be sorry. I will kill him."

She felt the color drain from her face. "Well, that's a terrible idea."

He scowled. "I suppose you'd like me to confront Mr. Rochester about his crime and have the authorities deal with it."

"Why, yes," she affirmed. "That sounds much more reasonable."

"Do you suppose that Mr. Rochester will simply confess? That I'll accuse him of this vile act, which is a crime worthy of death—and then he'll respond with, 'Yes, yes, that is exactly what happened. Arrest me, please'?"

"You need proof, obviously," she agreed. "You will need to build a case against him."

"I heard him arguing with my father. I saw him leave the building, just before the explosion. I saw him."

"None of that proves that he actually murdered your father," Charlotte pointed out. "You have no evidence that isn't circumstantial."

"So again I say, I should simply kill him. It's what he deserves. Everything in my life has been leading up to this point."

She shook her head. "Then you will get arrested for murder

yourself, which would be a great embarrassment to the Society, I imagine. And it will fail to bring about the justice you seek. It's a terrible plan, do you see?"

"I suppose you have a better one."

"Of course I do." She smiled up at him, her mind grasping at several wild ideas. She settled on one. "You're going to carry on with the ruse. You are Mr. Eshton."

"Impossible," said Mr. Blackwood. "I cannot pretend any longer."

"Now is not the time, Mr. Blackwood, to cry revenge and reveal all of your cards. You must wait. Watch. Remaining here, quietly, will allow you access to his home and his private life. Then you can gather the evidence you need to put him away."

"I'm not a very good actor," he confessed.

"You're fine," Charlotte assured him. "You've handled yourself brilliantly so far."

"But it's different now."

"I know. This situation is entirely more important."

Some of the fire seemed to leave him. He was quiet for a long moment.

"All right. I'll remain Mr. Eshton. For now."

Over the course of their conversation she had slowly traversed the room, to where she was presently standing just before him. She put her hand on his arm. "I will help you."

"Thank you." He seemed suddenly aware of the inappropriateness of their current circumstance. He rubbed at his forehead, then stepped back. "I apologize. I should not have burst in here. I . . ."

"You needed someone to talk to."

He nodded. "I will go. It's very late." His brows squeezed together. "Why were you not asleep?"

"I was writing." She gestured toward the small desk and her notebook. The candle had long since sputtered out. "I've been feeling inspired, as of late."

"Inspired by what?" he asked.

She glanced away. "Um . . ." She couldn't very well tell him that she was writing a romance now. Starring, as it happened, Mr. Rochester. Oh, dear. Mr. Rochester was now potentially a murderer. Which would make him entirely inappropriate as a knight in shining armor for Jane.

This would ruin her story.

Or possibly improve upon it. Charlotte wasn't sure. It was important, though, that Jane be informed of Mr. Rochester's alleged crime. Oh, double dear. What an awful thing to have to tell her. How exactly does one tell one's friend that the man she's in love with could be a nefarious villain?

At that very moment, the night was pierced by a fearful shriek. (Charlotte would later write this moment and describe it as "a shrilly sound that ran from end to end of Thornfield Hall.")

She and Mr. Blackwood froze. The cry had come from the east wing.

"What was that noise?" Mr. Blackwood said.

"It sounded like someone in need of help," Charlotte replied, shivering.

"Help! Help! Help!" screamed the voice.

"See?"

"WILL NO ONE COME?"

They dashed out into the hall. It was crowded with the various guests of the house—Charlotte saw Bran looking dazed and the Ingrams and Colonel Dent—all milling around exclaiming things like, "Who is hurt?" "What has happened?" "Are there robbers about?"

Then Mr. Rochester appeared at the end of the gallery, holding a candle. Miss Ingram ran to him and seized his arm.

"What awful event has taken place?" she cried.

Mr. Rochester's expression was completely, bone-chillingly calm. "It's all right," he answered. "It's a mere rehearsal of *Much Ado About Nothing*."

What? Just . . . what? Why was he talking about a play?

"A servant has had a nightmare; that is all," he added. "Now all of you, go back to bed. I have things handled. There is nothing to fear."

Was it a rehearsal or was it a servant with a nightmare? This story was not making sense.

The guests began to shuffle back into their various rooms. Charlotte glanced over at Mr. Blackwood. His dark eyes were still fixed on Mr. Rochester. His jaw clenched. His hands in fists. She touched his shoulder.

"Not now," she whispered. "Remember the plan."

He blinked, then looked around like he'd forgotten where he was for a moment. Then he turned to Charlotte again.

"Where is Miss Eyre?" he asked.

Charlotte's breath caught. She turned around wildly, looking. Everyone was here—everyone . . . except Mr. Mason. And Jane.

Where was Jane?

Jane TWENTY

A loud knock came at Jane's bedchamber door. She startled.

"Jane." It was Mr. Rochester's voice. "Miss Eyre, I need your help."

Jane was still trying to recover from the scare of that scream. When she'd gone to see what had happened, Mrs. Fairfax had intercepted her and said the master of the house required her help, and she should stay in her bedchamber until called upon.

It had been a tense wait.

Jane pulled her robe tighter around and answered the door.

Mr. Rochester was there with a candle. "Follow me."

Helen whooshed to her side. "I don't like the sound of this. And why does he need *your* help?"

"And quietly," Rochester whispered.

He rushed through one hallway and down the next. Jane had

to work to keep up and stay quiet. Helen gave up walking and just floated.

"I've got a bad feeling about this," she said.

Jane didn't want to admit that she felt the same way, but it was the middle of the night, and there was that scream. Of course they should have a bad feeling about this.

Mr. Rochester opened a door at the bottom of the east wing and they began to climb a spiral staircase.

"Jane, do you faint at the sight of blood?"

"Well, that sounds ominous," Helen said.

"I don't think so," Jane said.

At the top of the stairs, Rochester opened the door into a smallish anteroom. Mr. Mason lay on the sofa there, looking pale and drenched in sweat. A ball of bloody rags lay beside him, the freshest still bright red.

"What has happened to her?" He moaned. "She . . . has . . . killed . . . me. She's gone mad."

Helen's mouth fell open. "What. Is. Wrong. With. The. Living?!"

"Jane, sit with Mason," Mr. Rochester said. "Press the rags into his wound. I will ride into town and bring the doctor." He pushed Jane into a chair and shoved more rags into her hand. "And do not say anything to Mason, nor he to you. He is too weak to speak. Do you hear me, Mason? You are too weak to speak."

With that he blew out the door. Jane pressed the rags to the wound, and Mason groaned.

"Helen? I'm scared," Jane whispered.

But Helen was no longer staring at Mason. Instead she was pacing the room and grabbing her hair. "Something's not right in here," she said. "Something feels strange."

"Stranger than the fact that this man is bleeding to death right in front of us?" Jane said.

"I am?" Mason groaned, apparently more lucid than Jane had thought.

"No, no, sir, you will be fine. Just . . . shhhhhhhhh."

Mason clenched a fist. "I should have known she wouldn't want me here. I wouldn't have come, but . . ."

Helen groaned. "Why would Mr. Rochester ask *you* to do this? You're a governess, not a doctor."

"Stay calm, Helen. We have to keep our wits about us," Jane said.

A door on the opposite end of the room rattled. Then rattled again. As though someone were kicking it.

"What's that?" Helen said.

"I don't know," Jane said. "Go through the wall and find out."

This time Mason lifted his head, causing a fresh stream of blood to spurt out. "Go through the wall? Are you telling me to leave this mortal world?"

"No, no," Jane said. "You are hallucinating. You'll be fine. Sleep. Shhhh."

Helen went toward the door, trembling the entire way, but just as she reached it, she stopped.

"It's not letting me go through," Helen said. She tried again.

Suddenly a scream came from the other side of the door.

And then Helen screamed. Jane froze.

"I can't get through the wall or the door!" Helen began to turn in circles, pulling at her hair again. "I don't know what is going on!"

The door rattled again and then a window blew open, the strong gust dousing the candles. The room fell dark and silent.

"Helen?" Jane whispered. There was no response. "Mr. Mason?" She reached out and felt for his forehead. It was cold and clammy. "Mr. Mason?"

Again, there was no response.

And then time stood still.

When you are counting the passage of time by the breaths from your lungs, it moves very slowly, and that was what Jane was doing. She was up into the hundreds of breaths. Maybe even thousands. But that's all she had in this tiny room. The sound of her breathing, and the feel of her hand pressed into Mr. Mason's wound.

What had happened here? Who was Mr. Mason talking about when he said *she'd* killed him? Grace Poole had set Mr. Rochester's bed on fire. Could it be the same culprit? Could Mr. Mason be talking about Grace Poole?

Helen came back in. For some reason, she could only stand staying in this room for minutes at a time. Jane had never seen her so distressed.

"Something is very wrong here," she said.

Jane had to agree.

The sound of footfalls came from the staircase, and Mr.

Rochester burst through the door, followed by the doctor. Finally, there was some candlelight.

Jane backed away and let the doctor near Mr. Mason.

The door at the other end of the room rattled loudly.

"What is that?" Jane said.

"I heard nothing, especially not the door," Rochester growled. His face grew stern.

Jane stood there, open mouthed, as Rochester and the doctor carried Mason out the door. When they were gone, she collapsed onto the chair next to the sofa. She knew she hadn't fainted, because she was very aware of not collapsing on the couch with all the blood on it.

"He almost died," she said to Helen.

"I know."

"Why does Mr. Rochester act like the things that should matter don't really matter at all, and the things that don't matter . . ." Jane couldn't even finish her sentence.

"I know," Helen said.

Jane's eyes stung, tears pricking the corners. "I'm so confused. And I'm scared."

Helen stood and held her hand out. "Come, friend. Let's get to bed and lock the door."

But then Mr. Rochester stormed in. "Jane. Would you accompany me on a walk?"

"No," Helen said.

"Yes, sir," Jane said.

Helen sighed loudly. "I'm going to bed."

Jane followed Mr. Rochester down the stairs and out to the garden. The sun was just starting to light the roses.

"Jane, I knew you would do me good, the moment I met you."

This was perhaps the third or fourth time he'd said those exact words to her. "You mean the moment I sprained your ankle?"

"You bewitched my horse. And not only my horse."

Jane looked at the ground.

"You have passed a strange night, here. Were you frightened when I left?"

"Yes, sir. What happened?"

"Sit, please." He motioned to a bench.

Jane obeyed.

"I cannot give you the details of what transpired this evening. It's a private family matter. But I can say that I made a mistake many years ago that I am still paying for. And for the longest time, I have been mired in hopelessness and despair. Until someone entered my life. Someone fresh and healthy, without soil or taint. Should I risk the judgment of others to get her?"

Could he be speaking of her? And the judgment over the discrepancy in their stations?

Jane was about to say, yes, risk the judgment, but then Colonel Dent appeared. Mr. Rochester shot to his feet.

"So, yes, I am very satisfied with Adele's educational needs. That will be all, Miss Eyre. Good morning, Colonel Dent. Mr. Mason has already risen and departed our company, but there are still many here to entertain you. Come, let's go to the stables."

And Jane was left sitting there, her heart in her throat. But she wasn't alone for long.

"Jane!" Charlotte appeared at the archway to the garden. She rushed to her side and took her hand. "We've been so worried."

Mr. Blackwood had followed her. He bowed his head.

"I'm fine," Jane said. "Why were you looking for me?"

"Why, because there was that awful scream in the middle of the night, and you were nowhere to be found. Didn't you hear it?"

"Yes. But I was fine. Mr. Mason had an accident, and I was attending to him while Rochester—Mr. Rochester—fetched a doctor."

"What kind of accident?" Mr. Blackwood said.

Jane pressed her lips together. Mr. Rochester had said it was a family matter. She would protect his privacy.

Mr. Blackwood cleared his throat. "I don't believe you understand the nature of what's going on here."

"I understand enough," Jane insisted. "And what I don't understand, I trust Mr. Rochester's intentions."

"But why?" Mr. Blackwood said. "You hardly know him."

"I know him better than you do." The words were louder than Jane had intended.

Charlotte put her hand on Jane's shoulder. "Jane, dear, please don't be upset. We are only thinking of you. There is something strange going on here, and if we can, we want to help. Can you tell us anything about what happened?"

Charlotte's expression was so sincere, so understanding. She knew Jane's heart and she hadn't judged her for it. Jane sighed.

"Someone injured Mr. Mason," Jane said, choosing her words carefully. "He bled profusely."

Mr. Blackwood clenched his fists. "Rochester," he grunted.

"He had nothing to do with it," Jane said. "He had me tend Mr. Mason's wounds while he went for help. Mr. Mason left with the doctor not very long ago."

"Mr. Rochester is not who you think," Mr. Blackwood said. "His intentions are neither noble nor honest."

Jane stood. "You do not know him," she said again.

"Nor do you, Miss Eyre."

Charlotte raised her hand to Mr. Blackwood. "Please, Mr. Blackwood." She turned to Jane and seemed to search for the right words. It was a long moment of silence. Finally, she blurted, "Jane, you're in danger, friend."

Jane's brow rumpled. "What do you mean?"

"Mr. Rochester might be a nefarious villain," Charlotte exclaimed.

"She's right," Mr. Blackwood said. "We still have to gather proof, but in the meantime, it would be safest if you left Thornfield Hall."

"Tell me why you say this?"

"I am not prepared to give you the details," Mr. Blackwood said.

Jane closed her eyes and shook her head. "What is it with men unable to give details? I am at home here. I have found my place and nothing you can say would entreat me to leave."

"You wish Jane to leave?" The gruff voice came from the archway of the garden. Mr. Rochester had returned quite unexpectedly.

"Yes," Alexander said, stiffening his spine. "I do not think this is a good situation for her."

"I see," Mr. Rochester said. "In that case, get out."

"What?" Mr. Blackwood said.

"You may remove yourself from Thornfield at once. You obviously know nothing of our life here, and appreciate it even less. As master of the house, I kindly request you to vacate the premises. And please take your cousins with you."

Jane stood speechless for a few moments. Her feelings for Rochester were strong, and yet she was not sure whose side she should be on.

"Jane?" Charlotte said.

Yes, it had indeed been a strange night. But Mr. Rochester had seen her. Had appreciated her. And Mr. Blackwood had no details and no proof of any wrongdoings. Her feelings were muddled, but her logic was sound. She turned her head away from Charlotte.

Mr. Blackwood bowed. "We will impose on your hospitality no longer."

He stalked away, Charlotte following reluctantly.

And even though Jane felt justified in her actions, she couldn't help but feel like an abandoned ship.

TWENTY-ONE
Alexander

Getting kicked out wasn't the worst thing that could happen.

The pros were that Alexander could finally put on his mask again (at last!), and . . . well, maybe that was it.

The list of cons was a little bigger.

Firstly, he'd obviously lost Miss Eyre.

Secondly (we love to follow firstlies with secondlies), Rochester. He was the murderer, Alexander was (mostly) certain of it. But he needed more proof than just the letter, and now he'd been removed from Thornfield and all the proof that might be hiding in there.

However, there was still Mr. Mason.

(That might count as a pro of getting thrown out, but it was really hard to say at this point. Alexander was quite conflicted about the whole thing.)

Mr. Mason definitely knew something about Rochester, and if Alexander could question him, all his suspicions about Rochester would be vindicated. But they'd gone to the doctor and Mason hadn't been there. The rumor about town (which Miss Brontë had collected in all of five minutes, of course) was that Mason was returning home to the West Indies.

So that meant Alexander and the Brontës needed to overtake Mason on the road, question him, and then they could all return to Thornfield and arrest Rochester. Surely, once it was known that Rochester was the most vile sort of villain, Miss Eyre would consider other job opportunities.

As the carriage bumped down the road—with Branwell narrating everything he saw out the window and Miss Brontë writing in her notebook—Alexander closed his eyes and turned his thoughts inward.

The letter burned a hole in his pocket. It was somewhat alarming. What did *save the Society and bring this travesty to an end* mean? And what about the mysterious "AW" they wanted to do something about? That could be Arthur Wellesley.

But Wellington would never do anything to harm the Society. He was a war hero. Why, Beethoven had composed a fifteen-minute piece in commemoration. (Called "Wellington's Victory." Look it up.) So what did it mean if his father wanted to do something about the leader of the Society?

Surely his father hadn't betrayed them.

"You're brooding," Miss Brontë commented. She watched

him, glasses raised, and tapped her pencil against her notebook. A frown turned her mouth downward.

"I don't brood. I was just closing my eyes. I didn't sleep last night."

"I know brooding when I see it, Mr. Blackwood. Don't deny it."

"Go home, Miss Brontë."

She snorted.

But he didn't want her to go home. She was smart and thoughtful and truly had all the makings of a proper Society agent. (Arguably, that was the highest praise Alexander knew how to give.) He was glad for her presence and her level head.

"I'm sorry I wasn't able to persuade Jane to our cause," she said after a few moments.

"It isn't your fault. Rochester is to blame."

It was Rochester who was the real problem in all this. Whatever the letter had meant about problems in the Society—Rochester was probably to blame for those, too.

"I know," Miss Brontë said, "but I promised I could do it and I haven't. I intend to make up for the failure, however. And it's not really a failure. It's a temporary setback." She scribbled something in her notebook and muttered, "Temporary setback." Then she looked up at him again. "Attitude is everything. We can't call it a failure, because it's not."

Alexander wasn't so sure, but he didn't have the energy to argue with her. He just wanted to catch up to Mason as quickly as possible and find out what the man knew about Rochester.

The group began only a few hours behind Mason, but a storm forced them to drive slowly the first day, so they missed him in Nottingham. A broken wheel delayed them the second day, so they missed him in Leicester. And one of the horses threw a shoe on the third day, so they missed him in Northampton. Alexander was afraid someone would come down with dysentery (wait, that's a different story), so they took a train the rest of the way to London.

From the train station, they went straight to the West India docks, where he left the Brontë siblings near a pub with all their luggage while he inquired about ship schedules.

That was harder than Alexander anticipated, because in spite of growing up in London, he knew very little about shipping or docks or even who he might need to talk to. So his quest began with asking strange men about their superiors.

"Go see Fred over there. He's in charge of this area," said one man. He pointed toward a small shack.

Alexander didn't see a man. "You mean that pigeon?"

"No, I mean—" The man looked around and shrugged. "I guess he's gone. Try the dockmaster, though."

"Where's the dockmaster?"

"He could be anywhere. He has a lot of docks to master."

Alexander nodded. "What about his office? Maybe I'll try there first."

"Good idea." The man offered a few simple directions and sent Alexander off, but the docks were much more confusing and busy than he'd been prepared for, and he was soon lost. Several more times, he had to ask directions to the dockmaster's office. The afternoon sun was punishing, and the crowds of men hollering and hauling only made the heat worse. The stench of fish and brine filled the air, suffocating, and several warehouse guards gave him suspicious looks. Probably because of his mask.

Finally, though, he reached the office (which was actually quite close to the dock entrance, and it was possible all the dockworkers he'd gotten directions from had been having a good time watching him go in circles). He stepped inside to find a haggard-looking man sitting at a large desk with stacks and stacks of papers. Yet more papers spilled from file cabinets.

Even with the windows open, the room was stuffy. Sweat beaded behind Alexander's mask as he approached the desk. "Good afternoon. I'm Alexander Blackwood, with the Society for the Relocation of Wayward Spirits."

"I'm sure you are. And I'm King William IV." The man looked up. "Oh. I see you are from the Society. I recognize you by your mask."

"I get that a lot."

"I'm Guy."

"Guy?"

"Yes. What can I help you with?"

"I'm looking for a Mr. Mason," Alexander said.

Guy jerked a thumb at the window at his back, toward the crowded docks. "Do you see that?"

Alexander nodded.

"There are at least six hundred ships in there. That's thousands of crewmen. Thousands of dockworkers. Hundreds of guards. I don't know all those people by name, and I certainly don't know your Mr. Mason."

"He's not *my* Mr. Mason." Wait, that was off topic. Alexander searched his memory for everything he'd learned about Mr. Mason during his stay in Thornfield. "Mason owns a business, and at least twenty ships. He might be on one of the vessels leaving soon."

"Oh," said Guy. "*That* Mr. Mason. I know him!"

"Really?"

"No." Guy dropped his face to one of the piles of papers and began flipping through. "But I do know of him, now that you mention it. His ships come through here with sugar, molasses, other goods like that. He's a popular fellow. Always kind, I hear. He has a charming nephew. A hard worker, that boy. He—"

"Ahem." That was great, but Alexander didn't need gossip now. He needed to find the man himself.

After a few minutes, Guy jabbed his finger at one of the pages. "Ah! Yes, he's on the *PurlAnn*. He was added to the passenger manifest just today, and the ship departs in"—he squinted at the page—"thirty minutes."

Alexander exhaled in relief. He hadn't missed him after all. But thirty minutes wasn't a great deal of time. He'd have to go after Mason immediately. "I don't suppose you can show me which ship the *PurlAnn* is?"

Guy heaved himself up off the desk and limped toward the door. His peg leg thunked on the floor.

"That one." Guy pointed toward a four-masted galleon. Blue and green sails snapped in the wind. "Good luck." Guy thumped back into his office.

"Thanks!"

Alexander started toward the *PurlAnn*, but instinct—an intuition that had never led him astray—told him to check on the Brontës. He glanced toward the dockyard exit and waited for a break in the crowd on the street.

There was Miss Brontë, writing in her notebook, as usual. Every now and then, she lifted her glasses and gazed around the street, as though just the right words would appear before her. And when she caught him looking, she smiled and waved.

Then there was Branwell, bent down and offering something to a homeless child.

A . . . teacup?

The teacup.

And he wasn't wearing gloves.

"No!" The shout broke from Alexander and he took off at a mad sprint. "Branwell, no!"

His cry drew eyes as he barreled through the crowded docks and pushed his way through the busy street. But it was too late. Branwell straightened, his shoulders thrown back.

He was possessed. By Brocklehurst.

Why wasn't that fool boy wearing his gloves? Hadn't Alexander told him that the cup (and pocket watch and the cane) was dangerous?

Alexander pushed his way through the crowd, shouting, "Miss

Brontë, watch out!" but it turned out she didn't need instructions or help.

He did.

Branwell/Brocklehurst spun toward Alexander just as the crowd broke and backed off, probably realizing something terrible was about to happen, and the possessed Society agent lifted the teacup into the air.

"Which teacup is it?" Branwell/Brocklehurst screamed, and charged toward Alexander.

The action started something of a stampede. People ran in every which way, trying to escape the madman with the teacup. Miss Brontë moved to intercept her brother.

The teacup landed with a thump on Alexander's head.

"Which teacup is it?" Brocklehurst shrieked from Branwell's body. "How do you like it?"

All around them, people screamed and tried to get away, but there were just enough people who wanted to watch a Society agent be assaulted with a teacup that true exodus was difficult.

Alexander grappled with Brocklehurst, trying to take the teacup, but the ghost pulled back and started yelling at people in the crowd: "Don't let him near your tea!"

Upstanding British men and women gasped, some holding paper bags to their chests. The crest of the local tea shop was emblazoned across the front.

"Don't let him near your china!" Brocklehurst shouted.

And this time, house servants with boxes pulled back in alarm.

"He'll trap you in teacups!"

Alexander tackled Brocklehurst and grabbed for the teacup, but the china bashed against his temple and made him blink back stars. It was a shockingly sturdy teacup.

"Give me the teacup!" Alexander's fingers scraped against the ceramic—not enough to take it, but enough that the handle slipped from Brocklehurst/Branwell's fingers and the teacup dropped to the ground.

And it shattered.

Not so sturdy after all.

At once, Brocklehurst shouted in triumph as a thousand pieces of ceramic scattered across the street. "Die, you evil teacup!"

Miss Brontë appeared in the periphery of Alexander's vision, a huge plank of wood drawn back, ready to swing.

Brocklehurst evacuated Branwell's body.

Before Alexander could raise a warning, the plank hit Branwell square in the head, and his assistant dropped to the cobblestones with a thud.

"Free at last!" shouted the ghost of Brocklehurst as he skipped down the street, invisible to most everyone now.

"Take that!" Miss Brontë shouted.

"Miss Brontë, Brocklehurst is gone." Alexander climbed to his feet and dusted ceramic shards off his trousers.

"So I got him?"

"You got your brother."

She lifted her glasses. "Not Brocklehurst?"

"As I said, he's gone."

"You're under arrest." A gloved hand clapped down on Alexander's shoulder.

Alexander groaned. Could this day get any worse?

He turned and straightened his mask. "Good afternoon, Officer. My name is Alexander Blackwood. I'm with the Society for the Relocation of Wayward Spirits."

The officer frowned. "The Society . . ."

"I work for the Duke of Wellington. I'm happy to put you in touch with him if you have questions."

The officer frowned harder, like he wanted to inform Alexander of the Society's decline, but they both knew he couldn't arrest anyone here. Ghost business was still Society business.

"And what about this fellow?" The officer motioned at Branwell, who was just now rousing himself. A lump already grew on his head.

"He's my assistant," Alexander admitted.

"And this lady?" The officer glanced at Miss Brontë.

"My assistant's assistant." Alexander glanced over the officer's shoulder, toward the docks and the *PurlAnn*. Was the ship in the same place as before? It was hard to tell. "Now, I really do need to go—"

"Very well." The officer started away. "Have a good evening."

Just then, Alexander caught sight of the *PurlAnn*, her blue and green sails full of wind as she vanished toward the Thames.

Mr. Mason was gone.

TWENTY-TWO
Charlotte

"So this is it," Mr. Blackwood muttered as the downtrodden group shuffled into the third-floor flat on Baker Street. "Home, sweet home. Make yourselves comfortable."

Charlotte lifted her spectacles to her face. Mr. Blackwood's flat was neat and meticulously maintained, much like Mr. Blackwood himself. But there was not much in the way of furniture. She spotted a pair of small chairs in the corner of the sitting room and perched herself upon one carefully, folding her hands into her lap. Bran stood near the door as if he half expected to be asked to leave, still utterly remorseful at what had transpired with the teacup and the ghost of Mr. Brocklehurst. Neither of the Brontës looked remotely comfortable.

"Well then," said Mr. Blackwood. "Can I offer you some tea?"

Bran groaned and dropped his face into his hands. "I don't think I will ever have tea again. I couldn't bear it."

"Bran, dear, no need to be so extreme." Charlotte tried a sympathetic smile. "It was a mistake. We all make mistakes."

"But I make mistakes more than anybody else."

That was true.

"That is true," Mr. Blackwood said, not unkindly. "But you're a new initiate. And you're learning."

Bran glanced at him hopefully. "Did *you* ever handle a talisman mistakenly and end up possessed by the spirit within?"

Mr. Blackwood cleared his throat. "I'll see about that tea."

He strode off into another room. Charlotte went to Bran and put her arm around him. "Chin up," she instructed. "All is not lost, dear brother." Although as she said this, she thought about how, with Mason gone, they couldn't definitively prove that Rochester was of shady character, or gather any substantial evidence in the case of the murder of Mr. Blackwood's father. Plus, they had returned to London without Jane Eyre. And now Jane was apparently in love with a nefarious villain.

It did, indeed, feel as though pretty much all was lost.

"I have ruined everything," sighed Bran.

"We'll put things right somehow."

"How?"

Charlotte didn't know the answer.

Mr. Blackwood returned with a silver tea tray loaded with a pot and the appropriate amount of cups, which he placed on the end table. Charlotte went to help him serve the tea, pouring and passing a cup to Bran, who took his without comment. They slurped quietly for several moments. Then Charlotte asked, "So what are we to do now?"

"We should go to Westminster and report our findings to the Society."

"Of course," Charlotte said. Nervous butterflies flapped about her stomach. The Society. At last. But now she felt that her opportunity to be a part of the Society had slipped away. "When shall we leave?"

Charlotte had never been to London before. She'd read the best descriptions from books, of course, but nothing had prepared her for the bustling grandeur of the city, especially of Westminster. She kept poking her head out of the carriage window, spectacles planted firmly in front of her nose to take in the smaller details—the flocks of birds that winged their way from space to space above them with a great clap of wings, the stone and marble majesty of the buildings, the miles upon miles of gleaming windows, the jostling people walking and talking and all manner of carriages rattling by on the cobblestone streets, the slightly putrid smell of the river, and the tinge of oily smoke that hung in the air. Her fingers itched to write—to document all of her impressions, but the carriage was much too bouncy. Their party (which still consisted of herself, Mr. Blackwood looking slightly cross, and Bran still looking downcast) had been quiet on the journey. Mr. Blackwood in particular seemed impatient to reach their destination.

Abruptly they came to a stop. Mr. Blackwood leapt down from the carriage and held out a hand to help Charlotte disembark.

"This way," he said, and went briskly up the stairs. Bran followed close behind, while Charlotte hung back for a moment to gawk at the sheer magnificence of the building. In that moment she wished that she could be a painter like Jane, so that she could attempt to capture the way the light caught the stone. Words were good. But sometimes they were simply inadequate.

"Come along," said Mr. Blackwood from the doorway.

Charlotte quickened her pace to catch up. She followed Bran and Mr. Blackwood to the main corridor of the House of Lords and then off to a far hallway, where a discrete set of stairs descended into the undercroft of what had once been the chapel. It was a bit musty down there, but still beautifully decorated, with arching ceilings and shining wooden floors.

"Why does the Society meet in the Parliament building?" Charlotte asked as they walked on.

"Because, once upon a time, before the rift with the king, so many non-seer members of the Society were also members of Parliament," Mr. Blackwood replied with a shrug. "For the sake of convenience."

At the end of the undercroft they reached a large oak door. Mr. Blackwood rapped upon it twice.

"What is your intention on this earth?" came a voice from the other side.

Charlotte thought that was a surprisingly personal question.

Mr. Blackwood gave a tight, embarrassed smile. "To investigate the great mysteries of the world and to serve the welfare of humankind, both living and departed," he said quickly.

The door creaked open. A gigantic orange-haired man was standing on the other side. "Good day to you, Mr. Blackwood. Branwell." His eyes flickered over to Charlotte. "Miss."

"Stephen," Mr. Blackwood acknowledged. "We're here to see the duke."

"He's expecting you." The man stepped back to allow them passage through the door.

They traversed another long hallway, went down another short set of stairs, and stopped outside yet another door. Mr. Blackwood didn't knock this time. He threw open the door and strode inside, Bran and Charlotte trailing behind. The room turned out to be a library, lined wall to wall with bookshelves, each shelf sagging under the weight of heavy, official-looking books. Books! But Charlotte's attention was then immediately caught by the large desk in the center of the room, at which sat a slender, impeccably dressed man with salt-and-pepper hair.

She knew him at once. Arthur Wellesley. Who had been, according to Charlotte's father, almost single-handedly responsible for the defeat of Napoleon at Waterloo. The world's keenest military mind, some said. The world's most corrupt politician, others said—especially if those others were of the Whig party, so of course they couldn't be trusted in their opinions. The Iron Duke, some called him. The Duke of Wellington.

(She was a bit starstruck, truth be told. She'd never been up close to someone famous before.)

And then the duke rose to embrace Mr. Blackwood as warmly as if he were his son.

"Alex, my boy," he said. "I am so pleased to see you. You're later than I expected."

"I was delayed," replied Mr. Blackwood. "I have much to tell you."

The duke turned to gaze at Charlotte. "But first . . . She's quite small of stature, just as you said. But lovely. The spectacles are . . . a nice touch."

Charlotte felt herself smiling and blushing. So Mr. Blackwood had written to Wellington about her. And favorably, it seemed. "Your Grace." She attempted an awkward curtsy. "How do you do?"

"My dear." The duke crossed to her and took her small hand between his large ones. He was smiling, too. "It is an honor to meet you at last. Alexander has told me of your many impressive abilities."

Her abilities? Well, yes, she definitely had abilities. At the moment she couldn't quite recall what they were, but she knew she possessed them. "Thank you, sir. It is an honor to meet you as well."

"I am delighted that you have decided to join our austere organization."

She glanced at Mr. Blackwood, then Bran, her spirits soaring. "So you wish me to be inducted into the Society," she said eagerly. "I knew it."

"Of course. It's highly unorthodox for us to initiate a woman," said the duke. "We hire female employees very rarely. We had a case with a female agent some years ago that did not end particularly well, but I am willing to credit that failure to the unsuitable constitution of that particular woman, rather than assign blame to the gender as a whole."

The duke was quite a reasonable man, Charlotte concluded.

"So with that I would bid you welcome to the Society for the Relocation of Wayward Spirits," finished the duke. "We are so very glad to have you, Miss Eyre."

Oh.

Oh, no.

"Your Grace . . ." she began, her stomach plummeting.

"There's been a mistake, sir." Mr. Blackwood stepped in. "This is not Miss Eyre."

The duke frowned and backed away from her. "What? Not Miss Eyre? Well, then who the devil is it?"

"This is Charlotte Brontë," Mr. Blackwood said stiffly, pronouncing the Brontë part of Charlotte's name as though it had a strange significance. "She has proven herself vitally useful in my current assignment."

"She is my sister, Your Grace," Bran added helpfully.

Charlotte lifted her glasses. The duke was staring at her with

249

an expression that Charlotte found completely unreadable. A mixture of annoyance and curiosity, perhaps?

"But what about Miss Eyre?" he asked. "Are you not still convinced that she is a Beacon?"

"Miss Eyre is definitely a Beacon."

"Then why do you bring me Miss Brontë, instead? Is *she* a Beacon? Or a seer, at the very least?"

"No, sir." Alexander cleared his throat lightly. "But as she is a relative of Mr. Bran—of Branwell Brontë's, perhaps the trait is also in her blood. I do not believe that Miss Brontë has ever experienced death or resurrection, so it is impossible to know for sure."

The duke gazed at Charlotte again, like it might be worthwhile to temporarily kill her, just to find out. She swallowed.

"Miss Brontë possesses a rare wit and a suitable disposition for the type of work that is done within the Society," Mr. Blackwood added quickly. "I would unreservedly recommend her for induction into our ranks."

"Oh, you would?" The duke looked from Mr. Blackwood to Charlotte and sighed. "And what do you do, Miss Brontë?"

"Well, sir, I—" *Write things* had been what she had been about to say, but then she thought better of it. "I excel in matters of observation. And I could use these powers of observation to solve mysteries."

"What mysteries?"

Well. She hadn't actually solved any mysteries yet. She glanced at the floor. "I am also very good at making plans. Strategy. When

Mr. Blackwood needed to make an entrance to Thornfield Hall, for instance, I—"

"I see." The duke looked less than impressed. He kept staring at her glasses, which she'd had to hold to her face for the duration of this entire conversation in order to see what was going on. She supposed she did appear rather silly.

She lifted her chin. "Sir, I would consider it the greatest honor to be of use to the Society."

"Of course you would," he said. "It is the greatest honor, and not to be bestowed on a whim." He turned abruptly back to Mr. Blackwood. "But what of Miss Eyre? If you still believe her to be a Beacon, why did you not return with her?"

"Miss Eyre is one of the most astute seers of the otherworldly persuasion that I have yet to come across," Mr. Blackwood said. "And yes, I believe her to be a Beacon."

"What's a Beacon?" Bran piped up.

Poor Bran, thought Charlotte. Nobody tells him anything. "A Beacon is a special type of seer, dear, who attracts the ghosts and can even command them."

"Command them?" Bran looked hurt that she would know such a thing, when he didn't.

"Ghosts seem incapable of refusing a direct order from a Beacon," said Alexander. "When a Beacon tells a ghost to do something, he must do it."

"Oh, I see," Bran said. "That would be very useful. So instead of having to chase a ghost about or 'bop' him—Miss Eyre could simply order the spirit to go into the talisman. And he would have no choice but to obey. I bet you wish that you were a Beacon, Mr. Blackwood. You'd be really good at it."

"Indeed." Mr. Blackwood's eyes were not happy, Charlotte noticed. Because, she realized at once, Jane could be more efficient at the capture of ghosts than Mr. Blackwood would ever be. And she knew that he prided himself on being the very best agent in the Society.

And yet, he'd made Jane the offer of employment. He'd tried to bring her here. How very noble of him, Charlotte thought. To serve the interests of the Society above his own. And now he said gruffly, "I did my best to persuade Miss Eyre to become an agent, but she is simply uninterested in the position. She cannot be convinced."

The duke seemed nonplussed by this information. "Everyone can be convinced, if you utilize the right incentive."

"Not Jane." Charlotte shook her head. "Her mind is made up. She wishes to stay at Thornfield."

He scoffed. "What could possibly be at Thornfield Hall that is better than what we have to offer her here?"

"Yes, especially since we offered Miss Eyre a salary of five thousand pounds a year," said Bran.

"What?" The duke swung about to look at Mr. Blackwood, whose face reddened.

"I thought we would recover the cost, once Miss Eyre helped us to restore the Society to its former glory," he mumbled.

"I see," said the duke. "And she still refused?"

Then the men were all looking at Charlotte, as if she represented all women and they expected her to know Jane's reason exactly. And Charlotte did know the reason, but it was so indelicate to speak of such things. It was none of their business, really. It was Jane's affair.

"Well," she said slowly. "The food at Thornfield is very good, and plentiful. Jane is not accustomed to so much in the way of fine dining. Our fare was quite modest at school."

"Five thousand pounds a year could provide Miss Eyre more delectable meals than she could possibly eat," said the duke.

"She . . . um . . . has a fondness for the child she's instructing."

"The child she only met a few weeks ago? Tosh. If Miss Eyre were to serve in our employment, she'd be living a high life. Tasteful living quarters. Fine gowns. A greatly improved reputation."

All things that Charlotte herself had pointed out to Jane, to no avail.

"Jane has no wish for a high life, sir," Charlotte said. "And she has a negative impression of the Society, I'm afraid."

The duke frowned. "Why?"

Mr. Blackwood stepped forward. "Perhaps it is my fault. The first time I encountered Miss Eyre, as you'll recall from our discussion, I captured the ghost of Claire Doolittle in Miss Eyre's presence. I—"

Charlotte gasped, quite forgetting herself. "You did? Whatever happened that night? I've been dying to know. How did you capture this ghost? Claire Doolittle, you say her name is? And where is she now?"

"Here." Mr. Blackwood drew a wrapped handkerchief from his pocket. Upon unwrapping it was revealed to be a rather common-looking pocket watch.

"The pocket watch! Well, that's one mystery solved!" Charlotte exclaimed, and because she could not help herself, she immediately pulled her notebook out of her pocket and started writing notes. When she looked up again they were all staring at her. "Er, Jane seems to doubt that the Society 'relocates' the spirits it captures in a manner that is entirely ethical." Charlotte lifted her spectacles to gaze earnestly at the duke. "So what *do* you do with them? What will you do with this ghost in the pocket watch?"

The duke and Mr. Blackwood exchanged glances. Then the duke said, "Well, I suppose there's no harm in showing you."

He led them back through the darkened corridor to another set of stairs leading into a part of the undercroft that Charlotte hadn't previously noticed, a small enclave filled with several ornately carved wooden shelves. On the shelves there was an assembly of various items: a fork, a comb, an accordion, a knight's visor, a silk hair ribbon, each resting on a special cushion or placed in a series of long drawers, the way someone might display butterflies or pieces of art.

"Don't touch anything," Mr. Blackwood said to Bran in a low voice.

"Of course not, sir, I—" Bran couldn't even finish his sentence, he was so ashamed. "Of course not, sir."

The duke and Mr. Blackwood approached an empty set of

shelves. Mr. Blackwood placed the pocket watch gently on a black velvet cushion. Charlotte's arm began to tremble with the strain of holding up her blasted glasses, but she couldn't lower them. She held her breath, keeping herself from blinking, because there was no way she was going to miss what happened next.

But for a moment, nothing happened.

And then for another moment, nothing happened.

And another moment. Nothing.

"So that's it?" she asked. "You just keep it here?"

"We call this the Collection Room," said the duke. "It is where we store all the artifacts we encounter."

Charlotte felt a frown coming on. "So, you collect the ghosts and then hold them here indefinitely. That cannot be correct, can it?"

Mr. Blackwood shifted uncomfortably. "It's not that simple."

"So, you're not 'relocating' them, per se. You're 'collecting' them."

"We're doing a service to the people whom the ghosts are bothering."

"But ghosts are people, too." Charlotte's frown had arrived in force now. "Perhaps Jane's concern was warranted. It's not right to imprison people, dead or alive."

"There's no other way," Mr. Blackwood said, while at the same time, the duke replied, "There is another way."

"What?" Mr. Blackwood looked confused.

"There's a room I haven't shown you," the duke said. "Come."

He led them only a short distance to yet another locked door. The duke took out a set of keys and unlocked it. Inside was a large chamber set with a series of candelabras and red velvet drapes. There was something that resembled an altar in the center of the room, and a strange, tingly feeling that immediately set Charlotte's nerves jittering.

"This is what we used to call the Move-On Room," said the duke. "Years ago, when the Society was at its peak, we would bring the collected ghost here, speak some words from the Book of the Dead, and compel said ghost to go over to the other world, the one beyond this one. Then the ghost was at peace. And our job was complete."

"So why do you not bring them here now?" Charlotte wanted to know.

The duke was smiling again, which struck her as strange. "The ceremony requires a Beacon. Only a Beacon can read the book. Only a Beacon can help the wayward soul to move on."

"A Beacon," Mr. Blackwood murmured. "Why did I never know this?"

"There hasn't been a Beacon in the Society since I took you under my wing," Wellington explained. "So there was no need for you to know about it. But as there's the possibility of obtaining a Beacon now—"

"What's this about a book?" Charlotte asked. "What kind of book is a book of the dead? Is it Egyptian? Can I see this book?"

"You see now how important it is to procure Miss Eyre,"

continued the duke to Mr. Blackwood as if Charlotte hadn't spoken. "If she is indeed a Beacon, she could set all these poor, unfortunate souls free."

Mr. Blackwood was nodding. "If we explained this to her, surely she'd see reason. She's fond of ghosts. She'd want to help them. She'd come."

"No, she still won't leave Thornfield," Charlotte said matter-of-factly.

"But . . ."

And here it was. She would have to tell them.

"Jane won't leave Thornfield because—" Charlotte took a breath. "Because she's in love."

"In love?" Wellington, Bran, and Mr. Blackwood all said together.

"With whom?" Mr. Blackwood asked.

Charlotte bit her lip. "With Mr. Rochester."

"Mr. Rochester?" Mr. Blackwood said incredulously. "But he's . . ."

"Older. So much older. I know. But the heart wants what it wants." She should not be discussing Jane's relationship with Rochester. It was improper. Scandalous, even. But it was the reason why Jane would never leave Thornfield. They needed to know.

"And you believe Miss Eyre's affection is reciprocated by Mr. Rochester?" the duke questioned.

"He has said some things to her, very nice things, that would make it seem so."

"Interesting." The duke was smiling yet again. It was a chilling sort of smile, which made the small hairs on the back of Charlotte's neck stand up. All at once she perceived that the duke was not exactly as he seemed. "Well, perhaps we could make use of that," he said almost to himself.

"What do you mean, make use of it?" asked Mr. Blackwood.

"I am acquainted with Mr. Rochester, as it happens," said the duke. "I did him a large favor some time ago, and he owes me a debt. Perhaps I can prevail upon him to influence Miss Eyre. Yes. What a fortunate turn of events. I'll send a message to Rochester at once."

Charlotte lifted her glasses to see Mr. Blackwood's face. He was pale. His mouth tight. She waited for him to tell Wellington about the letter and his suspicions that Rochester had murdered his father. But he did not say anything.

"Now, if you don't have anything else for me today, there is much to be done," the duke said.

"I wish to speak with you," said Mr. Blackwood urgently. "Alone."

"All right. Come back to my office. There's a job that requires your attention as well." The duke nodded curtly at Bran and Charlotte. "I must bid you farewell."

"But . . ." Bran gulped in a breath. "What about . . . what about my sister, sir, and her desire to join the Society?"

The duke waved him off. "Oh, well, plenty of people *wish* to join the Society, don't they? Have her prove to me that she can offer us something that no one else can, and perhaps I will consider it. Good day." The duke began to walk briskly back to the main corridor, but then paused. "Oh. You are still in possession of an artifact, are you not? The one containing the headmaster. Mr. Brocklehurst, I believe his name was. We should add that to the Collection Room before we return to the surface."

Alexander's face reddened. "I have the cane from the carriage ghost, sir, but I no longer have the teacup. It was lost."

Surprise registered on the duke's face. "You don't often make mistakes, my boy. What happened?"

"It was . . . lost," Alexander said.

Charlotte wanted to hug him. For all the strangeness he must be feeling now about Jane and Rochester. And for protecting Bran.

Bran, for his part, did not want to be protected. He cleared his throat.

"Sir, it was my fault. I handled the talisman improperly, and the spirit of Mr. Brocklehurst possessed me for a time, and then I . . . I broke the cup."

The duke removed his spectacles. "So the ghost escaped."

Bran swallowed, a hard jerk of his prominent Adam's apple. "Yes, sir."

"I see," said the duke.

"I await your discipline, sir, with eagerness, in fact, as I know I much deserve it," Bran said.

Charlotte stepped forward. "He meant well, sir. He was trying to help a child in need."

The duke turned and walked unceremoniously back to the library. He sat at the desk, relit his pipe, and took a long, hard look at Bran. "I'd like to speak to Mr. Brontë in private for a moment."

"Sir," Mr. Blackwood said in protest. "I am to blame as well. I should not have left him alone."

The duke didn't appear to have heard. He simply waited for them to comply with his request. Mr. Blackwood sighed and exited the room. Charlotte stayed. She felt she would burst with all that she wanted to say. It was just a mistake. Anybody could have made such a mistake. Well, maybe not anybody. But Bran meant well. He always meant well.

Charlotte's hands clenched into helpless fists.

"Charlie," Bran said. "Go."

Charlotte and Mr. Blackwood waited in the hall for several long minutes. Then Bran emerged again, pale-faced but smiling bravely.

"Are you all right?" Mr. Blackwood asked.

"Fine," Bran said. "It was just a slap on the wrist, it turns out. I'll be fine. All will be well."

"Well, that's a relief," said Mr. Blackwood. "You're fortunate. The duke is not generally the type to give second chances. I'll walk you out now. I have some further business to attend to with the duke myself." His eyes caught Charlotte's, and she tried to give him an encouraging smile.

"I'm sorry, Miss Brontë," he said as they made their way back to the main entrance. "I know that you wanted to become an agent."

She nodded. "Well. I did. I do. But . . ." She bit her lip again. "Mr. Blackwood, do you ever get the feeling that the duke is not telling you everything?"

"Wellington is like a second father to me," he said. "He practically raised me. Of course he tells me everything."

"He did not tell you about the Move-On Room," she pointed out.

"There was no occasion to tell me," Mr. Blackwood said stiffly, drawing away from her a bit. "Like he said, we have not had a Beacon in our employ since before I came to the Society."

"But that's a rather significant detail for him to leave out."

"It's a detail. Nothing more."

"And don't you find it odd that he's acquainted with Mr. Rochester? And don't you think—"

"Miss Brontë, I appreciate your concern," he said in a voice that conveyed that he did not, in fact, appreciate it. "But everything is fine with Wellington. I know him. I will talk to him and sort it all out."

"Of course. But there's something important that we don't yet know. I can feel it."

"You can always feel it." He crossed his arms. "You should stop poking your cute button nose where it does not belong."

"My what?" She shook her head. "But, Mr. Blackwood. Don't you think it's all just a tad suspicious? Don't you think—"

"No. I don't."

They were out on the street by now, and it was harder to hear him with the bustle of people moving about. Bran was just behind them. He had not said another word since his tête-à-tête with Wellington.

"Mr. Blackwood," Charlotte tried again.

"Just stop," he said. "Stop overthinking everything. Stop trying so hard. Just accept that things are what they appear to be. There is no great mystery here, Miss Brontë. There is no story."

"But—"

"Go home, Miss Brontë," he said.

And this time, she felt, he actually meant it.

She drew herself up to her full, unformidable height. "Very well. It was a pleasure working with you, Mr. Blackwood. I am sorry that we apparently will be unable to work together in the future. I can . . . I can see myself home."

He sighed. He could obviously tell that he had hurt her feelings. "Miss Brontë, I—"

"Good day, Mr. Blackwood." She gave a half-hearted curtsy, deliberately not lifting her spectacles to look at him.

"Miss Brontë." Mr. Blackwood tipped his hat and then spun on his heel and went back into the building, leaving Charlotte and Bran on the street.

"Are you all right, Charlie?" Bran asked after a moment.

"Don't call me Charlie." She sighed. "What a strange day." She was trembling, she discovered. And her eyes were a bit wet. "Come on, let's go. I'm excited to see your flat, Brother."

"It's a room, not an entire flat. And the landlady is mean."

She waited for him to order a carriage, but he said he'd rather walk. So they walked and walked, more than a mile, until they came to a dilapidated house on a darkened street—the kind of street where unpleasant things occurred on a nightly basis. Bran unlocked the front door and led Charlotte quickly and quietly through a hall up the back stairs. To a room the size of a closet.

Charlotte sat on the bed, because that was the only place available to sit. She caught the strong scent of mold. And mouse droppings. "It's very nice, Bran," she said faintly. "Very cozy."

Bran took off his hat and tossed it into a corner. He ran his hands through his wild red hair, making it ever wilder. Then he looked around and gave a bitter laugh. "Well, that's one good thing. I won't have to endure this wretched place any longer."

"What do you mean? Have they found you a better place?" She shivered. "A warmer one?" It was odd, how used to being warm she'd gotten, after only a few weeks at the Ingrams' and Thornfield.

"No," Bran said. "But I've been given until the end of the month to vacate this one."

"But why?" she asked.

"I've been relieved of my position as Mr. Blackwood's apprentice," he reported. "And I've been cast out from the Society."

Her heart ached for him. "Oh, Bran, I'm sorry."

Bran swallowed. "The duke said I don't possess the qualities of a true member."

She grabbed his hand and squeezed it. "He was angry, understandably, about the incident with the teacup. But perhaps he will reconsider. They need agents, after all. Perhaps—"

"No," Bran said hoarsely. "You heard what Mr. Blackwood said. The duke doesn't give second chances."

"What will you do?" she asked.

"Go home, I suppose. Help Father with the parsonage."

"No, you can't," Charlotte cried. "It was just one mistake. The duke can't fire you for one simple mistake."

"Oh, but he can," said Bran. "He wasn't angry. He didn't mean me any ill will, Charlie. But he cannot abide incompetence within the Society. They are like a clockwork machine, and I have proved to be a faulty gear. I must go."

"But, Bran," she said. "Surely—"

"He wants nothing to do with me. I always found it a wonder that I was inducted into the Society in the first place. Besides, I don't want to work for an institution that will not accept you as well. They're fools, if they cannot see how valuable you are, Charlie. You'd be a magnificent agent." He sighed and scooted over to her, slung his arm around her as if he were the one comforting her. "So. That's that. I'll go home. You'll go back to school. And things will return to normal."

"I don't like normal," she said.

"Neither do I," Bran said.

"I detest normal."

"I abhor it," he agreed.

"I simply loathe normal," she said, and Bran gave a weak laugh. And then they got up and made some tea.

Jane TWENTY-THREE

"There's a letter for you," Mrs. Fairfax said at breakfast.

"For me?" Jane said. Charlotte and Mr. Blackwood had only just left Thornfield, and Jane couldn't imagine anyone else sending her a letter.

Mrs. Fairfax pushed it across the table toward Jane, who opened it with curiosity.

It was from Bessie, Jane's nursemaid from Aunt Reed's house.

> *Dear Miss Eyre,*
>
> *Your aunt Reed has taken ill and is confined to her bed. She has requested to see you. Please make haste, as her time on this earth shan't be long.*

Jane frowned.

"Is everything all right, Miss Eyre?" Mrs. Fairfax inquired.

"No. It is my aunt. She is dying and has requested to see me."

"Oh, I am sorry. You shall pack your things at once. Eliza!" A kitchen maid entered. "Please help Miss Eyre pack her things."

"But can you spare me for such a trip?" Jane asked.

"We can and we will," Mrs. Fairfax said.

"I thank you. But I will not need Eliza's help. My belongings are few."

"Very well," Mrs. Fairfax said.

Jane lowered her gaze. "I will, however, need some money. I have not yet received my wages."

"You must take that up with the master," Mrs. Fairfax said, returning her attention to the morning's post.

"Right," Jane muttered, not looking forward to such an uncomfortable conversation.

She returned to her bedchamber to pack her meager belongings.

Helen was not quiet with her feelings about the trip. "Your aunt Reed doesn't deserve to spit in the same room as you."

"She's probably rather dehydrated, and will not be spitting at all," Jane said.

"Nevertheless, I'm glad you are leaving Thornfield Hall, and Mr. Rochester. He is not a good man."

Jane frowned. "You don't know that."

"He's deceitful."

"We can't be sure."

"Fortune-teller. Bloody man. Screams from behind the door."

Helen ticked these off on her fingers.

"Okay, maybe he has, on occasion, not been fully forthcoming with the truth. . . ." Jane had to admit the ghost had a point.

When she went to approach Mr. Rochester about her wages, she found him in the drawing room, speaking in hushed tones, with Blanche Ingram. Jane felt a pang in her chest.

"Does that servant want you?" Miss Ingram said.

Mr. Rochester glanced up and when he saw it was Jane he excused himself immediately, leaving Miss Ingram frowning behind him.

"What is it, Jane?"

"I have to leave."

"What?" He didn't bother hiding the disappointment in his voice. "Do not tell me that whole business with the Eshtons has changed your mind about staying here."

"No. I have a sick aunt. She has asked to see me." Jane pulled the letter out of her pocket and handed it to him.

He took it and glanced it over and handed it back. "This is the aunt that cast you off and sent you to Lowood?"

"Yes. I will not deny a dying woman her request. I should only be gone a week or so."

"A whole week or so?" He sighed and let his head drop. "If you must, you must."

"One more thing," Jane said, feeling incredibly awkward. "I have no money. You haven't paid me."

"I haven't paid you? But isn't that one of the things my staff says about me, that I pay in a timely fashion?" He smiled and her heart went boom. "How much do I owe you?"

She lowered her voice. "Fifteen pounds."

He pulled out his wallet and dug through its contents. "Here's fifty."

"I can't take fifty!"

He rolled his eyes and then looked through his wallet. "Then I only have ten."

"That will do, sir. But you still owe me five," Jane said with a smile.

"Then promise me, Jane, you will not spend one more minute than you have to with your awful aunt." He took her hand, and Jane saw Blanche Ingram look away. "Promise me you'll come back for your five pounds."

"I promise," Jane said in a breathless whisper.

"He didn't have five more pounds?" Helen said incredulously. They were in the carriage making the trip to Aunt Reed's, and Helen could not get over the fact that he hadn't paid her all of her wages.

"I'm sure he does, just not on him at the time."

"You know what's better than five more pounds? Five *thousand* more pounds."

The carriage bumped and jostled along the road, and in the few hours it took to get to Aunt Reed's, Helen wondered about Mr. Rochester's shortchanging of her wages no fewer than seven times.

At her aunt's house, Bessie met Jane at the door. "I'm so glad you are come, Miss Eyre. My, how you have grown into an elegant lady! Not quite a beauty, but never mind that. You have come just in time. She's already died once, just before she sent for you. I fear the next time, her death will be permanent."

She ushered Jane immediately to the bedchamber, where her aunt's frail figure barely formed a lump in the mattress. A tall translucent man stood beside her, watching her. It was the ghost of Jane's uncle.

Helen ducked behind Jane.

"Who's that?" came a gravelly voice from the bed.

"It's Jane Eyre," Jane said. "You sent for me, Aunt Reed."

"Jane Eyre. I hated that willful ungrateful child."

Helen snorted indignantly and stepped forward.

The ghost of Uncle Reed shook his head and spoke to the lump under the sheets. "That is not what we discussed, my dear."

Aunt Reed turned away from him. Oh, Jane realized. She can see him now. Her short bout with death had turned her into a seer. This should be interesting.

"Aunt, I am Jane Eyre. You sent for me."

Aunt Reed eyed her up and down. "You are Jane Eyre. And I can see you've brought one of your heathen friends."

Helen looked right and left. "Is she talking about me?" She rolled up the ghostly sleeve of her ghostly dress. "Are you talking about me?"

"Quiet, dear," Jane said. "Aunt Reed, how can I be of service?"

She coughed and wheezed. "I am supposed to confess and make amends before I die."

"What do you wish to confess?"

Aunt Reed stubbornly pressed her lips together, and Uncle Reed poked her under her ribs. She flinched.

"I promised your uncle I would take care of you. And love you. I didn't."

"I know. I already knew that, Aunt."

"And . . ." Uncle Reed prompted.

"And . . ." She said the next bit as if it were one word. One four-letter word. "Ibelieveyouaboutseeingghosts."

She winced, as if it were physically painful to admit such a thing.

"Thank you, Aunt." Jane made a move to leave, but her ghost uncle cleared his throat.

"One more thing," her aunt said. She gestured to her desk, on top of which was a letter. "Three years ago, I received a message from an uncle you never knew existed. He had asked for your whereabouts. He wanted you to live with him. Wanted you to inherit his fortune. I wrote back to him and told him you were dead."

"What?" Jane said.

"I am the reason you did not inherit his twenty thousand pounds."

"What??" Helen said.

But Jane wasn't preoccupied with the money part. "I have another uncle?" she said. "I have family and you kept him from me?"

"Yes. I couldn't stand seeing you happy."

Uncle Reed bowed his head. "I am sorry for you, Jane."

For a moment, Jane was angry. And really, given the revelation, she should've stayed angry. Family: it was the only thing she'd ever longed for, and now to learn she could have had it?

"Twenty thousand pounds?" Helen said. "You could've had *twenty thousand pounds?*" She took a few steps toward the bed. "No, we will *never* forgive you!"

"Helen, please," Jane said.

Because the truth was, she felt sorry for her aunt. To harbor such hatred. To house it inside her heart, and protect it with such passion that it ate her alive.

"I forgive you," Jane said.

"What??" Helen exclaimed.

"If I didn't forgive her, I would end up as wasted away as she is now," Jane said to Helen.

Uncle Reed let out a sigh of relief. Then he looked at Jane's face, as if seeing her for the first time. "Jane Eyre, you are a sight to behold. To have gone from such a plain child . . ."

"I love you, Uncle," Jane said. "I hope you can move on, now that this is done."

Uncle Reed nodded. "Take care, dear niece."

She wet a cloth in the basin next to Aunt Reed's bed, and then placed it on her forehead. "Sleep well, Aunt. And know that I hold no ill will for you."

Jane and Helen walked out, leaving her uncle to take leave of his wife on his own.

* * *

When they returned to Thornfield, the remaining guests had all left. Jane thought perhaps Mr. Rochester would be gone as well, but Mrs. Fairfax said he was in residence.

"But I don't expect him to be here for long," she said over tea. "I believe there to be a proposal very soon. Ingram Park is a day's ride, and I am sure the master will be taking great pains to make the trip very soon and very often."

Jane frowned.

"What's the matter, dear? You've hardly touched your biscuit."

That evening, Mr. Rochester found Jane in the library.

"Miss Eyre. It's about time you came back to us. What kept you?"

"I've been gone three days," Jane said. She literally could not have returned any sooner.

"It's too long. Come, let's go for a walk. It's a lovely evening."

They went to the garden, and Jane decided once and for all she could no longer take the not knowing. She could handle anything— Aunt Reed, her lost uncle, she could even handle Mr. Rochester getting married—but she could no longer handle the not knowing.

Helen pointed her finger at Rochester. "Are you going to marry Miss Ingram, yes or no?"

Jane signaled Helen to be quiet. But the ghost had a point.

"Sir," Jane began. "I am wondering about my future at this estate, and I hate to be indelicate, but should I advertise for a new governess position?"

Mr. Rochester stopped under a tree, the long branches of which blanketed the grass in shade.

"Jane, you know I am soon to be married." He reached into his pocket and pulled out a velvet pouch. He opened the drawstrings and took out a pearl necklace. "These are to be a gift for the future Mrs. Rochester. What do you think?"

Jane frowned, trying to imagine the necklace on Blanche Ingram. "They will suit her bird-neck—I mean, they will suit her very well." Because everything suited the likes of Blanche Ingram very well. "I guess I will advertise."

Mr. Rochester grunted. "Miss Eyre, listen to me. I believe there is a string below your rib, and it stretches across class and age to me, and it is attached beneath my rib. And if you find another suitable position, and leave me, you will pull it out. And I will bleed."

"What do you mean?" Jane said.

"It sounds rather obvious, and slightly disgusting," Helen said. "He'll bleed."

Mr. Rochester placed his hands on her shoulders. "Jane, I do not wish to marry Miss Ingram."

Jane glanced up. "Excuse me?"

"I wish to marry you."

Helen gasped. "What?"

Mr. Rochester grabbed Jane's hand. "Say yes, Jane. Say you will have me."

"No," Helen said. She made a move to grab Jane's other hand, but of course her hand passed right through Jane's. "Please, Jane, my oldest and dearest friend. Please don't answer right away."

Jane looked frantically from Mr. Rochester to Helen, back to Mr. Rochester, and back to Helen. He was everything she'd ever dreamed about. Tall. Dark. Brooding. But he also had a penchant for lying, and making Jane think she was crazy, and not telling her the full story.

"Please, Jane," Helen said. "For me. Say you need time to think."

He was handsome and charming, and Mrs. Fairfax did say his bursts of anger were often not often.

But Mr. Blackwood and Charlotte had doubted his good intentions and questioned his very nature.

As much as Jane believed herself to be in love with Mr. Rochester, a little time to think surely couldn't hurt. "Sir, I will consider your proposal."

Rochester looked incredulous. "What?" He squeezed her hand. "Jane, I have never been more earnest about anything in my life. Say you believe me."

Jane tried to wrestle free, but his grip tightened. (Yeah, we know. *shudder*) "Please, sir, may I have the night to gather myself and my thoughts?"

Rochester sighed deeply through his nostrils. His voice became an angry growl. "Bloody hell, Jane. It would've been so much easier if you'd just said yes."

He grabbed the strand of pearls, and before she could move

away, he threw it over her head and around her neck.

Here, dear reader, is where your faithful narrators must step away from Jane's mind, for the pearls were a talisman that held a spirit. And that spirit now inhabited Jane's body. Which meant Jane's spirit was squeezed to the side in a most uncomfortable and frustrating (for Jane) manner.

"My dearest," Mr. Rochester said. "We shall marry in a fortnight."

Alt-Jane looked at him, her smile wide. "I cannot wait."

TWENTY-FOUR
Alexander

Alexander had always felt like he belonged in Wellington's office, partly because everyone said Wellington was grooming him to take over one day (which meant Alexander should practice being comfortable in this room), and mostly because he never got in trouble. He was the star agent after all.

At least, he had been.

Alexander tried not to slouch as he approached the duke, who stood at his desk with his hands clasped behind his back and his shoulders set in a thoughtful manner. "What's on your mind, Alexander?"

What *wasn't* on his mind? His chest still ached with the cruel way he'd treated Miss Brontë as they parted. He should have been kinder. Her questions had been fair. Why hadn't Wellington told him everything about Beacons, or that he'd been acquainted with Rochester? There'd been plenty of time. The note he'd sent telling Alexander not to stay at Thornfield could have mentioned that fact.

He *should* have been kinder to Miss Brontë, though, and as it wasn't proper for a single man to write letters (let alone visit!) to a single young lady, this might very well be the way she remembered him for the rest of her life.

Alexander touched the letter in his pocket. "Sir, it's about Rochester."

Wellington nodded. "What about him?"

"I believe Edward Rochester is the man who murdered my father." Alexander pulled the letter from his pocket, careful not to rumple the paper even more.

Wellington took the letter and read through it twice before folding it and offering it back to Alexander. "This is your evidence?"

Alexander nodded and tucked the letter away again.

"It proves nothing."

"I remember seeing him that night."

"You were four years old." Wellington placed a hand over Alexander's shoulder. "I believe you. I do. But this won't be enough proof to do anything about it."

Alexander closed his eyes and exhaled. He knew that. He did. But he'd waited so long to learn the killer's identity and now it seemed he may have waited *too* long. "The letter makes it appear as though they were friends," he muttered. "And when I was introduced to Rochester in Thornfield Hall, he seemed familiar, as though we'd met before. But he didn't know me."

Wellington nodded. "They were friends. Here, sit down a moment." He motioned Alexander to the nearest chair, and together they sat. "You may not know this, though the records are public, but Rochester used to be a member of the Society. His wife, too."

"Is that how you know him?" Alexander guessed.

"Yes," Wellington said. "Mrs. Rochester was our Beacon at the time, and the best agent the Society had ever seen. Mr. Rochester joined us because of her. Although their marriage had been arranged, they seemed to feel real affection for each other."

"What happened to her?"

"The stress of the job became too much for her. Women have such delicate faculties."

That made no sense. Granted, Alexander had little experience with the fairer sex, but Miss Brontë and Miss Eyre were two of the strongest people he knew. "That hasn't been my experience, sir."

Wellington frowned, only for a moment. "Well, it was true for Bertha Rochester. She did very well until one day, the stress of this job wore her down. To put it bluntly, she went mad, and shortly after died."

"That's very sad."

"The loss of Bertha Rochester affected the entire Society. As I said, she was a Beacon, and her death dealt a great blow to our productivity. We still feel her loss today." Wellington leaned back in his chair and sighed. "I'm afraid her death is what drove Mr. Rochester to abandon the Society."

"Where does my father fit into this?"

"He was killed—" Wellington's voice caught. He paused, then tried again. "I've always believed that his death was one of the events that pushed Mrs. Rochester over the edge. They were friends, as you know. He died. She went mad and died. And then Rochester left."

"Why would Rochester kill my father, though? I don't understand."

"Neither do I." Wellington shook his head. "Perhaps . . ."

"Perhaps what?"

"In that letter"—Wellington motioned toward Alexander's pocket—"Nicholas wrote about the 'travesty' in the Society, and that I—for I'm most certainly the 'AW' mentioned—must be stopped."

Alexander sat very still. He'd been curious, of course, but unsure how to bring it up.

"I'm afraid the travesty was that I had sent Mrs. Rochester back to Thornfield to rest. She'd been working so much that the stress was beginning to get to her. I wanted her to have time to recover, then come back, but perhaps I hadn't been clear in my intentions. The three of them—both Rochesters and your father—believed I'd fired her because she was a woman. Your father wanted to confront me, while Mr. Rochester wanted to permanently leave the Society. I cannot fathom how that disagreement led to your father's death, though. I'm as shocked as anyone. And now our new Beacon is with him. . . ."

Alexander's head was reeling with all the information. And really, look how forthcoming Wellington had been. Miss Brontë had worried him for nothing.

"I'll write to Rochester," Wellington said. "We'll get our Beacon. Now, take a few moments to collect yourself, and then I need you on this assignment. It's time-sensitive."

"It can't wait? I'd like to pursue more evidence against Rochester." Alexander didn't usually resist Wellington's directives (that time he completely ignored the letter telling him to come home notwithstanding), but surely the Lord President still understood that this was a special case, one he'd been working on since he was four years old. He had leads. He had a suspect. This wasn't the time for random ghost jobs.

Wellington crossed his arms. "This won't take you long. And it is your duty. Your purpose."

Alexander sighed. Wellington was right. Of course he was. It was just so hard to be taken from the revenge business when the revenge that had evaded him for so long finally felt within his grasp.

"It's my privilege to obey your commands, sir." Alexander stood and waited for his orders.

"I'm glad you think so." Wellington opened a drawer in the massive desk and removed a large envelope. "As I said, this won't take you long. All the work is already done, except of course capturing the ghost. We have an address. We have a key. We even have the talisman. We only need the seer to see the ghost and capture it."

That did sound rather simple. Most jobs were not nearly so well prepared, and left him to do much of the investigation.

"I'll send a note to Branwell and have him meet me at the location."

"That won't be necessary," Wellington said quickly. Perhaps too quickly? "You don't need to bother him with this. Branwell has other things on his mind right now, I'm sure."

Guilt needled at Alexander. He should have tried harder to make his case for Branwell, but at least the boy hadn't been dismissed.

Wellington cleared his throat.

"I'll capture the ghost immediately, sir."

"I expect the talisman returned by the end of the day." Wellington slid the envelope across his desk, which Alexander took. "And, oh, by the way," Wellington said as Alexander began retreating from the office.

"Yes?"

"We'll get Rochester. It will just take time."

Alexander nodded. "Thank you, sir."

"Now," said Wellington, "fetch me that ghost."

Here was the strange thing.

The talisman.

Oh, true to Wellington's words, the envelope did contain everything that Alexander needed, including a list of grievances against the ghost, which ranged from loosening the cobblestones to trip people walking down the road, to making branches tap against windows they wouldn't normally reach, and generally creating a lot of noise.

But the talisman was a strange thing, because it was a ring. And not just any ring, but a heavy gold band with the King of England's crest engraved on top.

It was the king's signet ring.

That truly begged the question of why.

Generally, talismans were objects that had taken a part in murder (like the teacup), or items of importance to the ghost (the pocket watch), so this was unusual to say the least.

Perhaps it was a mistake.

Or a copy.

But no, Alexander had seen signet rings before, and this one had the weight and heft of real gold, and the details on the crest were correct. Though he was no expert, Alexander was reasonably certain this ring was authentic.

Though the information in the dossier had given him no insight, perhaps the ghost would be willing to offer answers. Alexander had dealt with more than a few ghosts who wanted to go on (and on and on) about their lives. Miss Brontë would say perhaps they simply wanted someone to listen, and if he did, they might be more willing to get bopped on the head.

This ghost was recently deceased, apparently, and the family could not sell the house until the bothersome spirit was gone. Which was where the Society came in.

Knowing that, and guessing that the ghost would be furious to realize his family was more concerned about selling the house, Alexander might be able to offer himself as a friendly listener and get a few answers, satisfying his curiosity.

The house in question was a modest dwelling not far from the heart of London, on a tree-lined street filled with children playing and flowers blooming. It was quite lovely, if one didn't know there was a rude ghost in residence.

Alexander approached the house with caution, taking stock of the exits, the number of people around, and even the angle of the sun relative to the windows, so that if the ghost tried to fight him, he wouldn't risk being blinded by sunlight with the wrong move.

He bounced on the balls of his feet, rolled his shoulders, and after a few deep breaths, he marched into the house.

The ghost was sitting on the sheet-covered sofa, waiting for him.

"Hello." He was a mousy chap, with limp brown hair and a permanent squint, and with trousers that didn't quite reach long enough down his legs, and jacket sleeves that didn't fit down his arms. . . . It wasn't even that he was a large man; rather, it was simply because he hadn't known how to dress himself well in life, and so he was trapped like this until the end of his afterlife.

Though he was the most unassuming ghost to cause such a

ruckus, that was hardly the most surprising thing about him.

No, the most interesting part of all this was that Alexander knew this ghost. "David Mitten?"

The ghost nodded. "How are you, dear boy? You look well. Just like your father."

"You're a ghost."

Mr. Mitten nodded again. "Quite put out about it, as you can imagine."

"You seem to be handling it well." Alexander took the ring in his gloved hand.

"Surely you've heard the noise complaints," said Mr. Mitten. "That's why you're here, right?"

Alexander shrugged. "Mr. Mitten, why are you a ghost?"

"Because I died."

"When?"

"Two days ago."

"How?"

"Slipped and hit my head."

Alexander scowled. "That seems unlike you, sir."

Mr. Mitten shrugged, and behind him, some sort of green sludge slid down the wall.

"What's that?" Alexander asked.

"What's what?"

"That slime behind you."

"There's no slime behind me." Mr. Mitten didn't even turn around. "What's that slime behind *you*?"

Alexander looked over his shoulder. Sure enough, the green goop dripped over the door. It was everywhere now. How unsanitary.

All right. So David Mitten was the ghost he was supposed to bring in. And Mr. Mitten was in a chatty mood. But this raised even more questions than before, because Mr. Mitten worked for the Society . . . and the king. He had been, in fact, the liaison and the king's secretary, which explained (maybe) his connection with the signet ring. He'd probably handled the thing more than the king himself.

So that meant the king *might* have given the ring to the Society, but wouldn't he expect it back? How would that work, what with a ghost trapped in it?

And why hadn't Wellington said it was only Mr. Mitten?

And why was Mr. Mitten behaving so badly (allegedly)?

And what was the deal with the slime?

"Well," said Mr. Mitten. "Get on with it. I'm ready."

"To go in here?" Alexander held the ring between his index finger and thumb.

Mr. Mitten nodded transparently.

"All right." But Alexander hesitated, because this was all so strange and he'd really have liked answers, but the clock chimed six and he knew Wellington was surely waiting. Plus, the slime was gross. "Well," Alexander said. "Hold still."

Cautiously, he approached the ghost, half expecting some sort of fight. But Mr. Mitten held perfectly still while Alexander tapped the signet ring on his head.

Immediately, the ghost was sucked in. The gold trembled and glowed, and that was that. David Mitten was trapped in the ring, ready to deliver to Wellington.

"Good work, as always." The duke placed the signet ring on his desk, then put the handkerchief he'd used while inspecting the ring back into his pocket. "You've done England a great service."

It had hardly seemed like anything at all. Capturing Mr. Mitten had been easy. "You didn't tell me it was Mr. Mitten, sir."

Wellington gasped. "Mr. Mitten. Dead." He shook his head, a frown tugging at the corners of his mouth. "I wasn't aware of the ghost's identity. If I'd known, I would have told you. Of course, I'm as sorry to hear about David Mitten's demise as anyone. It's a real tragedy what happened to him."

"He said he slipped and fell."

"It's just awful, isn't it? Life is so brief. It can end in an instant. You never know when your time is up, I suppose."

"I suppose." Alexander frowned. Members of the Society were dropping at an alarming rate. "What about the king?"

"What do you mean?"

"We can't give the ring back to the king. Not with Mr. Mitten trapped inside it.

"You're right, of course. It wouldn't be safe. The king is aware of the issue, and he's already commissioned a new ring. It should be ready by Thursday."

"How nice that His Majesty could put aside his dislike of the Society to help us with Mr. Mitten," Alexander said. Maybe the king did (sort of) believe in ghosts after all? Or, more likely, he didn't want to cause a huge public fuss with the Society, figuring it would be on its way out shortly and this was as good an excuse as any to get a new ring.

Alexander would have to ask to know for sure, but he wasn't the type of agent to question his superior. Asking nosy questions was Miss Brontë's job. She wouldn't have hesitated to ask why the king was suddenly so cooperative. Or why the signet ring was the talisman, or . . .

Wellington crossed his arms. "What is it?"

"It's just . . . you seemed in such a rush to get the ghost."

Wellington folded his hands together. "The family of the deceased—"

Mr. Mitten.

"—wanted to sell the house immediately. They couldn't afford to wait."

"But he worked for both the Society and the king. Surely he left them plenty of money. Why not wait until Thursday when the king's new signet ring arrived?" Alexander slipped his hands behind his back and dug his fingernails into his palms.

"You're very curious tonight, Alexander."

"It was Mr. Mitten," Alexander said. "It feels personal. We all cared about him."

"Of course we did," Wellington agreed.

(Never mind that Alexander—and most people—regularly forgot that David Mitten existed. He was practically invisible in life, already ghostlike. It seemed like it was only in death that anyone cared about him at all. A true tragedy.)

"So why not wait?" Blast Miss Brontë's influence, her contagious questions.

"You've always been a solid agent," Wellington said. "The star agent."

Alexander sensed a *but*.

"But that's because of your willingness to do your job without asking too many questions. We who can't see ghosts can only put our minds to work. We rely on you to take action, to investigate and capture because we cannot. You're so busy with the work you've been dealt. I wish you trusted that we all have thought of every possibility and that we make the best plans we can make. We are the mind, Alexander. You are the sword."

"I see. I'm sorry if I caused you any upset, sir."

Wellington waved him toward the door. "Get some rest. You've had an eventful month, and I'm sure you'd like some time alone after the constant company you've kept."

"Thank you, sir." Alexander headed out of the Society headquarters and walked toward his flat. Was this what it felt like to be reprimanded? The sensation was so unfamiliar he wasn't quite sure if it was disappointment in himself, or confusion over Wellington's words, or something else entirely.

But the duke was right. Maybe it would do him good to finally have some time to himself, some space to stretch his legs without worrying about the others, some freedom to walk around his home with his tie loosened, so to speak.

So he went home. Alone.

And he made tea. Alone.

And he sat in his parlor. Alone.

Just days ago, Miss Brontë had perched on that uncomfortable chair, and Branwell had sulked by the door. He hadn't minded their company.

But now he was alone.

He liked being alone.

Tea for one.

His flat was just . . . so quiet. There were no ghosts around tonight. And there wasn't even the sound of a pencil scratching on paper as Miss Brontë recorded everything that happened. Not that there was anything to record here, because nothing was happening.

"Hello?" He tested his voice to make sure it still had substance.

Not even an echo answered.

Yes, he was definitely alone. And, for the first time ever, maybe he was lonely, too. No one had ever been so lonely.

TWENTY-FIVE
Charlotte

Charlotte shifted the carpetbag with the broken handle to her other shoulder and sighed. A train pulled into the station, but it was not her train. Her train would not arrive for a good fifteen minutes yet. Charlotte generally liked to be early—to allow herself time to locate the places she was supposed to go, given her poor eyesight and her terrible sense of direction. But being early also meant being left with time to think. Normally she didn't mind—thinking was what Charlotte considered herself best at, after all. This afternoon, however, the thoughts swirling about her brain were dreadfully glum. She was out of options: she had to return to Lowood. Where she would probably end up starving to death or succumbing to the Graveyard Disease, she thought. Or at the very least she'd be cold and hungry and utterly bored.

Conditions at Lowood had been markedly better since Mr. Brocklehurst was murdered, she reminded herself. But the thought didn't cheer her as it should have. Brocklehurst's name only called to mind a bittersweet memory: Mr. Blackwood chasing about the drawing room waving a teacup in the air, the very first day they'd met. And then the teacup made her think of Bran.

Sigh. Bran. For two weeks she'd watched her brother stumble about his room, packing his meager belongings to return to their father and the parsonage. He'd tried to act cheerful for her sake.

"I find I've been missing home," he'd mused as he'd folded his nightclothes into a trunk. "I'll be glad to sleep in my own bed again. This bed never truly felt like mine."

"So I've been sacked. It could be worse," he'd murmured as they sat in the middle of the empty floor, drinking lukewarm, sugarless tea. But Bran didn't elaborate on how it could be worse.

"I know I'm likely to be a terrible parson," he'd sighed as he'd climbed onto his northbound train just a few moments ago. "But I don't need to be the parson right now, do I? Father's the parson, and Father is a paragon of good health. I have years and years before I'm needed in Father's place. So I can just keep up with my studies and maybe do a bit of drawing." Bran liked to draw, almost as much as Charlotte liked to write. In that way he was much like Jane.

Jane. They had parted so poorly. Charlotte didn't even know what to think about Jane's situation. Jane was in love, and part of Charlotte was keenly envious and part of her was happy for her friend. To fall in love, even in less than convenient circumstances, must be a marvelous thing. But then Mr. Rochester was, some might say, a flawed man. That much was clear. And there was also the great possibility that Mr. Rochester was a murderer.

What would become of Jane?

Charlotte sighed again. The non-broken half of the handle of her carpetbag bit into her flesh. The train that was not hers was about to depart. The conductor leaned out and shouted, "All aboard for Canterbury! Last call for Canterbury!"

After a few moments, the train began to chug slowly forward. And then a voice cried, "Wait! Wait for me! Stop!" and Charlotte was nearly thrown to the ground as someone bashed into her from behind.

That did it for the carpetbag. The other handle snapped at her shoulder, and her clothes and books and bottles of ink and pencils spilled out everywhere. Charlotte said a rather unladylike word under her breath and scrambled to pick up her things. The man who had crashed into her watched helplessly as the train departed without him. Then he turned and stooped to help her.

"That's quite all right," she said a bit snappishly. "I can manage."

"I'm so terribly sorry." He held up a pair of her pantaloons, and then dropped them like they were on fire. "I'm so sorry. I'm so sorry."

There was something familiar about his voice. She lifted her spectacles. And then gasped.

"Mr. Mason!"

He cocked his head to one side and frowned at her. "Are we acquainted, Miss . . . ?"

"Brontë," she filled in, then shook her head wildly. "You would know me as Miss Eshton, of course. But that wasn't my real name. But that's not important now, because you are Mr. Mason! But how? You were on a ship bound for the West Indies! But you weren't on the ship!"

"No," he agreed. "I was—"

"This is wonderful!" She pressed her hands to her face as if to keep her head from exploding. "We must tell Mr. Blackwood!"

"Mr. Blackwood?" Mr. Mason still looked very confused.

"Mr. Eshton, to you. Don't you remember? Oh, Mr. Blackwood will be so pleased we haven't lost you." She grasped Mr. Mason firmly by the hand. "Come. We must go speak to him immediately."

Mr. Mason opened his mouth as if to protest, but she shook her head again. "You have plenty of time. You just missed your train, and the next train to Canterbury doesn't arrive until six o'clock. So you will accompany me to Mr. Blackwood's."

And so it was decided.

"What does . . . Mr. Eshton . . . wish to . . . speak to me . . . regarding?" Mr. Mason panted after Charlotte dragged him to the nearest carriage for hire, thrust him into it, and then ordered the driver to take them to Baker Street posthaste.

"Mr. Rochester, of course!"

Mr. Mason looked suddenly green. But it could have been the

rocking of the carriage. They were proceeding at a rather breakneck speed toward Mr. Blackwood's flat.

Charlotte, on the other hand, was smiling.

She was going to be useful, after all.

When they reached Baker Street, Charlotte took the stairs to Mr. Blackwood's flat two at a time—an impressive feat considering the volume of her skirts. She couldn't wait to see his expression when she presented Mr. Mason. The man was the key to Rochester's mystery—she could feel it in her very bones.

It was getting late, nearly suppertime. Surely Mr. Blackwood would be home at this hour, she thought as she reached the top of the stairs, and then she barreled through the door without thinking to knock.

"Mr. Blackwood!" she cried. "Alexander!"

At her scream, he came running from a back room. "Charlotte—I mean, Miss Brontë! Are you all right? What's wrong?" His gaze swept over her from head to foot, searching for injury. "What's happened?"

"I found . . ." She shouldn't have taken the stairs quite so quickly. In a corset. She bent at the waist and focused on breathing for several moments. Then she straightened. "I found Mr. . . ." She lifted her spectacles to her face so she could catch his expression when she told him.

"Oh dear," she said. "You're not dressed."

He was wearing trousers, thank heavens. But she'd obviously

294

interrupted him in the middle of shaving—there were still traces of shaving cream on his face. His hair was wet and gleaming, dripping onto his bare shoulders. His bare shoulders. Because he was not wearing a shirt. Which meant that, by pre-Victorian standards, anyway, he was more or less completely naked.

A blush glowed on his cheeks. "Miss Brontë."

She could feel her own blush heating her face. "Oh dear." She dropped the spectacles. "I should have knocked."

At that very moment a knock sounded at the door. Mr. Blackwood swiveled to look at it. Charlotte was glad for the interruption.

"That would be Mr. Mason," she said.

"Mr. Mason?" Mr. Blackwood looked incredulous.

She nodded. "I came across him at the train station."

"But he was supposed to be on that ship headed for the West Indies," Mr. Blackwood said, frowning as if, more than anything else, he couldn't believe he'd been given faulty information.

"I know."

"But why wasn't he?"

"Because he . . ." She stopped. "Actually, I don't know. We should ask him."

She went to open the door. On the other side stood, predictably, Mr. Mason. He immediately looked from Charlotte to Mr. Blackwood in his unclothed state and gave a small, scandalized gasp. Because pre-Victorians.

"Oh, it's quite all right. I can't see a thing without my glasses," Charlotte felt compelled to explain.

Mr. Blackwood cleared his throat. "Mr. Mason. I am surprised to see you."

"And I, you," Mr. Mason said. "Mr. Blackwood? I thought you were Mr. Eshton. A magistrate, correct?"

Oh, so he remembered Alexander, Charlotte observed a little bitterly. She'd obviously just been furniture dressing to the man.

"I'm an agent in the Society for the Relocation of Wayward Spirits," Mr. Blackwood clarified. "I was at Thornfield on assignment."

"I see," Mr. Mason said, but he clearly did not. "What kind of assignment?"

"Society business," Mr. Blackwood said tightly. "But while we were at Thornfield, we came to believe that Mr. Rochester was . . ." Charlotte lifted her spectacles. His brow was furrowed. He was thinking about his poor father. Then she was reminded again that he wasn't dressed and dropped the spectacles again. "Guilty of certain crimes," he concluded.

Mr. Mason nodded. "I would believe almost anything of Mr. Rochester. After this recent encounter with him I think him to be nothing short of a nefarious villain."

"That's what we think!" Charlotte exclaimed. "The most nefarious!"

"But why do you think him so?" Mr. Blackwood asked. "What harm has he caused you?"

"Not to me, sir," Mr. Mason said. "Outside of the harm of keeping me from someone I dearly love."

Charlotte couldn't help but lift her glasses to her face. "Someone you love?"

"My sister," Mr. Mason said.

"Who's your sister?" Mr. Blackwood demanded to know. He was practically quivering with the excitement of it all, every muscle in his back tensed like he was preparing to confront Mr. Rochester at this very moment.

"Mr. Blackwood!" Charlotte burst out. "Would you please put on a shirt!"

Mr. Blackwood's face colored again. "Mr. Mason, Miss Brontë, please forgive my lack of appropriate dress. Won't you be seated in the parlor until I can rectify the situation?"

"Of course," Mr. Mason said.

"Thank heavens!" Charlotte agreed.

Mr. Blackwood nodded briskly. "Please make yourselves comfortable," he directed, and hurried out of the room. Charlotte led Mr. Mason to the two less-than-comfortable chairs in the corner. They sat. Mr. Mason crossed his legs, then uncrossed them. He glanced around at the walls, but there were no paintings to examine, no decorations. He glanced at Charlotte and then looked away. Then he spotted a newspaper on the small table next to him. Relieved to have found something to occupy himself, he snatched it up and began to read.

They waited. Mr. Blackwood did not appear. A clock on the opposing wall ticked oppressively, counting the seconds of his absence. Charlotte shifted uncomfortably. (These chairs were, truly, the most uncomfortable chairs in all of England. We checked.) If Mr. Mason was a gentleman, she thought, he should offer her a part of the newspaper. Still, it would not be proper to suggest such a thing. She could get up and make them a cup of tea. Tea would be very calming. But to make the tea herself would have to assume some scandalous level of familiarity with Mr. Blackwood's kitchen. As usual, Charlotte found herself hopelessly penned in by etiquette.

"Would you like to read?" Mr. Mason offered a section of the paper. She almost sighed in relief. He was a gentleman, after all.

But what he handed her was the weddings and obituaries page. It was, to say the least, not the most enthralling reading.

She sighed and lifted her spectacles.

Mr. and Mrs. Charles Durst, Esquire, are pleased to announce the engagement of their daughter, Miss Cecilia Cecily Durst, to the esteemed Earl of Lancaster, Jonathan Fraser Northrop, the wedding to take place at their country estate on the fifteenth of September, 1834.

Charlotte's nose wrinkled. She amused herself for the next several minutes rewording the wedding announcements to liven up the stories they told.

Mr. Henry Woodhouse is overjoyed to announce the entanglement of his most precious and comely younger daughter, Miss Emma Woodhouse to Mr. George Knightley, the wedding to take place at the nearest available church house, immediately. The bride is both beautiful and rich, and enjoyed a brief flirtation with a Mr. Churchill that had everyone quite concerned, but in the end she saw the error of her ways and picked the right chap.

Mr. Edgar Linton, of Thrushcross Grange, would like to announce his engagement to the lovely Miss Catherine Earnshaw, the wedding to take place on the twenty-first of September, even though the lady would much rather marry a ruffian named Heathcliff. But she will forego her passion in order to secure social ambition.

Charlotte suppressed a giggle. At least she was competent—when the situation called for it—at entertaining herself. She was moving on to the next one when Mr. Blackwood reemerged, this time fully clothed. He smiled at her with a touch of nervousness. She beamed back at him.

"Can I offer you some tea?" he asked in a voice that portrayed that he was only offering because this was England and it was the polite thing to do, but he'd much prefer to get on with the interrogation.

"I'd love a cup of tea," Mr. Mason replied with an uneasy laugh.

Charlotte sighed and dropped her gaze back to the newspaper. Where the next wedding announcement seemed to leap out at her.

"Miss Brontë?" Mr. Blackwood inquired.

"No!" she gasped.

"No tea?"

"It's not possible!"

"Come now, tea is always possible," he said.

"No!" She jumped to her feet and shoved the paper into his hands. "Look! Look!"

His eyes scanned down the page. "What am I supposed to be . . ."

And then he saw it.

"Mr. Edward Fairfax Rochester, of Thornfield Hall, is pleased to announce his engagement to Miss Jane Eyre, also of Thornfield Hall, the wedding to occur on the tenth of September. . . ." His voice died away. "It's not possible."

"Mr. Rochester?" Mr. Mason was on his feet now, too. His face had drained of color. "Mr. Rochester is getting married?"

"Oh, Jane," Charlotte breathed.

"Mr. Rochester cannot marry," Mr. Mason said furiously. "He can't."

"Why?" Mr. Blackwood asked.

He told them why. And they immediately set out for Thornfield Hall.

They were almost too late. Jane and Rochester were nearly to the "Wilt thou have this woman for thy wedded wife?" part of the wedding ceremony when Mr. Blackwood and Charlotte (and Mr. Mason, trailing a bit behind) burst into the tiny stone church.

"Stop!" Mr. Blackwood strode up the center aisle. Jane and Rochester slowly turned to look at him.

Charlotte lifted her glasses. In her elegant silk wedding gown Jane was as lovely as Charlotte had ever seen her. A simple but pretty veil covered her hair. A stunning pearl necklace gleamed at her throat. Plain girls could clean up well when the situation called for it. Charlotte smiled and waved. *Nice dress,* she mouthed.

Jane stared back at her blankly. It was almost as if she didn't recognize Charlotte.

"What is the meaning of this?" asked the priest.

"The marriage cannot go on," Mr. Blackwood said. "I declare the existence of an impediment."

But Rochester turned away and took Jane's hand again. "Continue," he directed the priest.

"Yes," murmured Jane. "Continue. We don't know these people."

Well, that hurt.

"But . . ." The priest obviously wanted to know what the devil was going on.

"Say man and wife," hissed Rochester. "Man and wife!"

"Man and . . ." The priest frowned. "No." He addressed Mr. Blackwood. "What is this impediment you speak of?"

"Mr. Rochester cannot be married today, as he is already married."

"It doesn't matter," exclaimed Jane passionately. "I love him, and he loves me, and now we'll be together forever."

"Wait, you knew about his wife?" Charlotte gasped.

Rochester was shaking his head. "I don't have a wife. Who says I have a wife? Everybody around here knows that I'm single. Right, darling?"

"Oh," said Jane. "Right. I don't know about any wife. Except me, very shortly."

"You can't prove anything," said Rochester.

Mr. Blackwood took a piece of paper from his pocket. "I have a statement here." He cleared his throat. "'I affirm and can prove that on the twentieth of October, AD'" (A date some twenty years back—did we mention that Rochester was really old?) "'Edward Fairfax Rochester, of Thornfield Hall was married to my sister, Bertha Antoinetta Mason, daughter of Jonas Mason, merchant, and of Antoinetta, his wife, at St. Mary's Church, Spanish Town, Jamaica. The record of the marriage will be found in the register of the church—a copy of it is now in my possession. Signed, Richard Mason.'"

"Okay, so I was married . . . at one time," admitted Rochester. "But that document doesn't prove that the woman in question is still alive, now does it?" He turned back to the priest. "Say man and wife."

"She was alive three weeks ago," said Mr. Blackwood.

"How do you know?" asked the priest.

"We have a witness to the fact," Charlotte said. "Whose testimony even you, sir, will scarcely controvert." She turned and gestured to Mr. Mason, who'd been standing at the back of the church this entire time. "Mr. Mason, come forward please. We need to hear from you now."

Mr. Mason was pale. Trembling. He was clearly terrified of Mr. Rochester, with good reason, too, as the want-to-be-groom looked like he was going to rush the poor man at any moment and dispatch him with his bare hands.

"Have courage, Mr. Mason," Charlotte whispered to him. "Tell the truth."

"Bertha is my sister," said Mr. Mason in a small voice. "I visited Thornfield Hall not even a month ago, and I beheld her there with my own eyes. My sister—Mr. Rochester's wife—is very much alive. She's mad, perhaps, but who wouldn't be mad after all he's done to her. He's had her locked in the attic for fifteen years!"

Everyone in the church gasped.

"I assure you, I have a very good explanation for all of this!" Rochester exclaimed, but then he gave a sudden roar and lurched toward Mr. Mason like his solution to this rather insurmountable impediment to his nuptials was to do away with the witness. Mr. Mason blanched and then promptly slumped to the floor in a dead faint. Mr. Blackwood and the clerk of the church moved to restrain Mr. Rochester.

Charlotte rushed to Jane. "Oh, Jane, I'm so sorry to be the bearer of this news. I truly am. But thank goodness we arrived here in time to stop you."

"Stop me? Who are you?" Jane said coldly, grasping Charlotte by the shoulders. "This is your doing, isn't it? I was supposed to be free, at last. Alive again. With the love I thought I'd lost. But now you've spoiled everything."

"Well, it wasn't all my doing," Charlotte deferred. "Although I was the one who located Mr. Mason. It's kind of a funny story, actually. . . ."

Then Jane's small hands were around Charlotte's throat, and she stopped believing it to be so funny. "Jane," she gasped out. "If I said something to offend you, I do apologize. But surely you see that it's better now not to marry Mr. Roch-est—"

She couldn't get the last syllable out. She had no air. Jane was surprisingly strong for a girl of her diminutive size. And everybody in this quite crowded room was looking at Mr. Rochester, who was struggling with Mr. Blackwood, or at Mr. Mason, out cold on the floor.

"Jane," Charlotte croaked.

Jane squeezed harder. Dark spots swam before Charlotte's eyes. The world was fading. She gave one last desperate push at her attacker . . . and her fingers caught the pearl necklace around Jane's slender neck. She pulled, and the necklace broke free.

Pearls tumbled down all around them. Jane's hands dropped, and suddenly Charlotte could breathe again. Then Jane's eyes rolled back in her head, and she crumpled unceremoniously to the floor.

Jane
TWENTY-SIX

There was a fog in front of Jane's eyes. A dense fog that prevented her from seeing anything, or hearing anyone. Voices would speak to her, but before the sounds could coalesce into words, the fog would capture them and wrap them up in cottony nothingness, stripping them of all meaning.

The head cloud stayed for days and days, and then all at once, it was gone and Jane was flat on her back on a hard, cold surface, looking up at several faces.

Mr. Blackwood. Charlotte. Rochester. Mr. Mason? And a man in white robes holding a bible?

"Charlotte?" Jane said. "Where am I?"

"Oh, dear," Charlotte croaked and then coughed. "Do you not remember anything?"

"No," Jane said. "I must have hit my head. Oh, no. Did I hit my head? Is that it?"

Mr. Blackwood crouched by her. "Maybe we should help her up."

"Maybe we should tell her what happened before she . . . stands all the way up." Charlotte said.

After further discussion, it was decided that they would help Jane to a chair, where she should sit—definitely not stand—to hear what happened. The whole thing made Jane very nervous, but not as nervous as the very next moment when she discovered what she was wearing.

"Why am I all dressed up?" Jane asked, smoothing her hand down the softest silk she'd ever felt in her life. "I didn't steal it." She felt the need to clarify *that* fact upfront.

Rochester paced on the other side of the room defensively.

"Somebody please tell me what happened," Jane insisted.

"Well," Charlotte said. "To put it as succinctly as possible . . . You were possessed by a ghost, who then, using your body, agreed to marry Mr. Rochester, who, it turns out, has a secret wife locked away in the attic, and just as you were about to say your vows, we rushed in and stopped the wedding and I tore off your pearls, which seemed to be the talisman for your ghost, and then you collapsed, and . . . well . . . here we are."

"Yes, aren't we, though," Rochester grumbled.

Mr. Blackwood clenched his fists. "You, sir, have no right to say anything."

Charlotte went to his side. "We should call for the authorities."

"And tell them what?" Rochester smirked.

"Wait," Jane said, rubbing her forehead. "Wait."

"I know, I know," Charlotte said, returning to Jane. "Being possessed by a ghost cannot be a pleasant experience."

Jane shrugged Charlotte's hand away and stood. "Rochester's married? You're *married*?"

Rochester's gaze darted nervously from face to face. "It's not what you think." His voice cracked.

"Oh, is that right? Because what I think is *that you are married and you tried to get engaged to a woman who was not your wife and then had her possessed*!"

"Well, I guess in that regard, it is what you think. But I can explain."

Jane folded her arms, and then next to her, Charlotte folded her arms, and at that point, Jane noticed someone missing.

"Where's Helen?" Jane said.

"Who's Helen?" Rochester said.

"Here I am," Helen said, flying into the room. "When you were possessed, and I realized even I couldn't get through to you, I thought I would go to find help. But I didn't know where to go, or what to do without my Jane. I decided the task was going to take a lot of thinking, so I wandered Thornfield estate, thinking. Until I saw the carriages racing here today. For the wedding."

"I'm back now." Jane turned to Rochester. "Explain yourself."

"Please, please come with me." Rochester held out his hand. Jane didn't take it. He dropped his hand. "I will show you everything."

"You shouldn't go with him," Helen said.

"I have to know."

Jane and the rest of the wedding party followed Rochester out of the church and down the hill and back to Thornfield Hall.

They all entered the manor in a flourish. Housemaids and servants threw rice and flower petals at the couple.

"Curse your happy wishes!" Rochester growled. "There was no wedding today."

The staff scurried away like roaches in a sudden light.

Jane and company followed Rochester up the spiral staircase to the top floor of the east wing, where Jane had gone so many nights ago when Mr. Mason was injured.

When Helen realized where they were going, she turned around.

"I'll wait down here," she said. "I can't stand being in that room."

Rochester did, indeed, lead them to that very anteroom where Mason had lain, bleeding. Inside, Grace Poole was sitting near the sofa, fabric on her lap, a needle in her hand. She put down her embroidery when everyone walked in. "How is our charge?" Rochester said.

"She's a might touchy, sir," Grace Poole answered.

"Please show us in," Rochester said.

Grace frowned. "I'm not sure that's a good idea. She's rather snappish of late."

Jane remembered the noises coming from beyond that door the night Mason was injured. The rattling of the knob. The moans that mingled with the wind. A shiver ran through her as she watched Grace open the door.

Rochester stepped through the threshold, followed by Jane and the rest of the party. Inside was a large bed, draped with deep red fabric. Red tapestries hung from the ceiling. One such tapestry was sticking out of an open window as if someone were going to attempt an escape, but they were too far up. In the corner, a small table stood. On top of it were two glasses. One lay on its side, liquid pooled around it.

Jane couldn't see anyone in the room, until a strong breeze forced a gossamer drape aside, and behind it was a woman with ebony-black hair, sitting in a chair. She was thin to the point of being malnourished. There were scratches and cuts up and down her arms, and her head hung low as if she were asleep. Even so, Jane couldn't stop looking at her. She was luminous, as if a brilliant glow came from deep within her.

"Meet my wife," Rochester said. "I was married to her before I found out hysteria runs in her family."

At his voice, the woman raised her head. "You are not my husband," she said wearily. Then she noticed Mr. Mason.

"You." She lunged for the man, but wrist restraints jerked her back. "You promised to stay away! *Tu as promis!*"

She repeated herself in French, Jane noted.

"Bertha, it is all right. This is your brother." Rochester turned to Mason. "You'd better leave. You're upsetting her. In fact, we should all leave."

"No!" Mrs. Rochester cried. "No. This is not my husband. Please."

"See?" Rochester gestured to her. "There is no cure for this kind of madness. She is hysterical. Now, everyone kindly leave so I can tend to my wife."

Mrs. Rochester looked frustrated. Exhausted. Resigned.

But she didn't look crazy.

Reader, you might have noticed there was a propensity at this time to label women as "hysterical." The term was thrown around quite frequently, and, in the humble opinion of your narrators, far too easily. Then it became a vicious cycle. The more they protested, the "crazier" they were labeled. We are going on record here to say that we feel this treatment was completely unfair.

Mr. Blackwood took a step toward Rochester. "We will be waiting for you, *sir*."

Mr. Mason, Mr. Blackwood, Charlotte, and Jane left.

"She attacked me that night," Mr. Mason said. "I had no idea such madness had overtaken her."

Jane took Charlotte's hand. "I am feeling rather faint."

"Yes, poor Jane. You have been traumatized."

Mr. Blackwood and Mr. Mason bowed as the ladies walked out, as if pre-Victorian protocol mattered a whit at this point.

* * *

Charlotte walked Jane to her bedchamber. They were quiet as Charlotte helped Jane unbutton her gown and fold it carefully, and take off her veil and place it on top of the dress.

Jane put on her usual gray dress and then they both sat on the edge of her bed.

"So I was possessed?" Jane said.

Charlotte nodded. "I can't believe he did that to you. He should be arrested."

"There's no way they would believe it." Jane could hear the exhaustion in her own voice.

"Do you remember anything while you were possessed?"

Jane shook her head. "No. One minute I was talking to Mr. Rochester, and the next . . . nothing."

"And then you find out he has a wife," Charlotte said. She pulled her notebook out of her pocket.

"Really?" Jane said.

Charlotte blushed and set it aside.

"We must leave here at once." Jane went to her wardrobe, took out her other dress, and began to fold. "About the wife. Mr. Rochester kept saying she was mad, but I didn't find her to be so." She hoisted her trunk onto the bed. "Frustrated, yes. Exhausted, yes. But mad?"

Charlotte took Jane's stockings out of a drawer and folded them. "I agree, dear. But then, I've never met someone who was supposed to be mad."

"It almost seemed . . ." Jane paused. "It almost seemed like if we loosened her restraints and sat down to tea, we could have a—"

She was interrupted by a rap at the door.

"Jane?" Rochester's voice came through the thick oak.

Jane held a finger to her lips and met Charlotte's eyes.

"I just want to leave," Jane whispered. Charlotte nodded and placed the stockings in the trunk.

Helen ghosted in and noticed the packing. "Oh, good, we're leaving."

Three more strikes against the door.

"Jane, please. I'm sorry it all happened as it did, but I was desperate. Have you ever been so desperate, Jane? Have you ever been so hungry, you would do anything for bread? So cold, you would do anything for warmth? So tired, you would do anything for rest?"

Jane closed her eyes. She knew that feeling. She knew Charlotte knew that feeling as well. Helen's head burst into flames.

Helen had a point. Jane never would have deceived someone so, as Mr. Rochester had deceived her. Not to mention the fact that she never would've had someone possessed to get her way.

The thought made her stomach roll.

Another knock. "Jane. You are the most radiant thing I've ever seen. Remember when you bewitched my horse on that road?"

Charlotte raised her eyebrows at Jane, and Jane shook her head and pointed at Helen, who shook her flaming head and pointed at Jane.

"I knew then that you had come here to change my life. I

knew then that the happiness, which had eluded me so far, had come to me at last."

Jane couldn't take it anymore. "How can you say such things? I am, by all living accounts, plain."

"Did you see what I was married to?" Rochester said.

"Oh, bother," Helen said.

Jane rolled up her sketches and paintings and Charlotte tucked away her brushes.

"Jane, it doesn't matter if I'm married, because I would be satisfied having you merely as a companion. A sister, almost. We could live in a villa I have in the South of France." He knocked again, this time with more force. "Jane, we would have separate living compartments, and we would only spare a kiss on the cheek for birthdays."

"Please, stop talking, Mr. Rochester," Jane said. "I am not interested in that."

"You are the love of my life."

"Which life is that? Because you seem to be living so many."

"But we had something special, didn't we? I know you felt it, too."

Jane stamped her foot. "You lie and manipulate and twist until you get your way. You proposed to me, even though you have a wife, who's conveniently locked away in the attic, and when I asked for more time, you had me possessed! So no, I don't think I will live with you in the South of France as sodding brother and sister!"

The flames in Helen's hair sputtered out. Charlotte stood

frozen. Jane's eyes were wide as if she couldn't believe the words that had just come out of her mouth.

Jane was about to crack a smile, when a loud thump came at the door. And then another. And another.

"Jane, open the door!" Rochester's voice was enraged. "Open the door!"

Louder thuds sounded, as if Rochester were throwing the full weight of his body at the solid oak.

Jane looked around for something to defend them with, but there was only a hairbrush and then pieces of furniture that were too big for them to wield as weapons.

"Maybe the window?" Charlotte said.

"We can't possibly use the window as a weapon," Jane said.

"No, to escape."

They ran across the room and looked out the glass, but Jane's bedchamber was three floors up. And below them, the ground was all packed dirt and grass.

"I'll go first," Helen said. She ghosted through the window and floated to the ground. "Now you!"

Jane waved her off. "Quick, Charlotte. The dresser!"

Thud. "Jane, you may not see it now, but soon, I will make you see!" *Thud.*

Jane and Charlotte put their full weight against the side of the dresser. It moved an inch at a time. They shoved and shoved and then all of a sudden, the dresser toppled over onto its side, landing just short of the door and in no way blocking it.

"No!" Jane exclaimed.

Thud. A piece of the doorframe went flying across the room.

Jane and Charlotte grabbed hold of each other.

Thud. The top of the door separated from the hinge and then the entire thing fell to the floor. Rochester stood there in silhouette against the light from the corridor.

"I asked you nicely," he growled.

"You can't really believe that, can you?" Jane said.

Rochester raised his foot to come toward them, but just then a figure came barreling against his side.

"Alexander!" Charlotte exclaimed.

"Ladies, run!" He huffed from exertion.

Rochester was momentarily stunned by the blow. Jane and Charlotte scrambled past him and sprinted down the corridor, followed by Mr. Blackwood. Moments later, Rochester's footsteps followed.

"Faster!" Mr. Blackwood said.

"We're going as fast as we can," Charlotte said back. "Have you seen the shoes we're expected to wear?"

The three of them made it to the great hall, and almost across it, but Rochester caught up and he tackled Mr. Blackwood. Both men flew to the ground.

Jane and Charlotte stopped.

The two men lay there, their chests heaving as they tried to regain their breath.

"Mr. Blackwood, are you all right?" Charlotte said.

"Yes," he said, mid-cough.

The men brushed themselves off and then stood, facing each other, knees bent, hands out, combat position.

"Go!" Mr. Blackwood said to Jane and Charlotte.

"Find us at Haworth," Charlotte said. "We'll go to Haworth!"

"I will find you! Now go!" Mr. Blackwood said as he lunged for a sword on the wall.

The two ladies flew through the door and out into the cold dark night.

TWENTY-SEVEN
Alexander

Alexander grabbed a sword off its mount on the wall. A sword wouldn't have been his first choice as a weapon, but he certainly knew how to use one. It wasn't as though people like Rochester kept pistols mounted to their walls. (Meanwhile, in America . . .) A pistol would have made the intimidation factor much higher, he thought.

Rochester's glare settled on him. The sword. The guarded stance he'd taken up. "You're ruining everything," Rochester growled. "She's supposed to be mine!"

"She won't have you," Alexander said.

"I'm going to get her back no matter what it takes."

"Get over it."

Rochester scanned the room for another weapon. There. A

second sword. "We were meant to be together!" Rochester slid the blade from its mount.

So it would be a duel, then. That was fine. Alexander could duel. "You had to possess her with a ghost to make her agree to marry you." And who had that woman been? She'd been young and beautiful, and dressed in some—ah—interesting attire that made Alexander immediately avert his eyes. Yet, somehow she seemed familiar, too. He'd seen that interesting attire before—briefly.

"She's like the sun and I am the earth feeling its rays!"

"The sun and the earth will never be together!" Alexander frowned. Miss Eyre was delightful, sure, but like the sun? That seemed a little over the top. "Who was that woman? That ghost you were about to marry."

"Someone who used to be mine." Rochester attacked with a flurry of maneuvers that would have startled Alexander if Alexander had been less prepared. But he blocked so quickly that steel rang and both men launched into a complicated dance of death.

Fire roared through his veins. This was what Alexander had wanted all along. "I know it was you," he said. "And now you're going to pay."

Rochester performed a Marionette's Demise, a move that involved several smaller moves and lots of feinting. "What did I do?"

Alexander countered Rochester's attack with an Artist's Curse. "My name is Alexander Blackwood. You killed my father. Prepare to—"

"Who was your father?"

"Nicholas—"

"I've never met anyone named Nicholas."

A lie. Alexander knew it was a lie. Lots of people were named Nicholas.

He attacked using a new move called the Three Ladies' Luck, thinking his opponent might not know how to counter it, but Rochester was clearly a man who'd continued his sword studies throughout his life, because two sharp clacks of the blades and Alexander was blocked.

"You're outmatched, boy. I'm a master swordsman, unlike my—I mean you. Unlike you." Rochester growled as their fight spilled across the room, around sofas and chairs, endangering paintings and potted plants.

"Prepare to die." Alexander shot forward, trying to surprise Rochester by going straight for the man's heart, but the villain darted aside and tapped Alexander's sword away. "My father was your friend!"

"I really don't know what you're talking about," said Rochester as the fight moved into the drawing room. "I haven't killed anyone."

Why was the man denying it? What was the point?

Alexander charged with the Three Ladies' Luck again, hoping Rochester wouldn't expect it a second time. The man did. He was a better swordsman, Alexander had to admit. But then Rochester slipped on a pair of spectacles someone had carelessly left lying around, and Alexander pressed his advantage while the man was off balance, shoving him to the floor.

Chest heaving, Alexander dug the tip of his sword to Rochester's throat. "I've waited fourteen years to avenge my father's murder."

"I don't know him," Rochester said. "Truly, I do not."

Alexander glared down, hatred making his hand shake. Blood pooled where the sword point pierced skin. He'd never killed a man before, and there was no coming back from it once he took this step.

"I didn't kill him," repeated Rochester.

At the man's throat, a small iron key gleamed, and several thoughts crashed through Alexander at once: Mrs. Rochester insisting this man wasn't her husband, the repeated confused claims about not knowing Alexander's father, and his description of Miss Eyre's beauty.

Alexander slashed the sword to the left, cutting through the chain. The key went skittering across the floor, and abruptly, the ghost of a younger man ripped from Rochester's body.

Rochester—the real Rochester—slumped to the side.

Alexander lunged for the key.

The ghost glared at him. "You meddling fool. This place was mine. I had everything I wanted. And I would have gotten away with it, too, if it hadn't been for—"

Alexander bopped the ghost on the head, sucking him back into the talisman.

* * *

Several minutes later, after Alexander had dragged Rochester into his room and laid him out on the bed, he went to find Mrs. Fairfax and the rest of the house staff. He didn't explain the situation. But now that he wore his mask, they seemed to understand that something of the otherworldly persuasion had occurred there today.

"Have you seen Miss Brontë and Miss Eyre?" he asked as he waited for Mrs. Fairfax to finish preparing a tray of tea.

"They ran through here like the hounds of hades were after them. Why, I've never seen girls move so fast in my entire life."

Alexander had a lot of questions concerning what she knew about the events there, but then the tea was finished and he took it upstairs, along with the lockbox containing the small iron key.

Rochester was just sitting up in his bed, looking confused as he surveyed the room. He lifted his hands and let his sheets slide between his fingers.

Alexander poured a cup of tea and offered it to the man. "Can you speak?"

The man nodded slowly. "I . . . think . . . yes." His voice wasn't gravelly. It had been used recently, of course. But after being possessed for years, he'd perhaps forgotten how to use it, how to shape the words on his own.

Tea would help, though. Tea always helped.

"Drink up." Alexander took his seat and nodded to the teacup Rochester had been staring at. "I have questions."

"I must—" Rochester tried to stand, but collapsed back to the bed a moment later. "My wife. Where . . . ?"

Before Alexander could find a kind way to tell him that his wife had been locked in the attic for a decade and a half, realization crossed Rochester's face.

"Oh, no." He dropped his face into his hands and groaned. "He locked her away. That bastard. He—"

"He?" Alexander said. "Who?"

"My brother, Rowland. Always Wellington's lackey."

"What do you mean?" Finally, Alexander could get some answers.

But Rochester lurched to his feet, staggering past Alexander and the tea. "I must go to my wife."

"Wait," Alexander said. "I still have questions!"

For someone who hadn't used his own legs in years, Rochester was fast.

Alexander followed, just in time to hear Rochester say, "You! You know better than to come here. Go back."

"Forgive me. I came because—"

At that moment, Alexander emerged from the room to find Rochester on the stairs to the third floor, and Mason standing just below him. Both men went silent upon Alexander's appearance.

"We'll talk later," Rochester hissed. Then he ran up the stairs two at a time.

"What was that?" Alexander said.

Mason shook his head. "It's nothing."

It had definitely been something.

Alexander didn't have time for more mysteries right now.

"Good luck with nothing, sir." Then he headed downstairs and out the door, hoping that he could catch up with Miss Brontë and Miss Eyre before they made it too far away. But he didn't see them on the road. Charlotte had said they would go on to Haworth. He would have to meet up with them there, later, of course, after he'd had time to properly question the real Mr. Rochester.

But when he went into the house again, he discovered the Rochesters had disappeared, and no one seemed to know to where. Even Grace Poole was missing.

How was Alexander supposed to get answers if everyone kept vanishing?

Just then, a pigeon landed on the windowsill and cooed at him. A small note was wrapped around its ankle.

Report to me immediately, it read in Wellington's handwriting.

Before Alexander left, he returned to the bedroom where the ghost of Rowland had attacked the young ladies. There, he found Miss Brontë's notebook and tucked it into his breast pocket, resting his hand over it for just a moment.

Then he gathered the lockbox and the rest of his belongings and left Thornfield.

At Westminster, he quickly went through all the rituals of gaining entrance to the building, the secret rooms, and strode toward the great library with the lockbox tucked under one arm. Anticipation made his heart beat faster when he knocked on the door and waited for Wellington to answer.

Then he stepped inside.

"Good evening, Mr. Blackwood," said the duke. "What have you brought for me?"

Alexander approached the desk and placed the lockbox on the side near him. "A ghost."

"The normal offerings, then." Wellington smiled warmly. "I'd wondered where you'd gone off to so quickly. I sent a messenger to your flat the other day, but your landlady said you'd left in a hurry with Miss Brontë and a strange man."

"Yes, sir. There was an urgent matter at Thornfield. I received word that Miss Eyre was in danger, and we rushed to her aid."

"And is she safe now?" Wellington asked.

Alexander nodded. "She was forced to flee Rochester. You wouldn't believe what he'd attempted to do."

Wellington's face shifted into curious dread, exactly what Alexander would normally expect. "What?" he said. "Don't hold me in suspense. What was that nefarious villain going to do with Miss Eyre?"

"He was going to marry her. He had her possessed."

"Oh."

"The talisman was a—" Then, standing here in the library, a discussion of the pearl necklace rushed back at him. They'd spoken of it before. Here. Years ago. It had been the very set of pearls with which he'd captured that opera singer, Selene, and brought the string to the duke. So how had the pearls reached Rochester?

Unless.

Unless Wellington had given the pearls to Rowland; Rochester had called his brother Wellington's lackey.

"Oh." Wellington's expression fell. "I see the understanding on your face. You just remembered the pearls, didn't you?"

"What pearls?" Alexander said as he hopefully scanned the room for a weapon, but there was nothing within reach. "You've been lying to me all this time. You're a lying liar who lies."

Wellington sighed. "Of course I've been lying. I'm a politician."

"But why?" Alexander's heart sank as his whole world began to crumble apart.

"For money. For power. To silence those who try to move against me."

"Like my father?"

"Your father lacked vision, and then he decided to stop me, along with the foolish Rochesters. I had to take care of it."

And with those simple words, Alexander's entire world was shattered.

"Your father was the easy part. It was those Rochesters who've given me trouble all these years, even after I had him possessed and her locked away. But I don't need them anymore, now that I've got Miss Eyre."

"Have you got Miss Eyre?" They would have reached Haworth by now, Alexander thought. Unless Wellington had somehow intercepted them.

"No, but I soon will." And at that moment, Wellington bashed Alexander over the head with the lockbox. Stars popped in his vision, and blood poured from a gash. And though Alexander scrambled to fight, he went down quickly.

Over the next several moments, he drifted in and out of consciousness, aware just enough to realize he was being dragged through an unfamiliar hall—tinged bright red with blood leaking into his eye—before the stink of the river overwhelmed him.

"I hoped it wouldn't come to this," Wellington said. "I did care about you. I hoped you would see things my way, since I'm the one who raised you, but you're too much like your father."

Then, the traitor rolled Alexander over and dumped him into the Thames.

Alexander's last thought was this: *at least Miss Brontë and Miss Eyre are safe.*

TWENTY-EIGHT
Charlotte

"We're going in circles," observed Jane.

"We can't be." Charlotte lifted a hand to shield her eyes and gazed out at the windswept moors, which spread around them on all sides. There was no town or house or even the merest sign of human activity to mar the landscape. Not that Charlotte could actually see the landscape. Sometime during the scuffle back at Thornfield Hall, she'd misplaced her glasses. (We'd like to pause here to observe a moment of silence for Charlotte Brontë's tortoiseshell spectacles, which met their untimely demise when she'd dropped them as she was fleeing Thornfield and been subsequently stepped on by Mr. Rochester, inadvertently saving Alexander's life.) So all Charlotte saw of the moors was a reddish/goldish blur . . . and the unusually large rock that was jutting out of the hill on one side of them. "I know this moss-darkened granite crag may seem familiar," she said to reassure Jane, "but it's not the same moss-darkened granite crag we passed an hour ago. This is a different crag. I'm fairly certain of it."

Jane just stared at her. "Helen says she cannot go any farther," she said hoarsely. "She must rest."

Charlotte did not have the energy to point out that Helen was deceased and incorporeal and therefore could not rest more than she was already doing. But Charlotte's legs ached, and she could barely keep her eyes open. So she nodded, and the tragic little group stopped next to the familiar (yes, it was definitely the same one; she saw that now) moss-darkened granite crag and sat for a moment in the marshy grass.

How had they come to such a desolate place? Things had gone well enough, the first day. After fleeing Thornfield they'd walked until they'd reached a road, where a carriage had just happened to be passing by. They'd waved to it, and the driver had stopped. They'd asked where he was going, and he'd named a town not far from Haworth, where Charlotte had told Alexander to meet them. Haworth was Charlotte's home, sort of, even though she hadn't spent much time there, and it was safe, and Father and Bran would be there. The carriage driver said he'd take them for thirty shillings. Between them, Charlotte and Jane had been able to scrape together but twenty. On that meager amount, the driver had taken them as far as Whitcross, which was not a town but merely a place where four roads met at a crossroads. But it was reasonably close to Haworth, and Charlotte had assumed they could easily walk the rest of the way. And it would be quicker, she'd suggested, to go straight across the moors instead of taking the long way by road.

And so here they were. Lost and cold and in peril.

"Helen also says she's hungry," Jane reported.

Charlotte's stomach gurgled. She was no stranger to hunger—nor was Jane, she knew—but this hunger was beyond anything she'd ever experienced before. They had not eaten anything save a handful of questionable berries in the two days since they'd left Thornfield Hall. The first day, the hunger had been a sharp, persistent presence in her stomach. Now it had reached a state of floaty light-headed emptiness.

And like we said before, there was not a town in sight.

"I'm sorry we're lost," Charlotte said. "I have never had the keenest sense of direction."

"It's all right," murmured Jane. "At least I'm in possession of my own body. That's something. There are worse things than being lost."

Like starving to death, Charlotte thought. Or dying of exposure. Both of which seemed like a distinct possibility in the near future. This was why Charlotte had always considered herself an indoors type of girl.

Just then they all distinctly heard the faraway tolling of a bell. Charlotte and Jane both sat up.

"Helen says, 'What was that?'" said Jane.

"A church bell!" Charlotte gasped. "Could you tell what direction it was coming from?"

"This way." Jane took the lead this time, slogging through the heather in the direction of the sound. But after a moment the tolling stopped, and the only noise they could hear was the persistent voice of the wind, and still they could see no town.

"Blast!" said Charlotte. "We can't be far from Haworth."

"Helen says her feet hurt," said Jane.

Charlotte had a blister on her big toe. She was pretty sure Helen didn't have a blister on her big toe. She sighed. It was getting dark. Soon it would be very dark, and even colder than it was now. And from the looks of the growing bank of dark clouds overhead, it was going to rain.

She felt a drop on her face. Then another on the crown of her head. They'd gone off without their bonnets. She didn't even have the carpetbag with the broken handle. She closed her eyes and tilted her head up as the rain started to come down in earnest, willing herself to just breathe and try not to think of the very real danger they were in. She imagined Mr. Blackwood on a horse. Looking for them. Worried. Calling their names. Maybe he'd arrived at Haworth already. If so, he would have found them missing, and he'd be searching for them. Perhaps any moment now he'd find them.

But Mr. Blackwood wasn't here. She swallowed down a lump in her throat. This was, she realized, the kind of transforming experience that the great writers always wrote about. This might very well be the depths of despair. It must be documented.

That's when she realized that she'd left her notebook behind as well. This was the keenest loss of all. But then, she couldn't have written anything down, even if she'd had her notebook. She was still missing her glasses. And there wasn't enough feeling in her cold fingers to hold a pen.

"I'm sorry, Charlotte," she heard Jane say in a quavering voice.

She opened her eyes. Jane was standing in front of her, her hair and the entire upper part of her dress soaked with rain, her expression a picture of the same utter dejection that Charlotte had just been feeling. It was hard to tell, what with the rain, but Jane may have even been crying.

"Why are you sorry?" Charlotte asked. "I'm the one who got us lost."

"But this is all my fault," Jane said. "You wouldn't even be out here if it weren't for me. And now we could die."

"We're not going to die." But Charlotte's teeth were starting to chatter with cold.

"I've seen three ghosts out here already," Jane said. "All of them died not far from this very spot."

"Can you ask them the way to Haworth?" Charlotte closed the distance between Jane and herself and took Jane's chilly hand in hers. They tried to smile bravely at each other.

"Helen says being dead isn't really so bad."

"Helen," said Charlotte gently, "is not being terribly helpful."

Jane frowned. "Helen also says there's a light right behind you."

Charlotte spun around. The sky was darkening fast, night falling, but Jane was right—against a faraway hillside, like a welcoming star, there was a light, shining dim but distant through the rain. Or at least she thought she saw it. She couldn't see too well.

"Helen says we should go toward the light," Jane said.

They dragged their exhausted limbs slowly in that general direction. To get to the light they had to go through a bog. Charlotte kept tripping and falling in the mud, but Jane was always there to help her up. Together they struggled through the marshy ground and onto what turned out to be a road. A road! And the road led to a gate, and the gate led to a house, and at the door of the house Charlotte's legs stopped working and she sank down at the wet doorstep. She felt Jane's body come down beside her. Inside the house they heard voices.

"Well, I will admit it's nice to be home," said one, a girl's voice. "Even if it's only for a little while."

"How long do you think we'll get to stay?" said another, much younger girl's voice.

"The house will have to be sold," said the first. "We'll probably have until then."

Their voices were familiar. Charlotte had the mad thought that those sweet voices belonged to her sisters, Emily and Anne, which of course was impossible, as her sisters were still at Lowood. They were angels' voices, she decided.

"We should knock," croaked Jane.

But they were too exhausted.

"You knock, Helen," Charlotte said. But no knock sounded.

So for the moment they lay on the doorstep next to each other, getting more and more drenched by the rain, until there were

332

sudden footsteps on the path that led up to the door, followed by a muffled exclamation of surprise. And when Charlotte opened her eyes again, Bran's face was looming over hers.

She hadn't expected an angel to look like Bran.

"Charlie!" Bran cried. "And . . . Jane—Miss Eyre! What are you doing home?"

She gave a strangled laugh. They were still alive, apparently. And home. All this time wandering aimlessly and now she'd landed on her own front doorstep. She laughed again, then groaned.

"Em! Annie!" Bran called. "Come quick!"

The next few minutes went by in a blur. Emily and Anne— yes, her sisters were here—came running and helped Bran half carry, half drag both Jane and Charlotte into the house and in front of the parlor fire. Then Bran retreated to the kitchen while Charlotte's sisters retrieved fresh and dry clothes for the unfortunate pair. There was a thin soup spooned into their mouths. Blankets were wrapped around them. A spot of brandy administered. And after a while Charlotte found that she had recovered enough to talk.

"What are you doing here?" she asked Emily and Anne first off. She had a sinking feeling in her stomach that had nothing to do with hunger. Emily and Anne should be at Lowood. There was no reason for them to be here at Haworth unless . . .

"Father has died," Annie said gently.

"It was very sudden," said Emily. "His heart."

"He was buried yesterday. We would have sent for you, of course," said Bran, "but you weren't at Lowood, and I didn't know where to find you. You were supposed to go back to school, Charlie, after I left you at the train station. Why did you not go back?" He pressed his lips together in a way that reminded Charlotte of her father's scowl. Which made her chest hurt. She and Father had never been particularly close—he'd been a distant, almost cold figure for much of her life. But still, he'd been her father. And now he was gone.

"I was diverted," she said to Bran.

"Never mind," he said, patting her hand. "You're here now, aren't you?"

"Yes. I'm here now. And you're here. In charge of everything."

He nodded bravely. He seemed to have accepted this sudden change in his life's calling. A parson. The man who'd see to the religious needs of the community. She wouldn't have believed him capable of such a thing. But in a mere week since they'd parted ways at the train station, her brother seemed to have changed. He was sixteen now—he'd had his birthday, which she'd also missed. But he was looking and acting like he was twenty, at the least. Somehow, in the time since she'd last seen him, her brother had grown up.

"Have you heard from Mr. Blackwood?" she asked him.

"Mr. Blackwood?" Bran's expression tightened slightly like the mention of Mr. Blackwood still brought up embarrassing recollections of his time in the Society. "No. Should I have heard from Mr. Blackwood?"

"He distracted Mr. Rochester so that Jane and I could make

our escape," Charlotte explained. "He said he would meet us here."

"No, I have not seen him," Bran said.

A shiver made its way down Charlotte's spine, like a remnant from the cold she'd suffered on the moors. "Well. He should be here soon, then. We can expect him any time now."

A week passed, but Mr. Blackwood didn't arrive. The first few days Charlotte jumped at every footfall she heard outside, sure that he had finally come, but it never turned out to be the illustrious Mr. Blackwood. And slowly it began to dawn on her that something had gone wrong, to delay him so. Something had happened.

"Mr. Blackwood can handle himself," Bran kept telling her, but Charlotte still worried.

"He probably returned to London to report to the Society," Jane said as they were walking out in the garden.

"But he said he'd come find us," Charlotte argued. "He said, and I quote, 'I will find you.'"

Jane shrugged. She'd been a bit on edge these last few days. They all had. The entire company—Bran and Charlotte, Emily and Annie, Jane and even Helen, apparently, from what Jane reported— were all feeling a sense of impending doom. They were, at the very least, in for a change. The house at Haworth was going to have to be sold, as the sisters had been discussing the night Charlotte and Jane arrived. Their father had left them no inheritance to speak of. Just the parsonage, which Bran would be taking over.

So Emily and Anne were going to be sent back to Lowood. Charlotte couldn't bear the thought of returning, so she'd secured herself a teaching position in the town, which came with a tiny little room attached to the schoolhouse. It wasn't a very glamorous job. But it was something.

"I suppose I should search for another position as governess," Jane said now as they plodded along the garden path. She shuddered. "One that doesn't require references."

"For what it's worth I thought you were an excellent governess," Charlotte said.

Jane didn't answer. She was looking off into a patch of dead rosebushes, but she was seeing something else. Thornfield Hall, perhaps. Helen was still clearly hanging about Jane, but the true ghost that seemed to haunt Charlotte's friend was Mr. Rochester.

Breaking up is hard to do.

Charlotte kicked at a loose stone on the path. She hated the idea of Jane going off to another job somewhere and never seeing her again. She would have loved it if they could have all stayed on at Haworth—Emily and Annie and Bran and Jane—and played a happy family.

But it was not to be. "I'll only stay another week, two at most," Jane was saying now. "And then I'll be off to find a new adventure in child-rearing. Hooray."

"Hooray," Charlotte agreed faintly.

Behind them, a voice cleared gruffly. Jane and Charlotte turned to see Bran standing there. Charlotte lifted her glasses. (We know, we know, her tortoiseshell glasses were lost in the scuffle at Thornfield Hall, but Charlotte had discovered a spare, slightly-more-worn pair of spectacles in her dresser drawer in her room at

Haworth.) So at this moment she could see her brother perfectly well.

He was dressed in some of Father's nicer clothes, although the pants fit him poorly. And he'd attempted to tame his wild mane of red hair with a comb and some water. He pushed his glasses up on his nose.

"Hello, Charlie. Miss Eyre." He gave an awkward little bow.

"Uh, hello, Bran," said Charlotte. "What are you doing?"

He shifted from foot to foot. "I was wondering . . . if it wouldn't be too much trouble . . . if you'd be so kind . . . as to give me a private audience for a moment?"

"Huh?" Charlotte didn't get it.

"With Miss Eyre." Bran's face was getting paler and paler. His freckles stood out horribly. "There is something I wish to speak to her regarding."

It was silent for several heartbeats, as both Charlotte and Jane were genuinely confused as to what Bran could possibly want. Then Charlotte said, "All right, whatever you say, dear," and tromped off toward the house, leaving Jane and Bran alone in the garden. Well, mostly alone. She stopped after she'd gone a few paces and tried to listen in on their conversation. But the wind was blowing—as it always seemed to be blowing in this part of England—and she could only make out a few words. *Parsonage*—he definitely said the word *parsonage*. *Lowly parson. Duty. Family.* And . . . *love?*

That's when Jane came charging up the path, shaking her head. Bran trailed behind her, his voice pleading. "At least say you'll think about it."

"No!" Jane burst out. "I will not marry you, Mr. Brontë! I cannot believe you would have the gall to ask me! Not after everything that's happened!"

"But don't you see it would solve so many problems," he panted. "Jane! If we were to marry, you could stay on at Haworth. You'd have a place here. You'd have a family. If you don't marry me, where will you go?"

She stopped walking so fast he nearly crashed into her. She spun around and stuck her finger right in his face. "Do you love me?" she practically screamed.

"Well . . . no." His face had gone from pale to bright red. "But what's love got to do with it, in this day and age? Our marriage could be like an arrangement between friends. If you like we could live like brother and sister. . . ."

Jane got a frenzied look in her eyes. "Well, that's just the most romantic thing anyone has ever said to me. At least since the last idiot who followed it up with trying to kill me!" Then she literally screamed and pushed him away from her. She turned and fled back down the path and into the house. Charlotte heard the door slam, and then another slightly muffled scream of rage.

Charlotte discovered that her mouth was hanging open. She shut it. Turned to her stunned, woefully foolish younger brother, who was just staring after where Jane had gone.

"Well, that didn't go very well, did it?" She managed a sympathetic smile.

"She does not want to marry me," he remarked.

"Clearly. And that's hardly surprising. Considering what she's been through."

His flush grew deeper. "Oh, I know," he said sharply. "I'm strange-looking, and I'm clumsy, and I make a mess of everything. But I was trying to do her a kindness. She has no one to turn to. I thought . . ."

"I know. I heard what you thought." Charlotte walked over and stuck her arm through his, turning him to move away from the house. "It was very thoughtful of you, Bran. But a little thoughtless as well."

"I'm sorry," he bleated.

"Don't tell me. Tell her. But give her time to cool off first," she added quickly as they heard another bellow of rage from the house, this time followed by a crash of some kind.

They walked for a while without speaking. Gradually Bran's face returned to its regular color. He pushed his glasses up on his nose.

"I'm a fool," he said with a rueful laugh.

"Yes. But I think you're going to be a wonderful parson," she said.

His eyes brightened. "You really believe so?"

She laughed. "I believe so. I believe it with all of my heart."

Jane TWENTY-NINE

Jane now knew why they called it a broken heart. It was a physical pain in her chest. It was a malady as strong as influenza, and for the first few days, she wondered if it *was* an illness.

"Feel my forehead," she'd said to Charlotte many times. Charlotte humored her each time, but Jane never had a fever.

"He was an evil man who treated you terribly," Charlotte said.

"I know," Jane said. "It's just that my heart hasn't yet received that information."

Helen sighed. "If only our hearts had brains."

"And what if he's the only man who will ever fancy me? I'm poor and plain, with little to recommend me. He was supposed to be my hero out of a Jane Austen novel."

"There, there," Charlotte said, patting her hand.

"I always knew something was wrong with that man," Helen said. "I mean, I don't want to say I told you so—"

"Then don't!" Jane exclaimed.

Charlotte raised her eyebrows.

"Sorry, Helen was in the middle of saying she told me so."

"That's not helpful, Helen," Charlotte said.

"I wish Mr. Blackwood would hurry up and get here," Jane said.

"Me too," Charlotte said. "Purely for informational purposes. And not for any other . . ." She cleared her throat.

Jane glanced up to see Charlotte's face had turned red. "Charlotte, dear friend, do you have feelings for Mr. Blackwood?"

Charlotte put her spectacles to her eyes and became very interested in counting the books on the bookshelf.

"Charlotte?" Jane prodded.

"Well, I know you weren't particularly fond of Mr. Blackwood."

"That was before he saved my life! Tell me, friend, what are your feelings?"

Charlotte didn't get a chance to answer because of the sound of hoofbeats approaching. Someone was coming up the road. Charlotte leapt up from her chair. She met Jane's eyes.

"Do you think that could be . . . ?"

"Mr. Blackwood," Charlotte murmured.

There was a knock. Charlotte tucked a strand of her hair

behind her ear. She opened the door, already smiling, but then her smile faded.

Because it wasn't Mr. Blackwood standing at their doorstep. It was the Duke of Wellington.

Charlotte raised her glasses, and nodded to herself as if to confirm that yes, this man was indeed not Mr. Blackwood. Her face fell. "Sir, what brings you to Haworth at such an hour?" Charlotte said.

Wellington removed his hat and held it in his hands. "Miss Brontë, Mr. Brontë. And you are Miss Eyre, I presume. Good evening. I wish I could be here under better circumstances, but I'm afraid it is tragic tidings that bring me."

Jane felt a knot in her stomach, and Charlotte let her glasses droop for a moment, her face ashen.

"What is it?" Charlotte said breathlessly.

"It is about Mr. Blackwood." The duke's face was grim. "He is dead."

"No!" Charlotte exclaimed. She started to sink to the floor, but Bran dashed to her and helped her to the sofa. "That cannot be."

"So Mr. Rochester killed him?" Jane said.

"Yes. Yes, that is exactly what happened."

Jane found her own legs to be weak, and sank onto the sofa. Then Bran found his legs to be weak, and plopped down next to her.

"No, not Mr. Blackwood," Charlotte said, tears pricking at her eyes. "It is too unbelievable."

Wellington shook his head. "I still cannot believe it myself.

I'm sure you all gathered from my treatment of Alexander that I considered him very nearly my own son. I raised him."

Jane heard a sniffle, and turned to see Bran wiping his eyes.

Charlotte seemed to be trying every position of contorting her body in an effort to stanch the flow of inevitable tears. "Well, hmmm." She stood, and then sat, and then stood and then paced the small parlor. "Oh, dear." She put her glasses to her eyes, and then back down to her waist. She looked left, then right. "Shall I make some tea?" She started toward the stove but then bumped right into a table. "Mr. Blackwood loved his tea." Sniffle.

Then she sat on the floor and the tears began to flow. "The smoke from that fire seems particularly strong this morning." She stood up and reached for a poker.

Jane rushed to her side and gently urged the poker out of her hand, before Charlotte burned the whole house down.

"Charlotte, sit. There, next to Bran."

Charlotte's brother took her hand and held her close.

"Please, Your Grace, give us this time to collect ourselves," Jane said.

"Of course." The duke took a chair in a darkened corner of the room.

The Brontës and Jane held one another, and, as often happens with a grieving family, they took turns wiping away tears. Mr. Blackwood had been so brave, so strong, facing Rochester. Jane could not believe it had ended so. Especially at the hands of the man she'd been in love with.

Bran seemed distraught, but for Charlotte, linear thinking did not seem possible, like a train jolted from its tracks.

"Let's see, we need some tea," she would say.

"We have tea, dear," Jane answered.

"We must make up a bed for Mr. Blackwood, I am sure he will be here."

Jane would run her hand over Charlotte's hair. "He is not coming."

"I see. Yes, I know, Jane. I know."

And then the wind would cause a branch to make a scratching sound against the window and Charlotte would spring from her chair.

"Perhaps that is he." Then she would put her spectacles to her eyes and stare at nothing in particular, but the spectacles seemed to help her see things clearly: that Alexander Blackwood was not coming back.

After the news sank in, the duke once more approached the group.

Jane spoke for them. "Sir, this is the most grievous news. But why come to tell us in person? Is Rochester in custody? I am sure the Society has much work to do now."

"That's just it," Wellington said. "We do have much work, but we are down a few good agents."

He looked at Jane pointedly. She waited patiently for him to continue.

"Miss Eyre. Your service is required."

"Excuse me?"

"Your king and country need you. Your skills are undeniable. You can see ghosts, and you are a Beacon, which means you can influence ghosts."

"I'm a what?"

"A Beacon. It's a special kind of seer. Didn't Mr. Blackwood tell you?"

Charlotte raised her hand. "I started to tell her, but she was just so stubborn." She put a hand to her mouth. "I mean she was not in the right frame of mind to hear me."

The duke sighed. "Ghosts are attracted to Beacons, and they can also be influenced by them."

Helen snorted, then placed her finger on her cheek, thoughtfully. "Wait a second."

"Beacons are extremely rare. We've been looking for one for decades. We've found you, and who knows if we'll ever find one again. Please, you must return to London with me."

Jane stood still for a long moment. Helen came to her and studied each side of her face. "I think she'll speak yet," she said, as if she were a doctor diagnosing a patient.

Jane shook her head briskly. "Sir Duke, I believe you know I was recently possessed and almost married."

"Yes," Wellington said.

"And that I then spent days on the moors, starving and cold."

"I figured as much."

"And that I was recently proposed to again?"

Bran's cheeks went red.

"No, I hadn't heard that one."

Jane took a deep breath. "My point is, I believe I have been through enough for one lifetime, let alone one month of one lifetime."

Wellington frowned. "At least consider it. I implore you."

Bran looked at Jane. "It's what Mr. Blackwood would have wanted."

Jane sighed. She had only just begun to like Mr. Blackwood. She wasn't ready to change her life for it.

Charlotte dabbed a handkerchief to her eyes. Jane's feelings for her were an entirely different matter. "We have only just learned of Mr. Blackwood's death, sir. I need time."

"Very well. Miss Brontë, may I impose on your hospitality for a night?"

Charlotte nodded. "Of course. Anne? Emily?" The sisters appeared from the kitchen. "Would you take the duke's bag up to the guest room?" She emphasized the words *guest room* and Jane inferred it to mean, *quickly clear out your room and make it look like a guest room.*

Jane poured the duke a cup of tea, while Charlotte and Bran scurried about preparing for a guest.

"So, what do you think of my offer?" the duke said.

"It has not been nearly enough time for me to consider it."

"Right. Right."

They sipped in silence for a moment.

"I am so sorry about Mr. Blackwood," Jane said. "I did not know him as long, or as well, as you, but he will be missed."

"Yes," the duke said. "His absence will be felt for some time to come. In mourning him, my mind turns toward one thought."

"What is that?" Jane asked.

"How best to avenge his death. And the best way is with your help."

"Sir!" Jane exclaimed. "I will not be made to decide tonight. In fact, I believe this is the appropriate time to bid you good evening."

She went to rush out, just as Bran was coming in. "Did someone say *avenge*?" Bran asked.

"One last thought before you sleep on this, Miss Eyre," the duke said. Jane paused at the door. "There is but one way to make Alexander's death have any worth."

She closed her eyes and heaved a deep sigh. How did the task of avenging Mr. Blackwood's death end up at the feet of a poor plain orphan? Up until a few months ago, Jane's only concern was staying alive. Finding enough food. And now she was supposed to avenge a death?

"Good night, sir," Jane said. She made her way to her shared room with Charlotte. But before she got very far, she overheard Bran say, "If things are so dire at the Society, perhaps you need more seers."

As Jane and Charlotte (and Helen) lay in bed, Jane could hear sniffles coming from her friend.

"Charlotte, you must be in such pain."

"Truly, I am in as much pain as one would anticipate, upon learning an acquaintance has died. Yes, that is the amount of pain I am feeling. The expected amount. No more. No less." *Sniffle.*

"What did he mean when he said Beacon?" Helen said. "You can command ghosts?"

"Helen, please," Jane said. "Quiet."

"All right," Helen said. After a few moments, she whispered softly, "Wait, am I saying all right because you commanded me? Or because I want to be quiet?"

"I am not commanding you," Jane insisted.

"Have I ever made any decisions for myself?" Helen said. Charlotte sniffled loudly.

"Helen, please. Charlotte needs us right now."

"No, I don't," Charlotte said. "I hardly knew him."

"I'll be quiet, but that's because I want to," Helen said.

"Thank you," Jane said. She turned to Charlotte. "You did know him. You spent quite a bit of time with him."

"Only as much as propriety called for. No more. No less." She sniffed again and then blew her nose. "My, this room must be dustier than I am used to. I do believe it has gotten in my eyes."

"It's dusty?" Helen said. "Maybe you should command me to wipe it down."

Jane sighed loudly. She decided not to spend any more time convincing Helen she wasn't commanding her and convincing Charlotte that Mr. Blackwood had meant something to her.

* * *

Jane spent the restless night considering her choice. She was not interested in revenge. She was not interested in prestige. She was not even interested in the five thousand pounds.

But she was interested in her friend's broken heart.

The following morning, at tea, the duke shifted uncomfortably in his chair. And then he shifted some more. He took a sip of tea, which was too hot, and spit it out. He stood and walked to the window and stared out trying with all his might to appear calm and pensive. Charlotte and Bran bustled about trying to look busy.

"I'll go," Jane said, deciding to put him out of his misery.

The duke whirled around. "You will? Miss Eyre, you will not regret it. With your seer ability, and your Beacon ability . . . you will be a star."

"A star of what?" Jane said.

"Why, a star agent!"

Jane set her teacup down. "I don't have any desire to be a star anything. I only wish . . . well, you don't need to know my reasons."

The duke bowed his head.

"I will pack at once." Jane gazed at Charlotte and Bran, wishing she didn't have to part with the closest people to family she'd ever known. Then she looked to Helen, who had been sitting in the corner, arms folded, pouting. "Do you want to come with me?"

Helen shrugged. "You tell me."

"I'm asking you," Jane said. "Old friend. Dear friend."

Helen sighed. "Yes, I will come with you."

Jane turned back to the duke. "Where are we going?"

The duke smiled widely. "London."

THIRTY

Alexander

Alexander existed in pure agony for what felt like days. Weeks. Months. The cut on his head throbbed in time with his shuddering heartbeat, slowing as blood flowed out and out, into the dirty river.

Vaguely, in a faraway sense, he knew he had to climb out of the water. That he would drown if he slipped off the carriage door he'd managed to grab. It had been a frantic scramble as he'd heaved the top part of his body onto it, and already, his shirtsleeves were shredded from the ragged wood edges, and splinters dug into his cheek and neck where they pressed against the damp wood.

Still, he could feel himself slipping, gravity dragging him deeper into the river. Objects bumped against his legs and feet. Trash tangled around his limbs, drawing him off the carriage door. But when he tried to kick, to gain just a little momentum and haul himself farther out of the water, his body refused to obey. Whether that was from the cold or his body's slow betrayal, it was hard to tell.

I need to climb onto the bank, he thought, but his mind was so sluggish that the thought could hardly form at all. *I need to go after Wellington. I need to find Miss Brontë and Miss Eyre.*

But his body did not respond.

He floated on the door until the force of the earth, the river, and all the debris finally succeeded in drawing him down far enough that the door tipped.

And he slipped under.

"Welcome," whispered the ghosts who'd drowned here.

What Alexander did not see—could not see—were their eyeless forms, the shriveled echoes of their skin picked to shreds by fish. They reached for him, translucent fingers drifting through his ribs and face.

He didn't see them because he'd fallen unconscious again, but even without his guidance, his body fought for survival. His lungs held fast against the urge to breathe in. His mouth pressed tight against the temptation of falling open. Even as his blood pumped into the water and his body began to shut down from the lack of air, that human desire to live kept him going.

Until even that failed.

"Welcome," said the ghosts that surrounded him.

* * *

Suddenly, water whooshed away and air surged into his body.

He felt heavier as he was heaved onto solid ground, and half the Thames exited his lungs in a sputtery cough.

Rocks dug into his hip and shoulder, but he was definitely alive. When his breathing became steady, he was distantly aware of being lifted into strong arms and carried.

Reader, though Alexander spent much of this time barely aware of his surroundings, focused mainly on his heartbeat and the throbbing in his head, we feel confident in painting this picture for you. What we describe is based on separate accounts of no fewer than one hundred ghosts:

A tall, radiant woman had approached the water, her hair gleaming, her skin glowing. She'd drawn the attention of every single ghost in the Thames, which meant when she asked about a missing young man, they were able to lead the way.

Then she'd dived into the water and pulled him onto the shore, where she and a man made sure he was alive. Satisfied, the radiant woman lifted the young man into her arms and bore him into a building off the river.

"Will you stand guard for me?" she asked, and every single ghost scrambled to do her bidding. They ringed the building, ready to alert her at the slightest suspicious activity.

Gentle reader, by now you've probably guessed the woman's identity: Bertha Rochester. Indeed, she and Mr. Rochester had left Thornfield almost immediately upon reuniting, rushing to London to confront Wellington. Instead, Wellington had dumped

Alexander in the river, but it wasn't as bad as it could have been. Alexander, it seemed, was going to live.

Even so, he was mostly dead all day.

When Alexander finally came to, the sun was down and only a candle glowed in the warehouse where Mr. and Mrs. Rochester had taken him. He'd been stripped of his outer clothes and wrapped in layer after layer of blankets, but in spite of those attempts to warm him, chills still racked through his body. Probably from the blood loss, he realized. And his head felt light and floaty. Also probably from the blood loss.

But he seemed to be alive, so that was something, and Wellington wasn't there. More good news.

Both Rochesters were sitting with their heads bent together, discussing something in hushed tones, but when Alexander groaned, they looked up.

"You're safe," said Mr. Rochester. "And we won't be disturbed."

Alexander wasn't sure how comfortable he could feel with Mr. and Mrs. Rochester looking over him and offering assurances, as one had been possessed for years and the other had been locked in the attic. But the former seemed a changed man from the one Alexander had known during his time in Thornfield, and the latter was clear-eyed and clean.

"Wh—" Alexander's voice cracked, which would have been humiliating if he'd had the energy to be humiliated. Instead, he just closed his eyes and breathed through the exertion.

"I forgot to mention," Rochester said. "Wellington is evil."

Alexander groaned as he forced himself up, struggling to hide the fact that his head was swimming and his whole body hurt. "Thanks." His throat felt like it was on fire with the word, but he'd rested enough while he'd been mostly dead. "Thank you for coming to help me. Are you both well now?"

Mrs. Rochester cut a glance at Rochester, her expression darkening for a moment. She already seemed much better than any mere mortal had any right to be after being locked in an attic, but she hadn't forgotten. That much was clear. Her husband's face had been the face of her captor for so long, and no one overcame that overnight. "Perhaps not yet," she said at last, "but we will be."

"This may sound strange," said Rochester, "but are you the son of Nicholas—"

"Yes! Yes, he's my father. You knew him, right?"

"You look just like him."

"He was a good man," added Mrs. Rochester.

"I found a letter." Alexander patted his breast pocket, but it wasn't there. Nor was Miss Brontë's notebook; he'd stashed both in a secret location outside Westminster—a last-moment impulse. Now he was glad he had, or they'd have been drowned with him. "It seemed to indicate that you were at odds with Wellington."

Rochester nodded. "He was betraying everything the Society stood for."

"I was the only one of us who could see ghosts," Mrs.

Rochester said, "and because I am a Beacon, Wellington saw the most value in me. I was the closest to him. The star agent."

Alexander knew that feeling.

"In those days, I could use the Book of the Dead to help ghosts move on to the afterlife. We had a Collection Room, but it was only used by other agents who needed to drop off their talismans before going on their next assignment. Whenever I returned to London, Wellington and I usually spent a day or two releasing all the ghosts. But after a time, I began to notice Wellington kept some of the talismans. I asked about it only once."

"What did he say?" Alexander breathed.

"That he wanted to keep them for emergencies." Mrs. Rochester rubbed her temples, as though the memory still gave her a headache. "I never said anything to him again. I let him believe I understood. But I told Mr. Rochester, and I told your father."

Mr. Rochester touched his wife's shoulder. "After more investigation, we discovered that some of the ghosts Mrs. Rochester and other agents had captured—they had worked for the Society before they died. That was the travesty we wanted to deal with."

A chill ran up Alexander's spine, like someone had just stepped on his grave. "David Mitten is dead. I captured him for Wellington just earlier this month."

"It was soon after we began tracking the deaths in the Society that your father died. Then Rowland took possession of me, and then locked Mrs. Rochester in the attic, hoping we might be useful again one day." Rochester's voice shook slightly.

Mrs. Rochester closed her eyes and reached for her husband's hand. "Mr. Blackwood, do you know what Wellington was doing with the ghosts he didn't take to the Move-On Room?"

Alexander shook his head, but a sense of doom niggled at him.

"The duke is ambitious," said Rochester. "He was always power-hungry."

Alexander's mind still felt full of river water, so the answer didn't come as quickly as it might otherwise.

"He had George IV possessed," Mrs. Rochester said. "The king was under Wellington's control—at least until he died and William ascended the throne."

"Oh." Alexander recalled the David Mitten job again. The ghost who wanted to be captured. The signet ring. Wellington's urgency. "Good God," he muttered. "He's going to have Mr. Mitten possess the King of England."

THIRTY-ONE
Charlotte

Charlotte stared up at the ceiling, unable to sleep. At Lowood, she'd slept lined up in rows with at least thirty others girls, and she'd fallen asleep each night to a chorus of their fretful sighs and gurgles. At Haworth she'd had her own more comfortable bed to rest in, a quilt her mother had sewn for her, and her sisters all cozy in the same room. When they couldn't sleep they'd told one another stories, whispered tales of dragons and the handsome knights who arrived to slay them. And after her sisters had gone back to school, Jane had taken Emily's bed. Jane had snored a little. (Don't tell her. It was hardly snoring. It was very delicate.) Charlotte had found the sound immensely comforting. But now everyone had gone: Bran to the parsonage, Emily and Anne to Lowood, Jane to London on some vastly important mission for the Society, and Charlotte found herself in a squeaky little bed in the teacher's cottage in the village. Alone. No one had ever been so alone, she thought.

And Mr. Blackwood was dead.

She turned onto her side. A tear rolled across her nose and dropped soundlessly onto the pillow, which was already quite damp.

Mr. Blackwood was *dead*. Part of her would not believe it. How could Mr. Rochester have bested him? How had it happened? How was it possible that she would never see him again?

She stifled a sob. She'd never see him walk that way he did when he meant business, his strides long and his shoulders thrown back, his black coat billowing out behind.

She'd never see the glitter of determination in his dark eyes.

He'd never again offer his hand to help her down from the carriage.

He'd never make tea. Or catch a ghost. Or play charades. Or argue with her.

He'd never say, "Go home, Miss Brontë."

The tears flowed freely now. It was aggravating, the way she could not seem to stop herself crying over Alexander Blackwood. He was just a boy, wasn't he? They'd had no attachment to speak of. What she'd felt for Mr. Blackwood hadn't been romance, as Charlotte had previously defined romance. There had been no stolen glances—not that she would have been able to see them. No flirtations. No tortured yearning of her soul, the way Jane felt for Mr. Rochester. No, between Charlotte and Alexander there had only been the highest level of regard, a camaraderie, a mutual enjoyment of each other's company. But when she'd heard Mr. Wellesley say that Mr. Blackwood had been killed, something had seemed to break inside her, and it remained broken day after day. So she wept, and after the tears came a fierce ache in her chest, even worse than the crying.

Our Charlotte was floundering in the true depths of despair, dear reader, although this time she felt no urge to write about it. This time it felt like she could clearly see her entire life stretched before her, and it was a lonely life, a tragic one, where the people she loved all died, first her mother, her two older sisters, then her father, now Mr. Blackwood, and soon perhaps her sisters would succumb to the Graveyard Disease at school—Anne was always coughing these days, Emily looked pale—and Bran was so accident-prone, something could happen, and then she'd be alone forever. Or maybe she'd die young, too.

She wiped her eyes. It was absurd, but what she wished for most right now was the ability to simply speak to Mr. Blackwood again. *You should tell Mr. Blackwood all that's happened,* some wayward part of her brain kept insisting. She had numerous questions she'd like to ask him. What was his opinion, for instance, on the silly way that she kept crying over him?

She took a shuddering breath. Crying, she told herself sternly, does not indicate that you are weak. Since birth, it has always been a sign that you are alive.

The shutters rattled. Outside an October storm was blowing

in. The wind was escalating into a howl, an eerie, lonesome sound. When she was a little girl that Yorkshire wind had frightened her. She'd known it was only the wind, but her overactive imagination had produced a theory that the sound was the ghosts of England's past, a menagerie of the dead stretching back through history, all of them come to bang at her window. But she hadn't known about ghosts then. She'd never seen a ghost, but what Charlotte had gleaned from this whole Society experience was that ghosts were just like regular people, with typical thoughts and feelings. They were dead, was all. It was almost like nothing else had changed. If you could see them, that is.

Wait. Hold on.

Charlotte sat up. She thought she might cry again, but what came out was a hoarse laugh. Then she scrambled out of bed and hurriedly began to dress. She'd had an idea, and this was the kind of idea that really couldn't wait until morning.

"Bran!" Charlotte banged on the door of the parsonage again. The wind whipped her loose hair into her face. "Wake up, Bran!"

She heard footsteps on the stairs. Then the door opened a crack and a face appeared—her brother's, she assumed, although she couldn't see; her glasses were streaked with rain.

"Charlie!" he exclaimed.

"I have asked you repeatedly not to call me Charlie," she chided as he ushered her inside.

"Well, you look like a madwoman," he observed, a hint of

worry in his voice, like he was considering that she might, in fact, have gone mad at last. "It's the middle of the night."

"I'm aware of what time it is, Bran." Charlotte cleaned her glasses on his nightshirt and lifted them to her face. Bran's red hair was sticking straight out to one side and there was a pillow crease in his cheek. His eyes were only half open. His own glasses were terribly smudged, so she grabbed them and cleaned them, too. Then she went up to his room, pulled his battered old suitcase from under his bed, and started packing his things for a journey.

"Charlie, am I going somewhere?" he asked from the doorway.

"We. We are going somewhere." She closed the suitcase and straightened. "You have a horse, right? Father's horse?"

Bran was shaking his head. "I have a horse, but I can't leave. I'm the parson now. The townspeople need me."

"I need you," she said. "They'll get by."

"What if someone dies and needs a funeral? Or wants to get married? Or needs me to pray over a sick child? And I have a sermon to give."

Charlotte gave her brother a Look. They both knew nobody was going to miss his sermons.

"Oh, all right." He sighed. He'd learned over the years not to cross Charlotte when she had her mind set on something. "Where are we going?"

"Why, to Thornfield Hall, of course," she said as if it was most obvious.

Bran frowned. "Thornfield Hall? What for?"

"To learn what happened, firsthand. Which is why I need you, brother."

"Why . . . do you need me?" he asked.

"To talk to Mr. Blackwood." She couldn't help a hopeful smile. "Because you'll be able to see him, and I won't."

Bran gasped. "Of course! Alexander could be a ghost!" He was finally catching on.

Charlotte nodded. "We'll find out what happened with Rochester. I suppose we'll have to be careful, since Rochester is probably still there. But we'll locate Mr. Blackwood, and you'll talk to him. And he'll . . ." Her voice wavered with the blasted tears. "He'll tell us what to do."

She could see by his expression that Bran didn't think this was the wisest idea. But he didn't argue. Instead, he went to the desk in the corner and wrote a note to post on the parsonage door, to the people of the village, explaining that he'd be back shortly.

"We will be back shortly, won't we?" he asked her.

She had no idea when they'd be back. It all depended on what they discovered when they got to their destination. "Of course," she answered. "We'll be back before you know it."

They reached Thornfield Hall a day or so later, only to find the great house in total ruin. There'd obviously been a fire—the stones were black and the smell of smoke was heavy in the air. The front of the house was still standing, but it looked fragile, as if the wind would momentarily blow it in. All the windowpanes were smashed, and the roof had collapsed. All that remained of the once grand and imposing structure was a wrecked shell.

Bran and Charlotte stood looking at the place, silently horrified. Then Charlotte whispered, "Find him, Bran," and they picked their way around the edges of the house, Bran calling out, "Mr. Blackwood! Are you there? We'd like to speak with you, Mr. Blackwood."

Charlotte's heart beat madly the entire time. On the journey, she'd composed a little speech she'd give to Mr. Blackwood, which went something like this:

Mr. Blackwood. Alexander. I would like to inform you that you are (you were, I suppose, so sorry) the keenest, most attractive, most intelligent and thoroughly engaging boy that I have ever met, and I am filled with sorrow on account of your untimely demise.

And then she'd ask her numerous questions about his death and Mr. Rochester and what they could do to bring the nefarious villain to justice.

But Mr. Blackwood never appeared. Bran called and called for more than an hour, and Charlotte joined him, but Bran couldn't perceive any ghostly presence at Thornfield Hall. Not a single spirit came out to meet them.

It was the greatest disappointment yet.

"I'm sorry, Charlie," Bran said as they trudged back to where the horse was grazing.

"It's quite all right." She didn't cry this time. "Obviously Mr. Blackwood has moved on. He's in a better place now. I wouldn't wish him to be a ghost just so I could . . ." She swallowed. "I'm glad for him."

"I'm sorry, Charlie," Bran said again, slinging his arm around her.

"Thank you, Bran. Let's go home."

They got a room for the night at the nearest inn. At dinnertime, they walked to the local pub and Charlotte gathered information regarding the ruin of Thornfield Hall. It was hard to get a straight story from anyone—the rumors abounded. After an hour of interviews with the local townspeople, this is what Charlotte had been able to ascertain:

Mr. Rochester had his wife locked up in the attic. (She knew that, of course.)

Mr. Rochester had tried to marry his governess, but it had all gone afoul when it was discovered that he had his wife locked up in the attic. (She knew that, too. Firsthand.)

People felt very sorry for Mr. Rochester and held a lot of mixed but largely negative opinions about this Jane Eyre person—who had reached above her station, who had deliberately set to entangle poor Mr. Rochester, a treacherous Eve type, she was, a tempting siren, but also small and plain and utterly unremarkable in every way. (Charlotte held her tongue. Barely.)

The events that followed were thus:

Mr. Rochester had gone a bit mad, after his failed attempt at bigamy, and he'd lit his own house on fire, killing everyone inside: Rochester, the wife, and the girl, all together.

OR

Mr. Rochester had burned his house down in order to dispose of his wife, and then he and the girl had gone to live in the South of France.

OR

The wife had set the place on fire, and succeeded in doing away with both herself and Mr. Rochester. No one knew what had become of the girl. But Mr. Rochester was most certainly dead.

OR

Mr. Rochester was most certainly alive. He'd nobly tried to save his wife from the fire, but she'd leapt to her death from the roof of the house. Mr. Rochester had been trapped in the inferno, and part of the house had collapsed upon him, but he'd been pulled out very much alive.

BUT

He'd lost one eye and the vision in the other, therefore being made totally blind. Helpless as a wee lamb. A beggar on the streets of London now. Very sad.

OR

His hand was crushed and had to be amputated. Now he had a hook and had been last seen applying for the job of a pirate.

OR

All of the above. (Somehow.)

As a storyteller, Charlotte liked the "nobly trying to save his wife" version of the tale best. It felt like the proper ending to redeem a man (sort of). But none of the townspeople had any knowledge whatsoever of a Mr. Blackwood. It was impossible to tell, under these circumstances, if Mr. Rochester was alive or dead or possibly a pirate. And she was no closer to finding out what had transpired with Mr. Blackwood.

"He's not dead," Bran said suddenly.

"You think so? Is he a pirate, then? Or a beggar? A pirate is a bit far-fetched, in my opinion. Just because one loses a hand doesn't make a person qualified for piracy."

"Not Rochester. Mr. Blackwood." Bran was staring at an empty space just past Charlotte's right shoulder.

Her breath left her. "Mr. Blackwood's not dead?"

Bran shushed her. "I'm trying to listen. To the ghost."

"The ghost?"

"The one standing right behind you. Mr. Rochester."

Charlotte glanced behind her, but of course saw nothing. "You're talking to Mr. Rochester? So he died in the fire, after all?"

Bran shook his head. "Mr. Rochester, it turns out, was possessed by a ghost. Apparently he's not a bad fellow at all, but was being held a prisoner in his own body."

"By whom?"

"By Mr. Rochester."

Charlotte frowned.

"The ghost of his older brother," Bran clarified. "During his clash with Mr. Rochester, Mr. Blackwood discovered the possession and was able to separate the man from his talisman, thereby releasing Mr. Rochester from his spiritual bondage."

"That sounds just like Mr. Blackwood," Charlotte agreed.

"Afterward, Mr. Blackwood departed for London."

Charlotte was crying again. She pulled out a handkerchief. "Thank heavens. But how, then, was the house destroyed?"

"Grace Poole, who was also apparently employed by Mr. Rochester—the evil one, I mean—burned down the house in an attempt to do away with the Rochesters, but they had already escaped."

"But I thought you said Mr. Rochester was a ghost? The one speaking to you, in fact."

"Oh. No." Bran smiled apologetically. "The ghost who is speaking to me now is also a Mr. Rochester, but not *the* Mr. Rochester. This is Mr. Rochester the eldest, our Mr. Rochester's father. He's been haunting this pub for years, apparently, ever since Mr. Rochester, the brother, died and took possession of Mr. Rochester—the one we know."

There were, in Charlotte's opinion, entirely too many Mr. Rochesters. But that was of no matter. Mr. Blackwood was alive! In London! She blew her nose, put her handkerchief away, and stood up.

"Well done, Bran," she said to her brother. "Excellent job ferreting out all of this vital information. Now we should go."

"To London, I suppose," Bran said faintly. "To find Mr. Blackwood."

"To find Mr. Blackwood," Charlotte said, beaming. "And to

talk to Jane. The story this ghost has told you does not match up at all with the Duke of Wellington's account. I fear that Jane is being led astray. She could be in danger. We need to get to the bottom of the matter immediately."

"All right," sighed Bran. "I'll get the horse."

Upon arriving in London, they went straightaway to Mr. Blackwood's flat, only to find that Mr. Blackwood was no longer residing there. A young lady had moved in, the neighbors reported. A small young woman, they said. Plain. Utterly unremarkable in every way.

They stood idly across the street for several hours waiting for Jane. Presently she arrived in a carriage that bore the crest of the Society on the door. She had a large garment bag draped over her arm and a strained expression, as if she was bravely facing up to an unpleasant chore. She ascended the stairs to the flat and disappeared. Charlotte and Bran crossed the street as if to follow, but at the last moment a cloaked figure darted out from an alleyway and pulled them both into the shadows.

Charlotte was about to scream, but the man clapped his hand over her mouth. "It's me," he whispered urgently. He held his other hand out to Bran, who'd just taken a wild swing at him. "It's me, Branwell! I must speak with you." He threw back the hood to reveal his face.

It was Mr. Blackwood. Trembling, Charlotte lifted her glasses to her eyes and drank in the sight of him. His appearance was more unkempt than usual: his clothing rumpled, his dark hair tousled, his face unshaven. He even smelled a bit like the docks. But Charlotte threw her arms around him. "Oh, Mr. Blackwood," she cried. "I am so . . . pleased to see you again. We were told you were dead."

"Wellington tried to kill me," he affirmed. All at once they both became aware that they were holding each other. Mr. Blackwood gazed down into Charlotte's face, the corner of his mouth tucking up into a smile. "He failed, obviously. I am . . . pleased to see you as well, Miss Brontë."

Charlotte nodded mutely. For a moment neither of them spoke.

"I saw the ghost of Mr. Rochester," Bran announced proudly. "He told me you'd be in London, and here you are."

Charlotte and Mr. Blackwood stepped away from each other. Mr. Blackwood frowned. "The ghost of Mr. Rochester? How's that? I saw Mr. Rochester alive and well but an hour ago. He and Mrs. Rochester saved my life."

"He means the ghost of the senior Mr. Rochester," Charlotte explained. "Mr. Rochester's father. I know. It's confusing."

"Oh. Well, yes, here I am. In London," Mr. Blackwood said, although he didn't seem entirely pleased about it. "Unfortunately, I cannot say I've made much progress in my new mission to foil the duke's plans and avenge my father's death. And it seems that Wellington has replaced me with Miss Eyre in order to accomplish his schemes."

"So Wellington is the true villain?" Charlotte thought this was a marvelous twist in her story. And also, of course, terrible news.

"The most nefarious," Mr. Blackwood muttered. "We believe he means to possess the king. I've been trying to get to Miss Eyre, to warn her, but she's always shadowed by the Society." He jerked his head to one side to indicate a pair of large, surly looking fellows lurking on the corner just outside of Mr. Blackwood's former flat.

"I could warn her," Charlotte volunteered. "Wellington doesn't know that I know of his treachery. I could simply pay a visit to Jane. A social visit. She is my dear friend, after all. What do friends do if not visit each other from time to time?"

"That would be most helpful," Mr. Blackwood said.

Charlotte blushed. "I'll go right now."

Before she could take a step, however, the door to Mr. Blackwood's former flat opened and Jane popped out in what was possibly the most extravagant gown that Charlotte had ever beheld. The entire dress was simply huge. Jane teetered dangerously several times as she made her way down the stairs, but always managed to catch herself. At the bottom she straightened her hat—the same rose hue as the dress with several bows and a large white feather sticking out the front. Then she pulled up the edge of one elbow-length white glove, and squeezed herself through the door into the waiting Society carriage.

The two surly looking fellows stepped up onto the back of the carriage.

"To Saint James's Palace?" the driver asked, and one of the surly men confirmed the address.

"This is it," Mr. Blackwood whispered urgently. "She's going to the king. We have to stop her."

The driver cracked his whip, and the carriage pulled away. They watched it helplessly as it swiftly disappeared around a corner.

"Well then, it's a fine night to pay a visit to the palace, wouldn't you say?" Charlotte suggested.

A muscle ticked in Mr. Blackwood's jaw. "Yes," he said. "A very fine night, indeed."

Jane THIRTY-TWO

According to Wellington, the entire future of the Society came down to the success (or failure) of Jane's mission tonight. Of course, the pressure might have been exacerbated by the dress. Can we talk about the dress? First off, the sheer weight of the thing. Jane was a slight person, yes, but surely even the tallest and stoutest of women would be bothered by the heaviness of the gown. Second, the corset. Jane had found a book on the proper way to string a corset, and the gist of it was this: tighten it until you could barely breathe. Then you were halfway there. Since she was dressing herself, she tied two ends to a bedpost and walked forward to tighten it. But then the bedpost broke, and when the neighbor came over to see what the ruckus was, Jane implored her to tighten the corset for her.

Her neighbor acquiesced and then left her with this piece of advice: "Friends don't let friends corset alone."

Next, there were the sleeves. They extended at least four inches out on either side of Jane's small shoulders, making it impossible for one to walk through a doorway without turning sideways. And then there were the shoulders. Which were bare. As in, showing. Jane fought the urge to cover them with something else, something inconspicuous, something like . . . shrubbery.

Then there was the crinoline, which was a steel-constructed dome-shaped attachment that replaced layers and layers of skirts. It was supposed to make using a chamber pot easier, but Jane wondered what good that would do when the entire dress would prevent her from being able to enter the room with the chamber pot, let alone use it. At her wrist hung a drawstring handbag, inside of which was a mysterious book Wellesley called the Book of the Dead. It was supposed to help her in her mission tonight. It hung awkwardly, but excepting some sort of contraption that would hold it under the crinoline, her wrist really was the best option.

There was only one conclusion Jane could draw from the style and design of the dress and it was this: it had to be thought up by men. Then women could in no way outrun them, and with the lack of oxygen to the brain due to a rib cage the size of a fist, they could not outthink them. And with the bright colors, they couldn't hide. No running, no thinking, no hiding.

But she had given her word to Wellington, and her silent word to Charlotte, that she would do this work. And Wellington insisted that this outfit was an appropriate one for visiting a palace.

Which she was about to, for the first time in her very plain and simple life. The carriage was bound for Saint James's Palace, where, apparently, the king required a bit of help with a wayward ghost, and where Jane was also tasked with returning a signet ring.

The king was reluctant to call for the Society, but it was a particularly obnoxious ghost who had been rattling the royal shrubbery and knocking over the royal vases. Fun fact: it was the same ghost that was responsible for the "madness" of King George. Asking for help was the first step.

The second step was to squeeze oneself into a ridiculous dress, Jane thought. The third step was to save the Society.

Jane felt uncomfortable carrying the weight of the Society's future on her very small shoulders, especially since she had no experience and no training, but the duke was convinced that the fact that she was a Beacon would make up for everything else, and the financial situation of the Society was of the utmost urgency.

She didn't want to be here.

She didn't want to be here.

But she *was* here, and it was all for Charlotte, she reminded herself.

The carriage bumped and jostled along the road, and Jane wished she actually were wearing lots of skirts instead of a steel crinoline. At least there would've been some cushioning.

One of her guards from the Society sat across from her, his back to the horse side, as was the protocol. He did not look to be in the mood to talk, which was just fine with Jane. Helen sat next to him, staring at Jane and The Dress and The Bows.

"You look like a court jester," she said.

"Thank you," Jane said.

"You're welcome," Helen responded. Helen was still grappling with the fact of Jane's being a Beacon. She routinely questioned every single one of her actions.

"Am I walking across the room because you want me to?" she would say.

"Don't be silly, dear," Jane would say.

"All right. Am I not being silly because you don't want me to be silly??"

It was rather exhausting.

The carriage descended upon the palace, and Jane got out and walked slowly up the stairs, because walking slowly was all she could do in the dress. The king was having a ball tonight, and only the elite could gain entrance. This was the most distressing part of all, for Jane was not educated in the ways of high society. She wished she were wearing a Society mask right now, but the king had asked for the utmost discretion. He did not want to scare his dinner guests.

"Miss Jane Eyre," she said to the guard at the entrance.

"Of where?" the guard replied.

"Lowood . . . Estate."

"Miss Jane Eyre, of the Lowood Estate."

Upon entering the palace, Jane curtsied to the king, just as she'd practiced. The king noted her dress, counting the bows, Jane guessed. The duke had sent word to the king that he would recognize Jane by the number of bows on her dress.

The king nodded at her, held her gaze for a split second and then dismissed her with a wave of his hand. Jane assumed he would send for her at his convenience.

She hoped it would be sooner rather than later.

The evening was horribly long. Not being properly acquainted with anyone, and therefore not being able to make conversation with anyone, Jane went around the room pretending she had seen someone she had recognized and was on her way to meet up with them, but the result was that she just wandered back and forth with an expectant smile on her face that never actually landed on anyone. And do you realize, reader, how hard it is to not smile at anyone in particular when you are in a room crowded with faces?

At least Helen was there, but it wasn't really the same as having company since Jane couldn't talk to Helen in public. Exhausted, Jane sidled out of the great room and found a small dark alcove, in which she decided to catch her breath, and totally not hide, because she was an agent and hiding would be cowardly.

"Miss Eyre," a king's guard said.

Helen made a move to elbow Jane in the ribs.

"Oh, yes, I was just admiring the . . . darkness."

The guard said nothing.

"It's lovely, in a palace. The darkness. So much more elegant than . . . regular darkness."

"Good recovery," Helen said.

"Follow me." The guard turned abruptly, and Jane scurried (as much as one could scurry in that dress) to keep up.

She followed the guard down a series of corridors, and ended up in a room that was comparatively smaller than the others she'd seen so far, but still big. Behind an ornate desk stood a wall of ornate robes, and on top of those robes rested long, curly brown locks of hair, and behind all that, Jane assumed, was the king. He started to turn around, and quickly Jane darted forward and placed the signet ring on the desk. She was back in position a moment before he saw her.

She immediately curtsied and didn't speak.

"You are from the Society?" the king said.

"Yes, Your Majesty." Jane raised her gaze to meet the king's. That was when she saw him. The ghost. Standing next to the king. One hand on his hip, just like the king.

"I am not fond of the Society," the king said.

"And I am the King of Prussia," the ghost said.

Jane tried not to smile.

"I do not believe in this ghost nonsense," the king said, waving his hand as if brushing a fly away.

"Nor do I," the ghost said, waving his hand as well.

Helen snorted. "He's funny."

The ghost then seemed to notice Jane for the first time, and a wide smile broke out on his face. "My, aren't you a stunning creature. Tell me, have you ever been with a king?"

Jane's cheeks went red.

"Oh my," Helen said.

"Sire," Jane started.

"Yes?" the king and the ghost said simultaneously.

"I can help you." She pulled a talisman out of her satchel. It was a brooch that Wellington said most likely belonged to the tree ghost's beloved grandmother. "But before I do, I need you to do something for me."

The attendants in the room looked to one another uncomfortably.

"Anything," the ghost said.

Jane ignored him. "You must know what a help and comfort the Society can be, especially given your current predicament."

"You are quite overbearing for someone so poor and plain," the king said.

"Who are you calling poor?" Helen said, gesturing to the myriad bows adorning Jane's ridiculous dress. "She makes five thousand pounds a year."

"I can be," Jane admitted. "Please permit me to help you see the existence of ghosts."

The king narrowed his eyes. "You mean you wish me to believe. It's not that I don't believe in ghosts. I just didn't understand how bothersome they could be, until this one came along."

The tree ghost bowed.

"Would it help to talk to him yourself? I can show him to you." She took the Book of the Dead out of her satchel and set it on the desk. She opened it to a page she'd had tagged and read the words as Helen ducked behind her. When she had finished, the king glanced around the room, noticing nothing out of the ordinary, until he looked behind him.

There was the tree ghost, glancing around the room as well.

"I see no one," the tree ghost said.

The king startled at hearing the ghost, and stepped backward.

"This is madness," said the ghost. He glided over to Jane. "I would have you detained were it not for your extraordinary beauty."

The king went from looking surprised to looking rather puzzled. He shook his head and approached the tree ghost.

"You, sir, must leave the palace at once."

"Why would I leave my home?" the ghost said.

The king closed his eyes and took a deep breath. When he opened them, he seemed much more calm. "There is a better place for you."

The ghost scoffed. "Better than a palace?"

The king nodded. "Better than a palace."

"I don't believe you. Off with his head!" The ghost flicked his hand toward the king.

The king took a step closer. "I understand you feel an attachment to this place. But you are not meant to be here, walking the grounds as a spirit."

Suddenly, Helen stepped forward, and the king noticed her for the first time.

"Forgive me, Sire," Jane said. "This is my . . . companion. She is also a ghost."

Helen stared at the king. "What do you mean, he is not meant to stay here?" Helen asked.

"Sire," Jane whispered. "Say 'Sire.'"

"Sire," Helen said.

The king waved his hand as if she shouldn't be concerned about such things. Now that he had seen ghosts for himself, protocols seemed unimportant. "He is a spirit," the king said. "Spirits are meant to move on to the next life, whatever that may be."

"I would not mind staying with her," the tree ghost said, raising his eyebrows and looking at Jane.

Before anyone could look surprised again, Jane spoke up.

"I am what's known as a Beacon," Jane said. "Ghosts are attracted to me."

To give the king credit, he hid his surprise well.

"You can come with me," Jane said to the ghost. "I can help you move on."

"Why is moving on so good?" Helen said. "Especially if you don't even know where moving on goes?"

"Helen," Jane whispered.

The king waved his hand again. "Because it's supposed to happen that way. We must believe that the god who put us here, with families and companions and food and beauty . . . he has a place for us when we are no longer living. We must have this faith. The faith that we will again be with those we've lost. But you won't discover this promise if you linger here among the living."

Jane relaxed. She hadn't had an explanation for what awaited the spirits moving on. She hadn't wanted to dwell on the thought.

Then she looked at Helen, who was staring at her with a pained expression.

Perhaps she was looking at the why.

"Ghost," the king said. "Would you like to say farewell now? And follow Miss Eyre? She will take you where you need to go."

The ghost frowned but then bowed. "I shall follow the instructions of my top advisor. Thank you, good fellow." He went to pat the king on the back, and actually made contact, his emotions were so strong.

"Excellent," the king said with a cough. "Miss Eyre, you will guide him from here?"

"Yes, Sire."

Jane spared one last glance at the ring on the king's desk, and figuring her mission was accomplished, walked out with the tree ghost and Helen in tow.

Once in the hallway, Helen stood in front of Jane, and had she been a solid human instead of a ghost, she would have prevented Jane from walking. Still, Jane stopped.

"Why am I here?" she said, her hand on her hip.

"Because you wanted to come to the palace with me," Jane said.

"That's not what I mean."

Jane had a sinking feeling she knew what Helen meant.

"Why are you helping ghosts to move on to the place we are supposed to move on to, and yet I stay? With you?"

"I don't know, dear," Jane said. "But maybe it is because I need my closest friend, and she needs me. Are you not happy?"

Helen frowned and her lower lip trembled. "I don't know. I don't know if happiness exists for ghosts here."

"That can't be," Jane implored. "I've seen you happy."

Helen sniffed. "But what if that's simply a reflection of you? You're a Beacon. I'm a ghost. Is that why I have stayed?" She raised her voice. "Is that why I linger?"

Jane glanced around to see if they had drawn attention, but there were only uninterested guards in this corridor. And, also, Helen was a ghost.

"Helen, please. You saved me at Lowood. You are my kindred. I can't imagine a life here without you."

Helen frowned. "But maybe you are meant to live it without me."

She turned and ran down the corridor, and Jane would have followed but it was definitely against royal protocol for a woman in a dress and heels to run. And she had the tree ghost now.

"Follow me," she said.

It was a long walk back to the ballroom and then down the stairs and then to the entrance of the palace, and during the walk, all Jane could think about was Helen. She would not leave Helen. Helen needed Jane as much as Jane needed Helen. Helen was an anchor. A lighthouse. A compass, showing Jane the better way.

Sure, she was still a bit naïve. And she hadn't progressed emotionally or intellectually, as Jane had. But she was a ghost. And that was fine.

But what if she left?

The tree ghost stayed close by Jane's side as they approached the grand doors. Jane held the talisman at the ready if he suddenly decided to bolt, but he didn't. "Where did your friend go?" he said.

"I don't know," Jane whispered, not moving her mouth because there were people around.

"Is she coming back?"

Jane didn't answer. She didn't want to think about the possibility that she would never see Helen again.

The guards heaved the doors open, and suddenly Helen came rushing in.

"Jane!" she said.

"Helen!" Jane replied, causing the guards to look at her with confusion. Jane quickly turned around and motioned Helen to follow her. "I knew you wouldn't leave me."

"It's not that," Helen said. "I saw Mr. Blackwood!"

"His ghost?" Jane said.

"No, him! He's alive. He said the duke is bad. He has a message for you." She ticked off her pointer finger as if she wanted to get the message perfectly correct. "He said don't put the ring in the king's study, because the duke wants to possess him. Phew." She put her hand to her stomach and took several deep breaths in. "That's it."

"Wait," Jane said, not even bothering to keep her voice quiet. "Wait. Mr. Blackwood is alive?" Jane felt a moment of relief that Mr. Rochester hadn't killed him.

Helen nodded, wheezing. "And don't forget the other part I told you."

"The duke is bad, and don't put the ring in the study because he wants to possess him?" Jane said.

"Oh, good, your memory is so good." She smiled. "We did it!"

"But, Helen, I already put the ring in the study!" Jane exclaimed.

"Oh right," Helen said.

The door guards started to approach her.

Jane, Helen, and the tree ghost started to walk away. "How could the duke possibly possess the king anyway?" Jane said.

"The ring is a talisman," Helen said. "It's holding a ghost who can control the king."

Jane's heart sank. "We have to get back to the study."

Just then, trumpets sounded, indicating the king had once again entered the ballroom.

The three of them rushed inside, and there was the king, sitting on his throne.

"Tree ghost, can you go to him? Distract him?"

But the tree ghost only backed away. "That is not the king."

"What? Of course he's—" Jane caught a glimpse of the king's hand, and on it was the ring. "No. We have to get out of here and find Mr. Blackwood," Jane said. "He'll know what to do. Stay with me, Helen?"

"Always," Helen said.

THIRTY-THREE
Alexander

Within the first ten days of Wellington controlling the King of England, Mr. Mitten (as the king) issued several royal proclamations. The first was that everyone should recognize that his coronation had been the most-attended coronation of all time. Period. (Even though it had been four years ago, and really, who even cares?) The second decree dismissed Parliament and appointed Wellington as prime minister.

Meanwhile, Alexander—and everyone else who knew the truth about the king's possession—were living in a warehouse off the river. It was undignified and unsanitary. And to make matters worse, they were out of tea.

But they were together, and that was something. After Miss Eyre had emerged from the palace, she and Miss Brontë had embraced and bounced and embraced some more. Miss Eyre relayed Miss Burn's happiness to see Miss Brontë, and then Alexander and the three young ladies returned to the warehouse.

Where Miss Eyre saw the Rochesters for the first time since Thornfield.

It was super awkward.

"Uh, hello." Mr. Rochester shifted his weight. "I'm Edward Rochester. Pleased to meet you."

Miss Eyre just stared at him.

Then Mrs. Rochester swept in and took Miss Eyre's hand. "Hello, *ma chérie*. Wonderful to see you again." Her smile was so warm and radiant that Miss Eyre returned it, obviously surprised.

"Good evening," she said.

"I know what you've been through, but we Beacons are strong and resilient. You shall overcome it."

"What about what *you've* been through?" Miss Eyre asked.

"As I said, *ma chérie*: overcome."

The joyful reunion was cut short when news of the royal decrees reached them.

To be perfectly honest, Alexander was feeling rather sick about the whole thing. He didn't sleep anymore; rather, he lay awake going over every conversation he'd ever had with Wellington, searching his memory for some hint that this had been coming. What had he missed? That was probably the most disappointing thing of all: his own failure to stop all of this before it happened.

After that, he'd taken to reading Miss Brontë's notebook,

which he'd retrieved from its hiding spot the first time the Rochesters allowed him out of the warehouse. He knew he should return it right away, but curiosity made him open it one night. After he came to a charming passage about burnt porridge on page twenty-seven, he couldn't stop reading.

Some pages were the budding story of fictional Miss Eyre and fictional Mr. Rochester, while others were beautiful descriptions of people and places. Alexander was certainly no literary expert, but he knew at once that Miss Brontë possessed some faculty of verse.

The final entry read: *Do you think, because I am poor, obscure, plain, and little, I am soulless and heartless? You think wrong! I have as much soul as you and full as much heart. And if God had gifted me with some beauty and much wealth, I should have made it as hard for you to leave me as it is now for me to leave you. I am not talking to you now through the medium of custom, conventionalities, nor even of mortal flesh—it is my spirit that addresses your spirit; just as if both had passed through the grave, and we stood at God's feet, equal—as we are.*

Alexander paused at that paragraph, dated the day of the doomed wedding, and turned every phrase over in his mind. He could hear Charlotte in those words, feel the passion and conviction of the author's feelings. Not just the characters she was writing about, but *hers*.

He'd read some secret part of her heart.

He really should give the notebook back.

He read the passage again and again, until he fell asleep.

* * *

The next morning, the group was collected on a circle of crates piled into uncomfortable imitations of sofas and chairs. Someone had managed to procure bundles of blankets and pillows, so they'd been able to put together a semblance of living quarters, one for the ladies, one for the men, and one for Mr. and Mrs. Rochester, who refused to be separated for any length of time now, even though the couple sharing a space was something of a scandal. (Remember, these were different times. Married couples of high rank didn't always share a room.)

Speaking of scandals, Miss Eyre spent a lot of time watching the Rochesters from the corner of her eye, unconscious of the frown she wore, and Miss Burns's occasional jabs. Like right now.

"They make such a handsome couple," Miss Burns mused. She was sitting on a crate next to Miss Eyre, tapping her forefinger on her chin. "Look how age-appropriate they are. I just love it."

Miss Eyre's frown deepened as she elbowed her ghostly friend, but of course she passed right through.

"Now you're just being rude," Miss Burns said. "I've told you a thousand times that it's rude to go inside ghosts."

"Sorry," Miss Eyre said.

Across the crate-parlor, Miss Brontë watched what to her must have looked like Miss Eyre antagonizing and apologizing to empty air.

"We're just sitting around," Alexander groused. "We should be doing something."

"Like what?" Branwell paced the length of the room, his arms crossed and his brow furrowed in thought. He'd become the parson of Haworth, if Alexander recalled, and already the position had matured the boy far more than his time at the Society. Good for him.

"We need to get the ring off the king's finger," Miss Brontë said. "Or, rather, Mr. Mitten's finger. Technically the king's, but I suppose it's under Mr. Mitten's control."

"Doesn't that make it Mr. Mitten's finger?" Branwell turned to Miss Eyre. "You were possessed. What do you think? Is it Mr. Mitten's finger or the king's finger?"

But before Miss Eyre could open her mouth, Miss Burns leaned forward. "Maybe we should ask Mr. Rochester. Since he was possessed the longest and made to do all sorts of things he wouldn't normally."

Miss Eyre, who'd been translating for the two in the room who couldn't see ghosts, abruptly stopped. Unfortunately for her, Branwell picked up where she left off, because Miss Burns wasn't done.

"Remember when Rowland possessed him and tried to make him marry Jane, even after being mean and manipulative?" Miss Burns shot a dark look at Rochester, the real Rochester, who'd done none of those things except as an unwitting vehicle for his dead brother's actions.

As Branwell finished echoing Miss Burns's words, he clamped his mouth shut and blushed furiously. "Sorry."

Meanwhile, Miss Burns smiled, triumphant.

Mrs. Rochester was also blushing, her gaze aimed straight at the floor as though she could will away all the terrible things that had happened, including her husband's possession.

"Can we just get back to the problem?" Miss Brontë said. "Saving England?"

"Right." Alexander fidgeted with his gloves, because talk of talismans always made him check to ensure those gloves were firmly in place. "The king is constantly surrounded by guards, and he's not going to let us waltz right up and take the ring off his finger."

"Of course not," Miss Brontë said over a cup of hot water. Everyone had a cup actually, though no one was drinking. The news about the tea had truly been a blow to the group. "Which means we need a plan. Fortunately, I have one in mind."

Alexander was not surprised.

Miss Brontë leaned forward. "I've always thought that good plans need to have firm goals. So we start with the ring."

"Everything should fall into place once the king is himself again," Alexander agreed. "It's just returning the king to himself that's the problem."

"Exactly!" Miss Brontë jumped to her feet. "So here's my idea."

Everyone waited. Even the Rochesters leaned forward in anticipation.

"We storm Saint James's Palace," Miss Brontë announced. "And Jane and Mrs. Rochester use their Beacon powers on Mr.

Mitten the Ghost and ask him nicely to take off the ring."

"That's a fine plan," said Mrs. Rochester, "but our Beacon powers of compulsion do not work on ghosts currently possessing someone. Otherwise I could have prevented Rowland from taking over Edward for so long. And Miss Eyre could have saved herself an incredible amount of trouble."

Miss Brontë frowned. "But ghosts still find Beacons irresistible when they're possessing people, right?"

"Yes," said Rochester. "That seems to be the reason Rowland was . . . attracted . . ." He coughed. "But there seems to be something about the living body getting in the way of the compulsion."

"All right," Miss Eyre said, "so we can't compel Mr. Mitten to leave the king. What's your next plan, Charlotte?"

"Um." Miss Brontë sat down.

"Maybe we can figure out the ring bit when we get there," Miss Eyre said. "The answer will just come to us. Like magic."

"There's no such thing as magic," Miss Burns muttered.

Everyone (except Miss Brontë and Rochester) looked at the ghost.

"I mean that kind of magic." She rolled her eyes.

"Anyway," Miss Eyre said, "we'll figure it out when we get there. I think we need to discuss how to storm the castle—"

"Technically it's a palace." That was Miss Brontë, of course.

"It looks like a castle." Miss Eyre crossed her arms.

"It's a palace that looks like a castle, but really it's a palace." Miss Brontë looked to Alexander, as though asking for help.

"Let's get back on track," he suggested. "I'd also like to propose that we don't need to storm the, ah, palace or castle, whatever you want to call it. After all, Miss Eyre, doesn't everyone believe you're still part of the Society? You can request an audience with the king."

"Oh." Miss Eyre frowned. "I suppose that's true."

"Mr. Blackwood, I believe I was the one announcing the plan." Miss Brontë stuck her hand on her hip.

"Go home, Miss Brontë."

She rolled her eyes. "As I was saying, we're definitely not storming the palace, since Jane can get us in the front door with a lot less mess. But we're going to call it storming the palace, because that sounds far more exciting. And once we've stormed the palace, we get the ring off Mr. Mitten's finger. Somehow. Possibly by magic."

"And that's it?" Rochester looked dubious. "We just walk in and take the ring from him. In front of his guards and all the court. I don't see how this will work."

Mrs. Rochester sat up straight. "Magic! *Le Livre de l'esprit errance.* We distract everyone with ghosts."

Miss Eyre frowned.

"They'd have to be able to see ghosts first," Branwell said, "and we can't do that without briefly killing them, and what if we mess up? I don't want to permanently kill someone."

"We can make them see ghosts, though." Mrs. Rochester clasped her hands together. "Miss Eyre and I can ask the ghosts of London to join us in the palace, and when the time is right, we make everyone see the dead. That's when we seize the opportunity to remove the ring from the king's finger. Voilà!"

"But how?" Miss Brontë glanced around the room, looking vaguely where Miss Burns sat. (She knew Miss Burns *had* been there, at least, because people kept looking there.) A longing filled her gaze. "How can non-seers see ghosts?"

"*Le Livre de l'esprit errance,*" said Mrs. Rochester. "With this, we could make everyone see ghosts. But it can be dangerous. People do not always react well to seeing the dead. There will be chaos."

Miss Eyre lifted a hand. "I—"

"But we want a little chaos," said Branwell. "To distract everyone while we wrest the ring from the king." He paused a moment. "I'm a poet, Charlie."

"Don't call me Charlie."

"But—"

"I do rather like this plan," said Alexander. "Seeing all the ghosts of London—that's certainly not something anyone would expect to see in the royal court."

"Unless they're also seers!" Miss Burns beamed.

"Then they'd be working for the Society," Alexander said. "Wellington never met a seer he didn't want to control."

"Except me." Branwell shrugged. "It's all right, though. Really. I quite like being a parson. Blessing sermons and writing babies."

"I—"

"So we need the *Le Livre de l'esprit errance*." Rochester turned to his wife. "Do you know where Wellington keeps that, my love?"

Miss Eyre opened her mouth, but Mrs. Rochester was faster.

"I'm afraid the *Le Livre de l'esprit errance* is quite impossible to obtain, *mon chéri*." Mrs. Rochester dropped her eyes. "He keeps it locked in a room guarded by a three-headed dog, which drops into a pit of strangling vines, followed by a life-or-death life-size game of chess, which opens into a room with a locked door and a hundred keys on wings, and then there's a mirror. . . ."

Branwell gasped. "That's horrible! That poor three-headed dog!"

"I bet he just keeps it in his desk," Alexander said. "Are you sure that obstacle course of death isn't something else?"

Mrs. Rochester tilted her head. "Oh, I think you're right."

Miss Eyre stood up. "I—"

"Even if the book is located in his desk," Miss Brontë said, "it might as well be behind a hungry lion. How will we get into the Society?"

"Miss Eyre might be able to get it," Alexander said.

"That's what I've been trying to tell you." She put her hands on her hips. "I have the Book of the Dead with me."

"What!" Alexander lurched to his feet. "Why didn't you lead with that? The Book of the Dead is our biggest asset! This changes everything."

Miss Eyre let out a huge sigh, then retreated to her crate room, and when she returned, she carried the Book of the Dead. "I took it to the castle—"

"Palace," Miss Brontë muttered.

"—with me to make the king able to see the tree ghost and I didn't have time to give it back before Helen told me you were all outside and that Wellington was evil." Miss Eyre smiled and opened the book. "Here, we can practice. I'll read this, and Charlotte, if you can see Helen, then it works!"

"All right." Miss Brontë stood and straightened her dress. "I'm ready."

Miss Burns stood, too—right in front of Miss Brontë.

Miss Eyre read the incantation aloud: "*'Ostende nobis quod est post mortem! Nos videre praestrigiae!'*"

Miss Brontë jumped. Of course. Because Miss Burns was standing right in front of her, grinning widely.

"Helen?" Miss Brontë's soft voice was filled with excitement as she looked right at the resident ghost. "You look just like Jane's paintings."

Miss Burns squealed and clapped her hands. "Finally!"

Miss Brontë smiled. She had a nice smile, Alexander thought. Slightly crooked, very charming, and wholly genuine in the way her face lit with joy. "Now," she said, "we storm the castle."

"I thought it was a palace." Miss Burns grinned.

"Whatever." Miss Brontë lifted her spectacles. "Let's storm it."

THIRTY-FOUR
Charlotte

"Are you ready?" came Mr. Blackwood's voice. "It's nearly time."

Charlotte shook her head. "Mr. Blackwood, I must protest. This isn't remotely proper."

"Let's see."

"I'd feel more comfortable in my normal attire."

"Let's see," he insisted.

She moved out from behind the wall of crates they'd piled up to serve as an impromptu dressing room. Her face burned. She was wearing *trousers*, something she'd never imagined herself doing in her life, plus a fine button-up shirt that used to belong to Mr. Rochester, and knee-high leather boots with tissue stuffed into the toes. She stared down at the boots, pulling her ponytail over her shoulder. She didn't have her spectacles in place, but she could still feel Mr. Blackwood staring at her. She wondered if he would laugh.

"We discussed this quite thoroughly this morning," he said at last. "The Society doesn't often employ women."

"Which makes no sense."

"Which makes no sense," he said gently, "but it's the reality we're faced with. As far as Wellington knows, Miss Eyre is still a faithful agent of the Society. So the rest of us will have to go in disguise. You're a footman."

"Very well," she grumbled. "But I don't like playing a boy. I am perfectly at ease as a woman."

"So you are," he agreed. "But the clothing suits you, in my opinion."

"Oh." She didn't know whether to be flattered or offended.

"I mean, I would never mistake you for a man. But you must admit it's far more practical than that birdcage you're always wearing."

"It feels strange." Strange didn't begin to describe how she felt. But at least she could breathe without impediment. She felt unbound, unmoored from the stifling constraints of her gender. She felt like she could be quite capable of anything.

She smiled, in spite of her mortification. Mr. Blackwood reached for her hand, which was clutching her glasses, and held them up for her. He was smiling, too. He'd been in a good mood all day, dashing about, preparing. Like this business of confronting the king was not terrifying, as Charlotte found it, but merely putting him a step closer to the revenge he'd been seeking half his life. His dream within his reach once again.

"I know there's not time now," he said, "but we should get you some proper spectacles. The sort that you wear on your face."

She shook her head. "I had those type once. They hurt my nose. And I looked . . ." *Dreadful*, she wanted to tell him, but she didn't wish him to picture it.

"What matters is for you to be able to see." He let go of her hand and held out a plain black jacket. Charlotte slipped her arms into the sleeves. The coat, like the boots, was much too large, but there was nothing to be done about it. Just then Jane came into the room, wearing the same enormous dress that she'd worn to see the king the previous time. She looked at Charlotte and heaved a great sigh.

"How is it?" Jane asked.

Charlotte shrugged. "Comfortable. I could go directly to sleep. However do men get anything done?"

"You look just like a fledgling agent." Mr. Blackwood reached into his pocket and withdrew a black Society mask. For a moment he seemed about to tie it on, but then he remembered that he was not playing the part of an agent tonight. He sighed and put it back into his pocket.

Jane blushed and donned her own mask. "Let's go now. I don't believe I can stand any more waiting."

"Do you have the book?"

Jane pulled the Book of the Dead out of her handbag. "And

I've read it cover to cover. I know the words."

"Excellent," he said. "Branwell!"

The Rochesters appeared in the warehouse doorway, also dressed as men (although that was only strange on Mrs. Rochester, who still seemed to gleam like a star in whatever she was wearing). Bran popped up behind them. His hair was messy, his glasses inexplicably smudged again, and half of his shirttail was hanging out. But his eyes were bright with excitement. "Are we going yet? It's nearly sunset."

"We're going." Alexander swung his own coat onto his body in one fluid motion. Charlotte lifted her glasses to her face to admire the view as he strode toward the door, his coat billowing behind him, his steps purposeful.

She gave a faint sigh.

"Mr. Blackwood . . ." As they went headlong into this danger, she was flooded with the urge to tell him all the things that had come to her when she'd thought he was dead. To say the words out loud.

He stopped. Turned. "Yes?"

But now was not the proper time.

"Oh, I nearly forgot." He reached once more into his pocket and withdrew . . .

Her notebook!

The one with her Jane Frere story in it.

The one she'd left behind when she and Jane had fled Thornfield.

The one she thought she'd lost forever.

"Where did you find this?" she gasped.

"It was in Miss Eyre's room. I picked it up after my duel with Rochester. I thought you'd need it back. I imagine it's going to be a famous novel someday."

"You didn't read it!"

"I read . . . a bit." (We know, dear reader, that this was a fib. Alexander had read it from cover to cover, some of it three or four times.)

"Oh." She didn't know what to say.

He ducked his head. "I'm sorry—I was unable to resist. I found it quite compelling, truly. You should finish it."

He put it into her hands. She clutched it to her chest for a moment and then slipped it into her jacket breast pocket. It was handy, she'd admit, to have a jacket breast pocket.

"You think you might have time for some casual writing?" His eyebrows lifted.

She grinned. "You never know."

The sun was sinking fast as the group approached the palace. Charlotte's nerves were jittering. At the gatehouse of Saint James, they stopped.

"Who goes there?" asked the chief officer from behind the gate.

"Jane," said Mrs. Rochester. "*C'est* your cue."

Jane lifted her chin and stepped forward.

"I am an agent of the Society for the Relocation of Wayward

Spirits," she announced. "I'm here on urgent Society business. I need to speak with the king at once."

"And who are they?" The guard narrowed his eyes as he looked around at their assembled party.

"This is my entourage." Jane's voice wavered. "I'm the star agent."

Mr. Blackwood coughed uncomfortably.

"Very well." The guard stepped aside and let them pass. And then they were inside the palace. It had been the fastest storming of a castle ever.

In the great hall, they found the king on his throne, sur-rounded by lavishly dressed nobles, eating fistfuls off a tray of sweets. The room was easily the most extravagant that Charlotte had ever been in. The high ceilings were embellished with real gold leafing. The carpet had the look and texture of red velvet. The walls were covered in a wine-red wallpaper, and every few feet were adorned by large portraits of the past kings and queens and other various royalty.

Beside her, Charlotte heard Jane draw in a sharp breath.

"Are you all right?" Charlotte asked.

"I've never liked red rooms," her friend said darkly. Charlotte made a mental note to ask her about that someday. It could be good material for her book.

She was so excited that she was now going to be able to fin-ish her book. She could practically taste the ending. (We know the feeling.)

"Your Highness, an agent from the Society here to see you," announced the guard. "She claims that it is urgent."

Charlotte gave her a little nudge. Jane moved forward again. "I'm Miss Eyre, Your Majesty. If you will recall, I was here to see you recently."

The king eyed Jane. "No. Can't say that I do recall." He glanced at Mr. Blackwood. "But you're somewhat familiar. You look . . . like someone's father."

"I have one of those faces," Mr. Blackwood said. "I look like everyone's father."

So now came the tricky part. The getting-the-ring-off-the-king's-finger part.

"Well, it's a pleasure to meet you, Sire," Jane said a bit awkwardly. "Again."

She stepped up to the throne and held out her hand as if to shake. The king took it, reluctantly. Then he gasped and drew back as if she'd bitten him.

"Did you just attempt to steal my ring, young lady?" he puffed.

Well, it'd been a long shot, the simply getting-the-ring approach.

"I only need it for a moment. Then I'll give it right back," she said.

"How dare you! Guards!" he cried.

And then they were immediately surrounded by a dozen guards with swords and guns.

"Well, that was fast," remarked Bran. "No time for niceties or anything."

"On to plan B," Mr. Rochester said quietly.

"Take them out of here," the king ordered. "Now. Perhaps a few days in the stocks would be appropriate."

Charlotte hoped plan B was going to work. Otherwise it would be an unpleasant weekend.

"We require that one ring," Mr. Blackwood said.

"It's my ring," said the king. "It's my precious. And I think I know you, sir. You are Mr. Blackwood."

"And you are Mr. Mitten. We will be taking the ring now," continued Mr. Blackwood smoothly.

The king smirked. "You and what army?"

"Precisely." Mr. Blackwood sighed. "Miss Eyre, it's ghost time."

Jane cleared her throat. "Hello," she said a bit timidly, glancing around her. "It's so nice to see you this evening. Would you, perhaps, if you're not too busy at the moment, assist us?"

"You should *command* them," Mr. Blackwood said out of the side of his mouth. "Call them. Order them to your side."

"That seems rude." She sighed. "Oh, very well." She raised her voice. "Hello? Can you hear me? If you can hear me, please come toward the sound of my voice."

Mrs. Rochester came to stand beside Jane. *"Allez, l'esprits,"* she said in her musical French Creole. "Come!"

As far as Charlotte could tell, nothing happened. But then Bran smiled.

"It's remarkable, isn't it?" he murmured, shaking his head at the wonder of it all. "There's so very many of them."

"So many ghosts?" Charlotte wasn't the type to be frightened by spirits, but the idea of there being "so many" ghosts all around them was a bit unsettling. What a place was London, where you only had to call out, and in seconds ghosts came from every direction. It was a city crowded with both the living and the dead. Even the palace.

"That's probably enough, ladies." Mr. Blackwood stretched out his arms to the main guard. "Now the book."

"Oh! The book." Jane lifted the book, opened it, and spoke the words in a clear, loud voice.

"*Ostende nobis quod est post mortem! Nos videre praestrigiae!*"

It was basic Latin. When Charlotte had translated it for them earlier, calling on her Latin studies at Lowood, she'd come up with the following meaning: *Show us what is beyond death! Let us see the ghosts!* Which felt a bit on the nose, really, as magical incantations went. A little disappointing, if she was being honest. But then she supposed all of the real power stemmed from Jane. And perhaps the book. The book was very interesting. When Wellington had mentioned the Book of the Dead, Charlotte had expected some large and ancient tome written in hieroglyphs or Sanskrit, full of spells to control the dead and a secret knowledge of the underworld. But for the most part, this slim volume was a simple instruction manual on how to manage ghosts, protect oneself against possessions, and guide wayward souls in their journey to the place beyond, observations compiled by the various leaders of the Society stretching back throughout the years. It was not a magical book (although we would argue, dear reader, that all books are slightly magical), but it was certainly useful.

The point was, the Latin worked. The air seemed colder. The candles flickered and then whooshed out. The guards and nobles immediately began to shout in alarm.

Charlotte lifted her spectacles and gazed around the throne room again, and this time she saw them: dozens—perhaps even hundreds—of spirits all around them, the people of London who had long since passed. Bran was right—the sight was truly remarkable. It seemed to her that every period in English history was represented in this crowd of ghosts. There were men in knee-length fur-lined tunics with floppy hats. Women in long, flowing gowns with draping sleeves and veils over their hair. Women in pointy cone hats. Men in tricornered caps. Knights in chain mail and knights in plate mail and English soldiers in red coats. A band of unruly Scots in plaid kilts with blue-painted faces.

A radiant girl with red hair caught Charlotte's eye. She was dressed in a gorgeous embroidered, jewel-encrusted gown and an Elizabethan headdress. In her hand she held a book. She smiled sweetly at Jane, and reached for the man beside her, who, to Charlotte's total astonishment, suddenly turned into a horse.

The horse transformation alarmed the poor guards, especially.

"Gytrash!" someone yelled.

"What is this witchcraft?" another cried.

"Oh, we haven't bewitched you," Mr. Blackwood clarified. "We've simply helped you to see things a bit more clearly."

The ghosts advanced. Charlotte shivered. Up close, on some of them, one could see evidence that they were not truly living beings. Some of them were translucent or glowing a strange unearthly green color. Others bore the wounds of the injuries that must have killed them—a noose around a neck that was bent at an odd angle, the black pustules that marked a bout of plague, an open, bleeding wound in the chest. Still others looked as though they had just dug their own way from their graves—their flesh was rotted, their clothes hanging from them in tatters.

They were frightening, Charlotte concluded. Especially that horse.

The crowd obviously felt the same way. Pandemonium broke out. The nobles stampeded toward the exit, often pushing right through the ghosts, which spurred them on in their frenzy. Mr. Blackwood darted off to one side, pushing and exacerbating the situation in whatever way he could. Bran and Jane and the Rochesters went off in other directions. It was all going according to the plan.

Except then Charlotte's glasses were knocked from her hand.

Which was not the plan.

The plan had been for her to creep up to the king during the confusion and snatch the ring.

It had been decided that she should do the snatching. Because she was the most unobtrusive of the group. For once, being little and obscure was going to serve her.

Only now she couldn't see a blasted thing.

"Blast!" she yelled. "Why can things never go according to my plan?"

She groped about on the floor for her spectacles.

"Miss Brontë," she heard Mr. Blackwood call out. "Any time now."

"I really should get the kind I wear on my face," she grumbled as she searched. "This vanity of mine is going to be the death of us all."

She encountered the barrel of a small gun and thrust it away from her. She'd never liked guns.

She found a discarded ivory fan. It was probably expensive.

She grabbed a woman's ankle and the woman screamed and tried to kick her.

"Blast!" But then her fingers touched glass. And then the handle of her spectacles.

She quickly whipped the spectacles up to her eyes. And her mouth dropped open.

In the time she'd been searching for her blasted glasses the room had emptied, save Mr. Blackwood, the Rochesters, Jane, and Bran.

And the king. The king was still seated on the throne, surveying the scene quite calmly. And beside him was the Duke of Wellington.

For a moment, they simply gaped at him.

"Well, that was an amusing little display," the duke said finally. "But do you take me for a fool?"

"I would never take you for a fool," Mr. Rochester growled. "A traitor, yes. A two-faced, serpent-tongued blaggart, absolutely. But not a fool."

"Now, now. No need for name calling," said the duke. "Why don't we all just sit down and have a little chat?"

Charlotte felt Mr. Blackwood coil like a spring beside her. "We've talked enough. Give us the ring."

Wellington tsked. "I wish I could say it's good to see you, dear boy. But you not being dead right now is inconvenient for me."

"I trusted you." Mr. Blackwood's voice betrayed his agony at the duke's deceit. "I thought of you as a . . . father to me, when my own was gone. And all this time, I should have sought revenge upon *you*."

"I never did like your father," said the duke. "He was the sanctimonious sort. It seems the apple doesn't fall far from that tree. Now sit down." He drew a pistol from his waistcoat and pointed it at Mr. Blackwood with an expression that made Charlotte's heart beat fast. "Please," he added.

But Mr. Blackwood had drawn his own gun. Where had he gotten a gun? For a moment, the two men faced each other down, but then the duke smiled and swung his arm around so that it was pointing, not at any of them, but at the king. "Put your weapon down, or I will murder him," he said. "I've done it before. George III was such a bother. And David here won't mind—he'll just inhabit the next in line for the throne. I already have that all arranged."

Mr. Blackwood took a step forward. Wellington cocked the pistol. "I will do it. I will be very cranky if I must do it. It will cost me time and immeasurable effort. But I will. And then you'll be responsible for the death of a king. And when the guards arrive I will tell them that you killed him. And who will they believe? I wonder."

Mr. Blackwood's arm dropped. "We could duel," he said softly. "You and me, here and now, and then it would be over."

The duke shook his head. "I know how good you are, my boy. I taught you myself. No, I think not. If we dueled, one of us would die. Probably you, but why chance it? And besides, perhaps I was hasty in trying to dispatch you earlier. You're of more value to me alive, dear Alexander. I've always been fond of you. If you would only see the importance in what I am doing here, we could be allies once again. Help me. Support my cause. Surely you can see all that I've accomplished, and all that I will accomplish, as prime minister, and as . . . advisor to the king."

"So it's true," Mrs. Rochester said. "You mean to rule England."

"Of course I do. The king is a moron. The members of Parliament, only more so. The people require a firm hand to guide them. To lead them."

"We will never join you," said Mr. Blackwood.

"Speak for yourself," said the duke.

"Never," said Mr. Rochester.

"Never again," murmured Mrs. Rochester. The Rochesters took hands. "*Jamais.* This time we will stop you," she said darkly. "We will see this evil ended."

"You two have always been tiresome," the duke said. "I should have done away with you at the same time I dealt with his father."

Mr. Blackwood gave a choked furious cry, but did not, to Charlotte's surprise, attack the man who had killed his father. "You will pay," he growled instead. "You will pay for all of it."

The duke ignored him. He turned to address Jane. "Miss Eyre, I meant every word I said about how much the Society needs you. I would entreat you to stay in your position with us, serve as my star agent, my Beacon of light, and help me to usher in an era of peace and prosperity the likes of which this nation has never seen."

"Go to hell," said Jane. (Which was really shocking language for a woman of this time. But she was obviously starting to become annoyed at people telling her what to do.)

"Oh, well. Perhaps . . . Mr. Brontë." The duke moved on. "I could reinstate you immediately. You could be a credit to your family, instead of an embarrassment."

"He is a credit to our family," Charlotte said before Bran could answer.

The duke's eyes flickered to her. "And you, the charming but unfortunately nearsighted sister. You could be initiated as well. I am sure you could be quite useful to us . . . in some way I haven't yet discerned. Did you know that I'm your uncle?" He chuckled darkly.

"I had two miserable sisters, once."

"What?" Charlotte gasped, shocked. "Our mother?"

"I'd be willing to make you my heirs. Think about it. That twenty thousand pounds a year, after I die. You'd be rich."

"Twenty thousand pounds!" came Helen's voice from behind them.

"Oh, Helen. You can't take it with you," said Jane.

"Go. To. Hell," Charlotte enunciated plainly.

The duke smiled. "Oh, dear. Do you at least have my book? You checked it out, Miss Eyre, but you did not return it in a timely fashion. Give it back to me at once, or there will be consequences."

A shudder made its way down Charlotte's spine. There was nothing so disturbing to her as an overdue book. Possible fines. It was very scary.

Jane held up the Book of the Dead. "We're going to keep it, thank you. You've clearly been abusing its power."

The duke sighed dramatically. "Well, this puts me in a rather awkward position. I, of course, wish to remain as I am, as the prime minister and the caretaker—you might say—to the king. You obviously mean to stop me, and will not be reasoned with. Therefore I must get rid of you. The easiest way would be to kill you all. I have a gun, but then so do you, and I find that I am outnumbered. Obviously that won't work." He sighed again. "So I'm afraid I'll have to stick to my initial plan of killing poor old William IV." He was still aiming the gun at the king's head.

"All right," said the king. "But it's going to hurt, isn't it?"

"Only for a moment."

"But then you'll put me back into the next king," the white-haired man said slowly.

"Yes. After I frame Mr. Blackwood and his friends for regicide."

"Wait a second." King Mitten hesitated. "Isn't the next in line for the throne actually a woman?"

"It's a girl. Victoria, I think her name is." The duke chuckled. "As if a woman could ever rule a country without a man behind her secretly pulling the strings."

Charlotte's mouth opened. "That doesn't make sense. Elizabeth was a great queen!"

"But . . . a girl?" Mitten looked doubtful.

"You'll get to be young again, and beautiful, and rich," said the duke.

But the man who resembled the king was frowning deeply. "I don't think I would be comfortable, you know, in a woman's body."

"You'd get used to it," argued the duke.

"No, I wouldn't. Even being in this old fellow is a bit odd. His back aches from all the sitting, and he has too much hair in his nose, but at least the equipment's all the same. I don't want to be a girl."

"You'll be what I say you'll be." Wellington sounded angry. "Now hold still."

"No!" The king (or the ghost inside of the king) jumped to his feet. "I don't want to be a girl! I won't! You can't make me."

The duke scowled and tried to shoot him, but at that moment Mr. Blackwood darted in and grabbed the duke's arm, at the same time that Bran leapt forward and tackled the king to the floor. Charlotte's heart seized at the thought that her brother might take the bullet himself, but instead it shattered a rather expensive-looking vase in the corner. The duke shoved Mr. Blackwood back and pointed his gun at Jane.

"Don't move or I'll shoot her!" he cried.

Everyone—even the king, who had continued to repeat how he did not want to be a girl—froze.

The duke smoothed his hair back. "I know you love her," he sneered at Mr. Blackwood. "Even though she's so remarkably plain, you love her, and if you try to get at me, I'll kill her right before your eyes."

"What?" Charlotte squeaked. "What did you say about love?"

"Him?" Jane said incredulously, at the very same moment that Mr. Blackwood said, "Her?"

"You're obviously in love," said the duke. "You kept talking about her—how resourceful she was, and quick-witted, and how you wanted her to be an agent. And you—" He turned to Jane. "You were so devastated when I told you that he was dead. Because you—"

"She's more of a friend, is all," said Mr. Blackwood. "But we're not—"

"Right, they're not in love," said Charlotte. "You're reading it all wrong."

"I have a thing for Rochester," confessed Jane. "It's not healthy."

Mr. Rochester coughed uncomfortably. "My dear, I am so sorry at what my brother put you through while he was in control of my body. I couldn't stop him. I wish there was something I could have—"

"Oh, no," Jane said demurely. "I know it wasn't your fault. I would never blame you."

Mr. Rochester gave a short laugh. "And goodness—I'm old enough to be your father, aren't I? As a matter of fact, we have a—"

"And you love your wife," Mrs. Rochester added loudly.

He turned to gaze at her. "Yes. I love my wife. More than anything."

"That's wonderful," murmured Jane. "I'm so happy for you. I—"

"I feel we're getting off topic," interrupted the duke. But then he didn't say anything more. Instead, he grabbed a large painting from the wall—this one actually turned out to be one of William IV, himself, and hurled it at them. They ducked, and the duke took the opportunity to flee, screaming for the guards that there had been an attempt on the life of the king.

"He'll go back to his lair—I mean, his library," Mr. Blackwood cried. "It's just across the park from here. We should try to catch him before he gets there." Mr. Blackwood clearly wanted to go after him. But there was still the issue of . . .

"The king," Mrs. Rochester said. "Is he all right?"

"I don't want to be a girl," whined Mr. Mitten/the king. "That wasn't in the agreement."

"You don't have to be a girl," Bran said kindly. "Although the dresses are pretty."

"He's getting away," hissed Mr. Rochester.

"Go," Charlotte said. "You and Jane can go after Wellesley. Bran and I will see to the king, and then we'll catch up."

Mr. Blackwood gave her a grateful smile. "Come on," he said to the Rochesters and Jane. "Let's go catch a duke."

Then they were gone. Everything seemed dreadfully quiet.

"Time to get this ring off you," Charlotte said, taking the king's hand.

But he pulled away. "If you take the ring off, I'll go back to being dead. I don't want to be a girl, but I don't want to be dead again, either."

There was no choice. Charlotte and Bran had to hold the man down and wrestle the ring off his finger. But that was a problem, too, because the king's fingers were rather fat, and the ring was a bit tight, and it wouldn't simply slide off. They tugged and tugged, the king squirming and hollering the entire while, but they couldn't remove the ring. Their efforts had caused the finger to swell. And Charlotte was getting impatient. Every minute they wasted here was a minute she could be helping Mr. Blackwood grapple with Wellesley.

"Perhaps we could try lathering it with soap?" Bran suggested, but there was not a bar of soap to be found.

"Soak it in cool water?"

That didn't work.

"Butter?"

He held the king down while Charlotte went to look for some, but she could not find butter.

"I found something else." She'd been acting logically, when she'd suggested that Mr. Blackwood and Jane go after Wellesley. Jane was gifted with ghosts. Mr. Blackwood had training in fighting and whatnot. Charlotte knew how to direct Bran. But it was (figuratively) killing her, that Mr. Blackwood could be in danger, and she wasn't there. She was out of time.

She pulled the pair of garden shears from behind her back. "I think this will work."

Bran's face went milky. The king started to struggle more than ever, but Bran held him.

"Charlie, be serious. You can't mean to . . ."

"I do mean to." And she did. Without another moment's hesitation she knelt beside the king, positioned the shears, and snipped the finger off. The ring (and the accompanying finger) skittered across the carpet. The king's eyes rolled up, and he went limp. Charlotte used his coat and a string from a nearby velvet curtain to bind his hand. She'd read something about amputation in a book once. She felt a bit woozy on account of all the blood, but she soldiered on.

"Keep it elevated," she instructed Bran. "When he wakes, give him the finger."

"The finger." Bran was looking a bit green himself.

She handed it to him. Then she turned for the door.

"Charlie," he said. "Where are you going?"

"To Mr. Blackwood, of course. I have to go to him. Now that I've got him back, I'm not going to lose him again."

Jane THIRTY-FIVE

The night air hung wet and cold above them, but Jane couldn't feel anything except her heart racing. Mr. Blackwood was running a few steps ahead of her and a few steps behind her was Bertha Rochester. Mr. Rochester brought up the rear, Helen floated among them, calling out words of encouragement.

They were headed toward Westminster.

"Wouldn't he want to hide?" Jane had asked Mr. Blackwood.

"I know him. His ego won't let him believe he's in any sort of danger."

Jane's foot caught on a tree root, and she stumbled but righted herself before she hit the ground. Mr. Blackwood turned to make sure she was okay, but then he tripped and fell flat on his back with an oomph.

Jane scurried to his side and held her hand out. He took it, bounced up, and they were off again, Mr. Blackwood with a slight limp.

Mr. Rochester, due to age, was falling farther behind. "Keep going!" he shouted.

"Mr. Blackwood," Jane said breathlessly. "If the duke knows that you know that he'll go to Westminster, aren't we running straight into a trap?" Jane said.

"But I know something he doesn't know."

"What's that?"

"I grew up in this place. I know of a secret tunnel!"

They continued the run through Saint James's Park, which Mr. Blackwood said was a shortcut to Westminster. When the looming spires appeared in the night sky, Mr. Blackwood took a left toward the river. Jane followed without question, mostly because she was too winded to form more words. Mr. Blackwood turned right at the river and then darted through some trees and finally came to the base of a wall, where there was an iron grate.

"Here it is," Mr. Blackwood said.

"Wait. That's not a secret passage. That's a coal chute."

"I know." He panted. "It just always sounded more exciting calling it a secret passage. Don't worry. It's an easy slide." He picked up a large stick on the ground, dug around in the dirt for a moment, and then pulled out a long iron rod. "It's still here!"

He wedged the end of the rod in between the chute door and the wall, and pulled. The door creaked open.

"We'll sneak in, and use the element of surprise to our advantage. If we approach him from an unexpected direction, I'm sure we can overtake him."

Jane furrowed her brows and looked at the dark and totally uninviting coal chute. Helen was next to her, shaking. "What's wrong, dear?"

"I can't go in," she said. "This place feels the way Mrs. Rochester's room felt."

Mr. Blackwood nodded. "Of course. The Society knows how to protect places from ghost entry. Helen will have to stay behind."

"Be safe," Helen whispered to Jane.

"You too," Jane said. She glanced at Mrs. Rochester. "Should we let the men go first?" she said.

Mr. Blackwood nodded. "I'll be there when you all land."

Considering where they were at that moment, and the mess they were in, Jane took no comfort in those words. By this time, Mr. Rochester had caught up. He held the chute door open as Mr. Blackwood went through it. Jane went next, feet first, into the chute.

It was a short trip, and contrary to what Alexander had promised, she landed hard on her feet, her knees buckling. Pain shot through her legs.

Mrs. Rochester landed next to her with a disgruntled sigh.

"Mr. Blackwood?" Jane asked.

"He is indisposed," a voice said. It was the duke, the flickering light of a candle illuminating his face.

And there was Mr. Blackwood next to him, with a knife at his throat, held by none other than Grace Poole.

"And you thought your little passageway was a secret," the duke said.

"Don't come down, my love!" Mrs. Rochester shouted.

But in the next moment, Mr. Rochester landed next to her, eliminating their last hope that someone on the outside could save them.

The duke, along with Grace Poole and several guards, led the four of them to a large and ornate room.

"Welcome to the Collection Room," the duke said.

The room was made up of shelves, aisles and aisles of them, and on the shelves were all sorts of objects; pocket watches, urns, necklaces, rings.

"Talismans," Jane said. She turned to the duke. "Why bother bringing us all the way up here? We know your evil motives. Why not just kill us?"

Mr. Blackwood shot her a harsh glance.

The duke used his pistol to urge the four prisoners against a wall.

"Miss Eyre, you and Mrs. Rochester are Beacons. I still don't think you understand how exceptional that is. Why do you think I kept Mrs. Rochester alive all those years? With Grace Poole keeping her captive? I would sooner destroy priceless works of art than damage a Beacon. Pliable ghosts like Mitten are rare and take a painfully long time to cultivate. Since you are here, I assume you have de-possessed the king. Frankly, I don't have the time or the inclination to groom someone new. And I won't need to, with the power of influence of *two* Beacons. This is your last chance."

"Ha!" Jane shook her head. "There is nothing in this world that could induce me to assist you."

The duke raised his revolver and pointed it at Mr. Blackwood's head, about an inch away from his nose. "How about now?"

"Wait," Jane said. "If you kill him, I will *never* join you."

"Moi aussi," Mrs. Rochester said.

"Oh, I won't kill just him. I will *start* with Mr. Blackwood, who was like a son to me. And then I will kill Mr. Rochester, who was like a brother to me. And I will not stop there. You see, Miss Eyre, I have come to discover you have quite a few people in your life who mean something to you."

For just a moment, and much at odds with the tension of the situation, Jane felt a fullness in her heart because the duke was right. She had many people she cared for, more than a penniless orphan would have ever dreamed.

But then the duke cocked the revolver and she remembered the whole kill-everyone-she-loved scenario.

"Wait," Jane said.

The duke raised an eyebrow. "Agree, or Alexander is dead."

"Wait," Jane said again, trying desperately to think of a way out of this mess. One that didn't involve the deaths of everyone she held dear. The only idea that came to her was to try and stall. "First, give me a glimpse of how the moving on works."

The duke narrowed his eyes. "Miss Poole," he said. "Bring her a talisman."

Grace Poole walked over to the nearest shelf and grabbed a jewelry box with her gloved hand. Then she walked over to Jane and unceremoniously shoved it in her face. Jane flinched and reflexively took a step back.

And she felt something.

A force of some sort.

It wasn't coming from the box.

It was coming from Bertha Rochester.

When Jane had stepped back, she had stepped closer to Bertha.

The box Grace Poole held began to shake. She looked at it curiously.

"What is it, Miss Poole?" Wellesley said. "Why are you shaking the box?"

"I'm not shaking it," she said.

Jane stole a glance at Bertha, who was staring at Jane with a subtle smile. Jane raised her eyebrows and Bertha nodded almost imperceptibly.

"Miss Poole, stop shaking the box," Wellesley demanded.

"I'm not," she insisted.

With Wellesley's attention on the box, Jane and Bertha took the opportunity. They scrambled toward each other, and clasped hands.

And that was when the entire room began to convulse with rattling talismans.

"What is happening?" the duke said. The guards glanced nervously at one another. A glass cup flew off a shelf and struck one of them in the head. He crumpled to the floor. The rest of the guards (there were only three left) abandoned their posts and bolted for the door.

They were definitely not getting paid enough for this.

Wellington's alarmed gaze fell on Jane and Bertha, and then down at their clasped hands. "Stop this!"

He lunged toward them but before he could separate them, a hairbrush flew off a shelf and hit him on the head.

"No possessing!" Bertha shouted to any ghosts who could hear her from inside the talismans.

"Right," Jane said. Beacons couldn't control a ghost who was possessing a human. It would be chaos.

Blackwood and Mr. Rochester watched the two women in amazement. "Get down!" Jane commanded them.

Jane could feel the energy swirling between herself and Bertha. At the same time, she could feel it draining as the room continued to shudder. They would not be able to keep it up for long.

The flying hairbrush had stunned the duke enough for him to drop his gun, but only momentarily. He reached down and grabbed it and swung it toward Mr. Rochester, but a shoe hit his hand, flinging the gun across the room.

The women were focused on Wellington, since he was the one with the gun, so they did not notice Grace Poole sneaking up on them.

The servant lunged toward Bertha and tackled her to the

ground, breaking the physical connection.

The room went still.

Mr. Blackwood and the duke both turned toward the gun and dove for it. Each of them got a hand on it, and they struggled to gain control. Mr. Rochester flew to Blackwood's aid, but the guard who had been hit with the glass cup had regained consciousness and he tackled Mr. Rochester before he got very far.

Grace Poole was on top of Bertha, and the sheer girth of her was enough to hold her down. She put her hands around Bertha's throat.

"I've dreamed of doing this," she said. "I wanted to kill you from the start. But they just couldn't get rid of a Beacon."

Jane jumped on Grace Poole's back and put her arms around her throat but the woman's neck was as thick and sturdy as a tree trunk. Jane's slight build wasn't going to be enough.

Bertha scratched and clawed at the hands around her throat, all the while making terrible choking sounds.

Jane looked frantically around, but the talismans were annoyingly small. She grabbed a perfume bottle and struck Grace Poole's head as hard as she could.

But the woman was a beast.

Bertha's eyes fluttered shut.

Mr. Rochester was subdued by the guard.

The duke and Mr. Blackwood continued their struggle, but the duke was gaining the upper hand. Several shots went off in the commotion.

Jane thought fast.

She laid down next to Bertha and grabbed her hand. The force between them was not as strong, as Bertha was near the point of passing out.

Jane closed her eyes and focused all of her strength and energy on the nearest shelves of talismans. She used everything she had inside of her. Every strike of her face at the hand of her abusive aunt Reed. Every gurgling sound her stomach had made through years of starvation. Every friend she'd lost to the Graveyard Disease. Every chill she'd felt in her bones due to years of nearly freezing to death. Every fear she'd felt in the Red Room.

She used it all.

The room began to shake once again.

Jane opened her eyes in time to see a string of talismans striking Grace Poole. They flew with such speed that they appeared only as streaks in the air.

Bertha opened her eyes and used her free hand to shove Grace off her.

The two Beacons stood, luminous and glowing, their clasped hands high in the air.

More talismans flew off shelves and struck the duke and the guard.

The duke was quickly subdued, and within moments, Alexander was standing over him with the gun.

Bertha and Jane finally released their hands, and both women dropped to the ground in complete exhaustion.

"You would not kill me, my boy," the duke said in a weak whisper.

"I am not your boy," Mr. Blackwood said.

The smell of smoke reached Jane's nostrils, and it was followed quickly by the sight of flames licking up the wall on the other side of the room. During the fight, candles must have been knocked over. The group would have to escape the room, and soon.

Mr. Blackwood focused on the duke as the women tried to catch their breath.

A faint voice came from the doorway. "Mr. Blackwood?"

The group turned toward the sound just in time to see Charlotte there, clutching her chest. Then she collapsed.

"Miss Brontë!" Mr. Blackwood shoved the gun into Mr. Rochester's hand and raced across the room. He crouched down and gathered Charlotte in his arms. Jane's heart fell at the sight.

"No, no!" Mr. Blackwood said. "She's been shot!"

The duke used the distraction to lunge for the gun, but Mr. Rochester turned and fired.

The duke crumpled to the floor.

Dead.

THIRTY-SIX
Alexander

The fire was growing. Alexander didn't wait. He lifted Miss Brontë's motionless body into his arms and ran.

This couldn't be happening. It just couldn't. But as Miss Eyre and the Rochesters led the way, and Miss Brontë continued not moving, he had to admit that it did seem to be happening. She'd been shot—hit by one of those stray bullets.

A wall collapsed, bringing oil lanterns crashing to the floor. More fires erupted, making him run faster as he carried Miss Brontë through the halls and up the stairs. He ran until his side ached, and then he kept running because Miss Brontë's face was pale and blood soaked her jacket. Sweat poured down his face.

The others pushed their way outside. Even out of the building, the heat was intense. It billowed off the House in angry waves, making the lantern-lit air shimmer. Smoke obscured the night, hiding the nearly full moon.

The fire would only get worse. "Let's go!" he shouted, but his voice was lost under the rush of flame and destruction. "Hurry!"

Miss Burns had joined the others ahead, all of them moving quickly, and not quickly enough.

People filled the streets, the fire reflecting in their wide eyes.

"What's happened?" someone asked.

"I heard it was a ghost attack on the Society!"

Another person called, "It was the king! He realized he'd made a mistake by dismissing Parliament and set the House on fire!"

Alexander staggered through the growing crowd of onlookers, his heart beating wildly in his ears. In his arms, Miss Brontë was as light as a doll, and just as motionless. Was she breathing? He couldn't tell. She was so still; her head lolled back and her eyes were shut.

He pushed through the crowd, caught in the wake made by Miss Eyre's flying elbows. "Make way!" Miss Eyre cried. "My friend has been shot! Is there a doctor?" People shouted at them, telling them to stay still and watch the fire like everyone else, but Alexander ignored them all.

Finally, they reached a break in the crowd, and Miss Eyre cleared a pair of children off a bench they'd been standing on. Alexander settled Miss Brontë there and dropped to his knees at her side. Miss Eyre, Miss Burns, and the Rochesters clustered around him.

"What do you think?" Miss Eyre asked.

Alexander tore off his gloves and touched Miss Brontë's throat, seeking her pulse. Nothing.

He let out a strangled cry. "Miss Brontë." She couldn't be dead. She just couldn't.

But his bookish friend was completely still, her pale face streaked with soot and ash.

"Miss Brontë," he whispered. "Please don't die. Please don't leave us."

The fire warmth of her skin was fading. He leaned in close, listening for her breath, but there was no sound of it, no evidence of life. Her black lashes fanned across pale cheeks, unmoving.

"No, no, no." His fingers searched her throat again, wanting more than anything to find a pulse. In the months he'd known Charlotte Brontë, had he really appreciated her as he should? In the back of his mind, without him truly realizing, he'd assumed Miss Brontë would always be in his life. Always influencing, planning, smiling, writing. Oh, Lord, could he imagine her always writing.

And the idea of losing her—it was a stab to the gut.

An eruption tore from the building, followed by terrified screams. Alexander looked up just in time to see an enormous fireball hurl into the sky, and the House—which might have been saved before—was now completely engulfed in flames.

Hot wind gusted off the building, making the crowd of onlookers scream and stagger back.

That was it. The Society—all its records and talismans and library—was gone now. But Alexander could hardly feel the pain of that loss, because when he turned back to Miss Brontë, she was still silent and unmoving.

He bent and rested his forehead on her shoulder. "I'm sorry," he breathed. "I should have—" The words clogged in his throat as tears spilled out of the corners of his eyes. Was he crying? Blast it all. "I care about you, Miss Brontë," he rasped. "And now I'm too late in saying so."

Furiously, he wiped at his eyes, but the tears kept coming and after a moment, he let the sobs heave out of him.

"Oh, stop watching," Miss Eyre said from behind him, "and get back in there."

Alexander sat up just in time to see Miss Brontë's ghost sniffle. "Shh, Jane, I'm trying to listen." But she disappeared back into her body.

Then the body gasped.

"Miss Brontë!" He cupped one hand over her cheek, feeling warmth bloom beneath her skin. Her color lifted and her pulse fluttered. "Miss Brontë, you're—"

She opened her eyes and looked around, though she wasn't wearing her glasses.

"Can you see anything? Shall I find your spectacles for you?" He didn't particularly want to leave her side, but he would search ten thousand burning buildings if it meant pleasing her.

"I—" She coughed a little.

"What?" He smoothed hair off her face. "What is it?"

"I was dead, wasn't I?"

"Yes," he breathed. "But you're going to be all right. I think. How do you feel?"

"You said . . ."

"Yes? I said a lot of things when you were dead." And suddenly he was running through every word. Then he remembered: he'd admitted (out loud, yes) that he cared for her. *Cared for her* cared for her, if you know what we mean.

Her eyes widened. "That means—"

"I know," he said. "I know it was forward of me to just say so, but in my defense, you were mostly dead."

"No, no, that's not it."

He was confused. "Then what?"

"I can see dead people!"

Alexander laughed and pulled out his mask, then placed it across her face. "Welcome, Seer Charlotte Brontë."

Or, rather, that was what he'd intended to say, but before he could finish speaking her name, she pushed herself up a little and pressed her lips against his.

His eyes widened in surprise, and immediately she backed away from him, giving an embarrassed cry.

"I'm very sorry," she said. "I couldn't see! I don't know what came over me. That was unforgivably rude. I shouldn't have—"

"You shouldn't have?" His heart was pounding.

"No!"

"Oh." Unfortunately, now he couldn't help but see the gentle curve of her lips, the tremble in her jaw, and the way she tucked a strand of hair behind her ear. When had she become so delicate and strong at the same time?

"It was too forward," she went on. "Please forgive me. I was just so happy and I shouldn't have assumed anything about your feelings and we've never discussed—"

He kissed her.

It was the same as her kiss to him—just a touch of his lips to hers. A question. A hope. A promise.

"Are we even now?" He felt the blood rising to his cheeks, too, praying he hadn't misread her. "Or should I prepare a heartfelt apology as well?"

"Don't you dare."

This time, they kissed each other. For kind of a long time. Only when Miss Eyre loudly cleared her throat did they pull away.

"We're still here," Miss Eyre said. "In case you forgot."

"That was terrible to watch." Miss Burns shuddered. "Please never do it again. At least, not in public."

Miss Brontë's cheeks were a lovely shade of pink as she sat up straight on the bench.

"How are you still alive?" Miss Eyre asked.

Miss Brontë pulled her notebook from her pocket. The leather sported a large hole right through the center. "I think this slowed the bullet just enough. I always knew my life was for books."

When Alexander's heart slowed to a normal pace, he climbed to his feet and offered Miss Eyre and Miss Burns space to sit on the bench, while he stood beside the Rochesters. The three young ladies—two living and one dead—all held hands as they watched the House of Lords and Commons burn against the night.

Two days later, they met in the flat on Baker Street. You know, the one that had been Alexander's, but was currently Miss Eyre's (for the rest of the month, at any rate, since Wellington hadn't covered the rent beyond that). Miss Eyre had generously offered the flat back to Alexander, as it had been his first, but Alexander had declined. Instead, he and Branwell had rented rooms nearby.

"Tea?" Miss Eyre asked.

Everyone accepted.

Miss Eyre and Miss Burns disappeared into the kitchen, while Miss Brontë and Branwell took the sofa and bent their heads together. "We need to decide what to do next," Miss Brontë murmured.

"I should go back to Haworth." Branwell sighed. "I do rather miss it there. Of course, not much happens in Haworth, but that's the point, isn't it? I think we've had enough adventure."

Miss Brontë nodded.

Alexander's heart twisted a little when he thought about Miss Brontë going all the way to Haworth. He'd spent the last two days waiting for a meeting with the king, trying to figure out the Society's future now that the building and Move-On Room and talismans were all gone (not to mention Wellington), but the king was still recovering from what Mr. Mitten and Wellington had done in the days before the Great Fire. The Society's future was on his list, but it certainly wasn't a priority. Not right now, anyway.

Which left Alexander sort of the Society's leader by default, but not really, and because all that was so messy, he couldn't take actions like inducting new members, even if they were seers.

Anyway, Charlotte had just agreed about the excess of adventure in London. Maybe she wanted to go back to Haworth.

He moved toward the kitchen to help Miss Eyre with the tea. Even though she currently lived here and was technically the hostess, this had been his kitchen until recently. So no harm in helping.

"It's not that I want you to go." Miss Eyre's voice came from behind the door, barely above a whisper. "I'll miss you. Of course I will."

Alexander paused in the doorway.

"But you think I should." Miss Burns's ghostly voice was tight. "That's it, isn't it? You think it's better if I go?"

He should return to the front parlor, he knew, but Alexander moved forward just enough so that he could see Miss Eyre and Miss Burns. They faced each other, their hands in each other's—almost.

There was something luminous about Miss Eyre ever since the Great Fire. It was the same sort of glow Mrs. Rochester had, the light of being a Beacon that even the living could see.

Tears shimmered down Miss Eyre's cheeks. "I think you've been staying here because I've needed you all these years."

"And now you don't?" Miss Burns wiped her cheek on her shoulder.

"Oh, my dearest friend, I'll always need you. But I have to

think about what you need, too. I've been selfish in keeping you here. Selfish in wanting you by my side always."

"I'm all right with that." Miss Burns let out a small hiccup. "I want to stay with you. I don't know what happens in the after-life."

"It's something good," Miss Eyre whispered hoarsely. "It has to be."

Alexander held his breath, watching the two. Wishing he could go back to the parlor like he'd never walked in on this exchange. Knowing that he could not, because pieces of this conversation echoed in his heart. For most of his life, he'd carried his father's ghost with him. Not a literal ghost, of course, but the figurative ghost.

"What happens when I'm eighty years old," Miss Eyre went on, "and you're still fourteen?"

"We'll be best friends." Miss Burns bit her lip. "Won't we?"

"Of course!" Miss Eyre threw her arms around Miss Burns, but the embrace passed right through. She backed away, tears shimmering on her cheeks. "We will always be best friends. Forever. But our friendship isn't limited by life and death."

"Obviously." Miss Burns forced a brave smile.

"And it's not defined by whether you're here or there. If you stay here, I will still love you. If you move on, I will still love you."

Alexander's heart ached for the two of them. His throat and chest felt tight with the tension of his own ghost. What Miss Eyre said was true, wasn't it? Death could not stop true love, whether that love was paternal or platonic or romantic. Love extended across worlds.

"You think I should move on, though." Miss Burns's voice was so small.

Miss Eyre nodded. "I think you deserve to find peace."

Miss Burns wrapped her arms around her waist. "I'm scared of being without you."

"I'm scared of being without you, too." Miss Eyre's smile wavered. "But we both have things to do. I must live my life, and I can't drag you through it with me. That's not fair to either one of us. So I have to be brave."

"Me too, then." Miss Burns straightened her spine. "I'm going to do it."

"When?" Now it was Miss Eyre's voice that cracked.

Warm light spread throughout the kitchen, coming from Miss Burns. "Now," she said. "I think I'm going now." She seemed less substantial than before. More there than here.

"Helen!" Miss Eyre's cry brought Miss Brontë and Branwell to the kitchen door, next to Alexander, but no one dared enter when they saw what was happening.

"I better not see you for eighty years." Tears sparkled on Miss Burns's cheeks as she looked up and up, and suddenly a wide smile formed—

And she was gone.

The room dimmed to a normal brightness.

"Good-bye," Miss Eyre whispered.

Then, Miss Brontë rushed forward toward her, and the pair embraced.

"We should . . ." Branwell wiped his face dry. "I don't know what to do."

"Take them to sit," Alexander said. "I'll make the tea."

When he was alone in the kitchen, preparing a tray of cups and sugar and cream, Alexander glanced at the place Miss Burns's ghost had occupied. It was amazing how quickly she'd gone, once she'd decided to go. And she did deserve peace.

Maybe Alexander deserved peace, too. From revenge. From the figurative ghost he'd been dragging through his life. From his single-minded devotion to the Society.

He decided to let it go. All of it. Oh, he'd stay with the RWS Society, in whatever form it took. He was good at relocating ghosts, and he enjoyed traveling. But it didn't have to be his whole life. Not anymore.

When the water boiled, he placed the teapot on the tray and returned to the parlor. To his friends.

"Mr. Blackwood?" inquired Miss Brontë in that curious voice he was coming to know so well. "I have a question of the utmost importance."

"Of course you do." He gave her a cup of tea.

"It's regarding the letter that your father wrote to Mr. Rochester. The one you found when you were rakishly breaking into the study at Thornfield."

"I recall the letter quite well."

"The man who wrote the letter signed his name as a Mr. Bell."

He had thought this detail had slipped her notice. But nothing ever slipped Charlotte Brontë's notice. "Yes. My father was Nicholas Bell. After he died, Wellington thought it would be prudent if I chose a new name for myself."

"So your name is Alexander Bell."

"Outside of Wellington and the Rochesters, you're the only one who knows the truth."

She smiled. "What's your middle name? I bet I can guess."

He bent his head. "You'd never guess."

"No, but I think I might. Alexander . . . Bell. It feels there's an obvious middle to that."

He tried not to grin. "My middle name is Currer."

"Oh." She laughed. "You're right. I never would have guessed." She held out her hand to him. "Then I am pleased to make your acquaintance, Mr. Alexander Currer Bell."

He took her hand. "And I yours, Miss Charlotte . . ."

"I have no middle name, I'm afraid. The only one of us who received a middle name was Emily. Emily Jane."

"Miss Brontë, then."

"Mr. Bell. Although I suppose I must go on calling you Mr. Blackwood."

"You could call me Alexander, if you wished."

Her eyes widened behind her spectacles. "And you could call me Charlotte."

Indeed.

Epilogue

The morning was dawning bright at the Brontë residence. Jane and Charlotte could already be found, even at this early hour, in the garden behind the house. Jane was wearing a painter's smock over a pale blue dress and an expression of fierce concentration as she made a series of rapid yet delicate brushstrokes onto the canvas before her. Charlotte was perched on a bench a few paces away from Jane, wearing her new spectacles—the kind that she could see out of without having to lift them, as in permanent, over-the-ears glasses. Which was a fortunate thing, as she was hard at work herself, scribbling away furiously into a new notebook. (One without a bullet hole.)

That notebook was almost full to the very last page of the most engaging story.

"Read that last part back again," Jane instructed.

Charlotte cleared her throat delicately.

"Reader . . ." she began.

Jane's brow furrowed. "Are you certain you should address the reader that way? It seems forward."

Charlotte smiled and said stubbornly, "I'm sure the readers like to be addressed. It draws them into the narrative, makes them part of it. Trust me."

"All right, then. Continue."

"Are you sure?" Charlotte's mouth twisted into a smirk. "No more suggestions for improvement of that one word I've read to you so far?"

Jane laughed. "No. Proceed."

"Ahem. *Reader, I married him. A quiet wedding we had: he and I, the parson and clerk, were alone present. My tale draws to its close: one word respecting my experience of married life, and one brief glance at the fortunes of those whose names have most frequently recurred in this narrative, and I have done. I have now been married ten years. I know what it is to live entirely for and with what I love best on earth. I hold myself supremely blest—blest beyond what language can express; because I am my husband's life as fully as he is mine. No woman was ever nearer to her mate than I am. I know no weariness of Mr. Rochester's society: he knows none of mine, any more than we each do of the pulsation of the heart that beats in our separate bosoms; consequently, we are ever together."*

Jane gave a wistful sigh. "That's so good, Charlotte."

"It's not too much? I think it might be too much."

Jane shook her head. "It's a little long. But it's romantic. I don't think I've ever heard a story that's so perfectly romantic. Your readers will eat it up."

Charlotte bit her lip nervously. "I don't have any readers, currently. Except family. And Alexander." She felt greatly embarrassed sometimes when she thought of Alexander reading the story, because so much of what she'd written about Jane Eyre's feelings for Mr. Rochester had been inspired by what she herself felt for a certain Mr. Blackwood.

But then she smiled at the thought of Alexander.

Jane smiled at the word *family*. She was part of Charlotte's family, you see, and not just because she lived at Haworth now, too, but officially. (And no, this was not because Jane Eyre had married Branwell Brontë.) No, the way Jane had become family to the Brontës was the result of a funny coincidence, actually.

Some weeks after they'd all returned from London, smoky and slightly singed but still victorious, a lawyer had arrived. He'd informed them that he was acting on the behalf of the estate of Arthur Wellesley, the recently and tragically deceased Duke of Wellington. Who had been the estranged uncle to the Brontës, didn't they know?

They did know, it turned out.

Their estranged uncle Arthur had left behind quite a fortune when he'd passed, the lawyer had informed them. In the sum of twenty thousand pounds.

"To us?" the Brontës had asked incredulously. That seemed unlikely. Considering.

"Well . . . no," said the lawyer. To a mysterious person the duke didn't know he'd ever met. The duke, it turned out, had another sibling—a lost sister who'd died in childbirth long ago, who'd left behind an orphan, who'd been missing this entire time, who'd been reported as deceased herself, but it had recently come to the late duke's attention that this girl was not, in fact, deceased. She was very much alive. A teacher at Lowood school. And to this modest little teacher, the duke had left his entire fortune. So the lawyer had gone searching for the girl at Lowood, and he'd tracked her to Haworth. Where he was now seeking none other than—you guessed it—our very own Jane Eyre.

It was a bit of a convoluted story, but this was the gist of it: Jane was a cousin to the Brontës. And now she was apparently loaded.

Well, that had changed things for everyone.

You'd think that Jane would have been overjoyed about the money. It was twenty thousand pounds. But Jane hadn't cared about the money. In fact, she'd immediately shared her inheritance with the Brontës, as she felt they stood to receive a portion of the duke's money equally. What had mattered to Jane, what had always been what mattered to Jane, it turned out, was that now she had family. She had actual blood relations, and she delighted in every new member of her familial circle—Charlotte and Bran, of course, and Emily and little Anne, who they'd brought home immediately from school. They'd all settled down at Haworth together, and spent their days writing stories and drawing pictures and painting and generally having the very best time imaginable.

Which brings us back to Jane and Charlotte in the garden, Charlotte reading to Jane a complete draft of what was going to become one of the most famous novels ever written.

"Are you sure you don't want me to write it as it really happened?" Charlotte asked Jane.

Jane shook her head, her expression thoughtful. "No. Your Jane Eyre should end up with Mr. Rochester, I think."

Mr. Rochester, they knew, had taken his wife and little Adele to the South of France, where they were, as far as the Brontë clan was aware, living in blissful obscurity and recovering from years of abuse and separation. But Jane still thought about Mr. Rochester from time to time. And it pained her. Charlotte could tell.

She sighed. "The truth was ever so much more exciting."

"But who'd believe it?" Jane argued. "Ghosts and possessions and people who trap the wayward spirits of the dead? What a tall tale, indeed. Besides, we've all agreed that the Society should be a secret. Now that Mr. Blackwood is running things. No, it's my story, in a way, my name anyway, and I want it to be a love story."

Charlotte nodded. It *was* Jane's story, and Charlotte had felt privileged to be allowed to write any part of it at all. But at the same time what she'd written made her feel sad for Jane. Jane had not actually been allowed to be part of any great love story. It was like she'd been robbed of her own well-deserved happy ending.

But Jane claimed that she was content with her life. She turned back to her painting, which was turning out to be the best she'd ever attempted. She stretched her arms and gazed out on the hillside before them, where the spring-green grasses of the moors swayed in the breeze. But Jane was not painting the moors. She was not painting a young woman with golden hair in a white dress, either. Today Jane was working in all reds and oranges, reconstructing the vision of a fire—the House of Lords and Commons ablaze against a night sky. When she looked at it she could still feel the heat of that fateful night, the smoke, the uncertainty and then relief of their victory over Wellington. It'd been a terrifying ordeal, but she also believed that it was the night her life had truly begun.

"There is one mystery left to be solved, however," Charlotte said to Jane.

"What mystery?"

"Who killed Mr. Brocklehurst?"

"Oh." Jane cringed. "That was Miss Temple."

"The obvious choice." Charlotte sounded disappointed.

"Well, Miss Temple gave him the tea. Miss Smith made the tea. Miss Scatcherd procured the poison."

"Oh. Oh . . . So it was a group effort." For once, Charlotte didn't ask another question, because at the same time both girls heard the sound of hoofbeats on the road. Then happy squeals from Emily and Anne inside the house. And presently Alexander appeared on the garden path. His gaze locked with Charlotte's, and she blushed, her eyes bright behind her glasses.

"Mr. Blackwood," she murmured.

"Miss Brontë. You're looking well."

"To what do we owe the pleasure?" Jane asked. "Is everything all right?"

"As good as it can be, although we're eagerly awaiting your

return," Alexander said. "We need our Beacon."

Jane nodded. "Soon. But for now I am enjoying my time here."

"I'll go," said Charlotte, and blushed again.

"We would gladly have you," Alexander replied, smiling with his eyes. "We can always use persons of great wit, intelligence, and veracity. And I would welcome it, especially." He straightened his cravat and cleared his throat. "But that's not what I've come about. There's been an interesting new development."

Charlotte and Jane exchanged glances. They didn't know how many more "interesting developments" they could handle.

"Come," Alexander bid them. "There's someone I'd like you to meet."

They followed him back into the house and into the parlor, where they found a slender, smartly dressed young man standing at the window with his hands clasped behind him.

"Edward," Alexander said. "May I present Miss Charlotte Brontë and Miss Jane Eyre?"

The boy turned. Jane's breath caught. It wasn't that he was attractive—although he undoubtedly was. He was young, probably sixteen or seventeen, at most. And he was tall. Dark. Handsome. His black hair had a charming curl to it as it fell to just below his ears, which made him seem slightly wild and windblown—or it could have been because he'd just been out in the Yorkshire wind, who knows. His smile contained a hint of playfulness. His forehead, Jane thought, was the kind to inspire sculpture.

But what had caused Jane to catch her breath was the young

man's eyes. There was something so entirely familiar about his dark, intelligent eyes. A certain brooding intensity. She was overcome by the sudden notion that this boy possessed the ability, not only to see her, standing there awkwardly in her blue dress and her paint-smeared smock gaping up at him, but into her as well. Like he could see into her very soul.

"I'd like you to meet Mr. Edward Rochester," Alexander said.

"Edward . . . Rochester?" Charlotte tilted her head, frowning.

"The Second," the boy clarified.

"As it happens, before Edward and Bertha Rochester withdrew from the Society, before Edward was possessed and Bertha imprisoned in the attic, they had a son," Alexander explained. "As her last act of defiance against the duke, Bertha sent the boy away to the West Indies with Mr. Mason, to be raised by her family and kept secret and safe. But now it's time for him to be restored to us."

"Edward Rochester," breathed Jane.

"The Second," added Charlotte.

"Hello," the boy said. He gave a slight bow. "I am so pleased to make your acquaintance, Miss Brontë." He looked at Jane and smiled. "Miss Eyre. I've heard so much about you."

"Say something, Jane," hissed Charlotte.

"Hello," said Jane.

Acknowledgments

Hello again! It's us, your friendly neighborhood Lady Janies. We're back to the part where we'd like to thank an incomplete list of the people who need to be thanked.

We'd like to start with the Society for the Revision of Wayward Novels, aka our agents (Katherine Fausset, Lauren MacLeod, and Michael Bourret) and editors (Erica Sussman and Stephanie Stein—sorry we killed you in fiction, but it's out of love). And thanks to our publicists (the incredible Rosanne Romanello and Olivia Russo) and our amazing cover designer (Jenna Stempel-Lobell, who created another winner for this book!).

To the incredible authors who blurbed *My Lady Jane*, Tahereh Mafi and Jessica Day George, we say thanks! Your words make us blush pre-Victorian blushes.

Thanks again to our families (Jeff, Dan, Will, Maddie, Shane, Carter, Beckham, and Sam) for dealing with us. And a big thank-you to Jack and Carol Ware (Cynthia's parents) for allowing us to use your lovely home in Virginia as a retreat to work on the book over the summer.

And where would we be without you, our clever, adventurous, and creative readers? Thanks for giving our silly book a chance.

Finally, to the ghosts.

MY
PLAIN
JANE
EXCLUSIVE
BONUS
CHAPTER

THE DOUBLE DATE

Oh, hey, reader, you're still here?

Why?

You want *more*? Okay, fine. We'll tell you what happened to our heroes after England and the Society were saved.

Shortly after Rochester Jr. arrived at Haworth and was introduced to Jane, they, along with Charlotte and Alexander, traveled together to London. "To show Rochester Jr. the wonders of British life," was the reason given by Alexander, as the poor boy had heretofore been living in the West Indies and had never even seen the Thames or eaten a single serving of fish and chips.

Jane thought the entire trip sounded like a wonderful chance for her to get to know Rochester the Second, whom she was having trouble differentiating from Rochester the First, the older one who was still very much in the south of France and in love with his wife. At first, Rochester Jr. had seemed like simply a younger, blessedly age-appropriate version of the Rochester Jane had fallen in love with. He had the same intense and soulful eyes, the same wind-ruffled hair, and the same chin. But as the group journeyed together, first by carriage, then by train, Jane came to realize something important:

Rochester Junior was an entirely different person from Rochester Senior.

He was strange, truth be told. Jane had never met a boy like him.

He was quiet, for one thing. Rochester Senior always had some grand announcement or fiery, soul-stirring speech to impart. But Rochester the Second was introspective. He listened to her whenever she spoke, *as if he were actually interested in hearing her opinions.*

He was also, Jane found, quite funny. He had a habit of suddenly piping up with an extremely clever and humorous comment, and when he delivered these delightful little jokes, his dark eyes would sparkle and the corners of his mouth would twist up in a way that transformed his entire face into a picture of mirth. For instance, just yesterday, they had been in a carriage headed to the Tower of London and Rochester Jr. had abruptly blurted out, "Why did the chicken cross the North Circular Road?"

"Oh. Why?" Jane had replied.

He stifled a mischievous smile. "To get from Finchley to Hendon."

(Alas, reader, we don't really get this joke. But Jane thought it was hilarious.)

Also, Rochester Jr. didn't try to control her. He seemed quite content to let her decide what she'd like to eat and how she'd like to dress and the places she'd like to go, *as if he thought she was capable of thinking for herself*. It was so bizarre.

Their trip to the Tower had also brought Jane's attention to another quality of Edward Rochester the Second: he couldn't see ghosts. As they'd traipsed around the Tower grounds, Jane had been practically swamped with all manner of troubled spirits all clamoring for her attention, but Rochester Jr. hadn't noticed.

It was refreshing that he simply thought of her as a regular girl, when everyone else kept insisting how spectacular she was.

By the end of the week, Jane had decided that she liked Rochester Jr. More than liked him, in fact. For who he was, and not who his father was.

But how to tell him? It didn't seem like it should be so difficult to let him know that she was interested in him "calling upon her," or whatnot. But every time an opportunity presented itself, Jane found herself at a loss for words.

She'd had only one experience with love before, and it had gone so very badly.

She didn't want to mess things up now.

And she had no idea if he liked her back. He seemed to enjoy her company, but then he seemed to enjoy *everyone's* company. After all, he'd spent the last fifteen years in near isolation in a foreign country.

Now it was the last day of their vacation. The group ambled along next to the ruins of the old Roman wall, Charlotte and

3

Alexander somewhere behind them, Rochester Jr. a few steps ahead. Suddenly he turned and said her name.

"Miss Eyre," he said. "I wonder . . ."

She stopped, her heart beating strangely. "Yes?"

"Would you—" he started, cleared his throat, and tried again. "That is, Miss Eyre, would you do me the honor of . . . attending the opera with me this evening?"

Jane was tempted to be utterly scandalized at the proposition. What kind of girl did he think she was? But then she reminded herself that Rochester Jr. had been raised away from English society, and therefore she should forgive him for not understanding. Under normal circumstances, a mother would pass the rules of courtship etiquette on to her children, but his own mother hadn't been able to, due to the fact that she'd been busy being locked in the attic and scratching at the wallpaper.

But Jane was obviously going to say yes, propriety be darned. She was darning a lot of propriety these days. Her cheeks turned a lovely shade of splotchy red, but before she could answer, Charlotte's raised voice came from behind them.

"The opera house?" she said. "Or the 'opera house,' like on page one hundred and eight?"

Rochester Jr. looked confused, but Jane, who had been reading the current draft of Charlotte's novel, immediately understood her friend's air quotes.

"The former," Jane clarified.

Charlotte looked relieved. "Oh! Like a romantic outing. But not too romantic."

"Um . . ." said Rochester eloquently.

"Of course you would need a chaperone," Charlotte mused, tapping her chin. "Otherwise it would be totally scandalous."

"Of course," Jane agreed. "Propriety."

An awkward moment passed between the three of them, the two girls staring at each other, as they both knew what was about to happen, and poor Rochester just standing there, adorable but oblivious.

"I could be your chaperone." Charlotte smiled brilliantly. "I've never been to an opera, and I think I'm well equipped to ensure the level of romance is just right."

"Wonderful," said Jane faintly.

Charlotte clapped her hands together. "Alexander!" she yelled, and then lowered her voice as Alexander, who was walking a few paces behind, jogged to catch up with her. "I mean, Mr. Blackwood. I've just had a marvelous idea. We could all go out."

"Go out?" Alexander tilted his head to one side. "But we *are* out."

"No, silly, to the opera."

"Opera? Now?"

Charlotte suppressed a sigh. "Tonight. Mr. Rochester has asked that Miss Eyre accompany him to the opera. And I thought perhaps you and I should also attend. That way we will all serve as one another's chaperones."

"Oh," Alexander said. "So it could be a kind of romantic outing."

(Hey, reader, it's us. This is a good time to let you know about the history of the word *date*. And, obviously, a double date. Since, apparently, that's where this is heading.

It may interest you to know that Jane, Charlotte, Alexander, and Jr. were actually the first couples to go on a literal *double date* and call it that. Before this point in history, the popular term was "courtship." The word "date" wasn't used until much later, but our plucky heroine picked it out of her brain and said, "So, the four of us will go to the opera this evening on this date." She grabbed her notebook and wrote down some intense emotions surrounding her excitement.

"It's a date I will always remember," Charlotte murmured, making history.

But nobody heard her, so the term didn't catch on. Tragically, Charlotte never got the recognition for coining the phrase. That honor went to George Ade, a columnist for the *Chicago Record*, in 1896. For decades, Americans held it over Britain's head, but then the Brits adopted the metric system, and any time Americans said, "Our guy coined a phrase!" the Brits would retaliate with, "Twelve inches to a foot? Three feet to a yard? Sixteen ounces to a pound? How is that reasonable?"

Anyway, that was a long parenthetical. Back to the story.)

"Excellent," said Alexander. "When should we pick you up?"

Several hours later, after much primping and hair curling and several discarded choices in dresses, Jane and Charlotte descended the stairs of the inn.

"Wow," breathed Alexander and Rochester Jr. at the same time, and the girls beamed.

The boys had gone shopping earlier, and so they each presented their date with a bouquet. But rather than flowers, Rochester Jr. offered Jane a bouquet of paintbrushes, with hand-carved handles and fine camel-hair bristles.

It was the most thoughtful gift anyone had ever given Jane.

Maybe he did like her back, she thought. She wished she had a way to simply ask him. Like writing him a note with the question: Do you wish to court me? Check yes or no.

But nobody had come up with this ingenious system of sussing out another person's feelings as of yet.

Before the opera, they stopped at a typical English pub to eat typical British cuisine. You might recognize this as the earliest instance of the dinner and a movie. Except this was eatery and an opera. We mean, have you ever wondered *why* these characters are so famous? (Except for Alexander, of course, for national security reasons.) It's because they invented not just double dating, but dinner and a movie, as well. Even before movies.

Allow us to set the scene: The four sat around a table, boy-girl, boy-girl. A man with a violin played on the other side of the room, while delicious aromas floated out from the kitchen.

And then there were the ghosts who were wandering around, more than usual because of Jane being a Beacon. Rochester Jr. had yet to fully grasp the concept of a Beacon (it was really impossible to *fully* grasp unless you could see the way ghosts behaved around her, which he couldn't), and while Rochester Jr. had handled seeing her walk around empty air (ghosts) at the Tower of London, tonight was different. Tonight was a *romantic outing*, and she didn't want anything to go wrong.

They were waiting for their food to arrive, but the uncomfortable small talk got there first.

"How's the book coming along?" Rochester Jr. asked Charlotte awkwardly, because he felt like he had to make conversation with everyone when he really just wanted to speak with Jane.

"Well, I will have to publish it as a man, because of sexism. It makes no sense," Charlotte answered politely. "I've been trying to come up with a decent nom de plume. I'm considering . . ." She met Alexander's eyes and smiled. "Currer Bell."

"That's a terrible name," Alexander replied, but he was also smiling.

"I don't get it," said Rochester Jr.

"You're writing a book? I've always wanted to write a book, but I'm afraid I don't have the time. Maybe you could write my idea for me?" asked a tall, translucent fellow. But then he noticed Jane. "Oh, excuse me, Your Highness, but I must know, how did you get your hair so shiny?"

"I—" Jane blushed as everyone (except Rochester Jr.) looked between her and the ghost. "This really isn't a good time," she said at last.

"I'm sorry?" asked Rochester Jr.

"It's nothing," Alexander said quickly. "Ghost things."

"Oh."

"Really," Jane said, careful to phrase her wishes as a request, not a command, "I would be grateful if you would go now."

Rochester Jr. blinked rapidly, then scooted out his chair and stood. "Miss Eyre, if I've done something to offend you . . ."

"Not you!" Jane grabbed at his sleeve. "Sit."

Rochester Jr. sank back into his seat. There it was again: the smile. He was playing around. He knew.

Jane found herself smiling too.

Then the ghost sat on Alexander's lap.

"Excuse me," Alexander protested, lurching from his chair, passing *through* the ghost.

"Rude!" The ghost pressed his hands against his chest. "Don't you know it's rude to go through ghosts?"

"You sat on my lap!"

"Who sat on your lap?" Rochester Jr. said.

"The ghost," Charlotte said.

"There are ghosts here?" the ghost said, swiveling his head about.

"You're the ghost," Jane said, pointing at him.

Rochester Jr. only saw that she pointed at an empty chair. He held out a hand as if to shake the ghost's invisible hand. "Pleased to make your acquaintance, Mr. Ghost."

The ghost ignored him. "I am not a ghost!"

"I agree with the lady," said Alexander. "You're clearly a ghost."

9

"Why do ghosts hate rain?" asked Rochester Jr.

"What? Why?" Jane asked.

"Because it dampens their spirits."

She couldn't help but laugh. Charlotte tittered. Alexander's lips twitched. Even the ghost looked highly amused at that one.

"Very funny," the ghost said. He leaned forward, toward Alexander. "Let's say this theory of yours has some merit. How can you tell a ghost is a ghost?"

"Because I went through you," Alexander said. "Plus, you already admitted you're a ghost."

"Yes, and I felt bothered, and if I feel emotion, do I not also exist?"

We should tell you that this ghost was a budding philosopher, who, in life, rambled on and on to friends and strangers about his theories of what it means to exist, and most of these friends and strangers found him to be quite annoying. When he died in a freak carriage accident, his friends and strangers said that pretentious fellow had it coming.

"Miss Eyre," Alexander said, "do you mind . . ." He rolled his hands around each other and made a finger explosion. "Poof?"

"I don't *poof* people! I'm not even a full agent yet, as you well know, and you can't make me poof anyone!"

"Poof?" asked Rochester Jr.

"Hasn't anyone told you anything?" Charlotte burst out. "Jane is a Beacon. She can force ghosts to move on."

The ghost, who had been quietly listening to this entire

exchange, took this as his cue to leave. "Oh dear, look at the time. I'm late. For . . . something ghostly." He promptly disappeared.

Jane blushed. "Well, I don't *force* them. . . ."

Charlotte rolled her eyes. "Don't disclaim your gift."

Jane turned to Rochester Jr. "When a ghost is having a difficult time transitioning to the next phase of existing, I can sometimes help him. Or her."

"So you help ghosts move on, even if they don't want to?"

Jane winced. "Yes."

"Well then, it sounds like you do them a service."

Jane's face lit up.

Rochester Jr. gazed into her eyes. "If I were a ghost, and I were trapped here, and there was a better place waiting for me, then I should . . ."

His voice trailed off.

"Yes?" Jane said.

"I should be honored if you would perform such a service for me."

"Really?" Jane said, confounded. "I mean, sir, I would be honored to cast you into the next life whenever your circumstances should require it."

And that was the closest declaration of love that Jane had ever made.

Rochester Jr., in a manner that wasn't necessarily following the rules of propriety, but was totally in line with the rules of your humble narrators' propriety, clasped Jane's hand. He looked into her eyes. And smiled again. "I am unknowing in the ways of Seers and Beacons, but I look forward to a full education."

This was a pre-Victorian way of saying that he liked her.

She squeezed his hand, beaming. "Mr. Rochester Jr., I would be happy to educate you."

"Oh dear," said Charlotte. "I should be writing this down."